HEROES IN TRAINING

No. 3

GRAPHIC NOVEL

HADES AND THE HELM OF DARKNESS

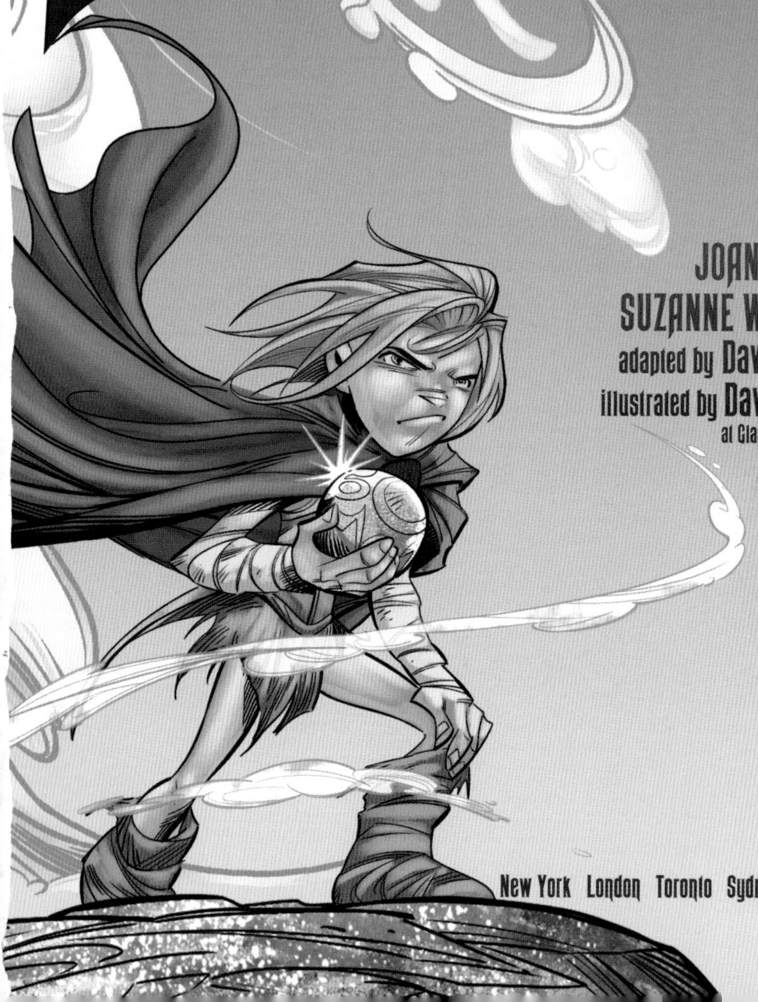

created by
JOAN HOLUB &
SUZANNE WILLIAMS
adapted by David Campiti
illustrated by Dave Santana
at Glass House Graphics

Aladdin
New York London Toronto Sydney New Delhi

ALADDIN
An imprint of Simon & Schuster Children's Publishing Division
1230 Avenue of the Americas, New York, New York 10020
First Aladdin edition August 2022
Text copyright © 2022 by Joan Holub and Suzanne Williams
Illustrations copyright © 2022 by Glass House Graphics
Art by Dave Santana. Inks by Flávio Soares with João Zod and Juan Araujo. Colors by Felipe Felix and João Zod. Lettering by Marcos Inoue. Art services by Glass House Graphics.
All rights reserved, including the right of
reproduction in whole or in part in any form.
ALADDIN and related logo are registered
trademarks of Simon & Schuster, Inc.
For information about special discounts for bulk purchases, please contact Simon & Schuster Special Sales
at 1-866-506-1949 or business@simonandschuster.com.
The Simon & Schuster Speakers Bureau can bring authors to your live event. For more information or to book an event contact the Simon & Schuster Speakers Bureau at 1-866-248-3049
or visit our website at www.simonspeakers.com.
Designed by Nicholas Sciacca
The text of this book was set in CCMonologus.
Manufactured in China 0522 SCP
10 9 8 7 6 5 4 3 2 1
Library of Congress Control Number 2021945037
ISBN 9781534481213 (hc)
ISBN 9781534481206 (pbk)
ISBN 9781534481220 (ebook)

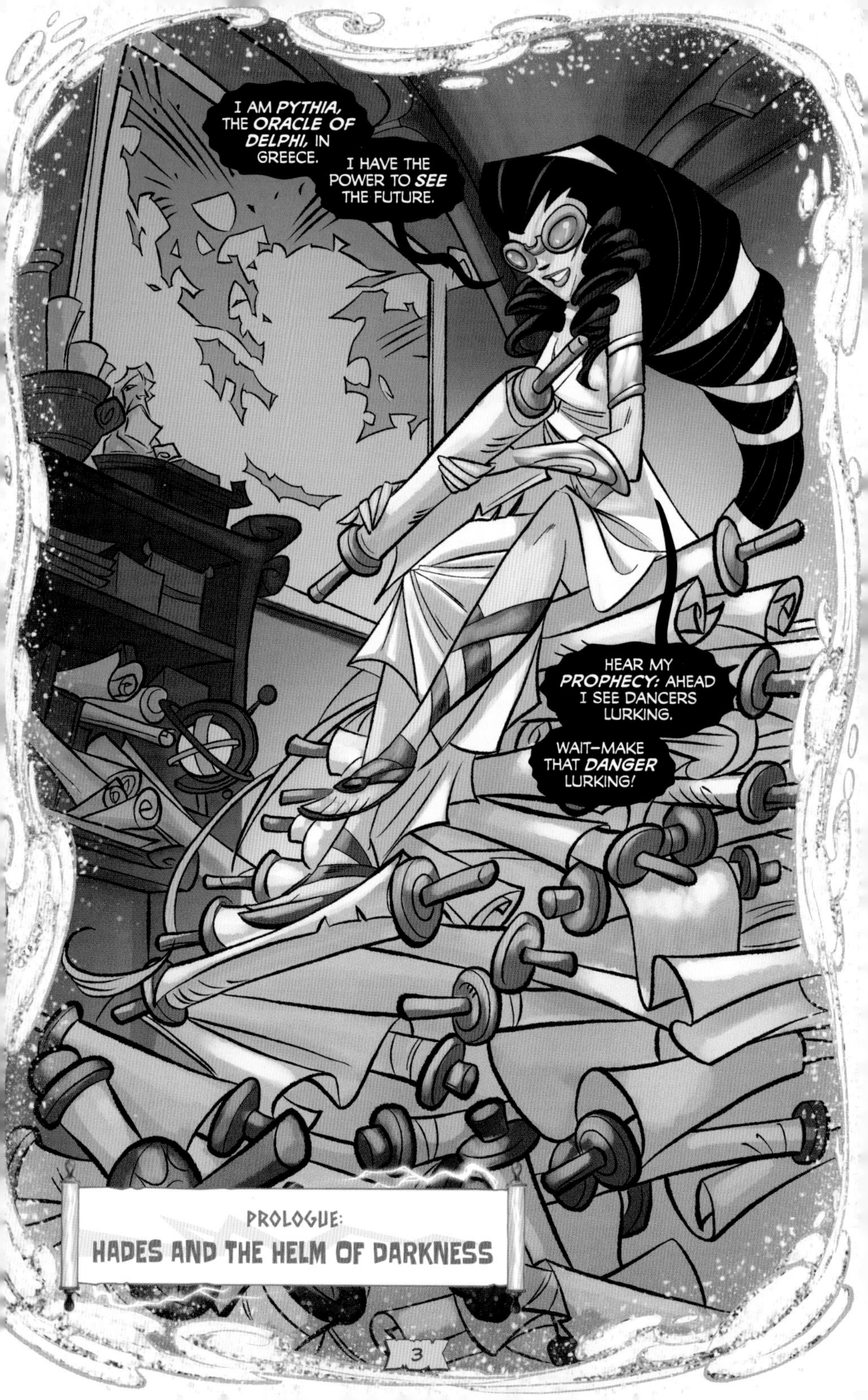

I AM PYTHIA, THE ORACLE OF DELPHI, IN GREECE.
I HAVE THE POWER TO SEE THE FUTURE.
HEAR MY PROPHECY: AHEAD I SEE DANCERS LURKING.
WAIT—MAKE THAT DANGER LURKING!
PROLOGUE:
HADES AND THE HELM OF DARKNESS

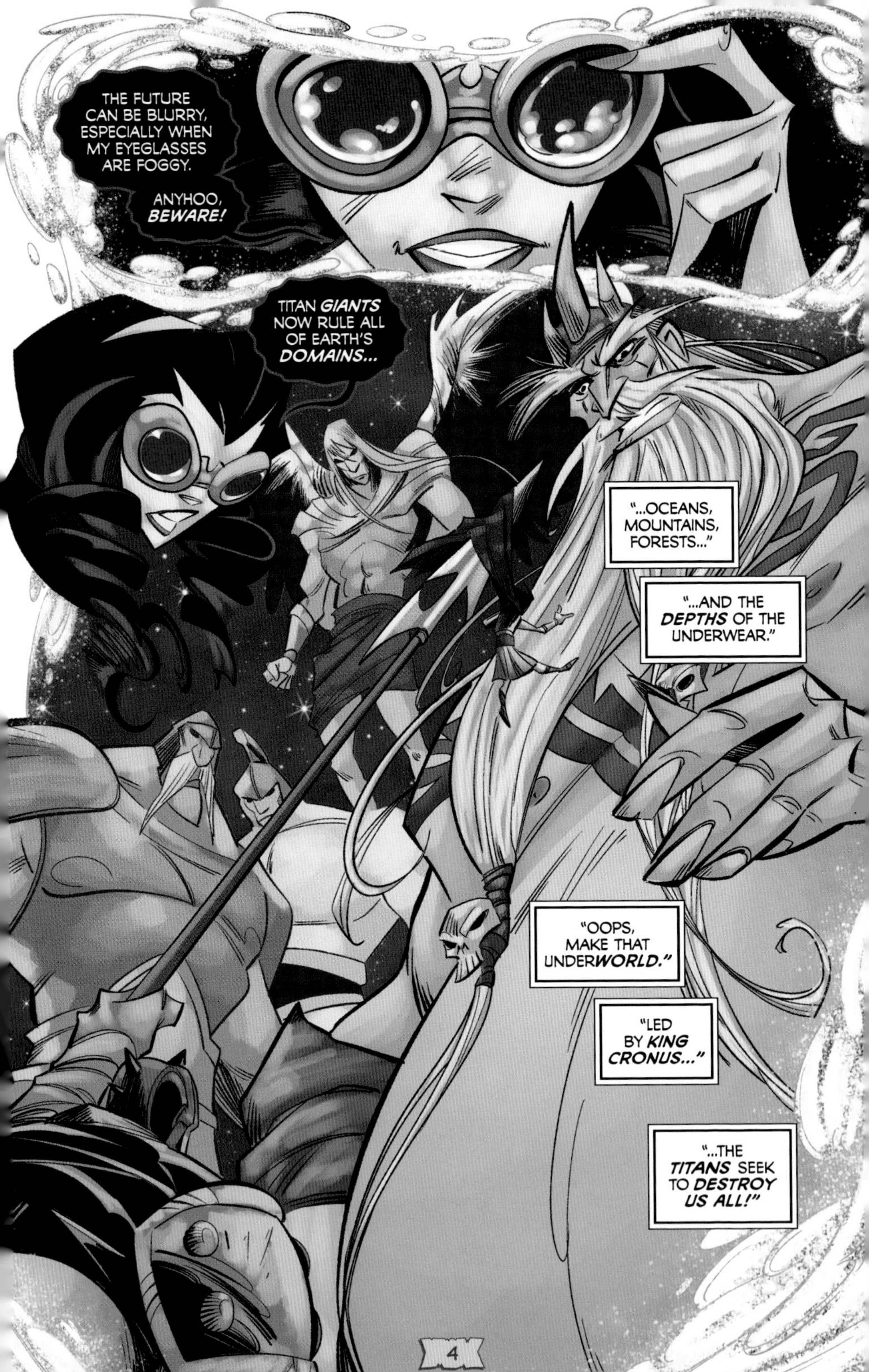
THE FUTURE CAN BE BLURRY, ESPECIALLY WHEN MY EYEGLASSES ARE FOGGY.
ANYHOO, *BEWARE!*
TITAN *GIANTS* NOW RULE ALL OF EARTH'S *DOMAINS...*
"...OCEANS, MOUNTAINS, FORESTS..."
"...AND THE *DEPTHS* OF THE UNDERWEAR."
"OOPS, MAKE THAT UNDER*WORLD.*"
"LED BY *KING CRONUS...*"
"...THE *TITANS* SEEK TO *DESTROY US ALL!*"

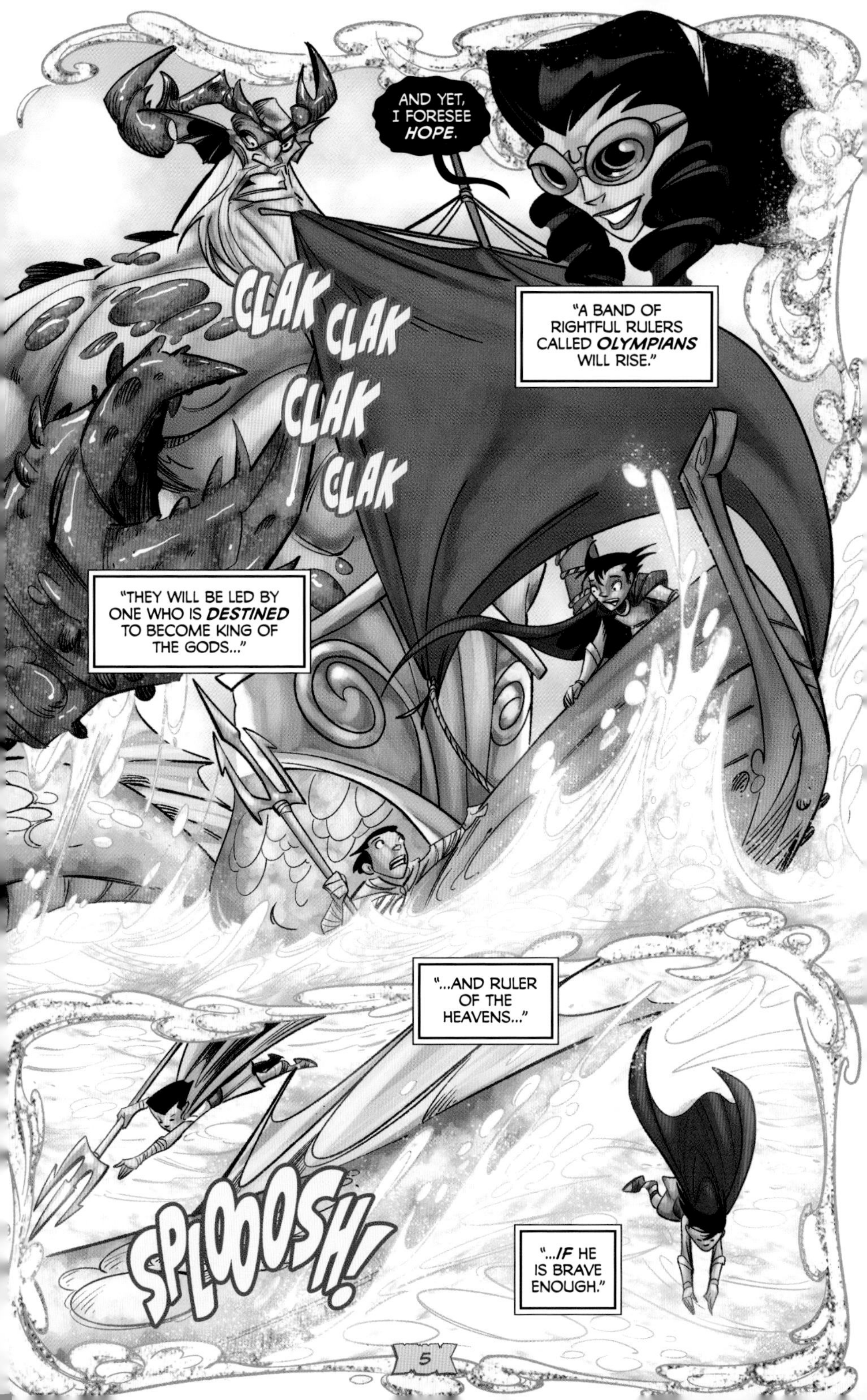
AND YET, I FORESEE *HOPE*.
CLAK CLAK CLAK CLAK
"A BAND OF RIGHTFUL RULERS CALLED *OLYMPIANS* WILL RISE."
"THEY WILL BE LED BY ONE WHO IS *DESTINED* TO BECOME KING OF THE GODS..."
"...AND RULER OF THE HEAVENS..."
SPLOOOSH!
"...*IF* HE IS BRAVE ENOUGH."

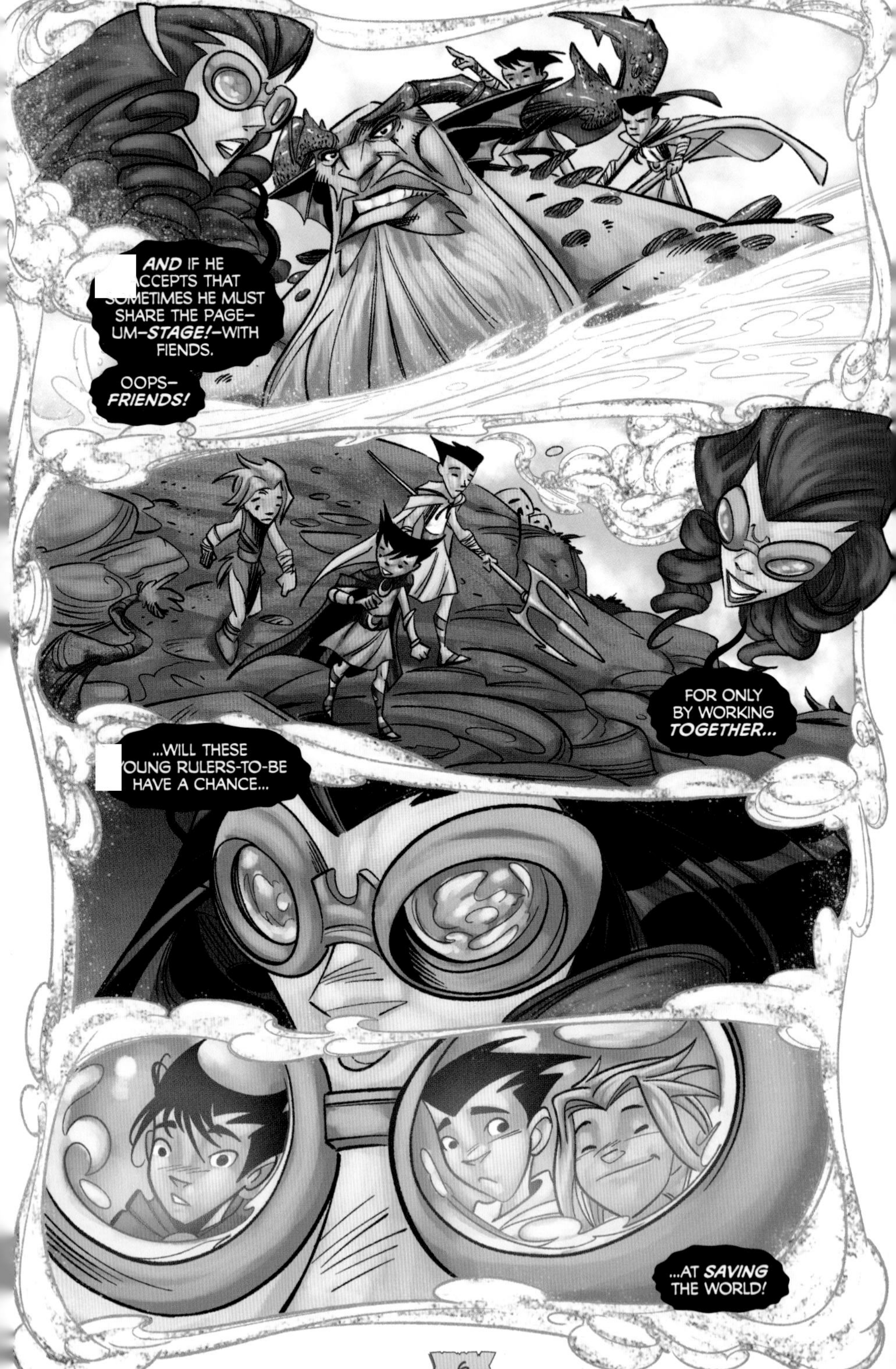
AND IF HE ACCEPTS THAT SOMETIMES HE MUST SHARE THE PAGE— UM—STAGE!—WITH FIENDS.
OOPS— FRIENDS!
FOR ONLY BY WORKING TOGETHER...
...WILL THESE YOUNG RULERS-TO-BE HAVE A CHANCE...
...AT SAVING THE WORLD!

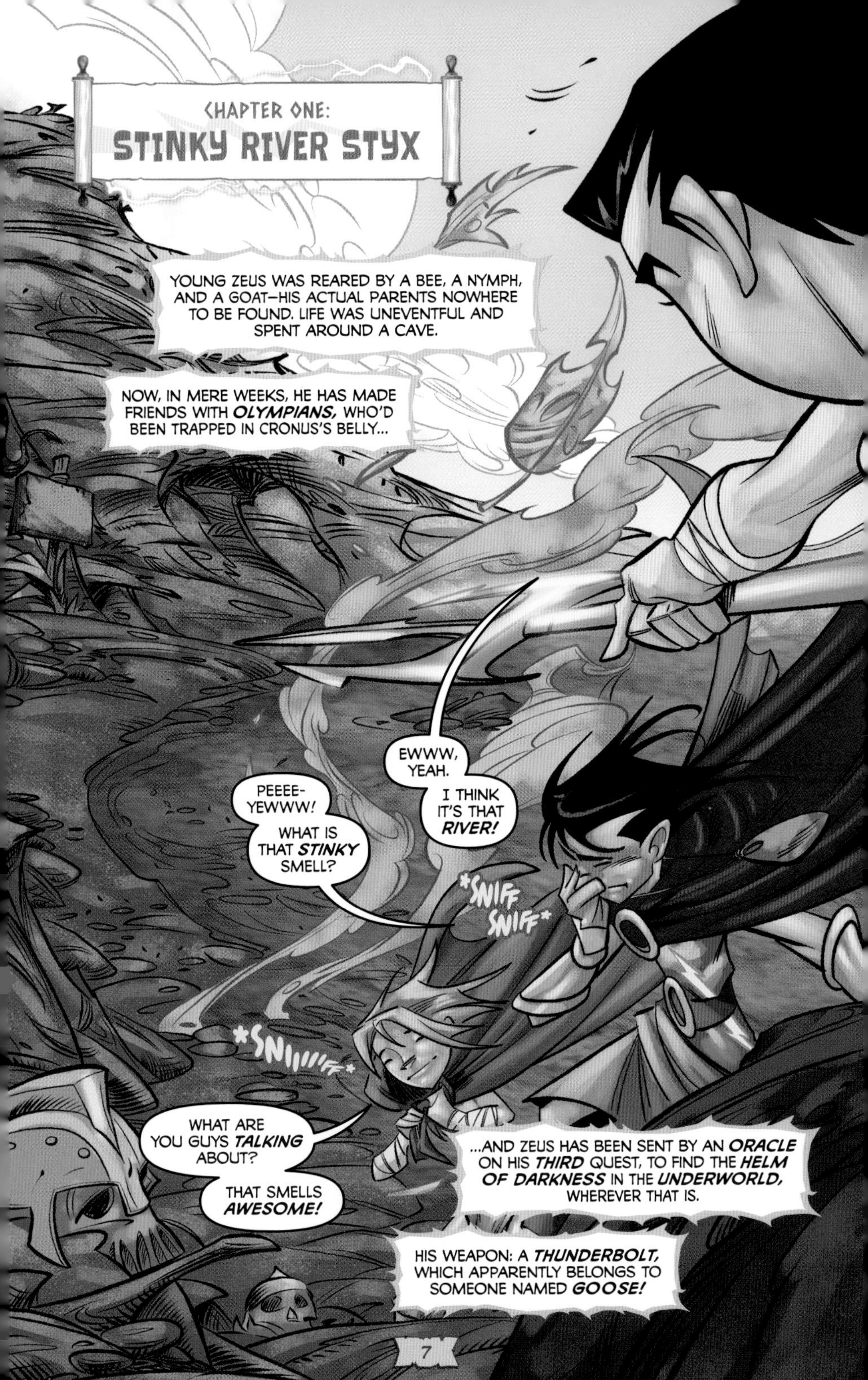
CHAPTER ONE:
STINKY RIVER STYX
YOUNG ZEUS WAS REARED BY A BEE, A NYMPH, AND A GOAT—HIS ACTUAL PARENTS NOWHERE TO BE FOUND. LIFE WAS UNEVENTFUL AND SPENT AROUND A CAVE.
NOW, IN MERE WEEKS, HE HAS MADE FRIENDS WITH OLYMPIANS, WHO'D BEEN TRAPPED IN CRONUS'S BELLY...
EWWW, YEAH.
I THINK IT'S THAT RIVER!
PEEEE-YEWWW!
WHAT IS THAT STINKY SMELL?
SNIFF SNIFF
SNIIIIIFF
WHAT ARE YOU GUYS TALKING ABOUT?
THAT SMELLS AWESOME!
...AND ZEUS HAS BEEN SENT BY AN ORACLE ON HIS THIRD QUEST, TO FIND THE HELM OF DARKNESS IN THE UNDERWORLD, WHEREVER THAT IS.
HIS WEAPON: A THUNDERBOLT, WHICH APPARENTLY BELONGS TO SOMEONE NAMED GOOSE!

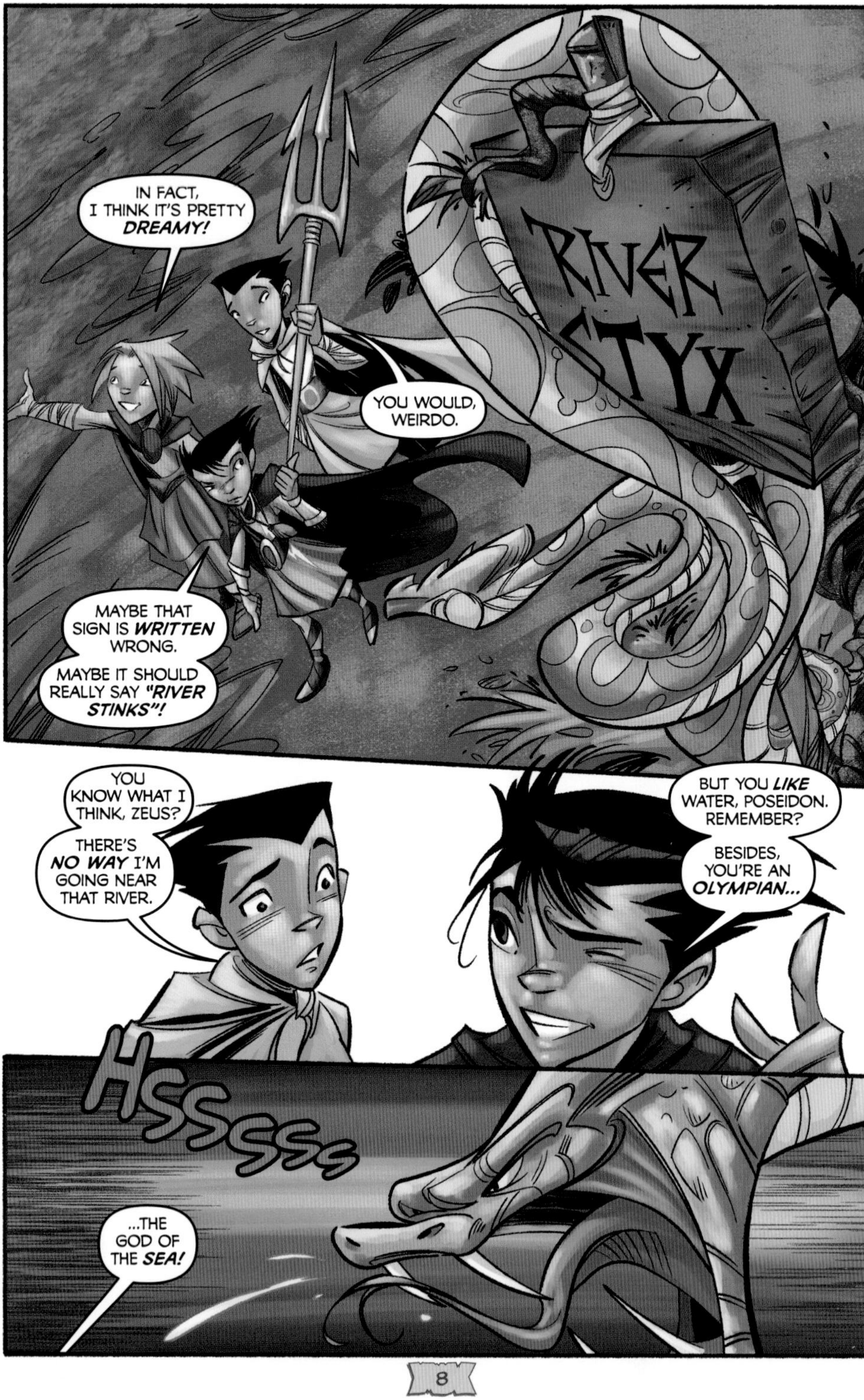

IN FACT, I THINK IT'S PRETTY ***DREAMY!***
RIVER STYX
YOU WOULD, WEIRDO.
MAYBE THAT SIGN IS ***WRITTEN*** WRONG.
MAYBE IT SHOULD REALLY SAY ***"RIVER STINKS"!***
YOU KNOW WHAT I THINK, ZEUS?
THERE'S ***NO WAY*** I'M GOING NEAR THAT RIVER.
BUT YOU ***LIKE*** WATER, POSEIDON. REMEMBER?
BESIDES, YOU'RE AN ***OLYMPIAN...***
HSSSSSS
...THE GOD OF THE ***SEA!***

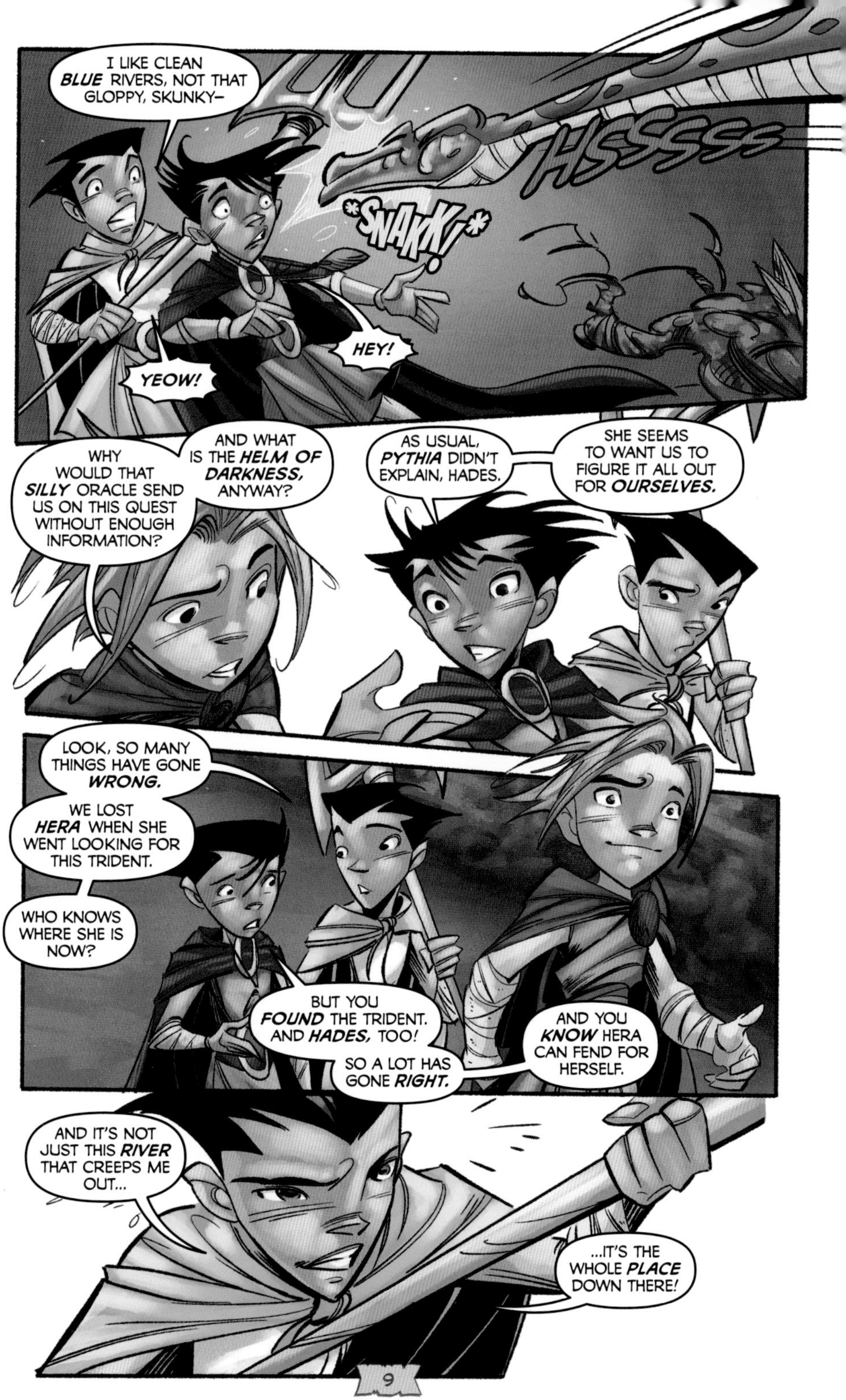
I LIKE CLEAN BLUE RIVERS, NOT THAT GLOPPY, SKUNKY–
HSSSSS
SNAKK!
YEOW!
HEY!
WHY WOULD THAT SILLY ORACLE SEND US ON THIS QUEST WITHOUT ENOUGH INFORMATION?
AND WHAT IS THE HELM OF DARKNESS, ANYWAY?
AS USUAL, PYTHIA DIDN'T EXPLAIN, HADES.
SHE SEEMS TO WANT US TO FIGURE IT ALL OUT FOR OURSELVES.
LOOK, SO MANY THINGS HAVE GONE WRONG.
WE LOST HERA WHEN SHE WENT LOOKING FOR THIS TRIDENT.
WHO KNOWS WHERE SHE IS NOW?
BUT YOU FOUND THE TRIDENT. AND HADES, TOO!
SO A LOT HAS GONE RIGHT.
AND YOU KNOW HERA CAN FEND FOR HERSELF.
AND IT'S NOT JUST THIS RIVER THAT CREEPS ME OUT...
...IT'S THE WHOLE PLACE DOWN THERE!

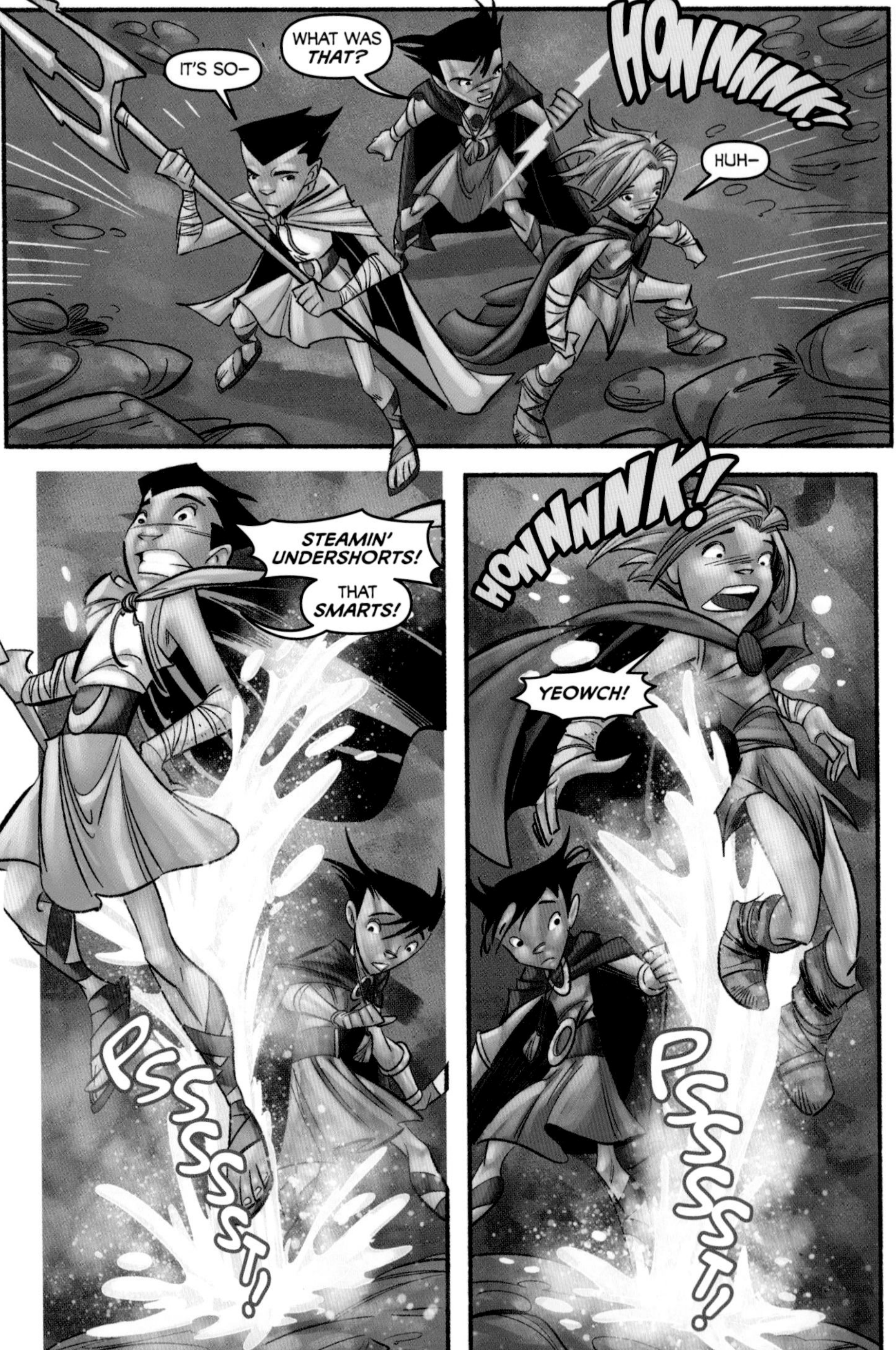

IT'S SO–
WHAT WAS *THAT?*
HONNNNK!
HUH–
STEAMIN' UNDERSHORTS!
THAT *SMARTS!*
PSSSSST!
HONNNNK!
YEOWCH!
PSSSSST!

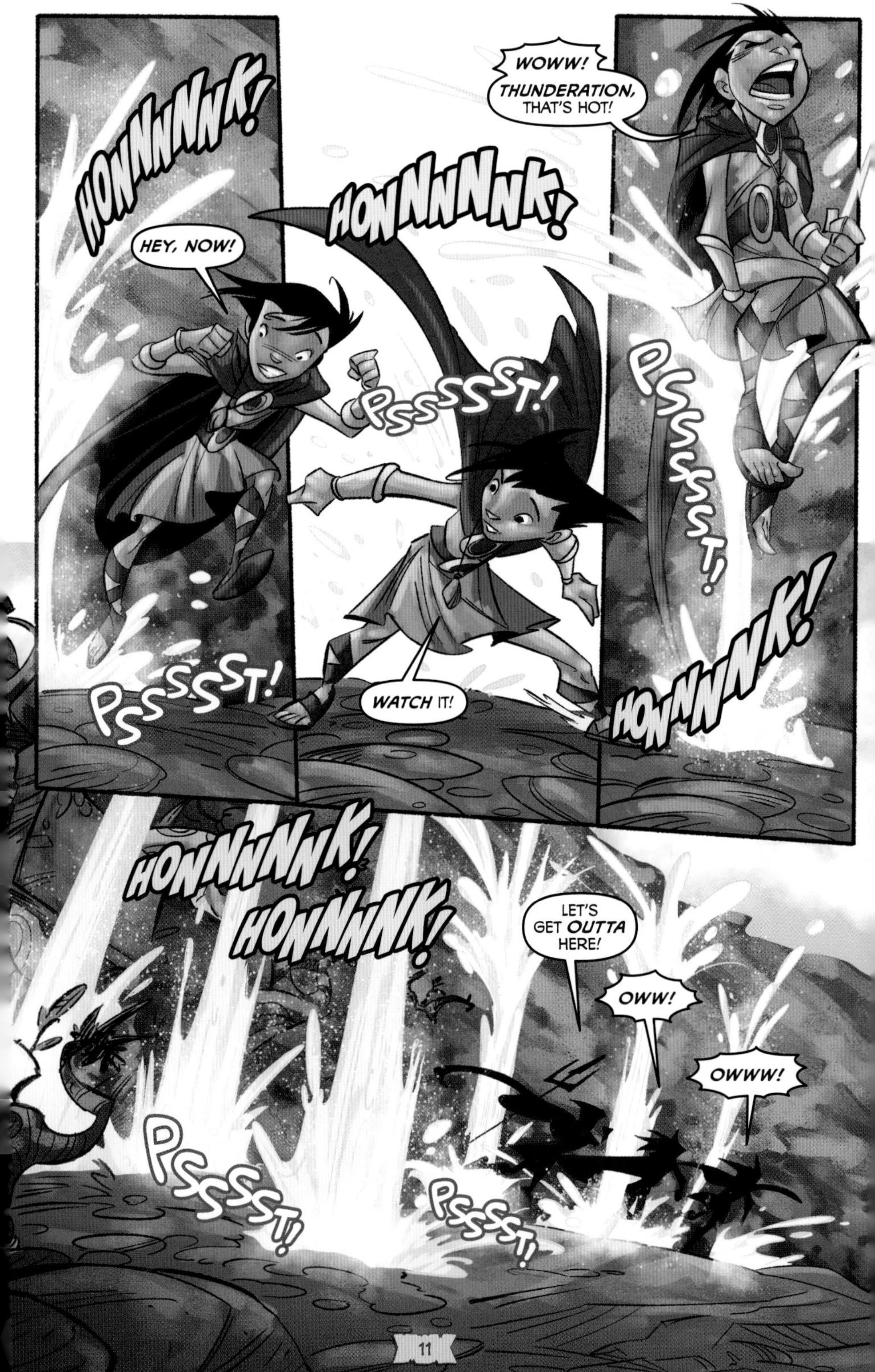
HONNNNNK!
HEY, NOW!
HONNNNNK!
PSSSSST!
PSSSSST!
WATCH IT!
WOWW! THUNDERATION, THAT'S HOT!
PSSSSSST!
HONNNNK!
HONNNNNK!
HONNNNK!
LET'S GET OUTTA HERE!
OWW!
OWWW!
PSSSST!
PSSSST!

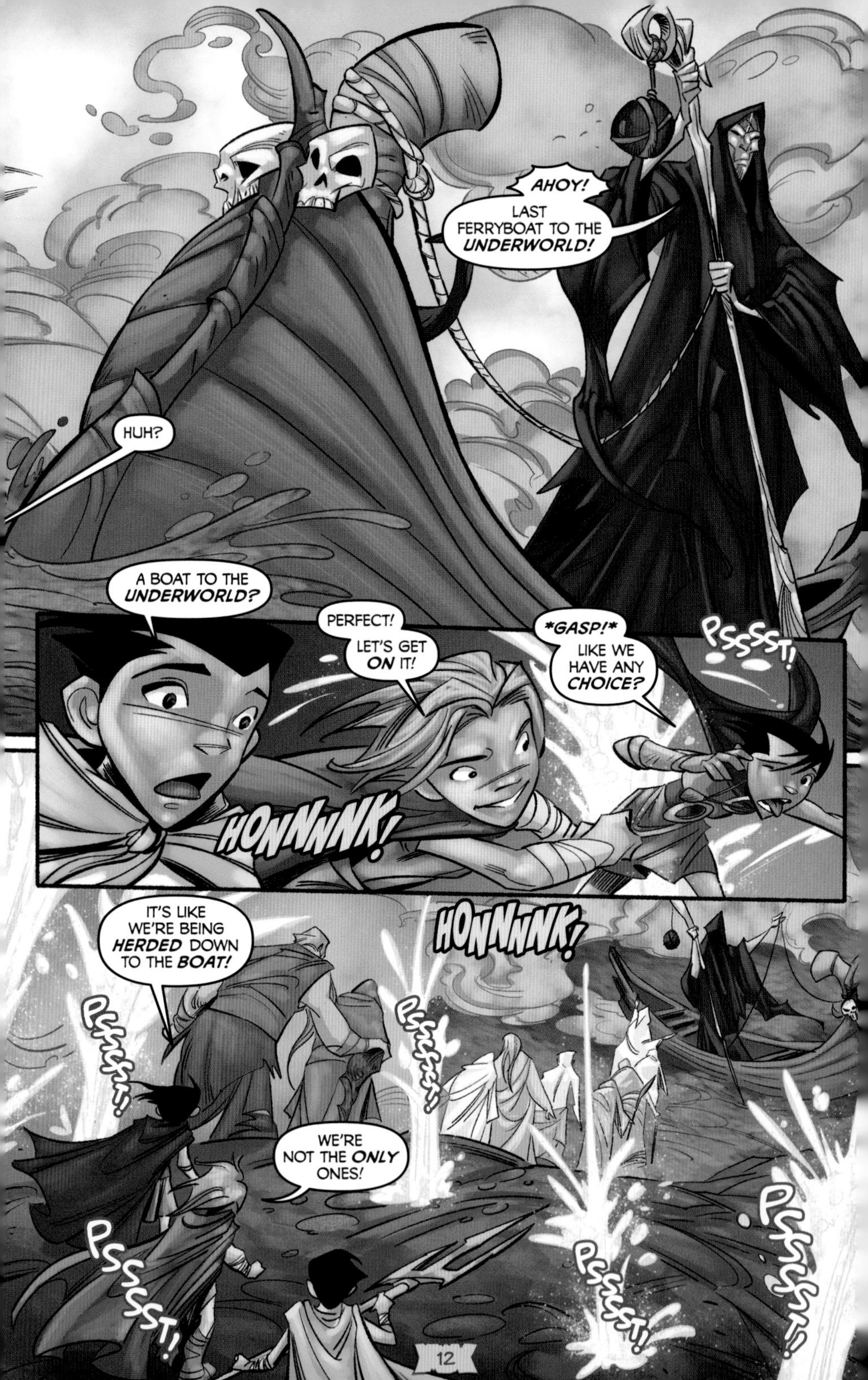

AHOY!
LAST FERRYBOAT TO THE UNDERWORLD!
HUH?
A BOAT TO THE UNDERWORLD?
PERFECT!
LET'S GET ON IT!
GASP!
LIKE WE HAVE ANY CHOICE?
PSSSST!
HONNNNK!
IT'S LIKE WE'RE BEING HERDED DOWN TO THE BOAT!
HONNNNK!
PSSSST!
PSSSST!
WE'RE NOT THE ONLY ONES!
PSSSST!
PSSSST!
PSSSST!

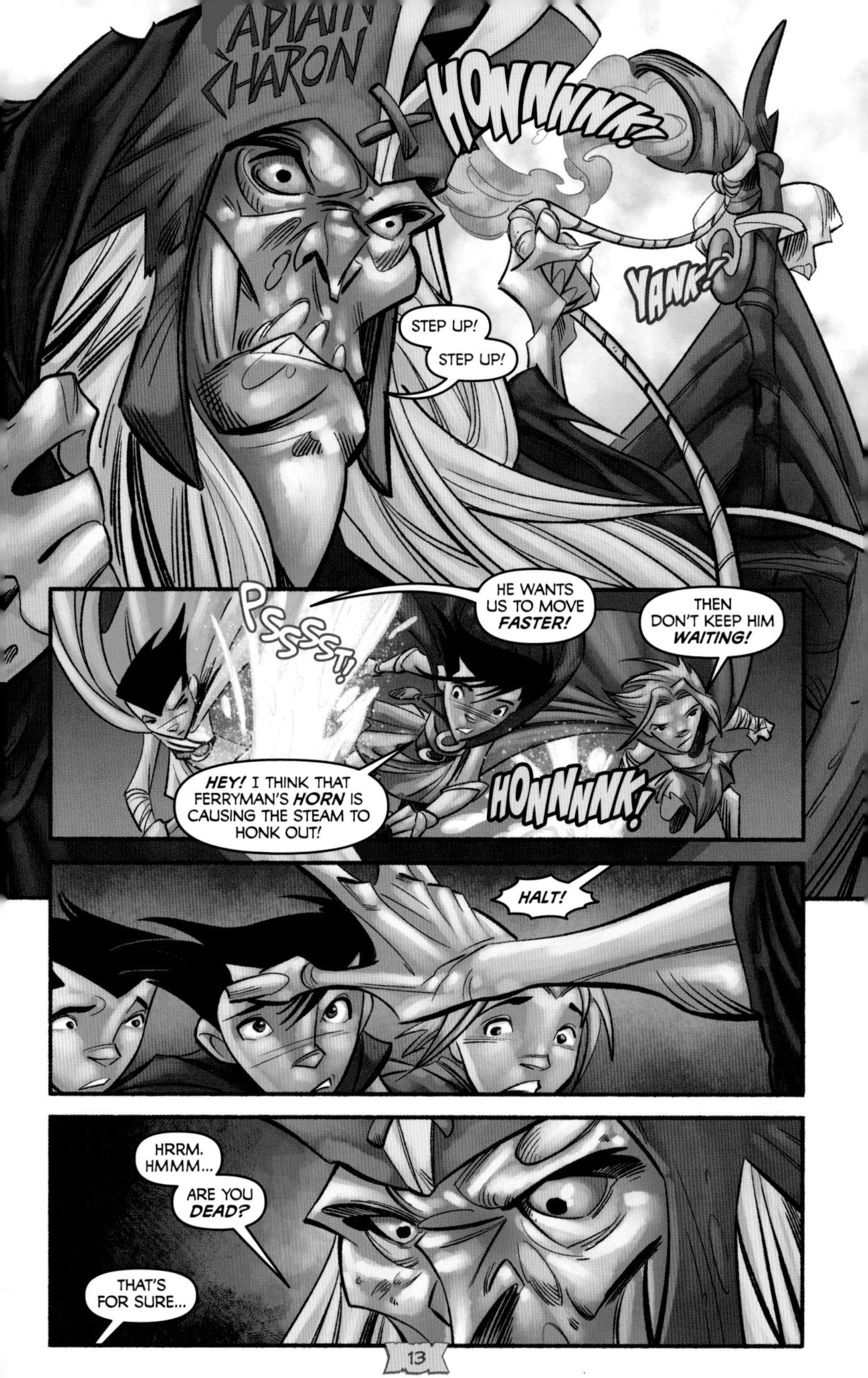
CAPTAIN CHARON
HONNNNK!
YANK!
STEP UP!
STEP UP!
PSSSST!
HE WANTS US TO MOVE FASTER!
THEN DON'T KEEP HIM WAITING!
HEY! I THINK THAT FERRYMAN'S HORN IS CAUSING THE STEAM TO HONK OUT!
HONNNNK!
HALT!
HRRM. HMMM...
ARE YOU DEAD?
THAT'S FOR SURE...

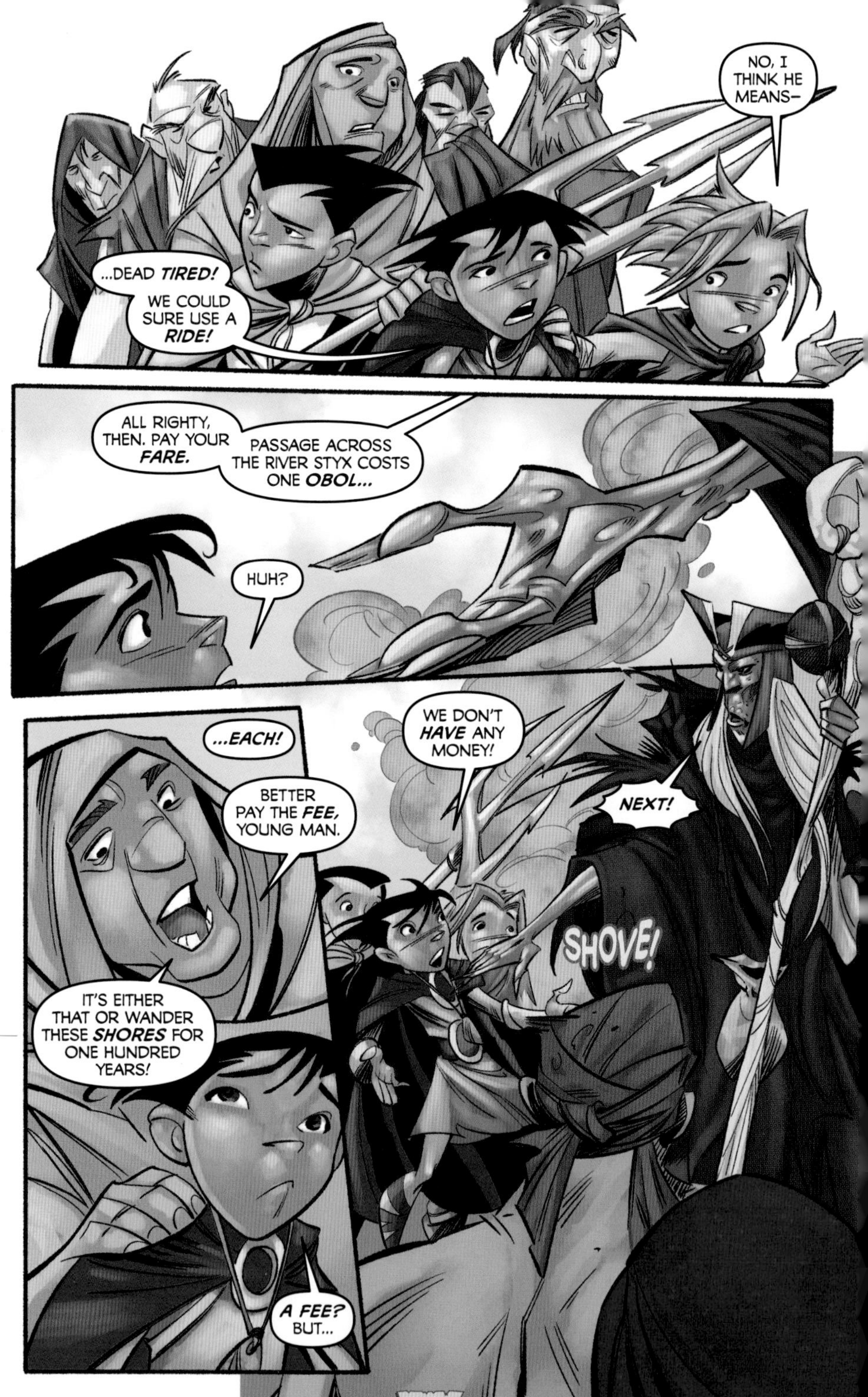

NO, I THINK HE MEANS—
...DEAD TIRED!
WE COULD SURE USE A RIDE!
ALL RIGHTY, THEN. PAY YOUR FARE.
PASSAGE ACROSS THE RIVER STYX COSTS ONE OBOL...
HUH?
...EACH!
BETTER PAY THE FEE, YOUNG MAN.
IT'S EITHER THAT OR WANDER THESE SHORES FOR ONE HUNDRED YEARS!
A FEE? BUT...
WE DON'T HAVE ANY MONEY!
NEXT!
SHOVE!

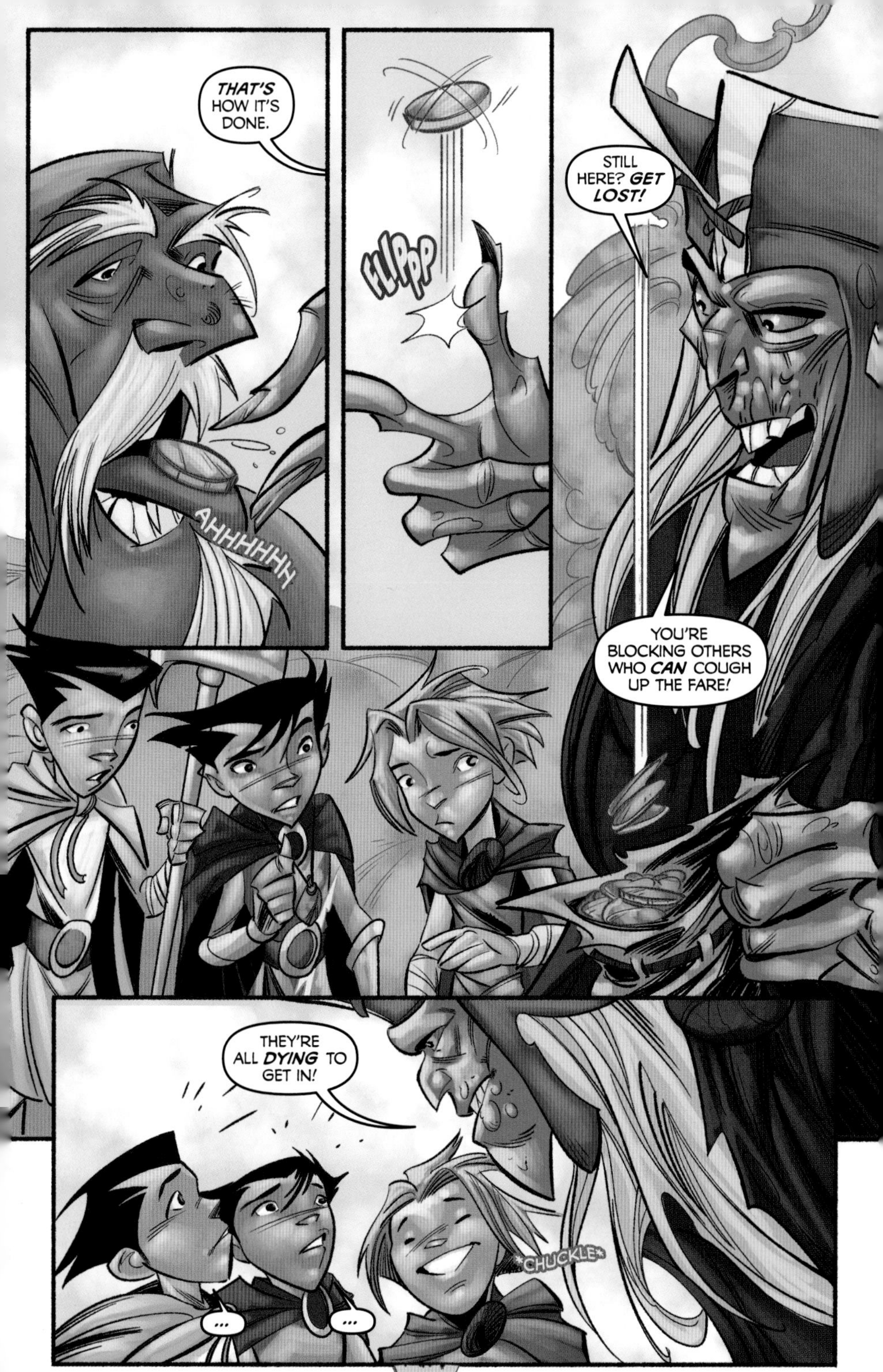
THAT'S HOW IT'S DONE.
AHHHHHH
FLIPPP
STILL HERE? GET LOST!
YOU'RE BLOCKING OTHERS WHO CAN COUGH UP THE FARE!
THEY'RE ALL DYING TO GET IN!
...
...
CHUCKLE

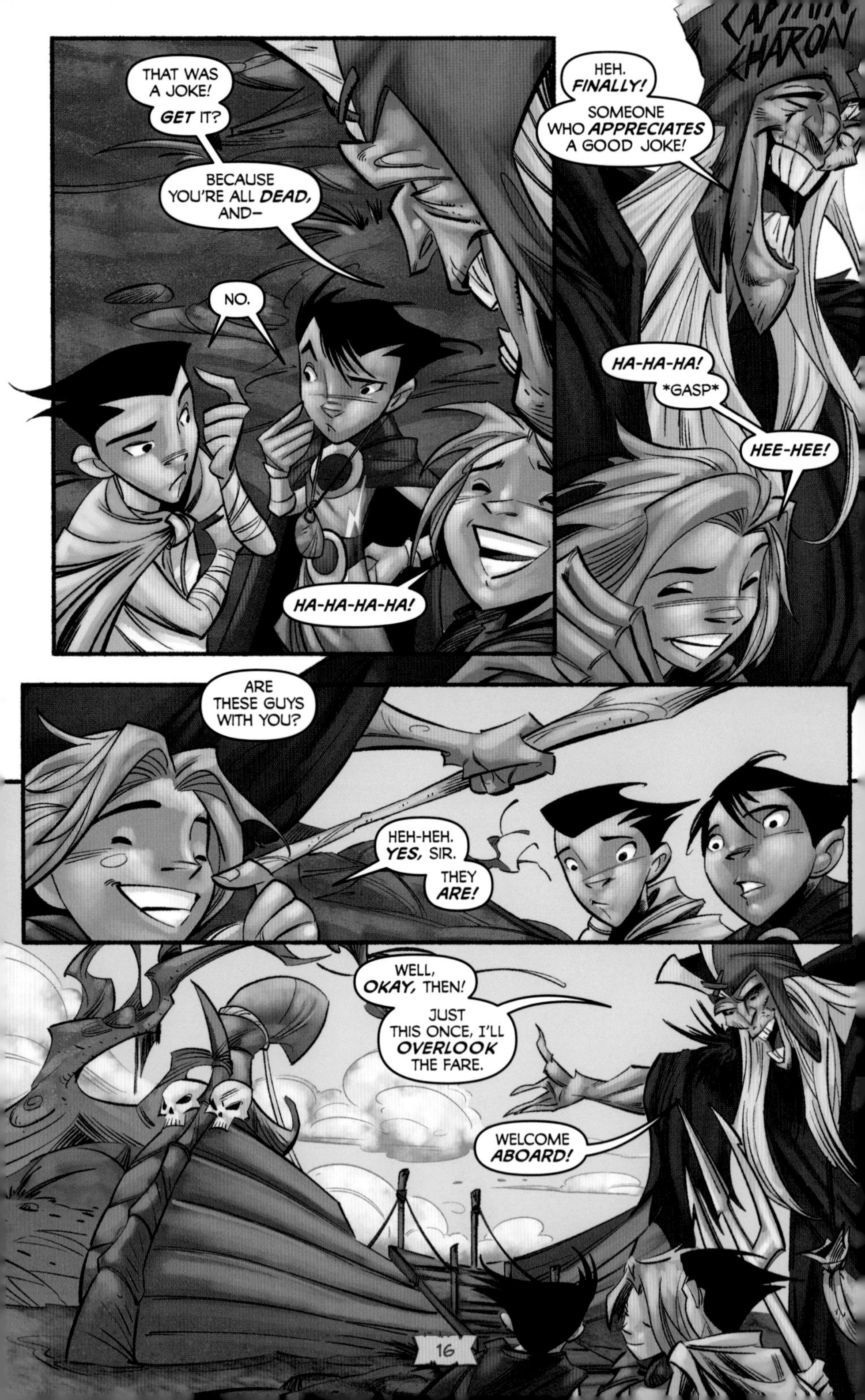
CAP'N CHARON
THAT WAS A JOKE! GET IT?
BECAUSE YOU'RE ALL DEAD, AND–
NO.
HA-HA-HA-HA!
HEH. FINALLY!
SOMEONE WHO APPRECIATES A GOOD JOKE!
HA-HA-HA!
GASP
HEE-HEE!
ARE THESE GUYS WITH YOU?
HEH-HEH. YES, SIR.
THEY ARE!
WELL, OKAY, THEN!
JUST THIS ONCE, I'LL OVERLOOK THE FARE.
WELCOME ABOARD!
16

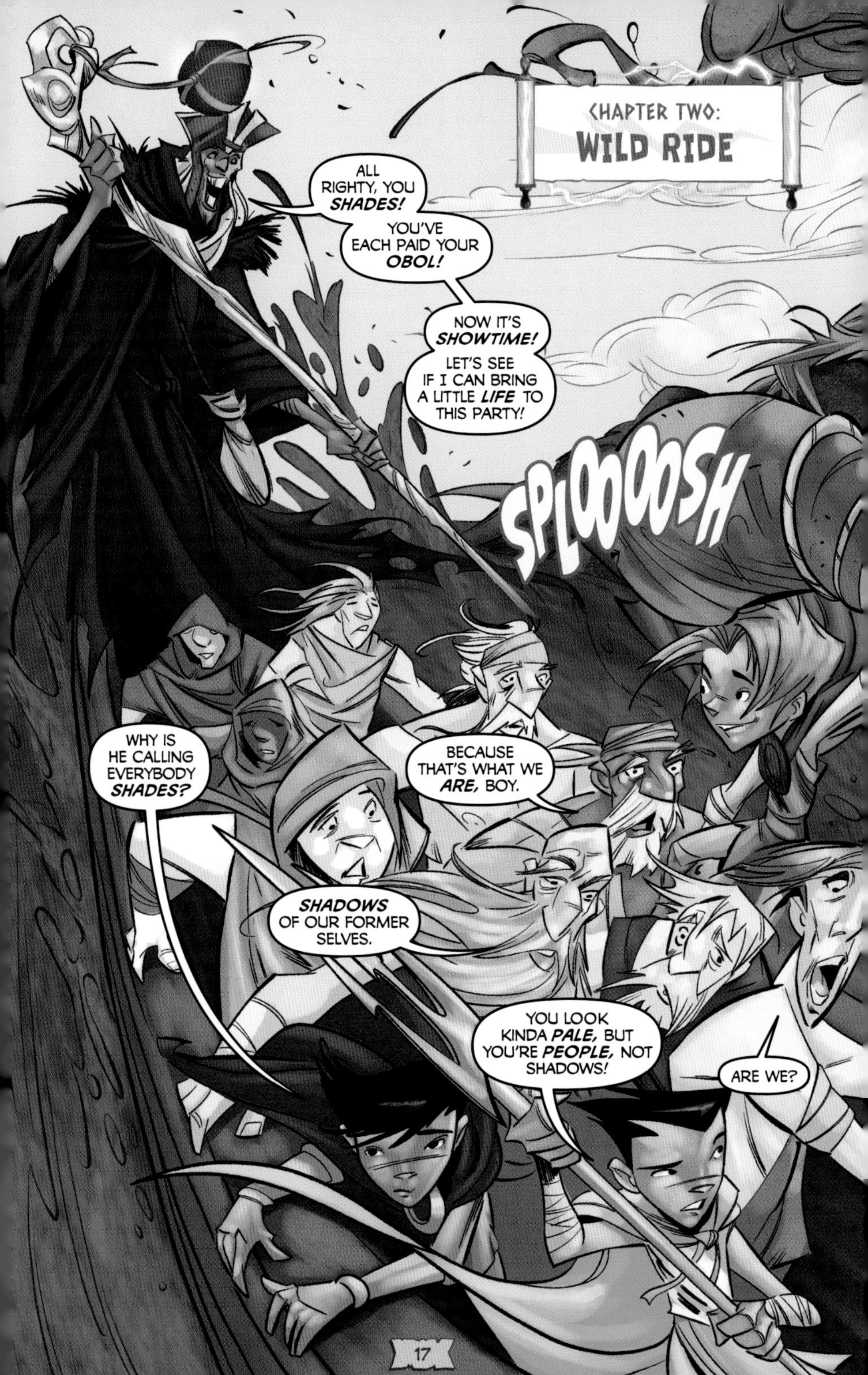
CHAPTER TWO:
WILD RIDE
ALL RIGHTY, YOU SHADES!
YOU'VE EACH PAID YOUR OBOL!
NOW IT'S SHOWTIME!
LET'S SEE IF I CAN BRING A LITTLE LIFE TO THIS PARTY!
SPLOOOOSH
WHY IS HE CALLING EVERYBODY SHADES?
BECAUSE THAT'S WHAT WE ARE, BOY.
SHADOWS OF OUR FORMER SELVES.
YOU LOOK KINDA PALE, BUT YOU'RE PEOPLE, NOT SHADOWS!
ARE WE?

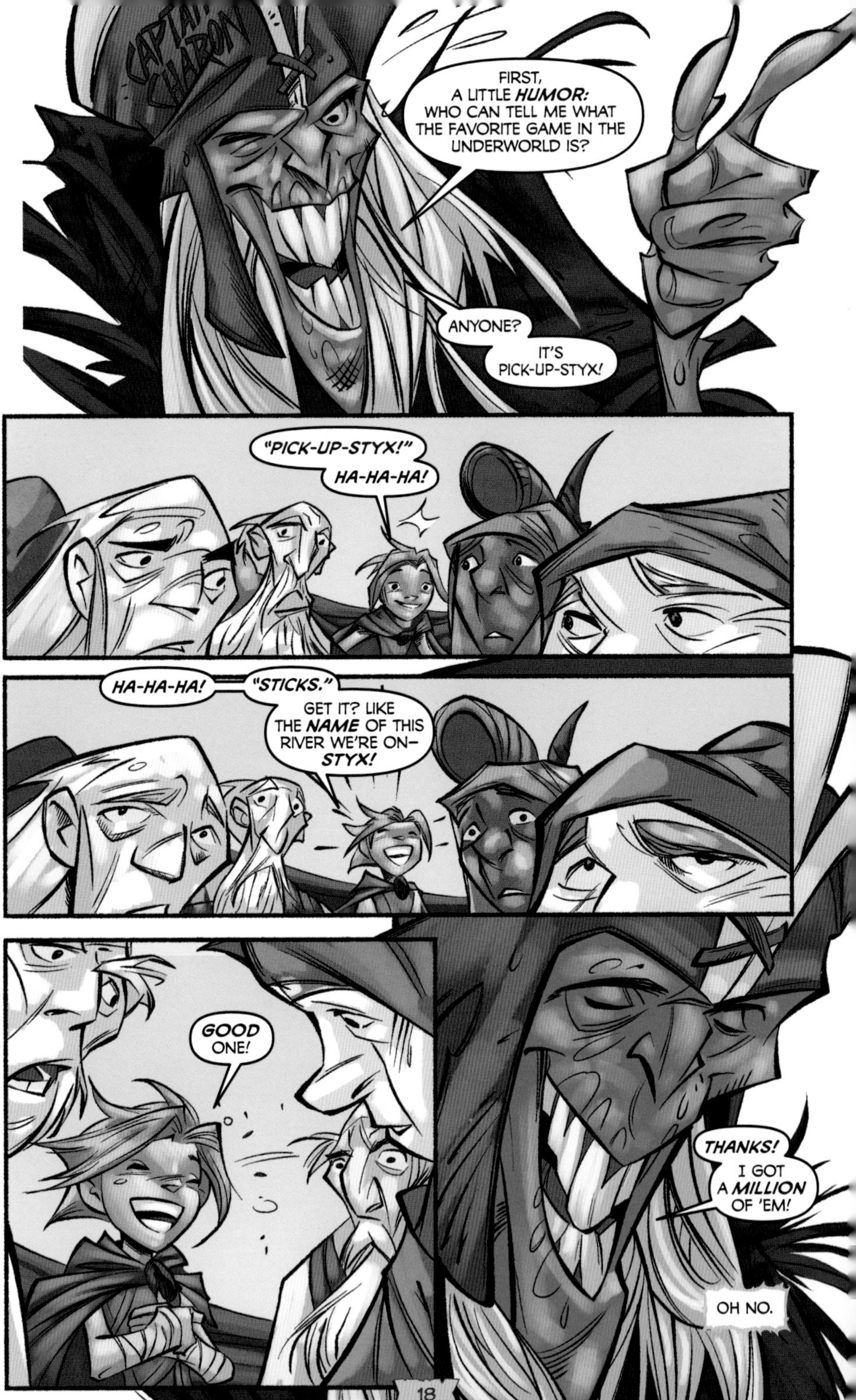
CAPTAIN CHARON
FIRST, A LITTLE HUMOR: WHO CAN TELL ME WHAT THE FAVORITE GAME IN THE UNDERWORLD IS?
ANYONE?
IT'S PICK-UP-STYX!
"PICK-UP-STYX!"
HA-HA-HA!
HA-HA-HA!
"STICKS."
GET IT? LIKE THE NAME OF THIS RIVER WE'RE ON— STYX!
GOOD ONE!
THANKS!
I GOT A MILLION OF 'EM!
OH NO.

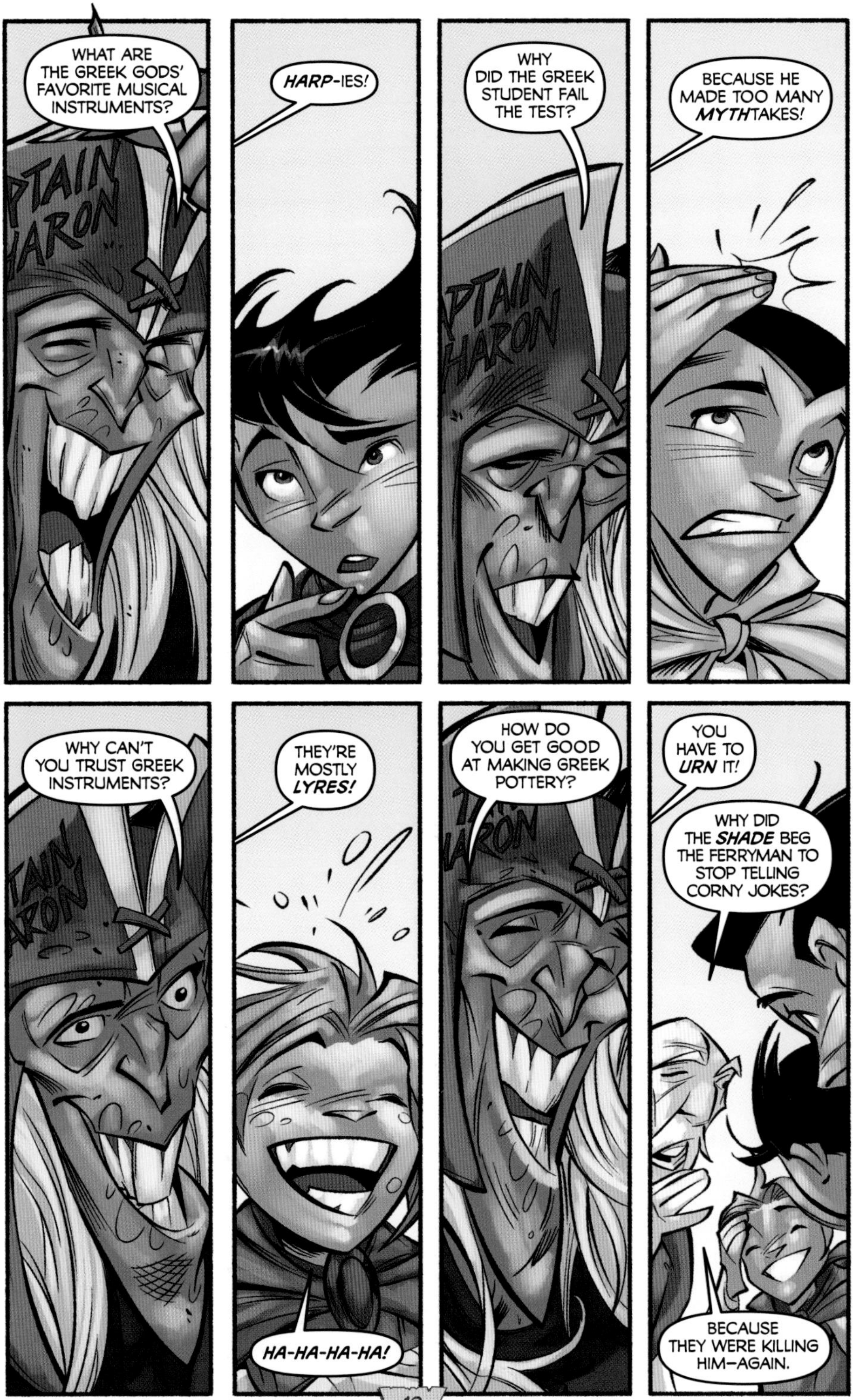
WHAT ARE THE GREEK GODS' FAVORITE MUSICAL INSTRUMENTS?
CAPTAIN CHARON
HARP-IES!
WHY DID THE GREEK STUDENT FAIL THE TEST?
CAPTAIN CHARON
BECAUSE HE MADE TOO MANY MYTHTAKES!
WHY CAN'T YOU TRUST GREEK INSTRUMENTS?
CAPTAIN CHARON
THEY'RE MOSTLY LYRES!
HA-HA-HA-HA!
HOW DO YOU GET GOOD AT MAKING GREEK POTTERY?
YOU HAVE TO URN IT!
WHY DID THE SHADE BEG THE FERRYMAN TO STOP TELLING CORNY JOKES?
BECAUSE THEY WERE KILLING HIM—AGAIN.

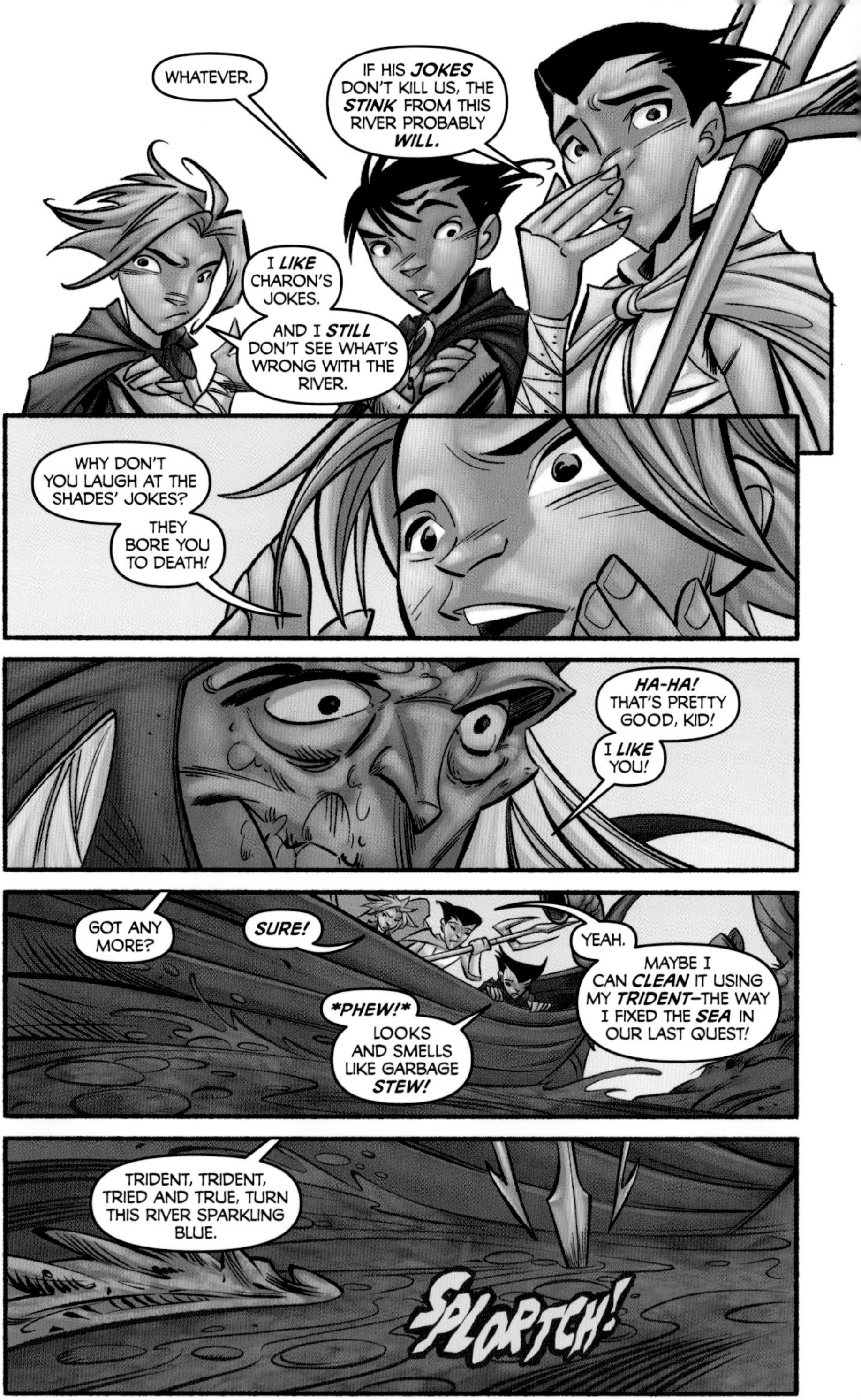

WHATEVER.
IF HIS JOKES DON'T KILL US, THE STINK FROM THIS RIVER PROBABLY WILL.
I LIKE CHARON'S JOKES.
AND I STILL DON'T SEE WHAT'S WRONG WITH THE RIVER.
WHY DON'T YOU LAUGH AT THE SHADES' JOKES?
THEY BORE YOU TO DEATH!
HA-HA! THAT'S PRETTY GOOD, KID!
I LIKE YOU!
GOT ANY MORE?
SURE!
PHEW! LOOKS AND SMELLS LIKE GARBAGE STEW!
YEAH.
MAYBE I CAN CLEAN IT USING MY TRIDENT—THE WAY I FIXED THE SEA IN OUR LAST QUEST!
TRIDENT, TRIDENT, TRIED AND TRUE, TURN THIS RIVER SPARKLING BLUE.
SPLORTCH!

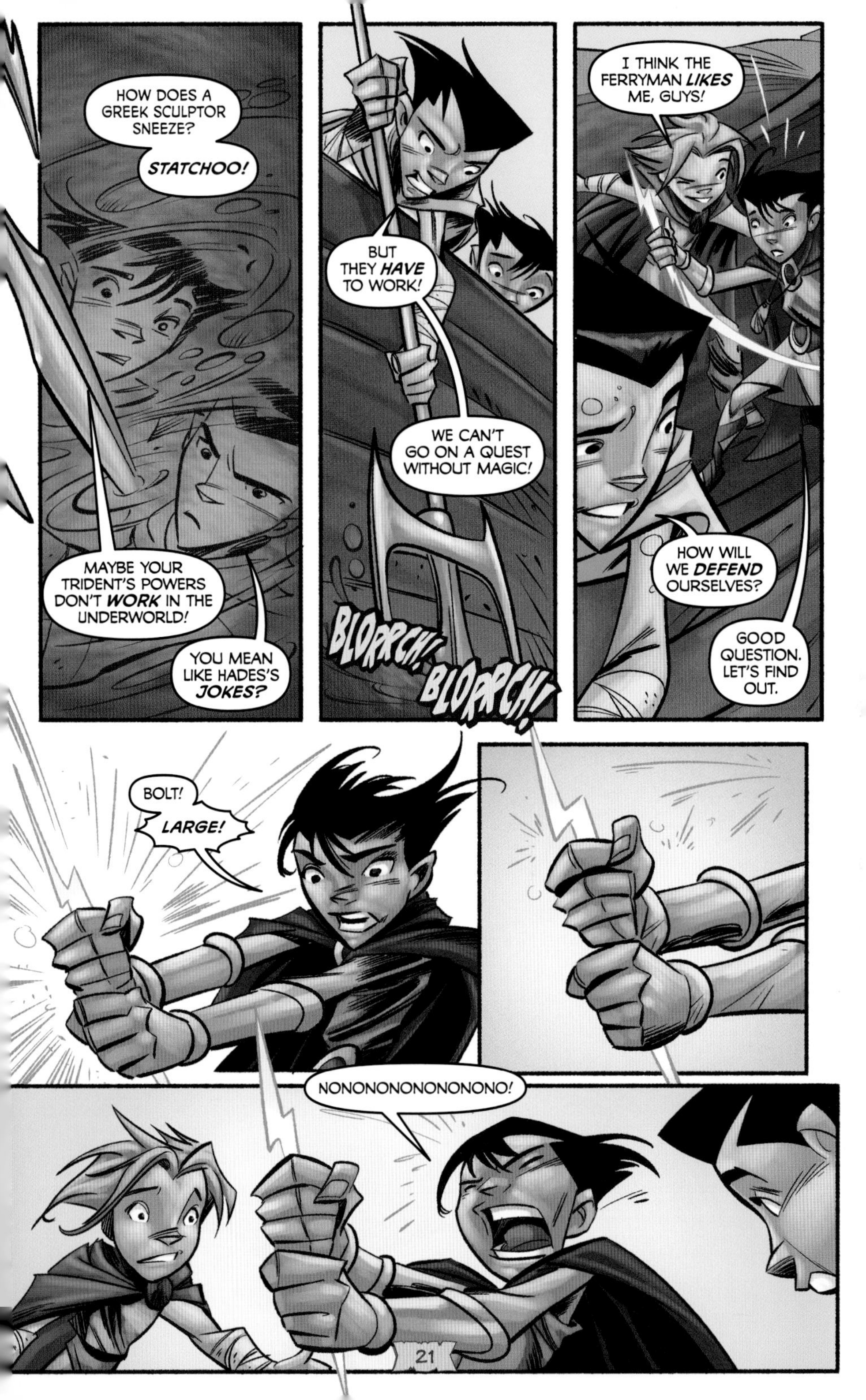

HOW DOES A GREEK SCULPTOR SNEEZE?
STATCHOO!
MAYBE YOUR TRIDENT'S POWERS DON'T WORK IN THE UNDERWORLD!
YOU MEAN LIKE HADES'S JOKES?
BUT THEY HAVE TO WORK!
WE CAN'T GO ON A QUEST WITHOUT MAGIC!
BLORRCH! BLORRCH!
I THINK THE FERRYMAN LIKES ME, GUYS!
HOW WILL WE DEFEND OURSELVES?
GOOD QUESTION. LET'S FIND OUT.
BOLT!
LARGE!
NONONONONONONONO!

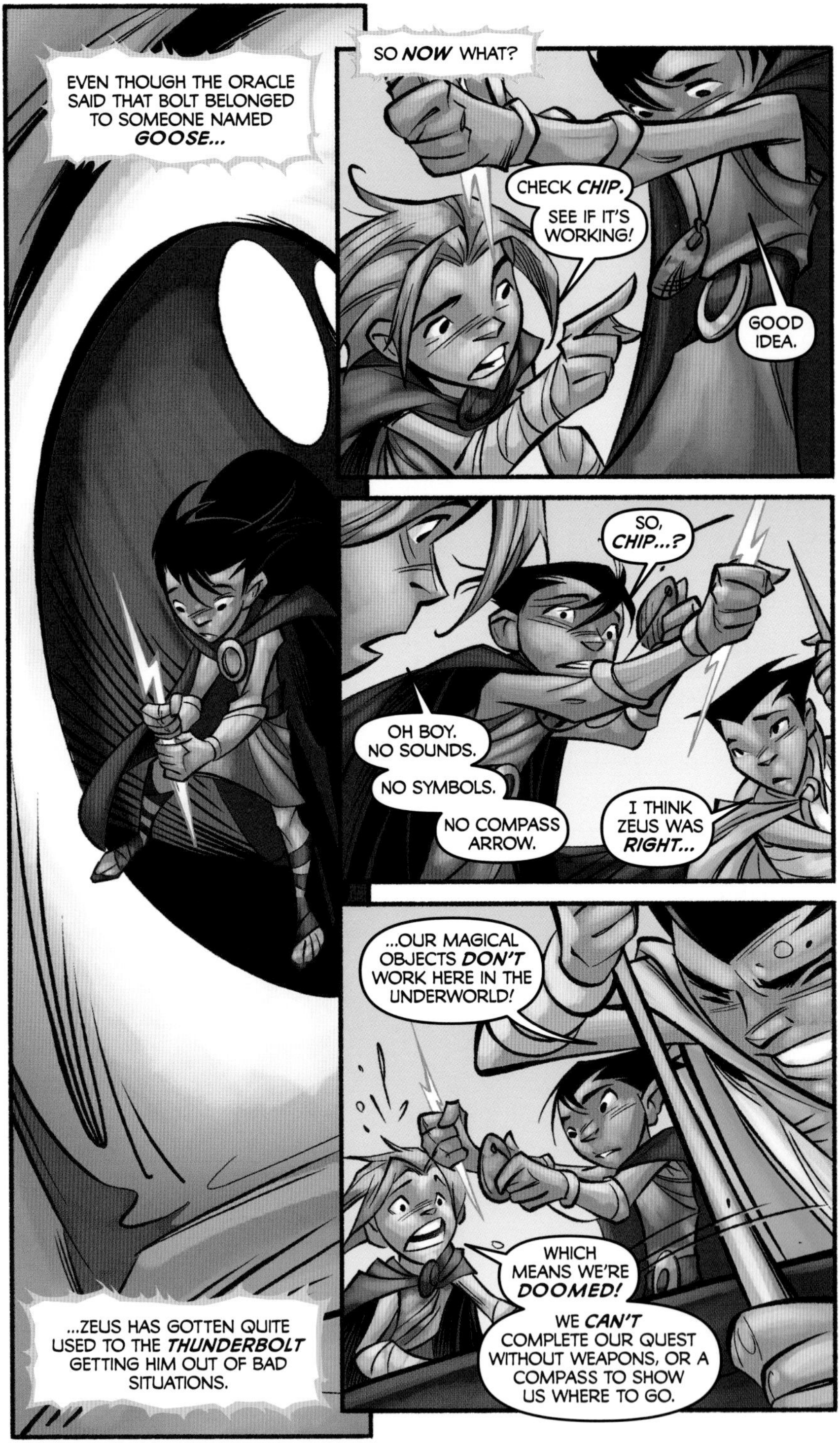
EVEN THOUGH THE ORACLE SAID THAT BOLT BELONGED TO SOMEONE NAMED GOOSE...
...ZEUS HAS GOTTEN QUITE USED TO THE THUNDERBOLT GETTING HIM OUT OF BAD SITUATIONS.
SO NOW WHAT?
CHECK CHIP.
SEE IF IT'S WORKING!
GOOD IDEA.
SO, CHIP...?
OH BOY. NO SOUNDS.
NO SYMBOLS.
NO COMPASS ARROW.
I THINK ZEUS WAS RIGHT...
...OUR MAGICAL OBJECTS DON'T WORK HERE IN THE UNDERWORLD!
WHICH MEANS WE'RE DOOMED!
WE CAN'T COMPLETE OUR QUEST WITHOUT WEAPONS, OR A COMPASS TO SHOW US WHERE TO GO.

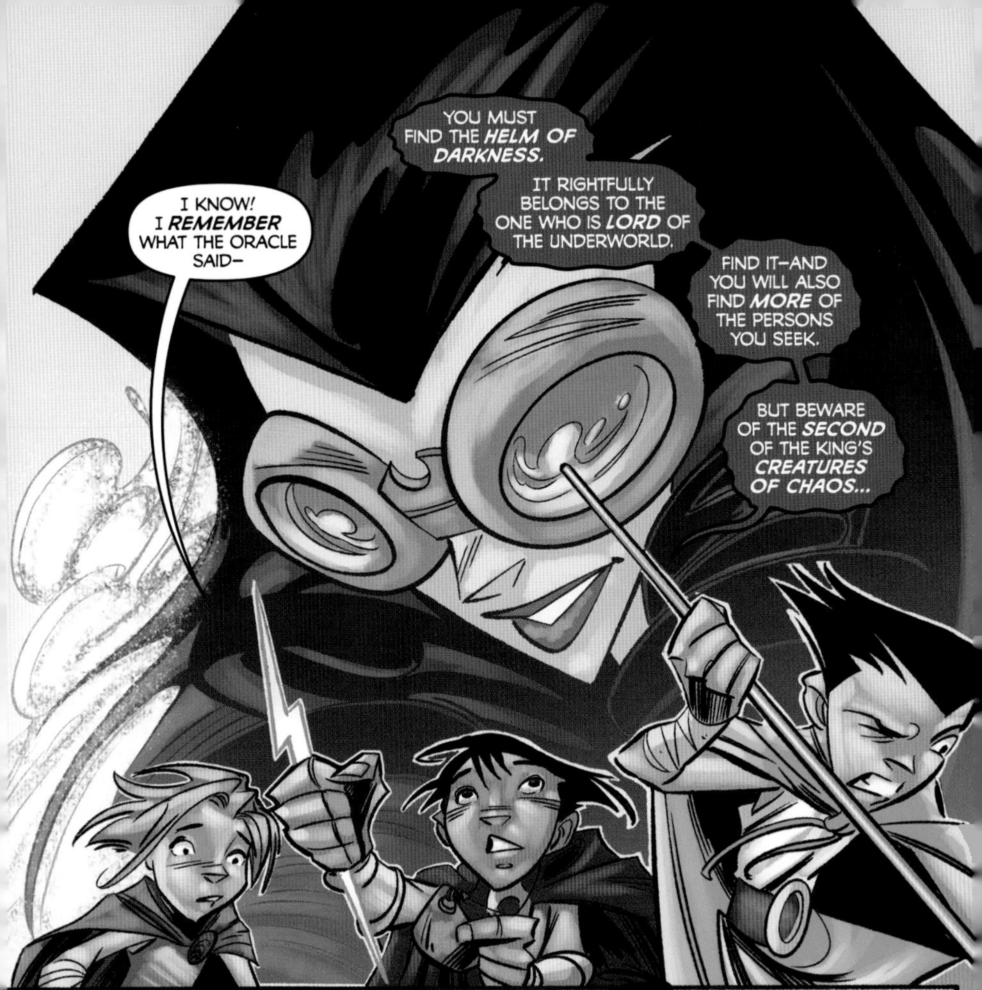
YOU MUST FIND THE HELM OF DARKNESS.
IT RIGHTFULLY BELONGS TO THE ONE WHO IS LORD OF THE UNDERWORLD.
I KNOW! I REMEMBER WHAT THE ORACLE SAID–
FIND IT–AND YOU WILL ALSO FIND MORE OF THE PERSONS YOU SEEK.
BUT BEWARE OF THE SECOND OF THE KING'S CREATURES OF CHAOS...

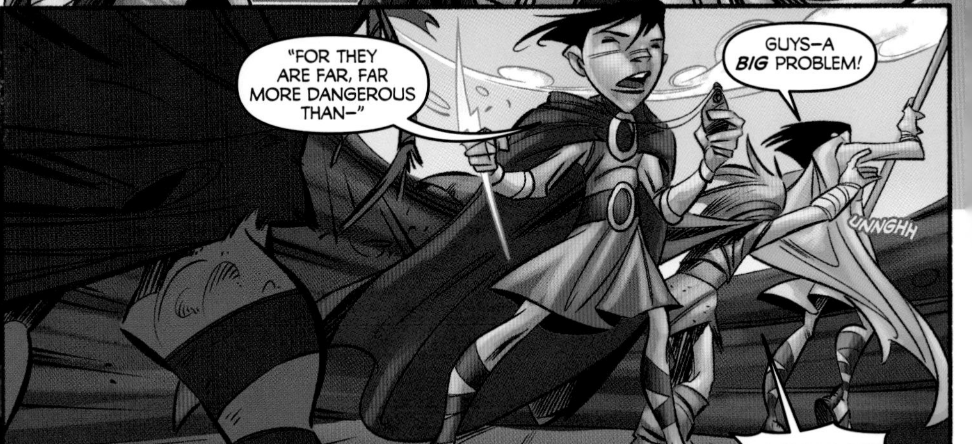
"FOR THEY ARE FAR, FAR MORE DANGEROUS THAN–"
GUYS–A BIG PROBLEM!
UNNGHH
INCOMING!

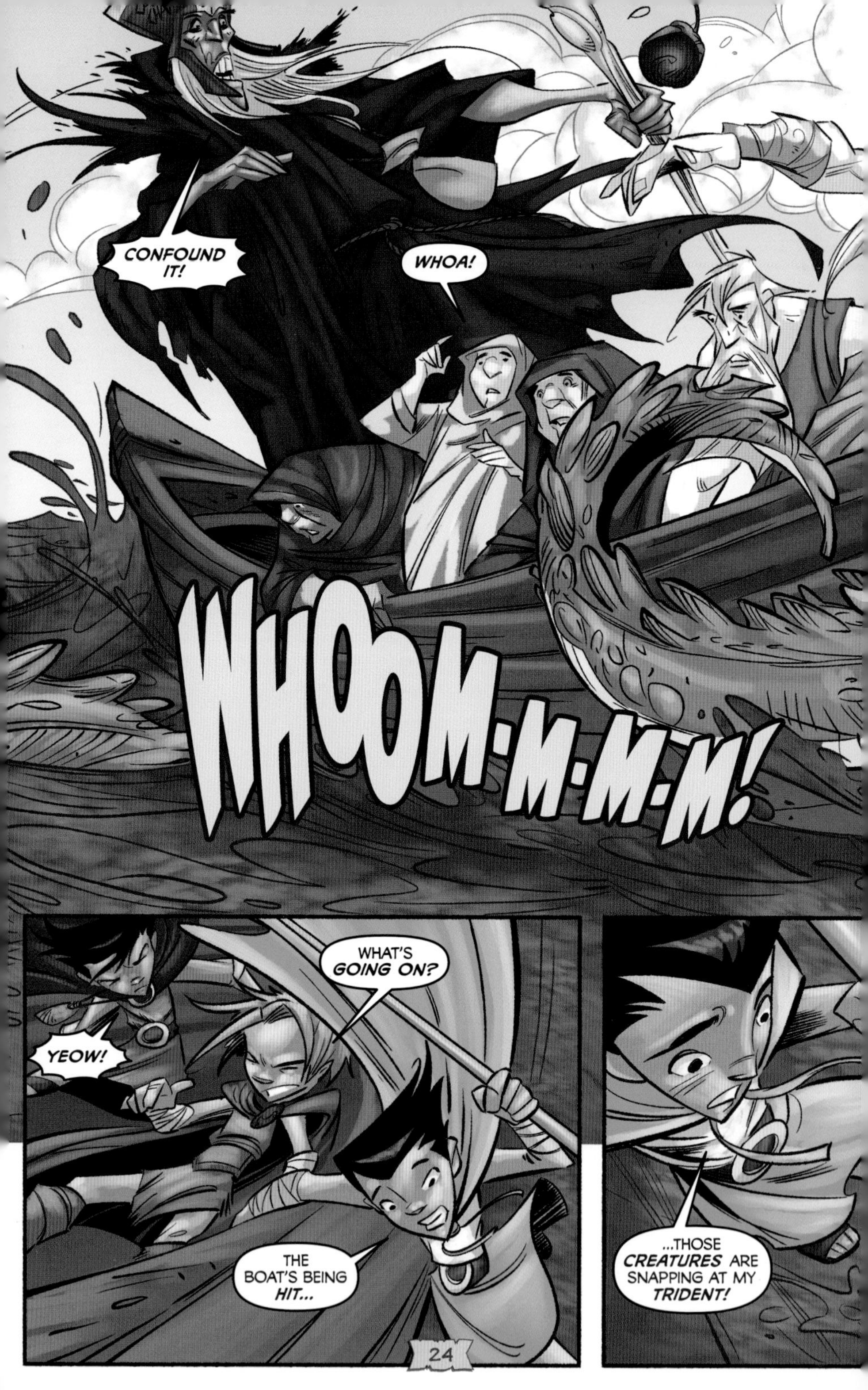
CONFOUND IT!
WHOA!
WHOOM-M-M-M!
WHAT'S GOING ON?
YEOW!
THE BOAT'S BEING HIT...
...THOSE CREATURES ARE SNAPPING AT MY TRIDENT!

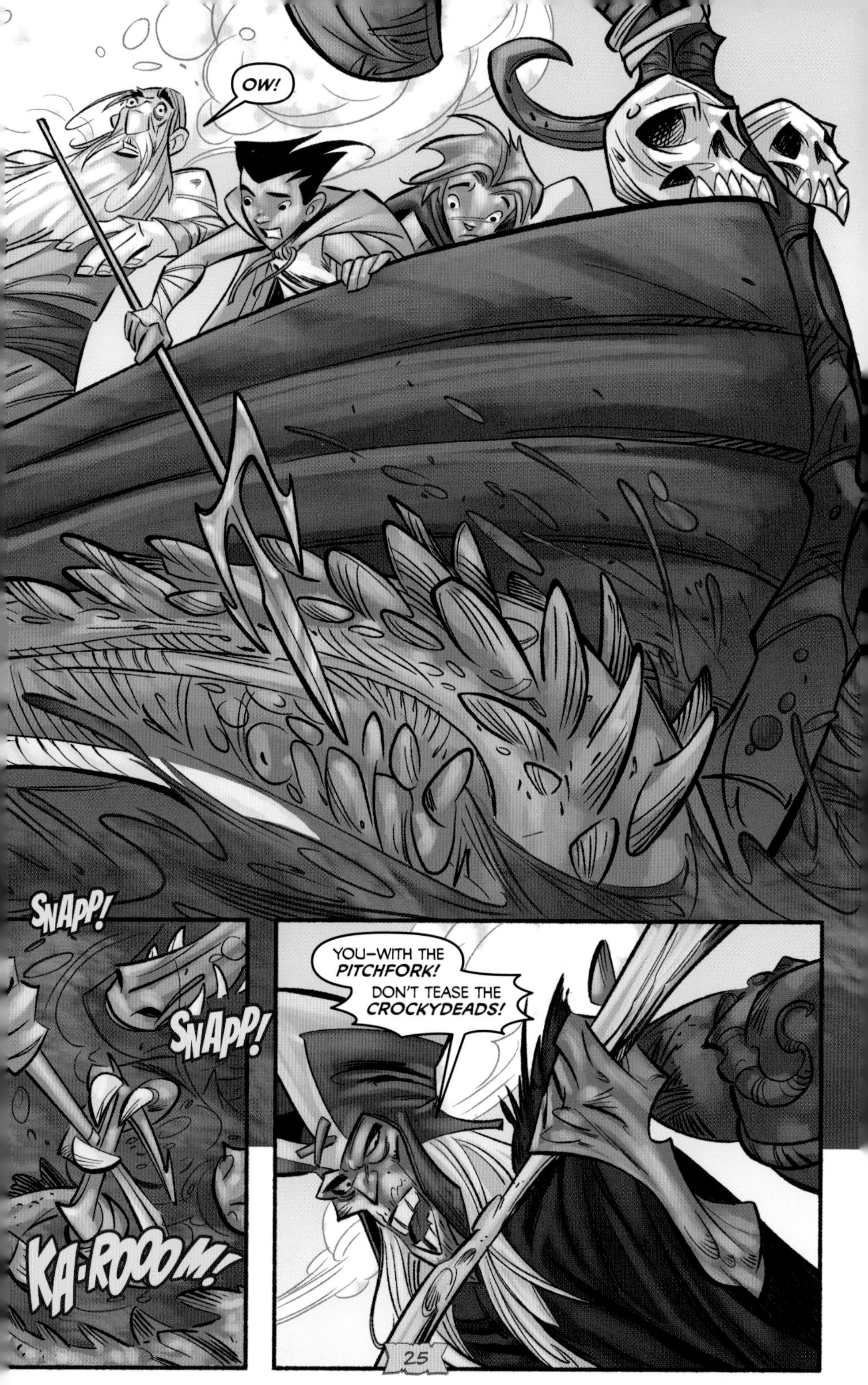
OW!
SNAPP!
SNAPP!
KA-ROOOM!
YOU—WITH THE PITCHFORK!
DON'T TEASE THE CROCKYDEADS!

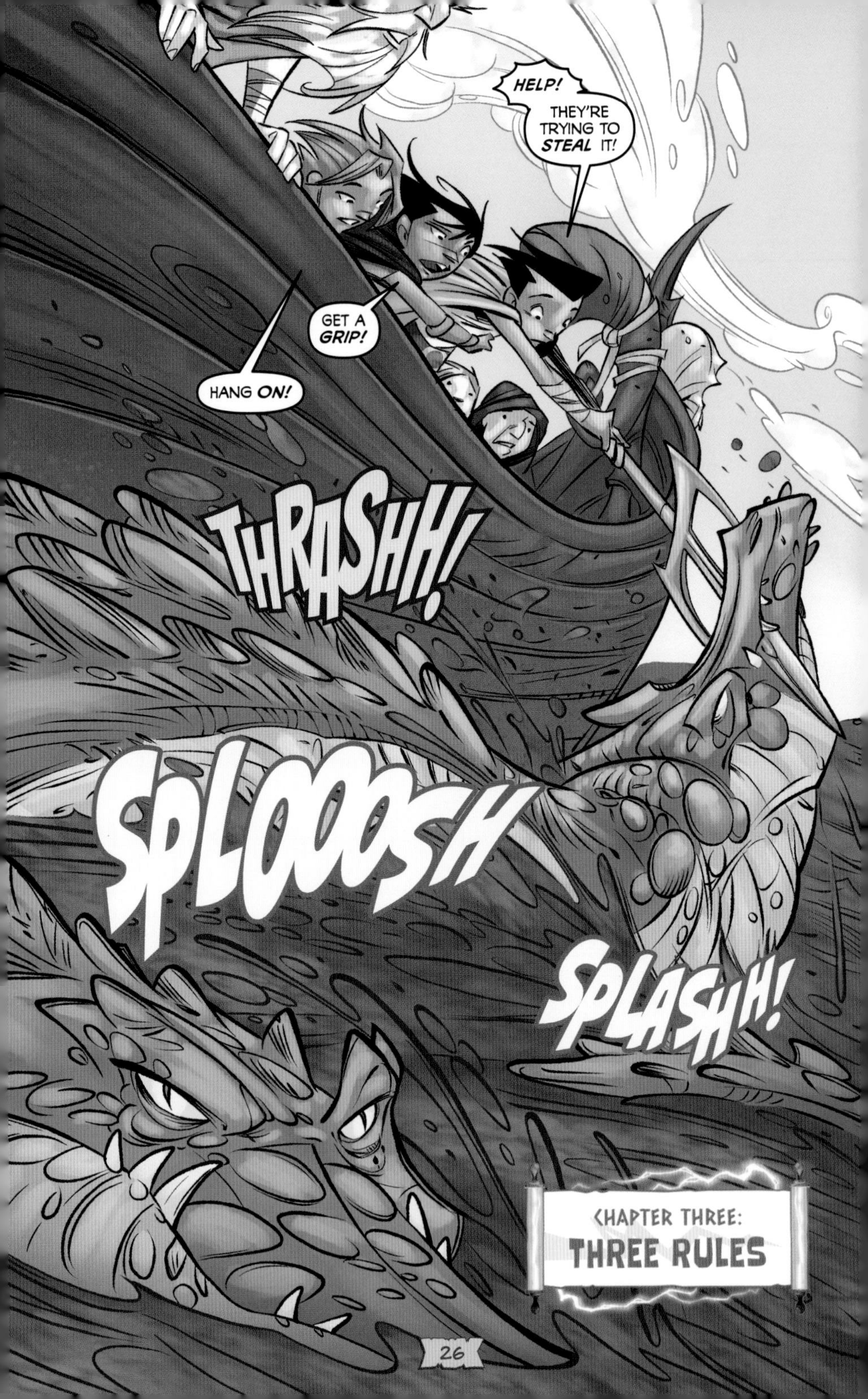
HELP! THEY'RE TRYING TO STEAL IT!
GET A GRIP!
HANG ON!
THRASHH!
SPLOOOSH
SPLASHH!

CHAPTER THREE: THREE RULES

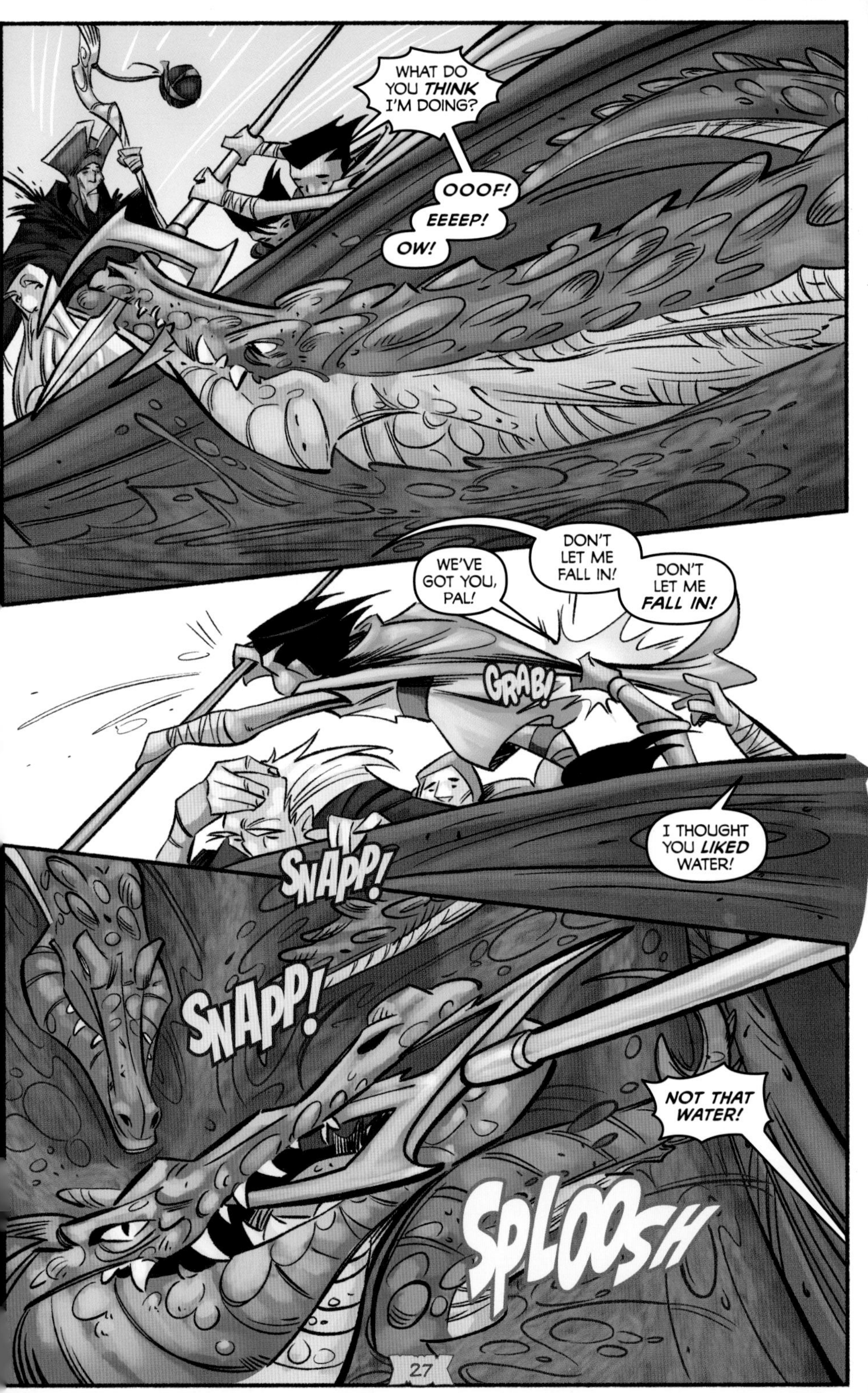
WHAT DO YOU *THINK* I'M DOING?
OOOF!
EEEEP!
OW!
WE'VE GOT YOU, PAL!
DON'T LET ME FALL IN!
DON'T LET ME *FALL IN!*
GRAB!
I THOUGHT YOU *LIKED* WATER!
SNAPP!
SNAPP!
NOT THAT WATER!
SPLOOSH

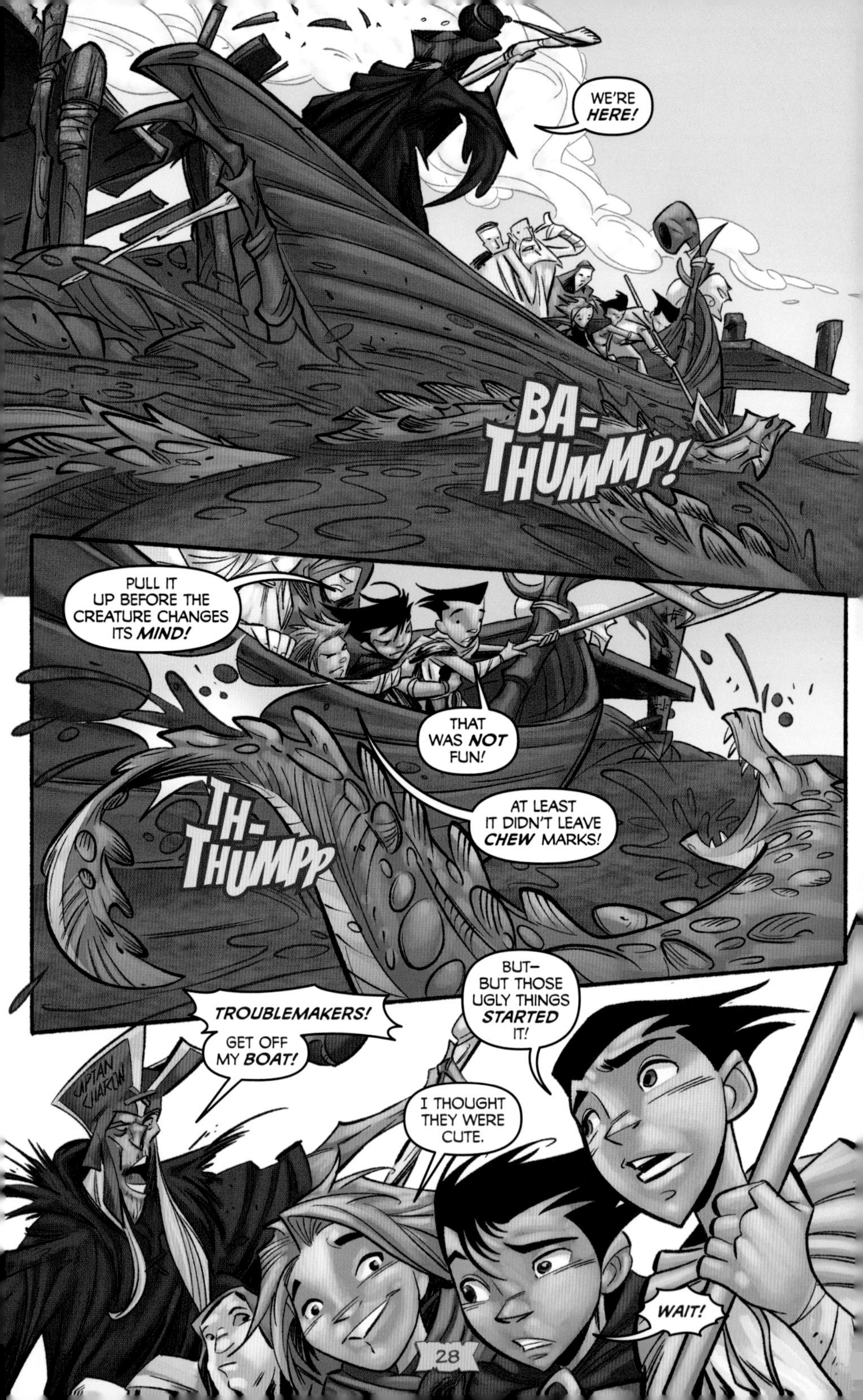
WE'RE HERE!
BA-THUMMP!
PULL IT UP BEFORE THE CREATURE CHANGES ITS MIND!
THAT WAS NOT FUN!
AT LEAST IT DIDN'T LEAVE CHEW MARKS!
TH-THUMPP
TROUBLEMAKERS!
GET OFF MY BOAT!
BUT— BUT THOSE UGLY THINGS STARTED IT!
I THOUGHT THEY WERE CUTE.
WAIT!

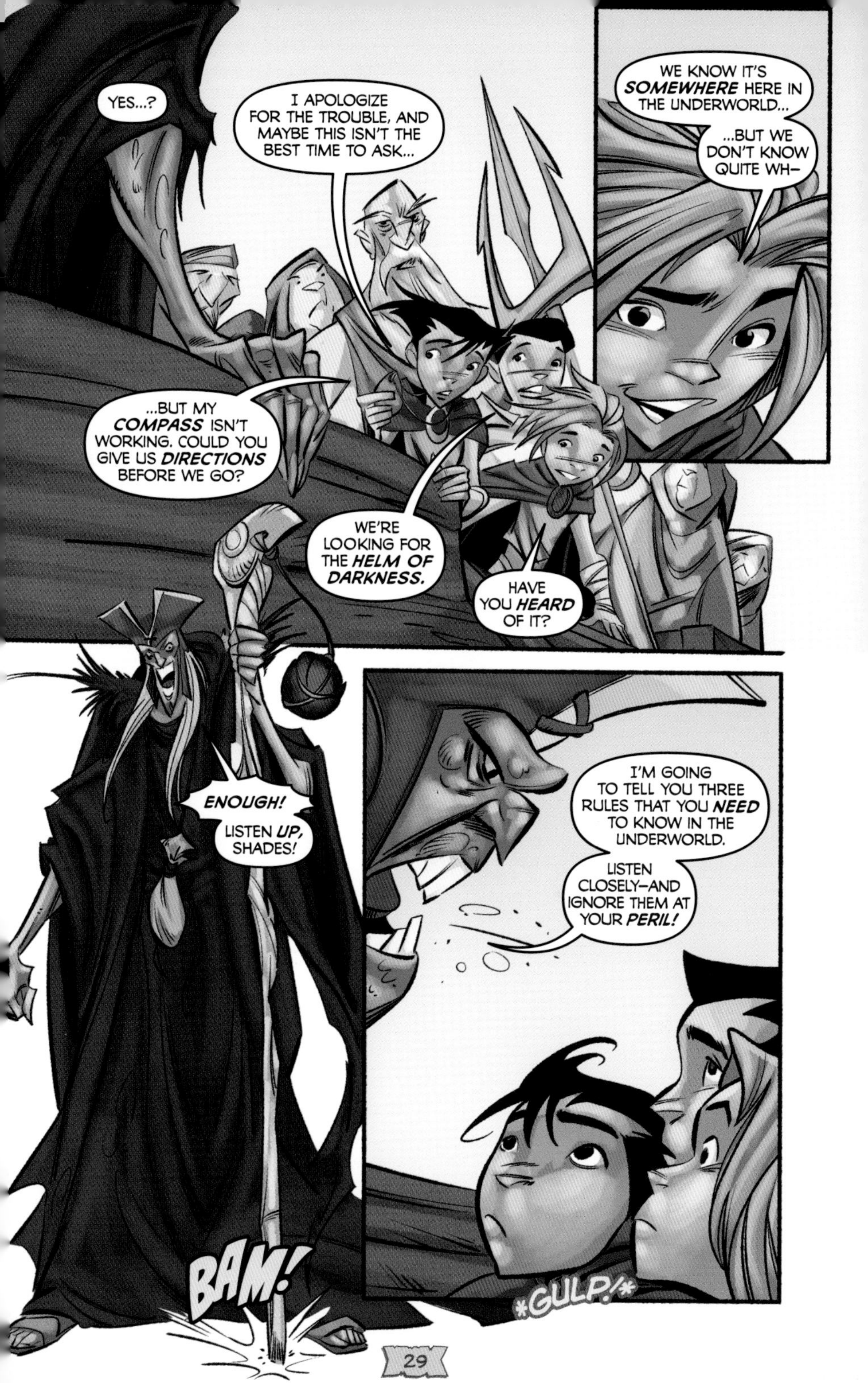

YES...?
I APOLOGIZE FOR THE TROUBLE, AND MAYBE THIS ISN'T THE BEST TIME TO ASK...
WE KNOW IT'S *SOMEWHERE* HERE IN THE UNDERWORLD...
...BUT WE DON'T KNOW QUITE WH–
...BUT MY *COMPASS* ISN'T WORKING. COULD YOU GIVE US *DIRECTIONS* BEFORE WE GO?
WE'RE LOOKING FOR THE *HELM OF DARKNESS.*
HAVE YOU *HEARD* OF IT?
ENOUGH!
LISTEN *UP,* SHADES!
BAM!
I'M GOING TO TELL YOU THREE RULES THAT YOU *NEED* TO KNOW IN THE UNDERWORLD.
LISTEN CLOSELY–AND IGNORE THEM AT YOUR *PERIL!*
GULP!

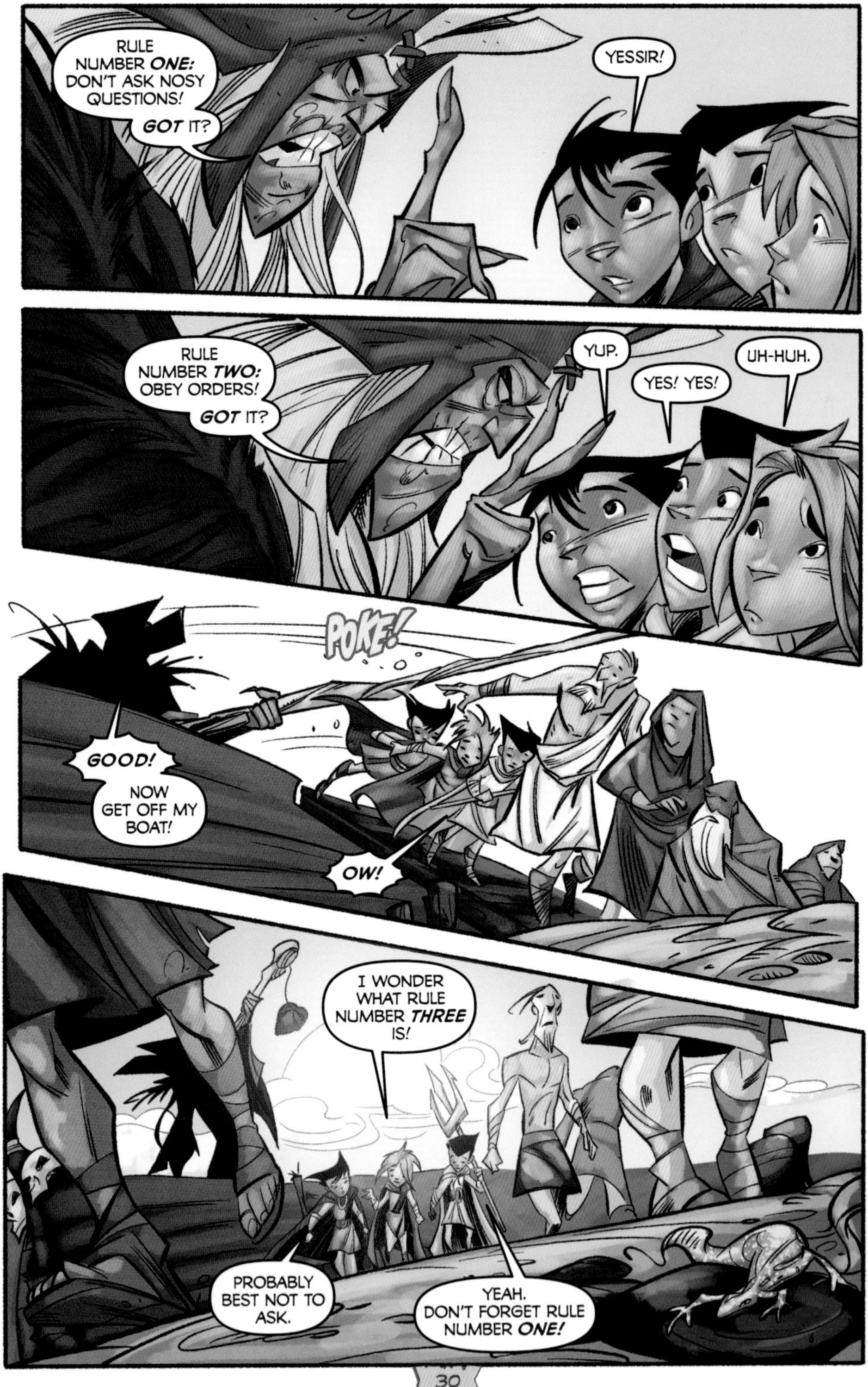
RULE NUMBER ONE: DON'T ASK NOSY QUESTIONS! GOT IT?
YESSIR!
RULE NUMBER TWO: OBEY ORDERS! GOT IT?
YUP.
YES! YES!
UH-HUH.
POKE!
GOOD! NOW GET OFF MY BOAT!
OW!
I WONDER WHAT RULE NUMBER THREE IS!
PROBABLY BEST NOT TO ASK.
YEAH. DON'T FORGET RULE NUMBER ONE!

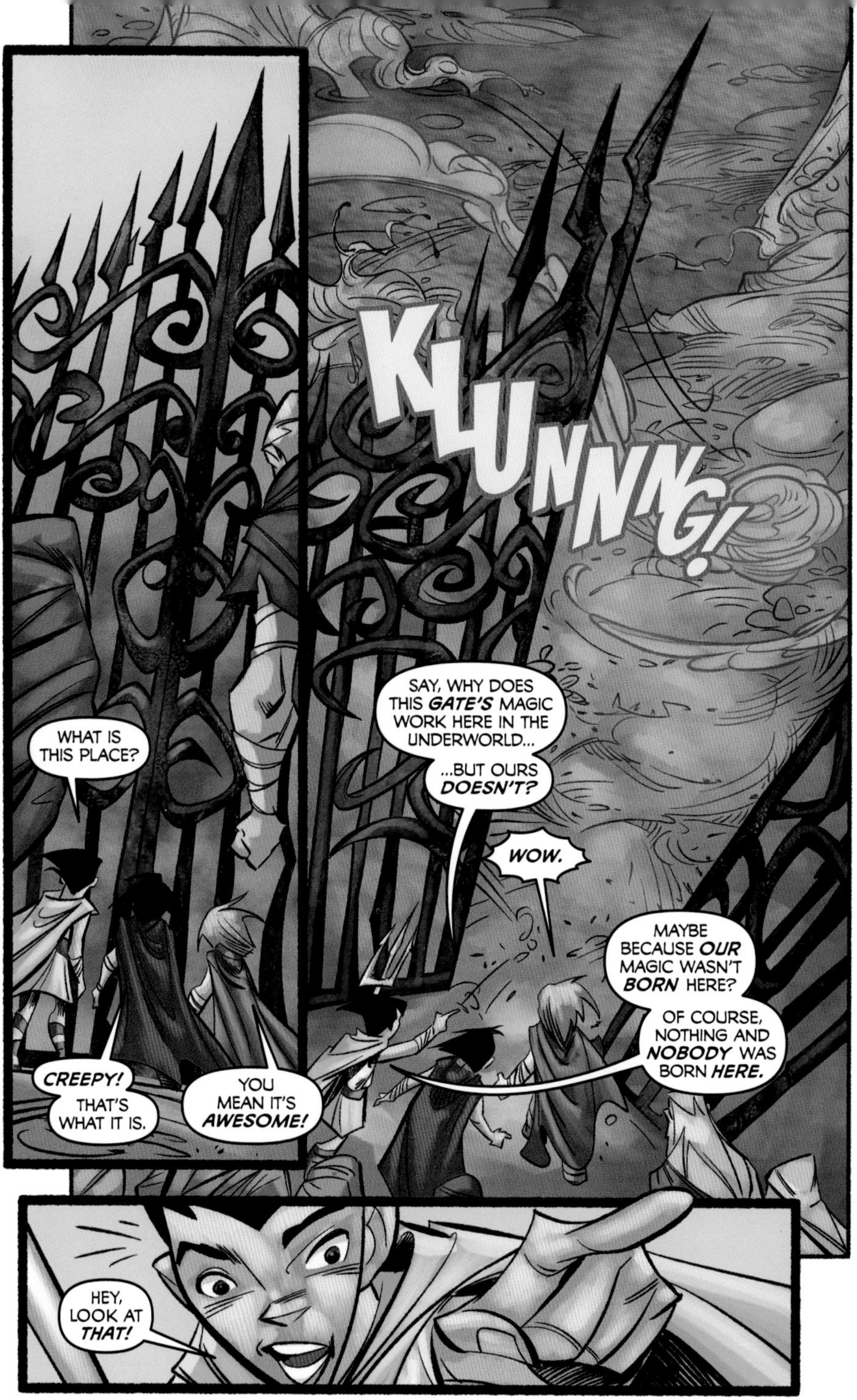
KLUNNNG!
WHAT IS THIS PLACE?
CREEPY! THAT'S WHAT IT IS.
YOU MEAN IT'S AWESOME!
SAY, WHY DOES THIS GATE'S MAGIC WORK HERE IN THE UNDERWORLD...
...BUT OURS DOESN'T?
WOW.
MAYBE BECAUSE OUR MAGIC WASN'T BORN HERE?
OF COURSE, NOTHING AND NOBODY WAS BORN HERE.
HEY, LOOK AT THAT!

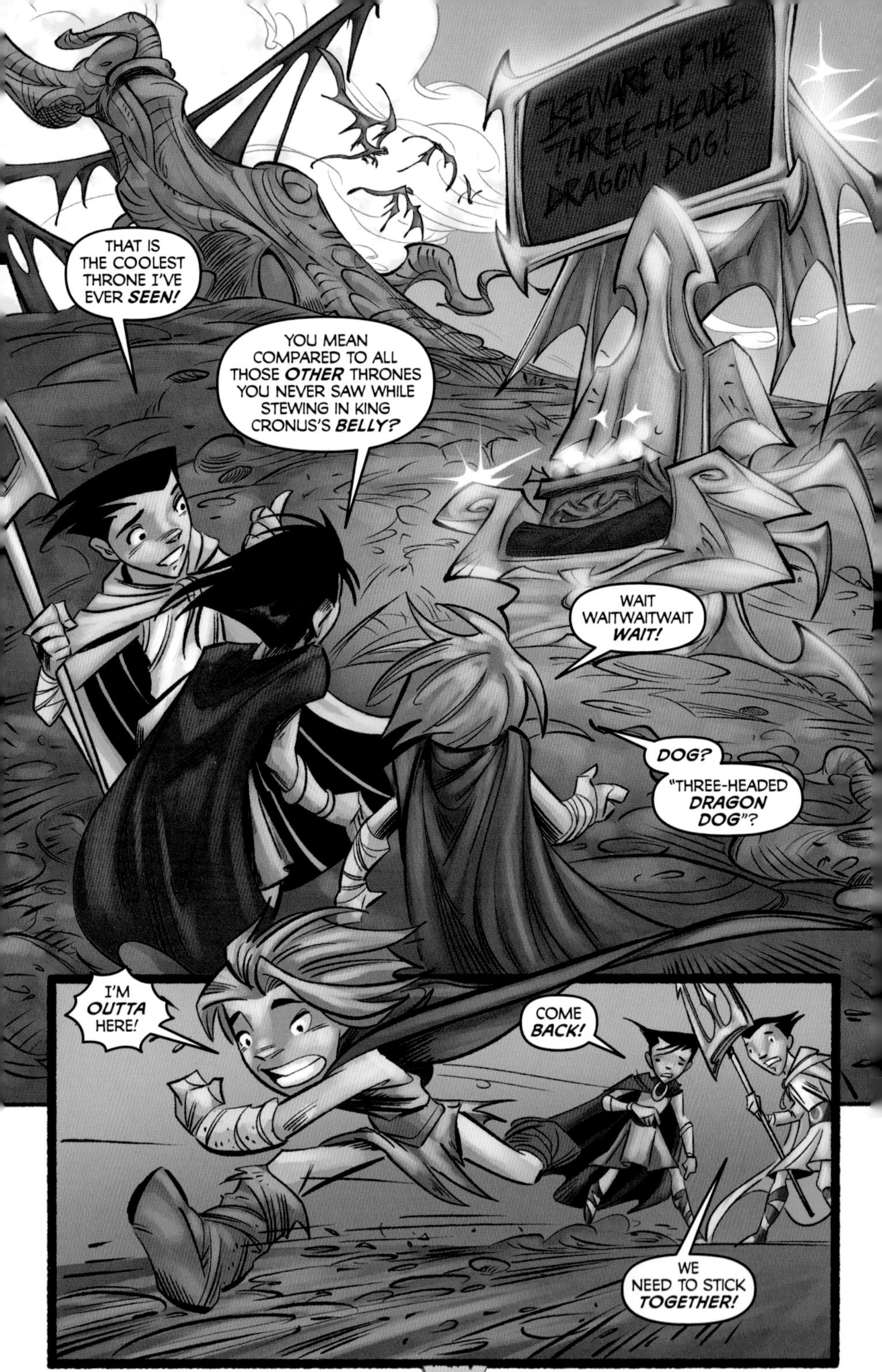
BEWARE OF THE THREE-HEADED DRAGON DOG!
THAT IS THE COOLEST THRONE I'VE EVER *SEEN!*
YOU MEAN COMPARED TO ALL THOSE *OTHER* THRONES YOU NEVER SAW WHILE STEWING IN KING CRONUS'S *BELLY?*
WAIT WAITWAITWAIT *WAIT!*
DOG?
"THREE-HEADED *DRAGON DOG*"?
I'M *OUTTA* HERE!
COME *BACK!*
WE NEED TO STICK *TOGETHER!*

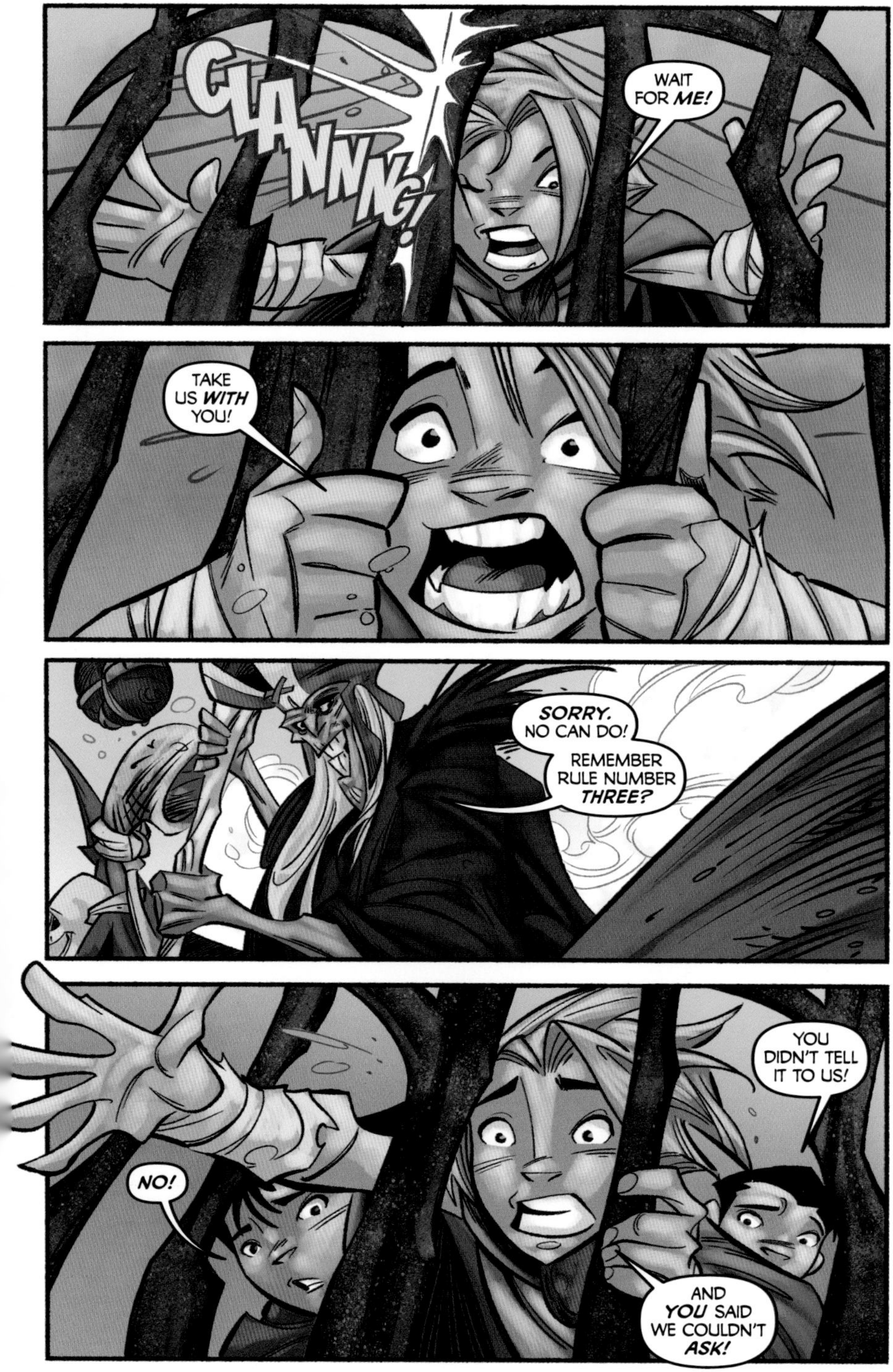
CLANNNG!
WAIT FOR ME!
TAKE US WITH YOU!
SORRY. NO CAN DO!
REMEMBER RULE NUMBER THREE?
YOU DIDN'T TELL IT TO US!
NO!
AND YOU SAID WE COULDN'T ASK!

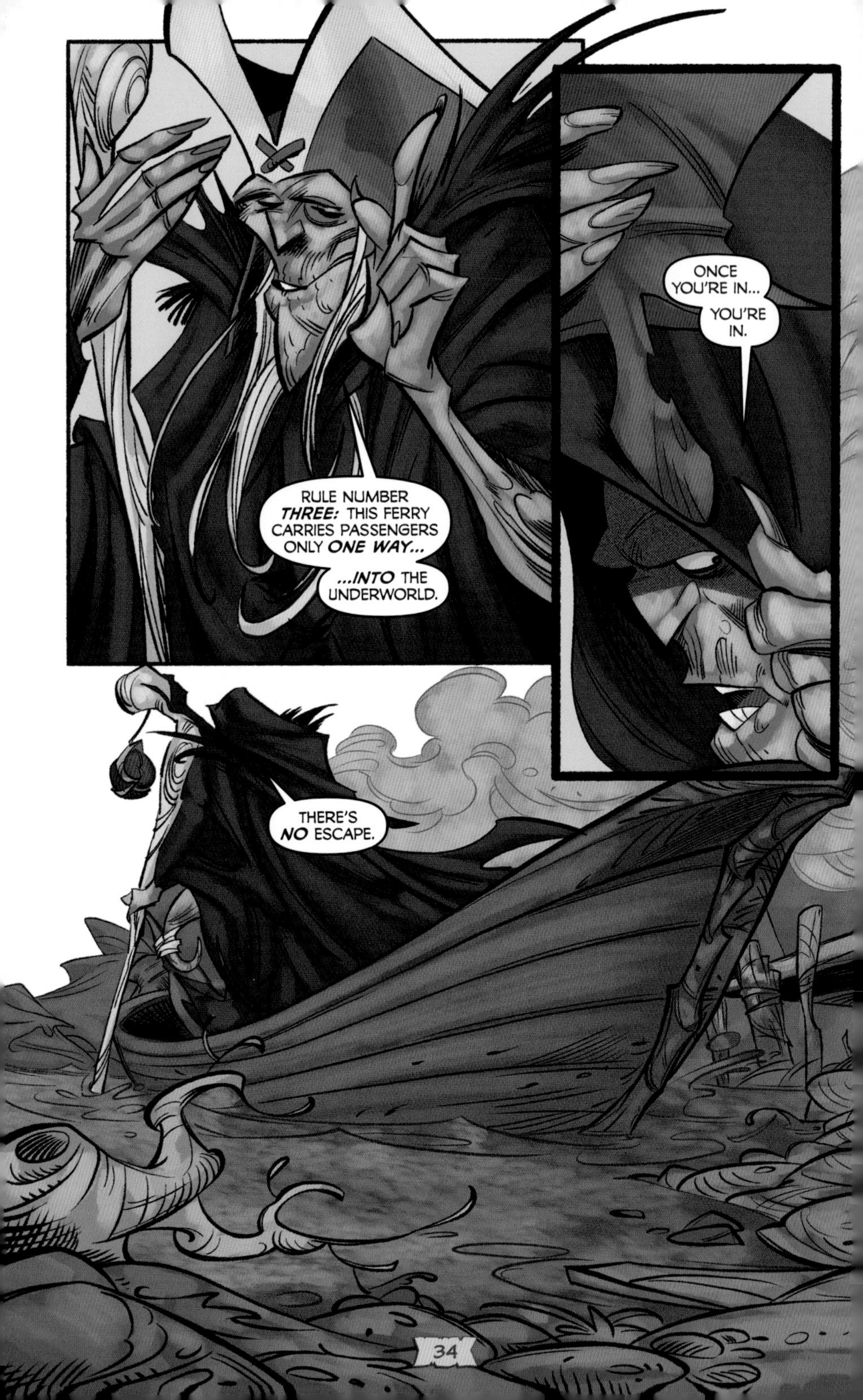
RULE NUMBER *THREE:* THIS FERRY CARRIES PASSENGERS ONLY *ONE WAY...*
...INTO THE UNDERWORLD.
ONCE YOU'RE IN...
YOU'RE IN.
THERE'S *NO* ESCAPE.

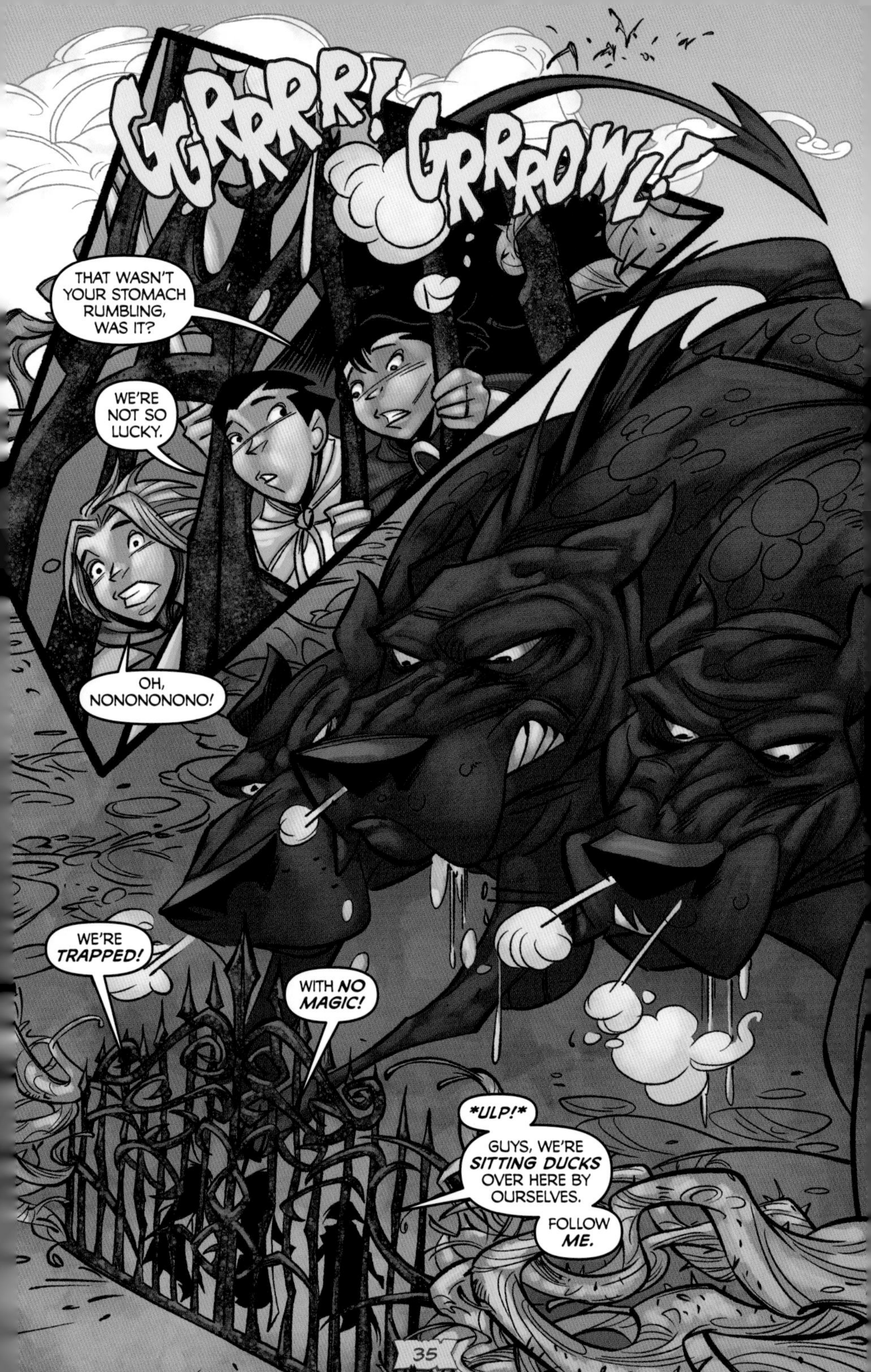
GGRRRR! GRRROWL!
THAT WASN'T YOUR STOMACH RUMBLING, WAS IT?
WE'RE NOT SO LUCKY.
OH, NONONONONO!
WE'RE TRAPPED!
WITH NO MAGIC!
ULP!
GUYS, WE'RE SITTING DUCKS OVER HERE BY OURSELVES.
FOLLOW ME.

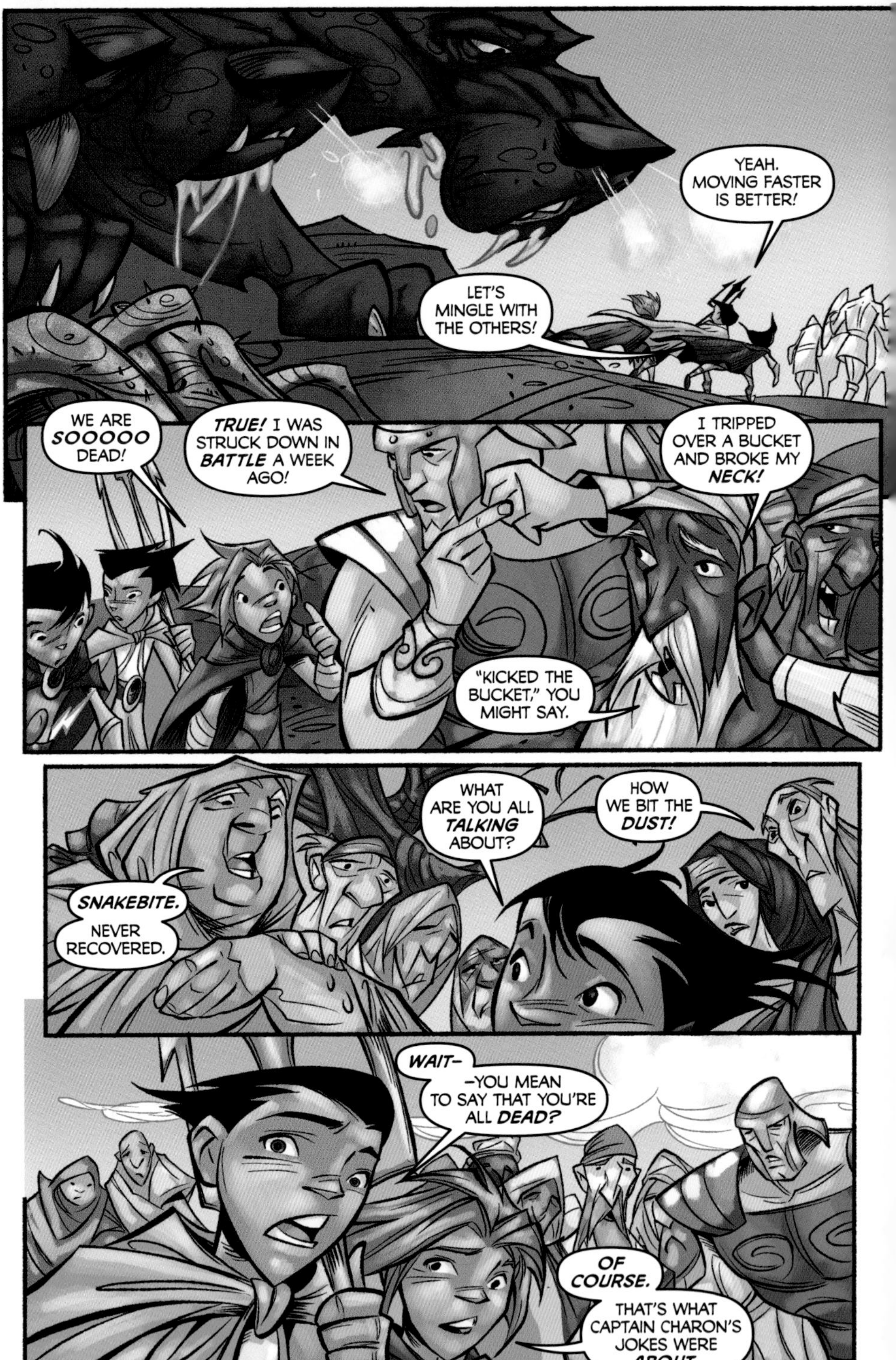
YEAH. MOVING FASTER IS BETTER!
LET'S MINGLE WITH THE OTHERS!
WE ARE SOOOOO DEAD!
TRUE! I WAS STRUCK DOWN IN BATTLE A WEEK AGO!
I TRIPPED OVER A BUCKET AND BROKE MY NECK!
"KICKED THE BUCKET," YOU MIGHT SAY.
SNAKEBITE.
NEVER RECOVERED.
WHAT ARE YOU ALL TALKING ABOUT?
HOW WE BIT THE DUST!
WAIT–
–YOU MEAN TO SAY THAT YOU'RE ALL DEAD?
OF COURSE.
THAT'S WHAT CAPTAIN CHARON'S JOKES WERE ABOUT.

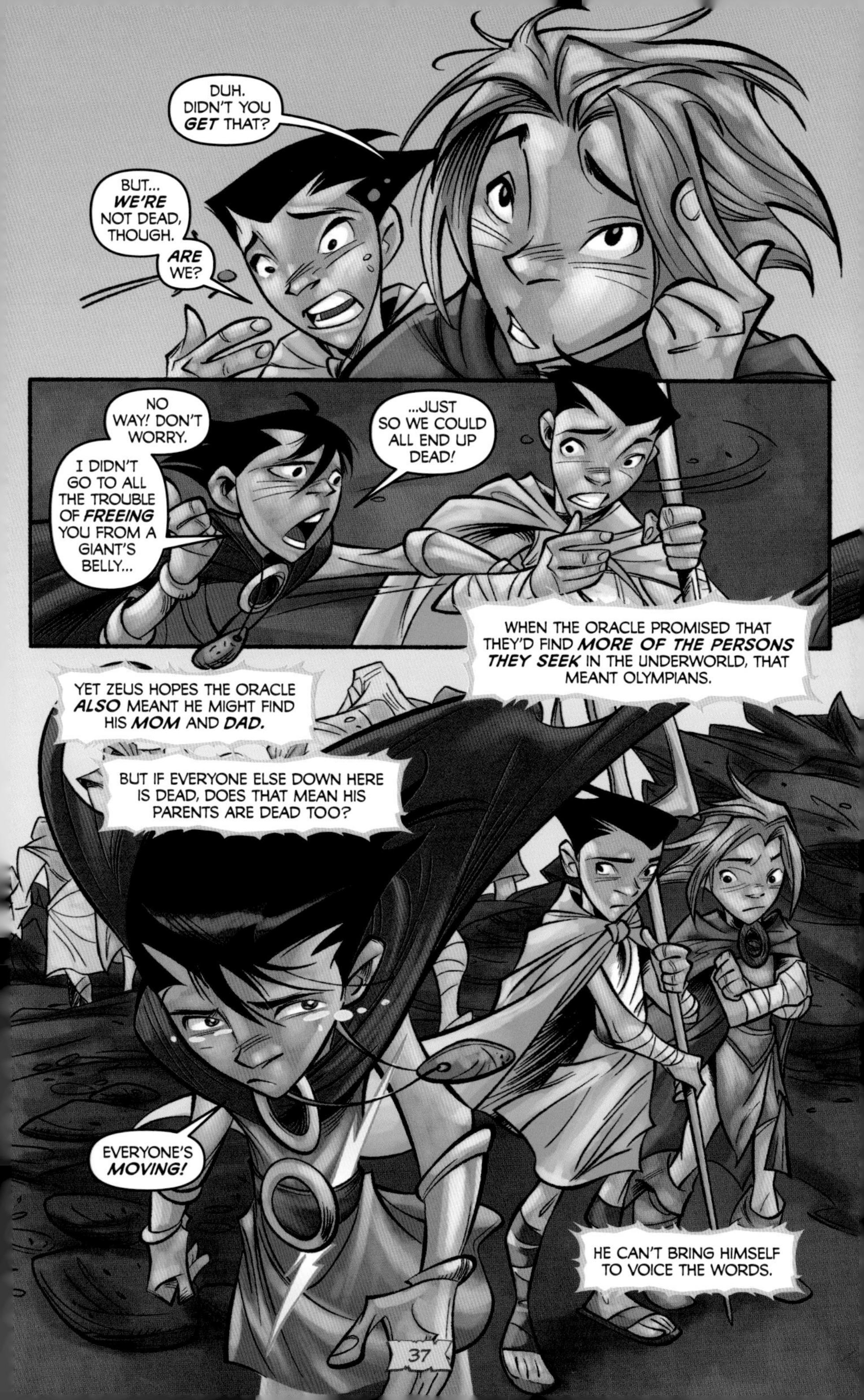
DUH. DIDN'T YOU GET THAT?
BUT... WE'RE NOT DEAD, THOUGH. ARE WE?
NO WAY! DON'T WORRY.
I DIDN'T GO TO ALL THE TROUBLE OF FREEING YOU FROM A GIANT'S BELLY...
...JUST SO WE COULD ALL END UP DEAD!
WHEN THE ORACLE PROMISED THAT THEY'D FIND MORE OF THE PERSONS THEY SEEK IN THE UNDERWORLD, THAT MEANT OLYMPIANS.
YET ZEUS HOPES THE ORACLE ALSO MEANT HE MIGHT FIND HIS MOM AND DAD.
BUT IF EVERYONE ELSE DOWN HERE IS DEAD, DOES THAT MEAN HIS PARENTS ARE DEAD TOO?
EVERYONE'S MOVING!
HE CAN'T BRING HIMSELF TO VOICE THE WORDS.

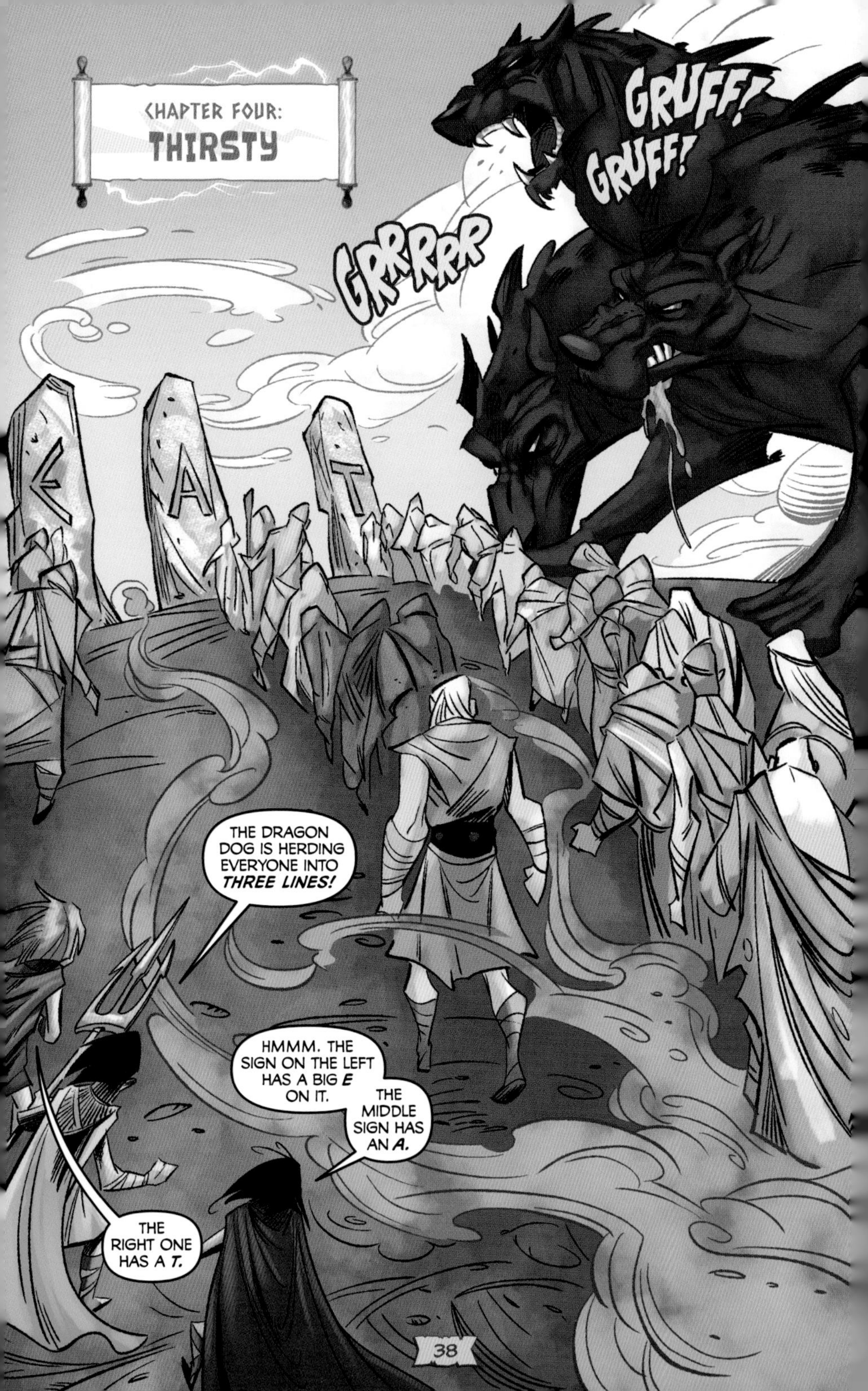
CHAPTER FOUR:
THIRSTY
GRUFF!
GRUFF!
GRRRRR
E
A
T
THE DRAGON DOG IS HERDING EVERYONE INTO *THREE LINES!*
HMMM. THE SIGN ON THE LEFT HAS A BIG *E* ON IT.
THE MIDDLE SIGN HAS AN *A.*
THE RIGHT ONE HAS A *T.*

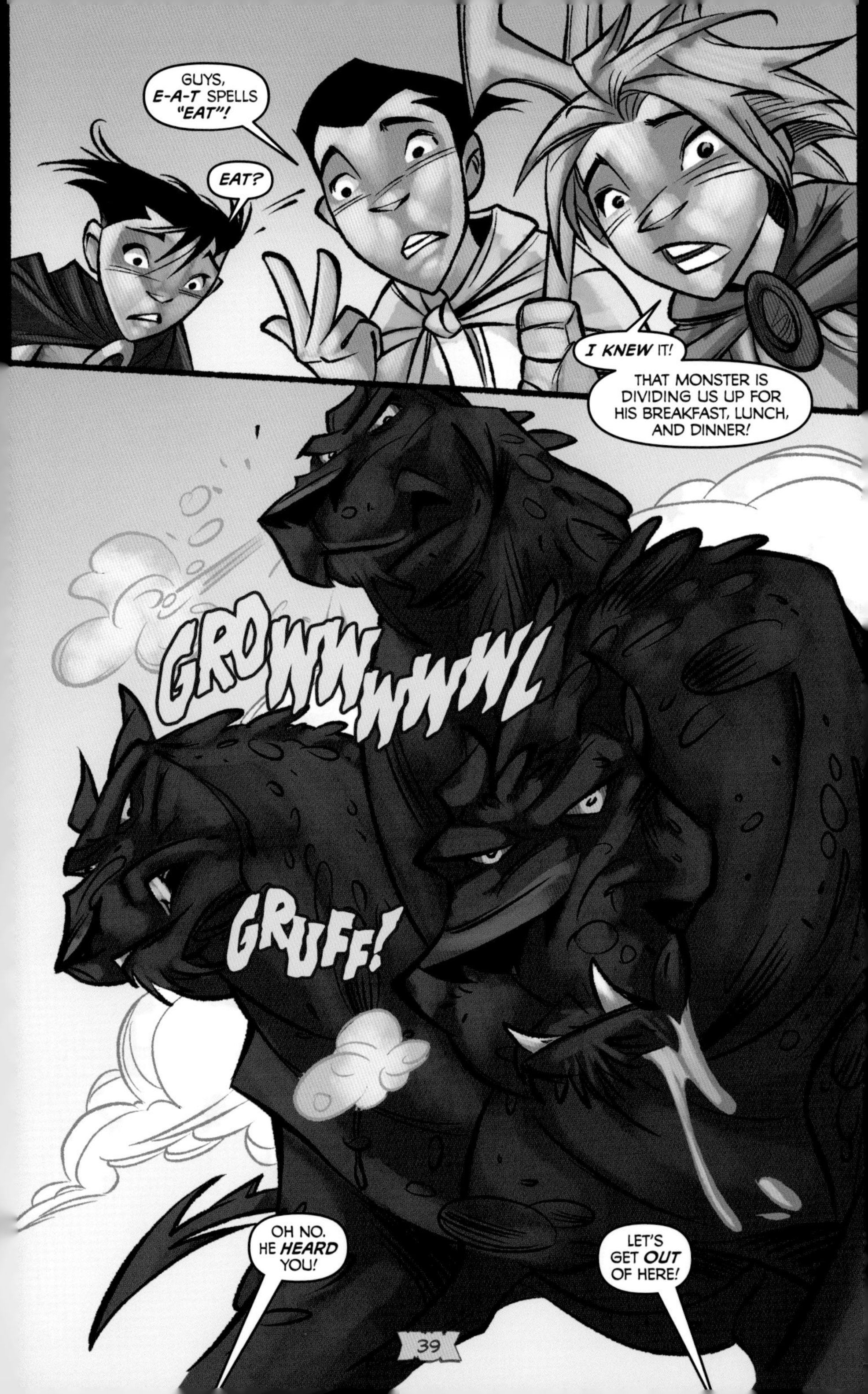
GUYS, E-A-T SPELLS "EAT"!
EAT?
I KNEW IT!
THAT MONSTER IS DIVIDING US UP FOR HIS BREAKFAST, LUNCH, AND DINNER!
GROWWWWWWL
GRUFF!
OH NO. HE HEARD YOU!
LET'S GET OUT OF HERE!

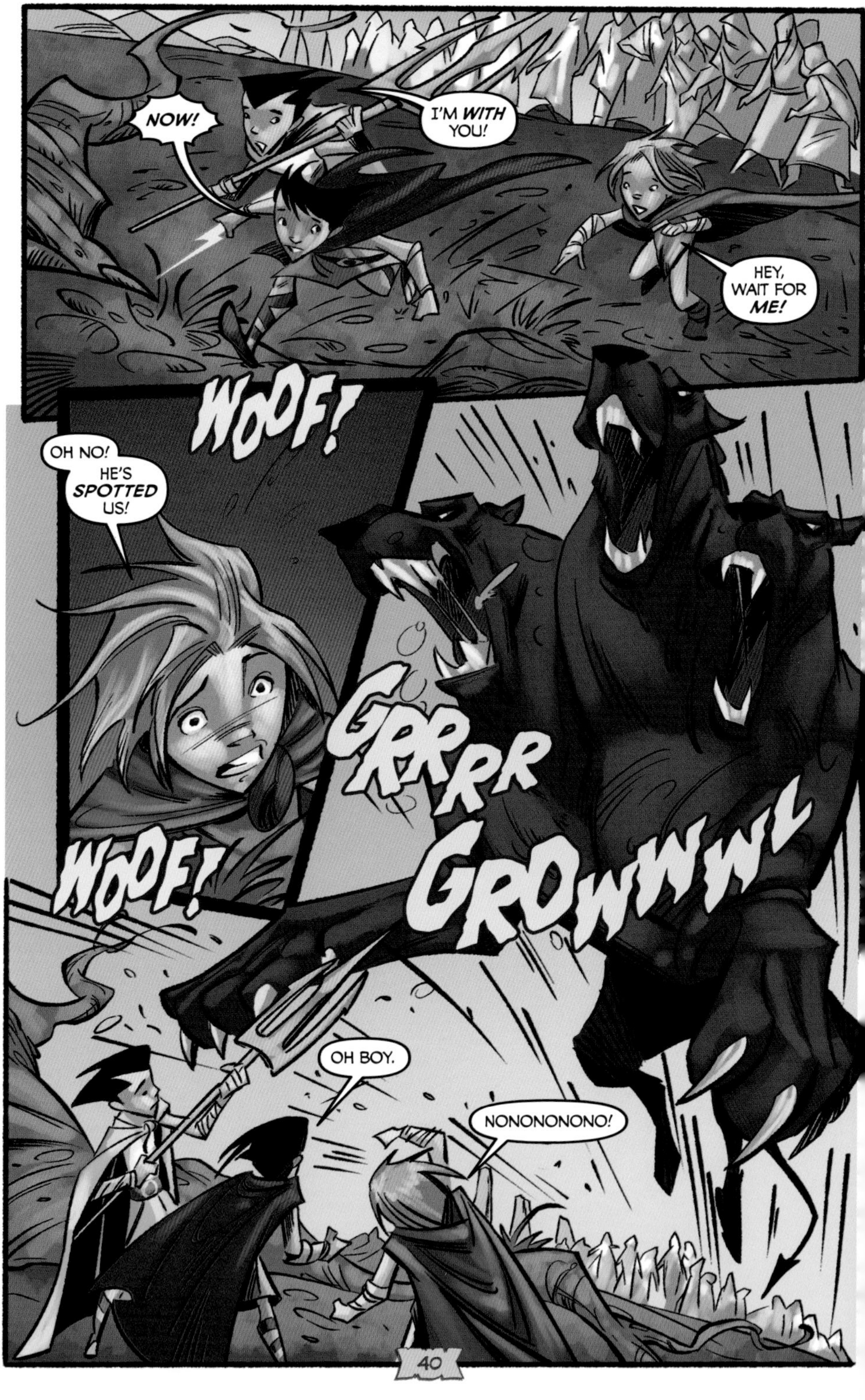
NOW!
I'M *WITH* YOU!
HEY, WAIT FOR *ME!*
WOOF!
OH NO! HE'S *SPOTTED* US!
GRRRR
WOOF!
GROWWWL
OH BOY.
NONONONONO!

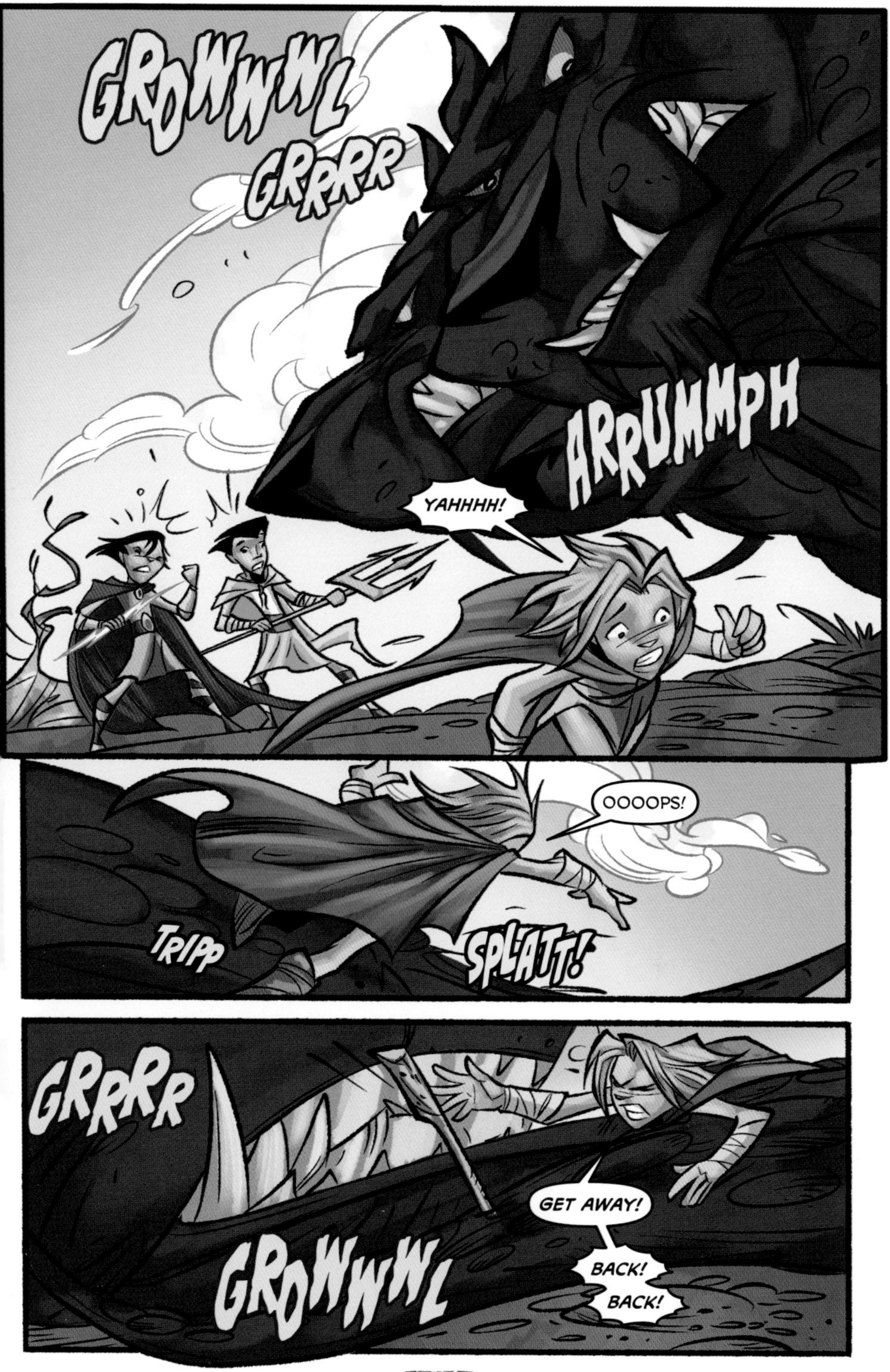
GROWWWL
GRRRR
ARRUMMPH
YAHHHH!
OOOOPS!
TRIPP
SPLATT!
GRRRR
GET AWAY!
GROWWWL
BACK!
BACK!

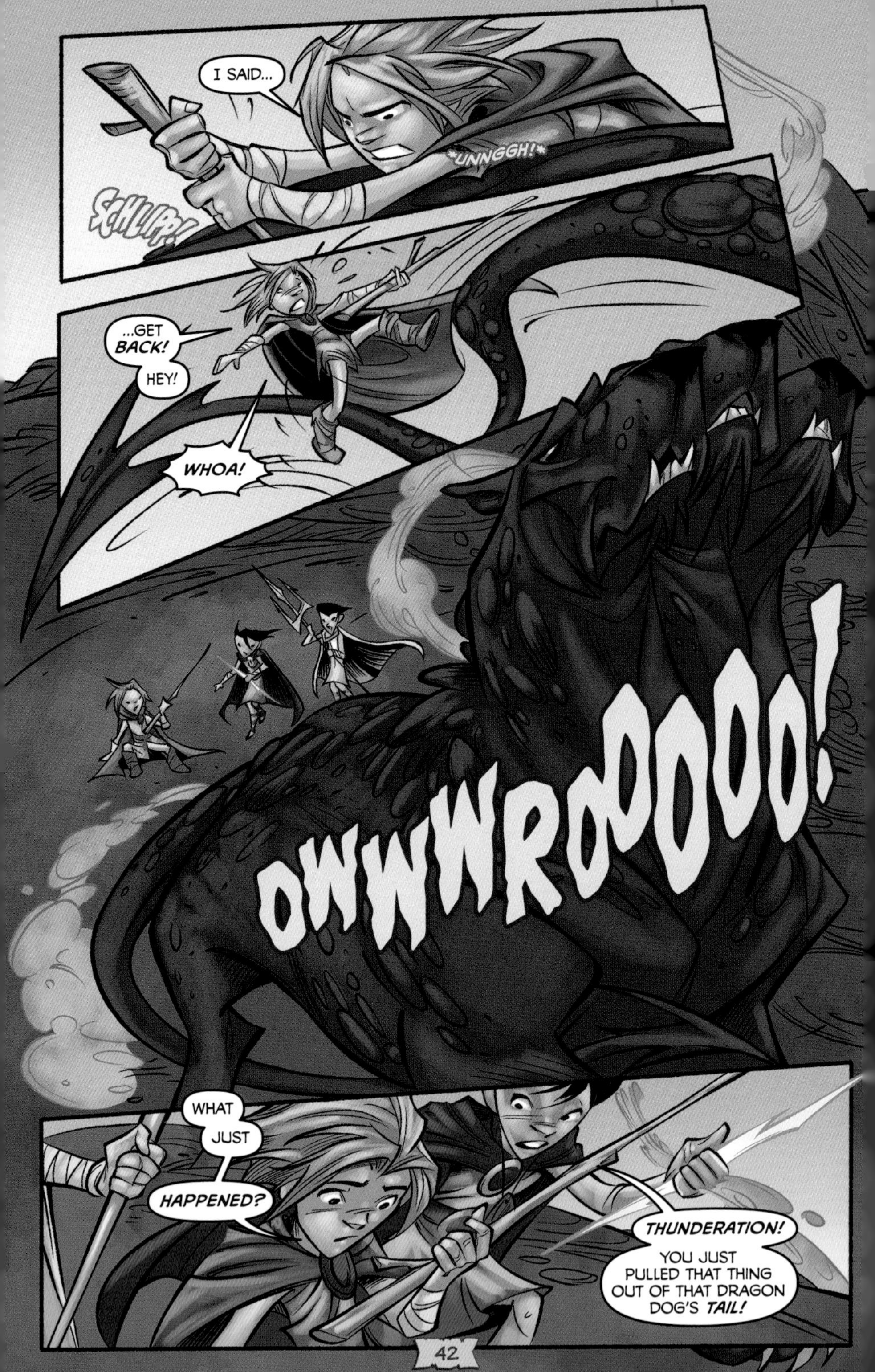
I SAID...
UNNGGH!
SCHLIPP!
...GET BACK!
HEY!
WHOA!
OWWWROOOOOO!
WHAT JUST HAPPENED?
THUNDERATION!
YOU JUST PULLED THAT THING OUT OF THAT DRAGON DOG'S TAIL!

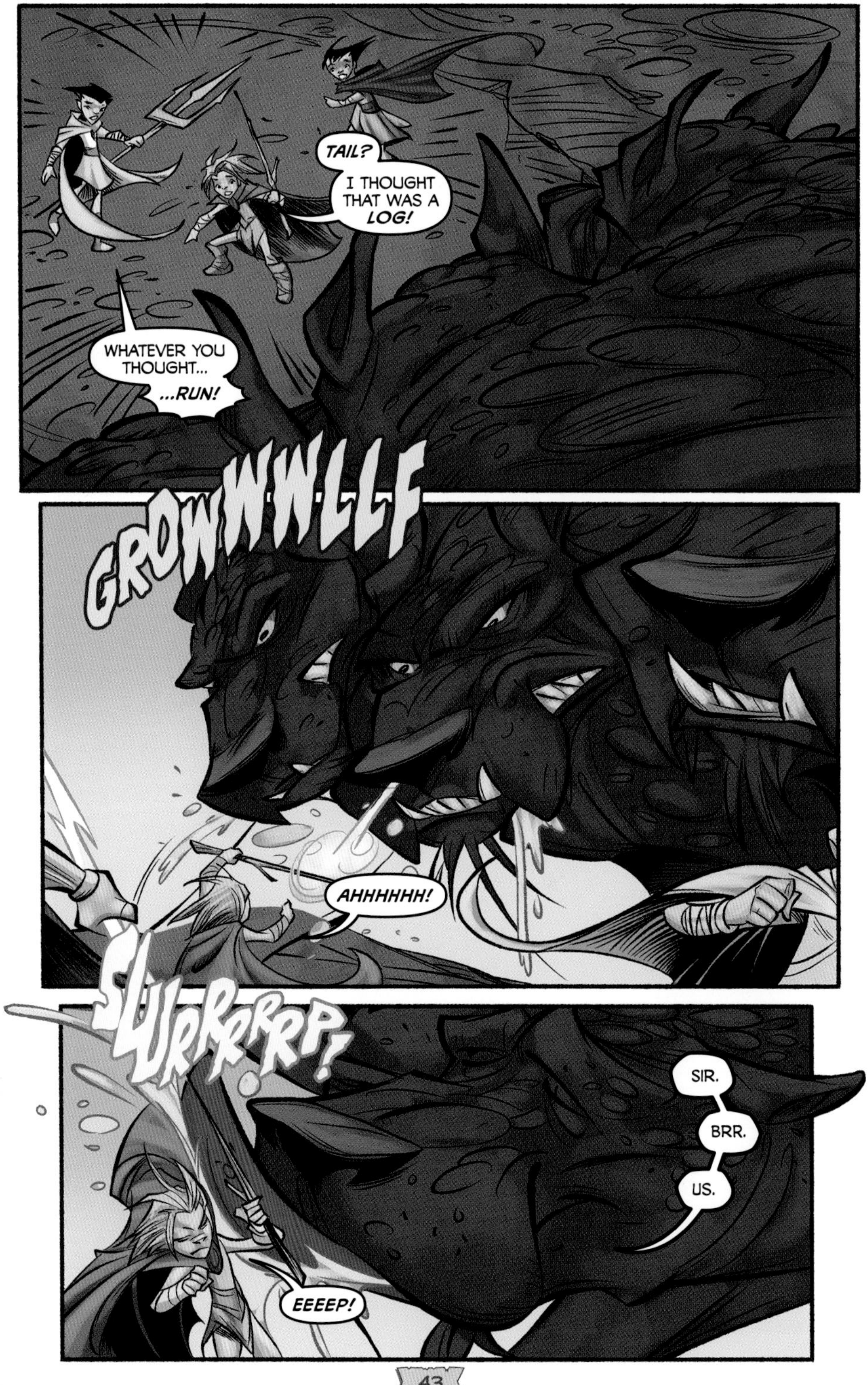
TAIL?
I THOUGHT THAT WAS A LOG!
WHATEVER YOU THOUGHT...
...RUN!
GROWWWLLF
AHHHHHH!
SLURRRRRP!
SIR.
BRR.
US.
EEEEP!

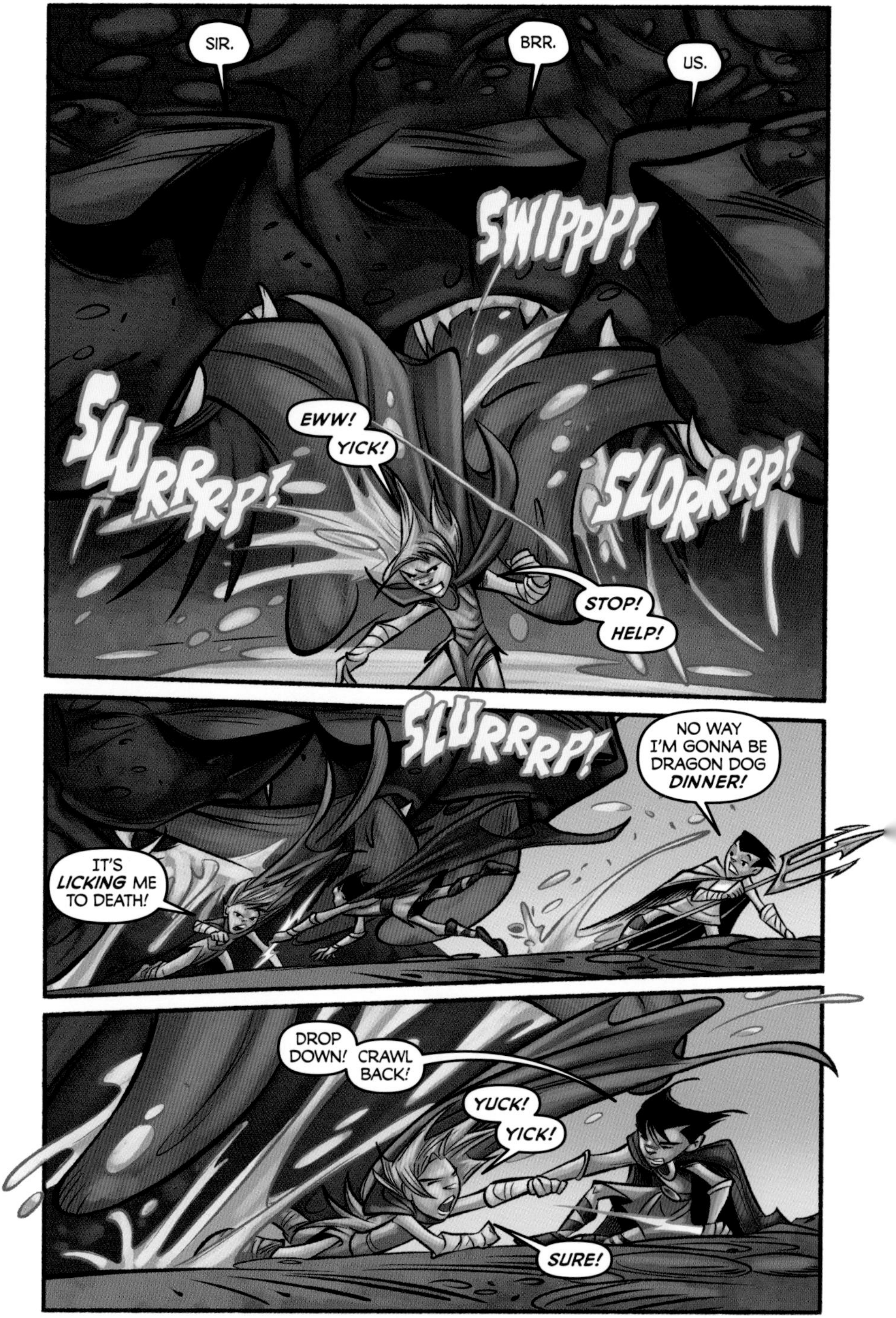
SIR.
BRR.
US.
SWIPPP!
SLURRRP!
EWW!
YICK!
SLORRRP!
STOP!
HELP!
SLURRRP!
NO WAY I'M GONNA BE DRAGON DOG *DINNER!*
IT'S *LICKING* ME TO DEATH!
DROP DOWN!
CRAWL BACK!
YUCK!
YICK!
SURE!

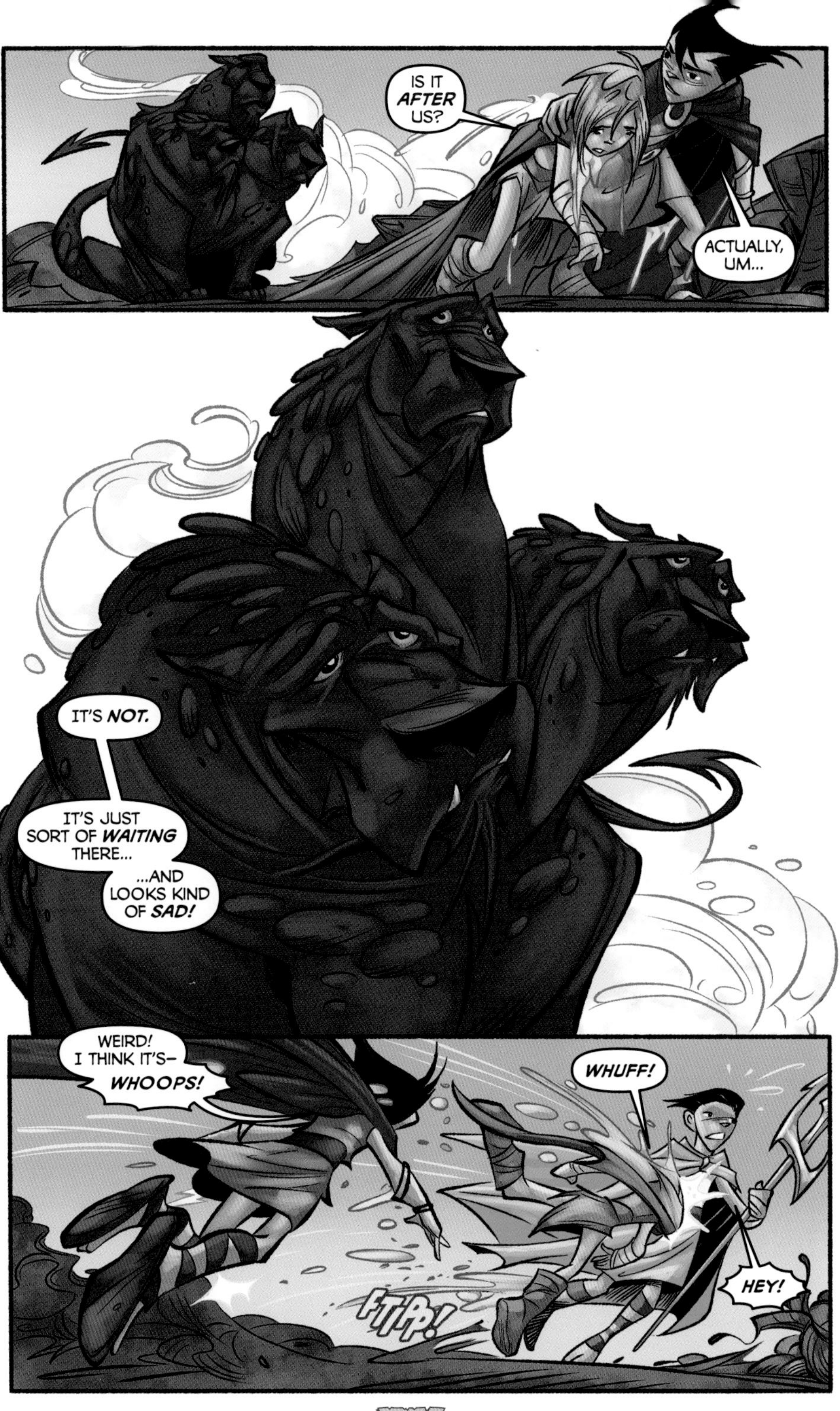
IS IT *AFTER* US?
ACTUALLY, UM...
IT'S *NOT.*
IT'S JUST SORT OF *WAITING* THERE...
...AND LOOKS KIND OF *SAD!*
WEIRD! I THINK IT'S— *WHOOPS!*
WHUFF!
FTIPP!
HEY!

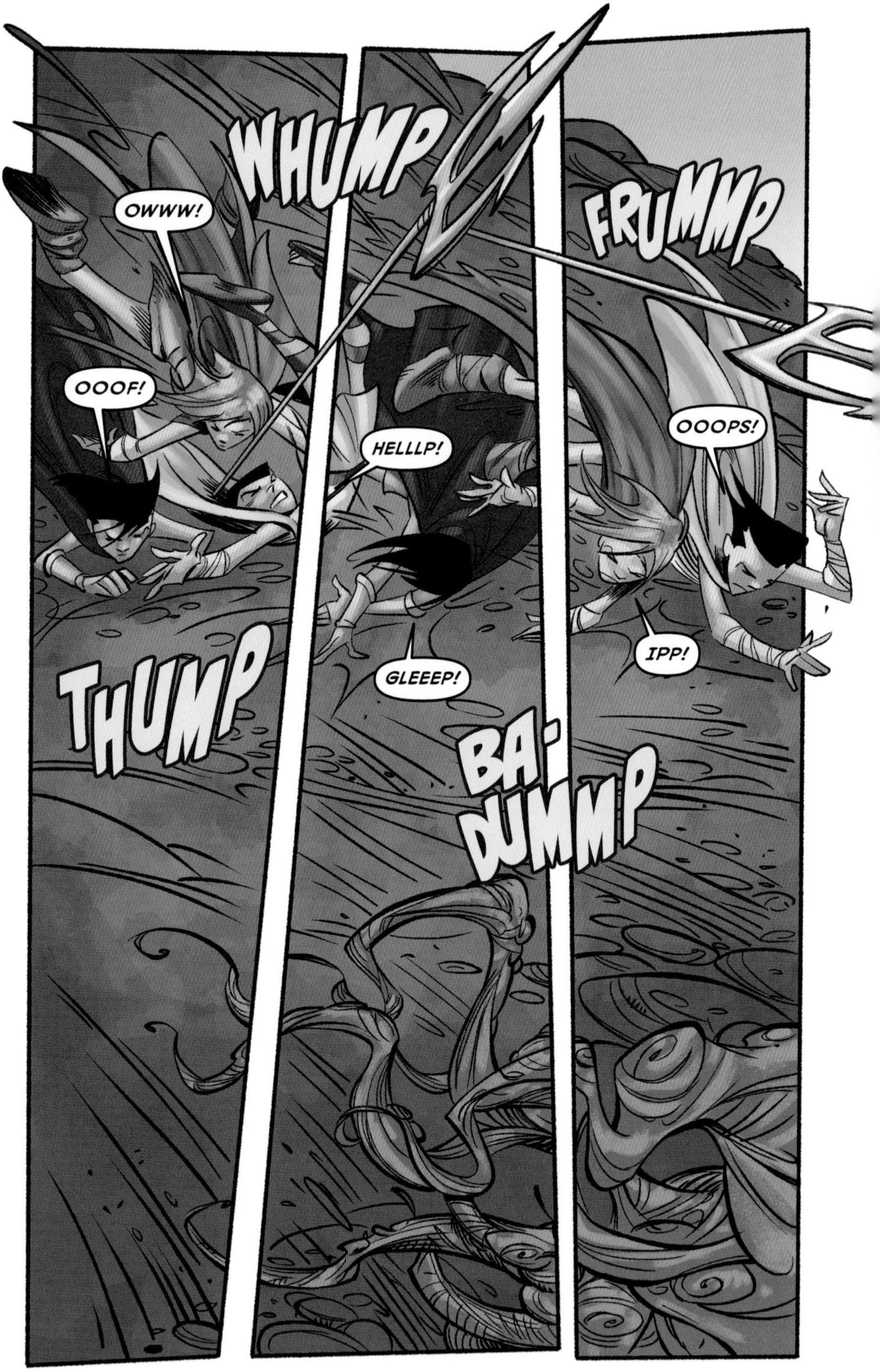
WHUMP
OWWW!
OOOF!
HELLLP!
FRUMMP
OOOPS!
THUMP
GLEEEP!
IPP!
BA-DUMMP

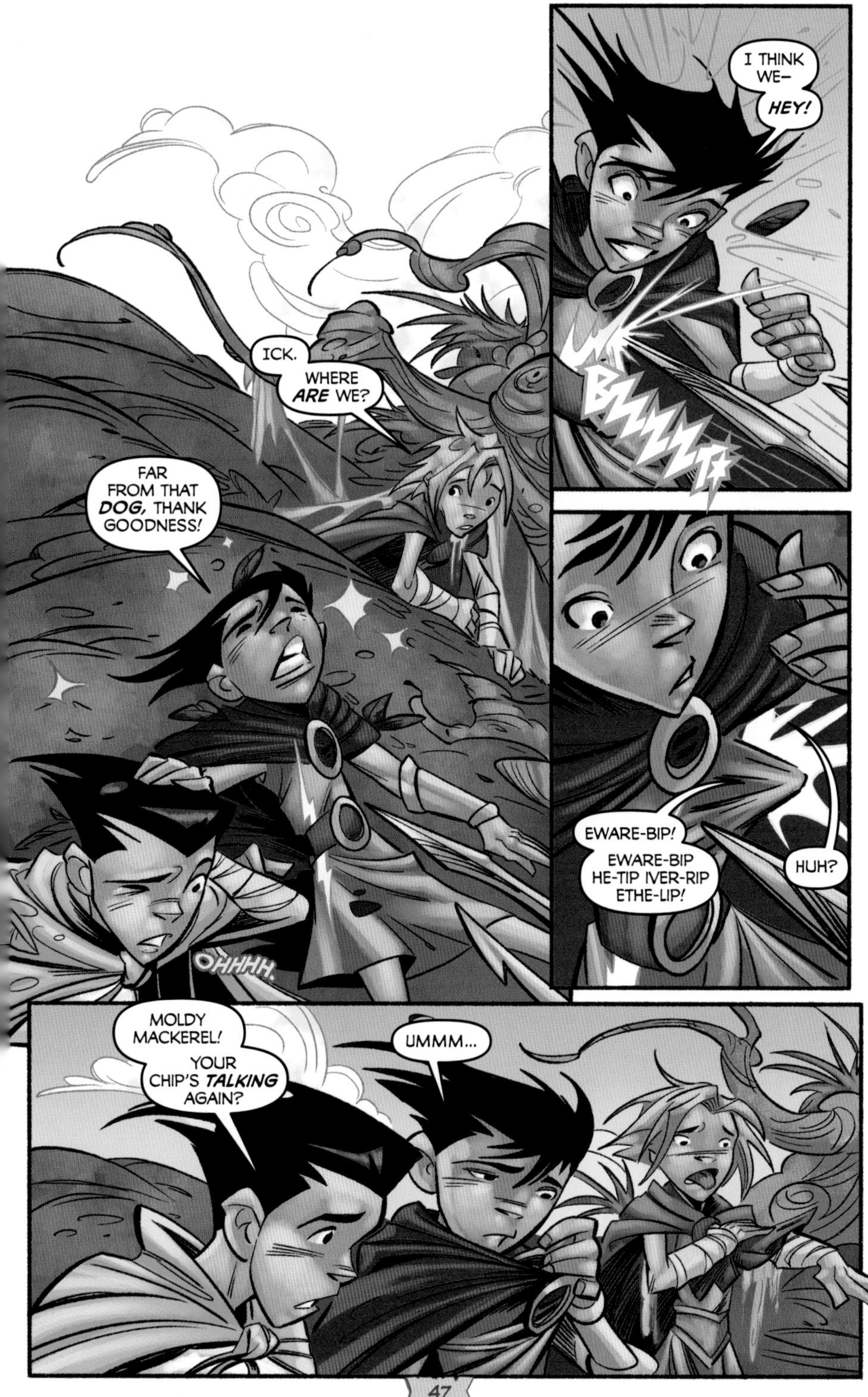
ICK.
WHERE ARE WE?
FAR FROM THAT DOG, THANK GOODNESS!
OHHHH.
I THINK WE–
HEY!
BZZZZT!
EWARE-BIP!
EWARE-BIP HE-TIP IVER-RIP ETHE-LIP!
HUH?
MOLDY MACKEREL!
YOUR CHIP'S TALKING AGAIN?
UMMM...

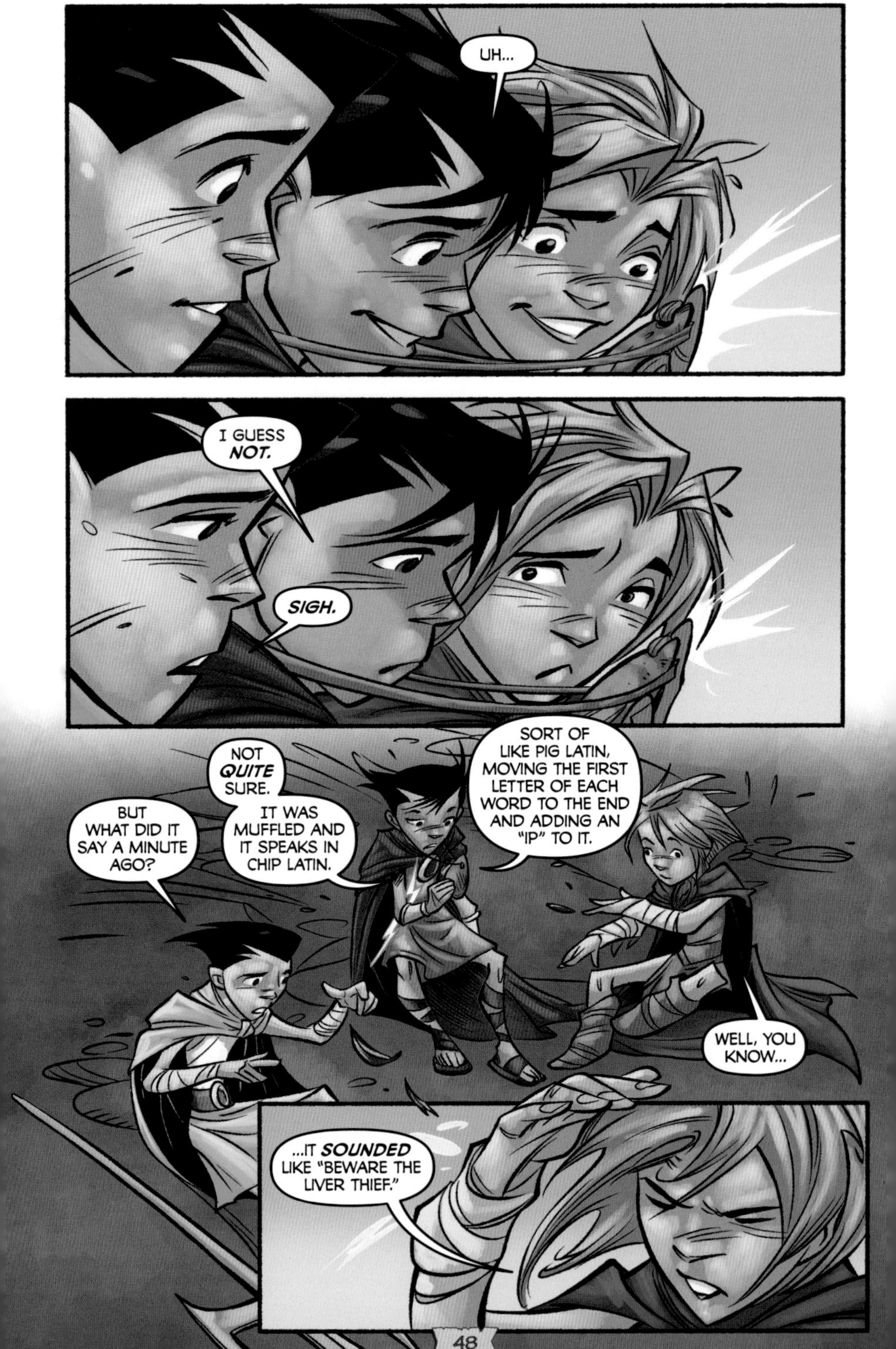
UH...
I GUESS NOT.
SIGH.
BUT WHAT DID IT SAY A MINUTE AGO?
NOT QUITE SURE.
IT WAS MUFFLED AND IT SPEAKS IN CHIP LATIN.
SORT OF LIKE PIG LATIN, MOVING THE FIRST LETTER OF EACH WORD TO THE END AND ADDING AN "IP" TO IT.
WELL, YOU KNOW...
...IT SOUNDED LIKE "BEWARE THE LIVER THIEF."

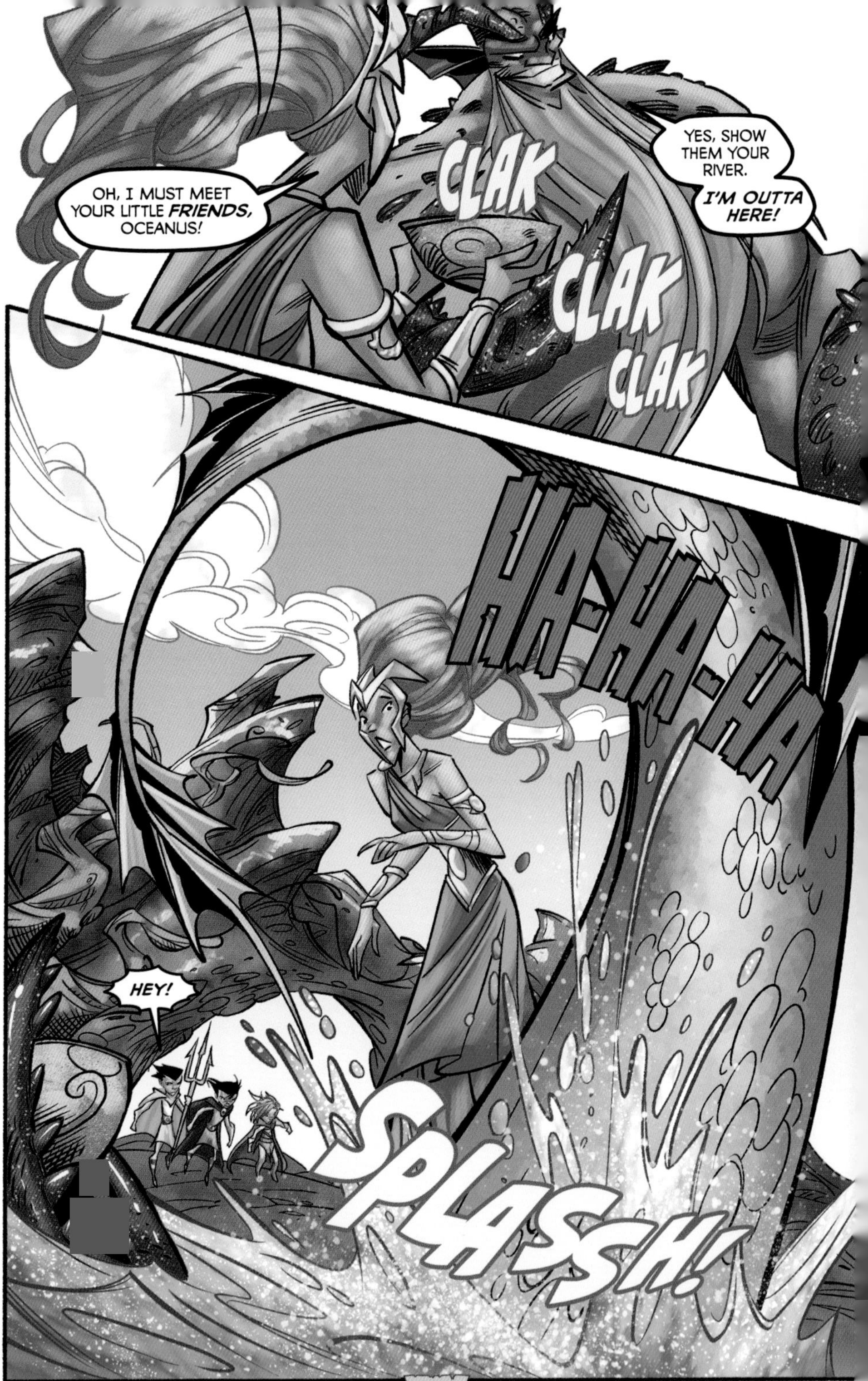

OH, I MUST MEET YOUR LITTLE *FRIENDS,* OCEANUS!
YES, SHOW THEM YOUR RIVER.
I'M OUTTA HERE!
CLAK
CLAK
CLAK
HA-HA-HA
HEY!
SPLASH!

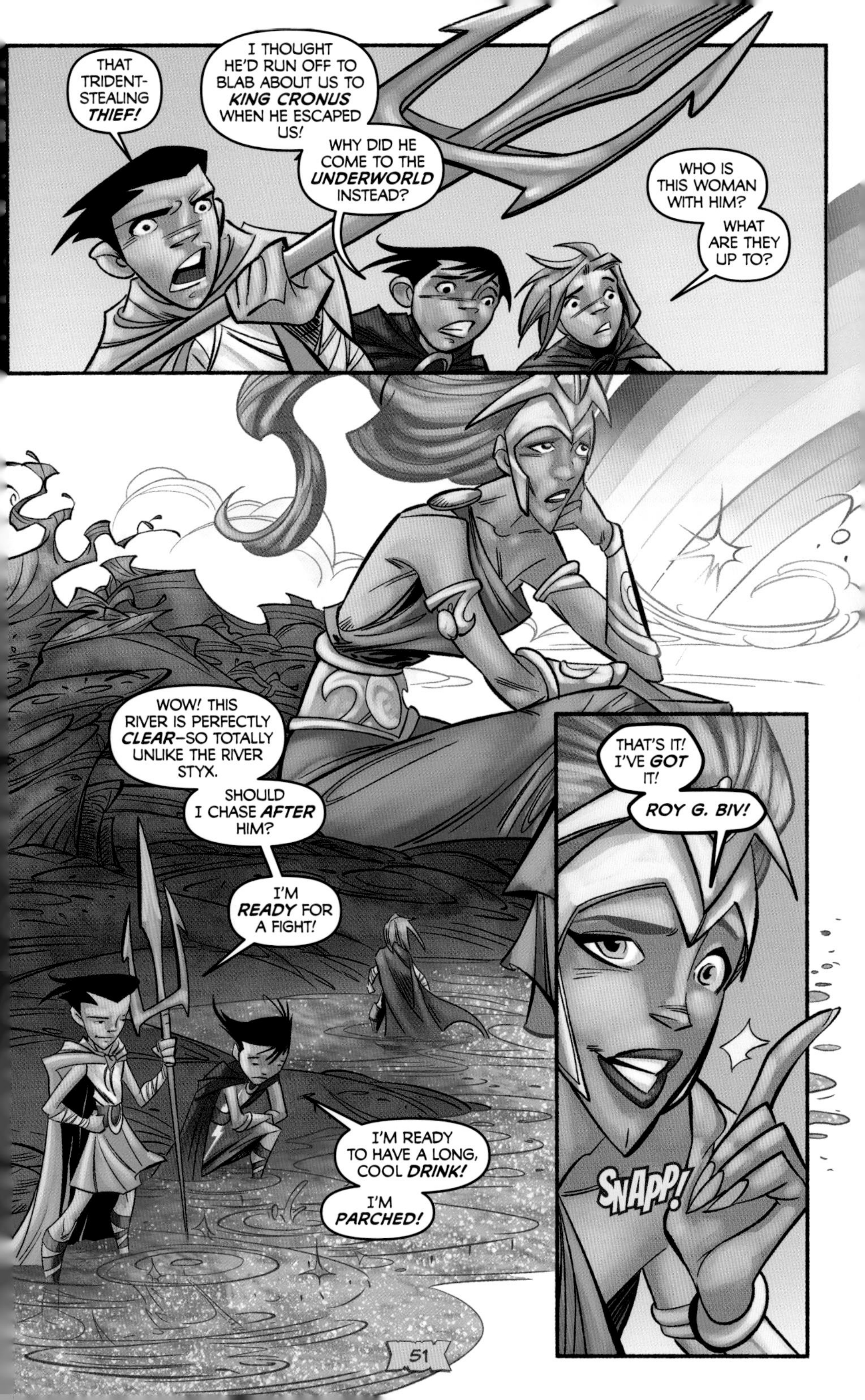
THAT TRIDENT-STEALING *THIEF!*
I THOUGHT HE'D RUN OFF TO BLAB ABOUT US TO *KING CRONUS* WHEN HE ESCAPED US!
WHY DID HE COME TO THE *UNDERWORLD* INSTEAD?
WHO IS THIS WOMAN WITH HIM?
WHAT ARE THEY UP TO?
WOW! THIS RIVER IS PERFECTLY *CLEAR*—SO TOTALLY UNLIKE THE RIVER STYX.
SHOULD I CHASE *AFTER* HIM?
I'M *READY* FOR A FIGHT!
I'M READY TO HAVE A LONG, COOL *DRINK!*
I'M *PARCHED!*
THAT'S IT! I'VE *GOT* IT!
ROY G. BIV!
SNAPP!

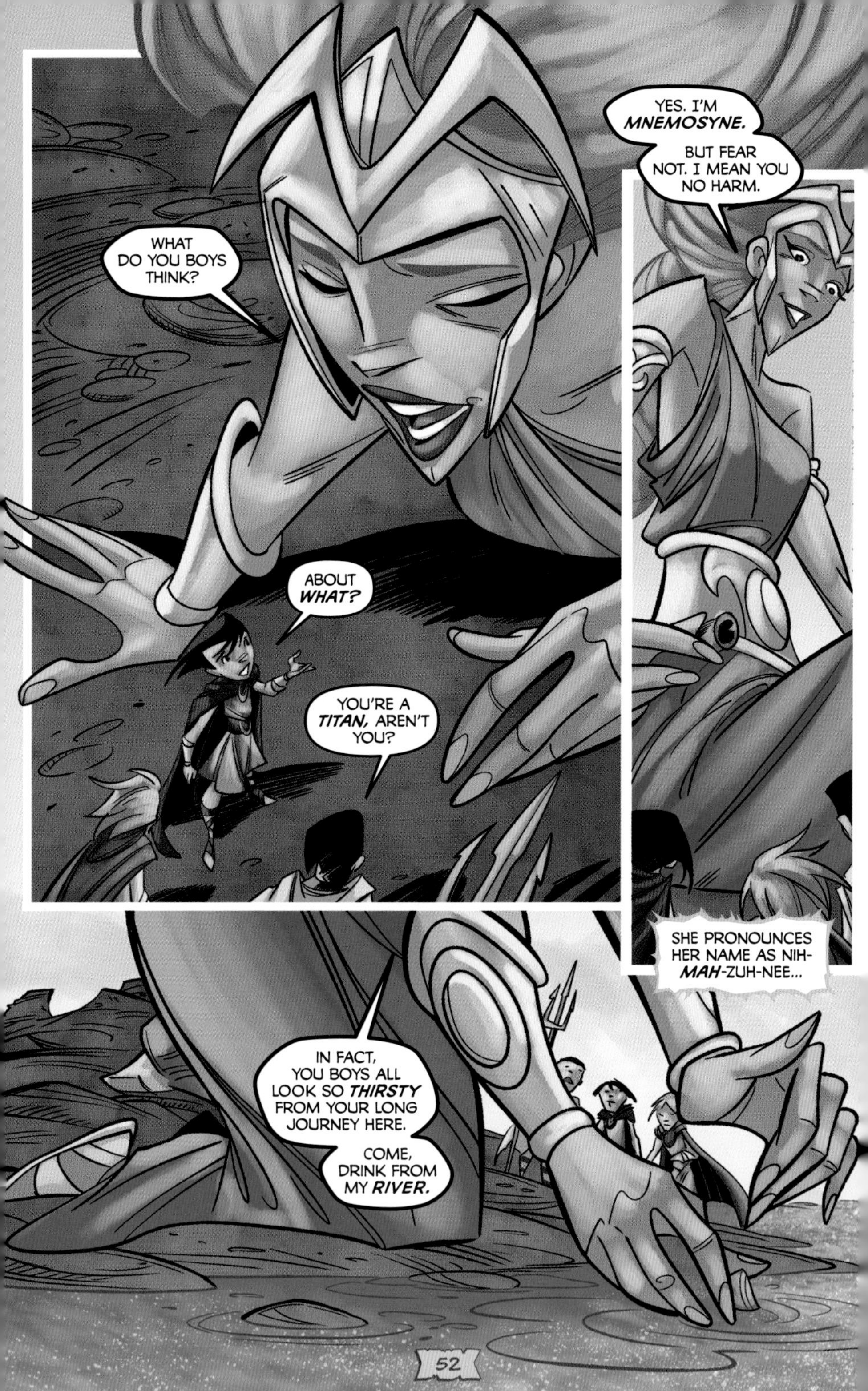

WHAT DO YOU BOYS THINK?
ABOUT *WHAT?*
YOU'RE A *TITAN,* AREN'T YOU?
YES. I'M *MNEMOSYNE.*
BUT FEAR NOT. I MEAN YOU NO HARM.
SHE PRONOUNCES HER NAME AS NIH-*MAH*-ZUH-NEE...
IN FACT, YOU BOYS ALL LOOK SO *THIRSTY* FROM YOUR LONG JOURNEY HERE.
COME, DRINK FROM MY *RIVER.*

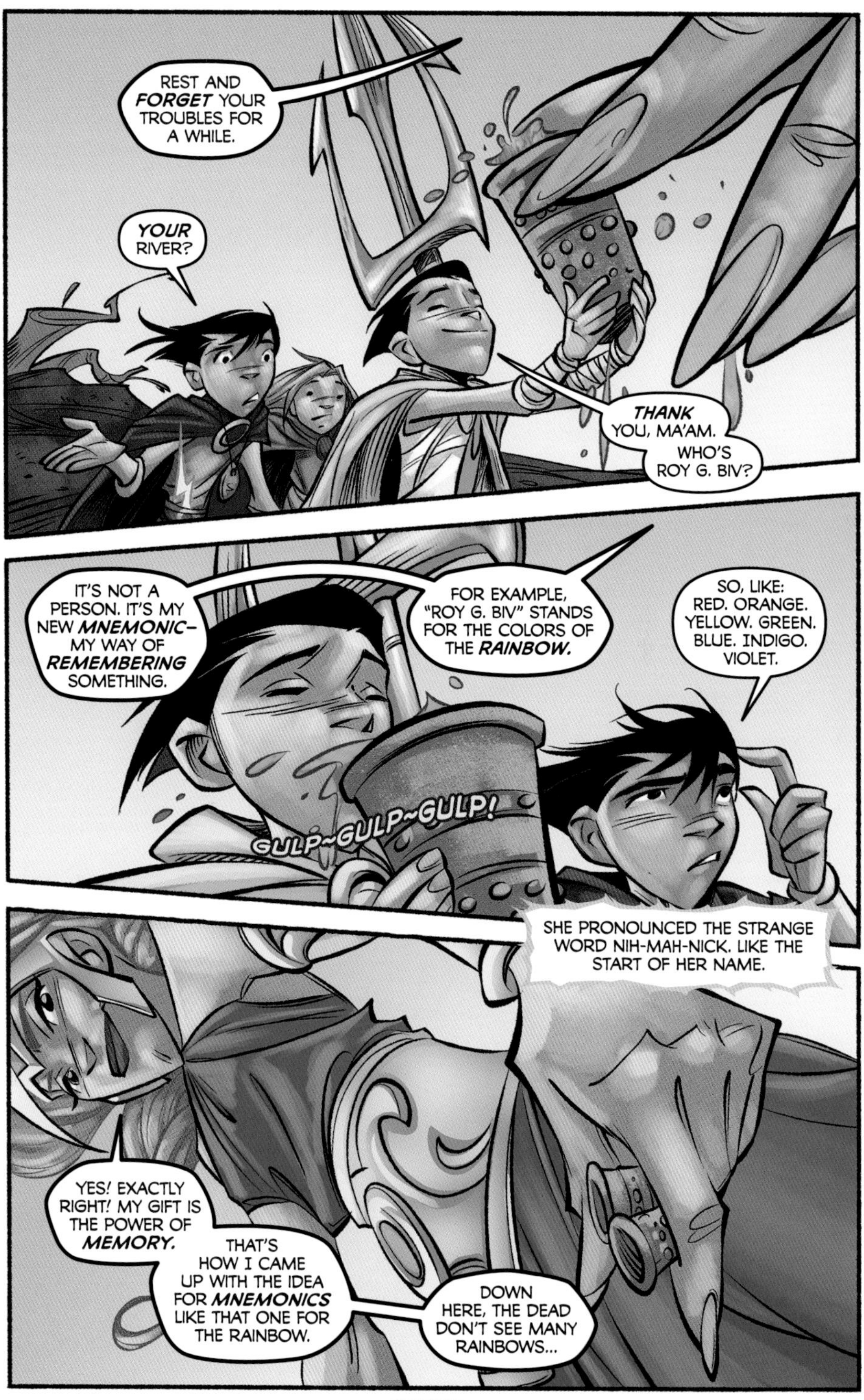
REST AND FORGET YOUR TROUBLES FOR A WHILE.
YOUR RIVER?
THANK YOU, MA'AM. WHO'S ROY G. BIV?
IT'S NOT A PERSON. IT'S MY NEW MNEMONIC– MY WAY OF REMEMBERING SOMETHING.
FOR EXAMPLE, "ROY G. BIV" STANDS FOR THE COLORS OF THE RAINBOW.
SO, LIKE: RED. ORANGE. YELLOW. GREEN. BLUE. INDIGO. VIOLET.
GULP~GULP~GULP!
SHE PRONOUNCED THE STRANGE WORD NIH-MAH-NICK. LIKE THE START OF HER NAME.
YES! EXACTLY RIGHT! MY GIFT IS THE POWER OF MEMORY.
THAT'S HOW I CAME UP WITH THE IDEA FOR MNEMONICS LIKE THAT ONE FOR THE RAINBOW.
DOWN HERE, THE DEAD DON'T SEE MANY RAINBOWS...

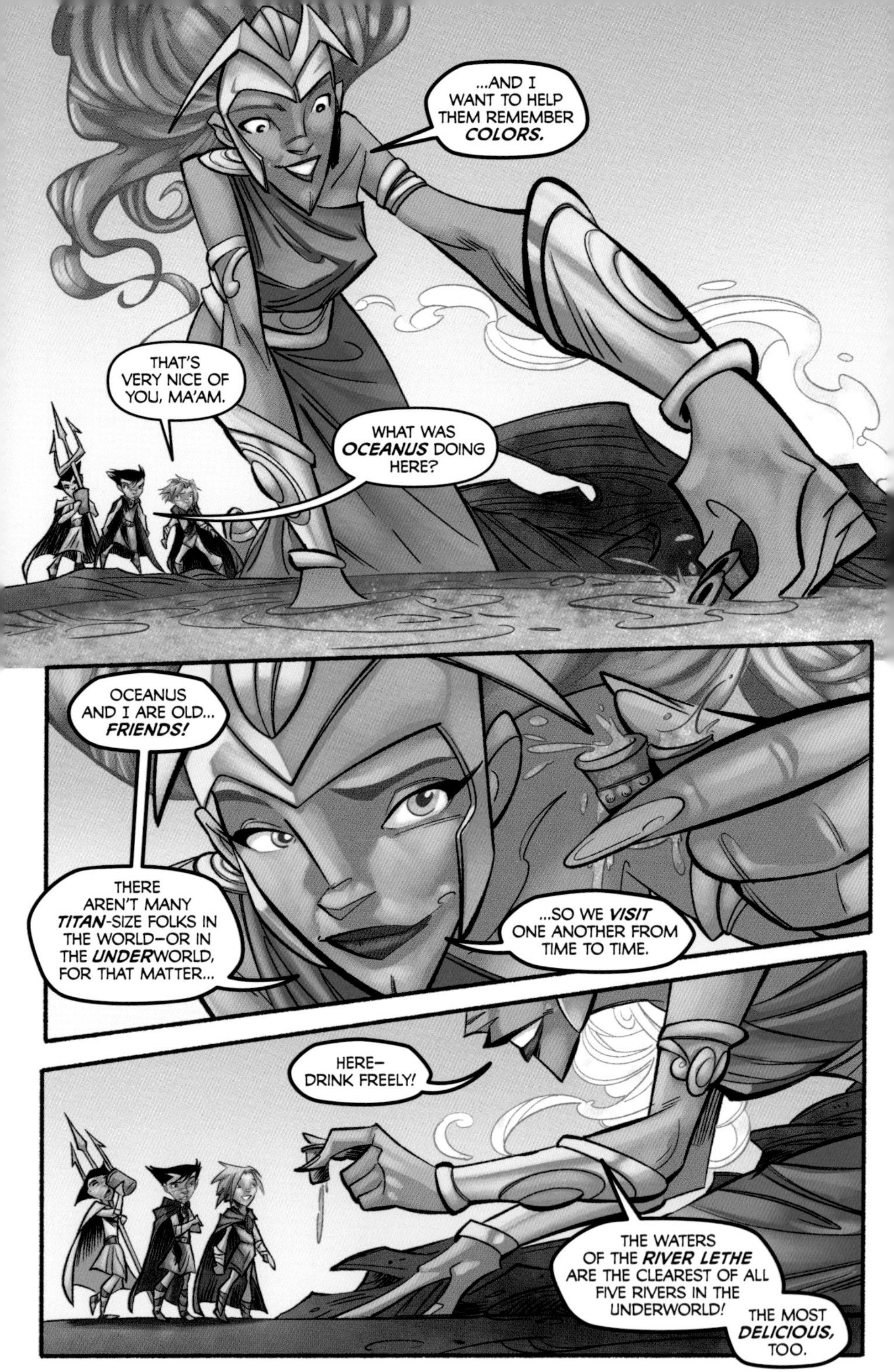
...AND I WANT TO HELP THEM REMEMBER COLORS.
THAT'S VERY NICE OF YOU, MA'AM.
WHAT WAS OCEANUS DOING HERE?
OCEANUS AND I ARE OLD... FRIENDS!
THERE AREN'T MANY TITAN-SIZE FOLKS IN THE WORLD—OR IN THE UNDERWORLD, FOR THAT MATTER...
...SO WE VISIT ONE ANOTHER FROM TIME TO TIME.
HERE—DRINK FREELY!
THE WATERS OF THE RIVER LETHE ARE THE CLEAREST OF ALL FIVE RIVERS IN THE UNDERWORLD!
THE MOST DELICIOUS, TOO.

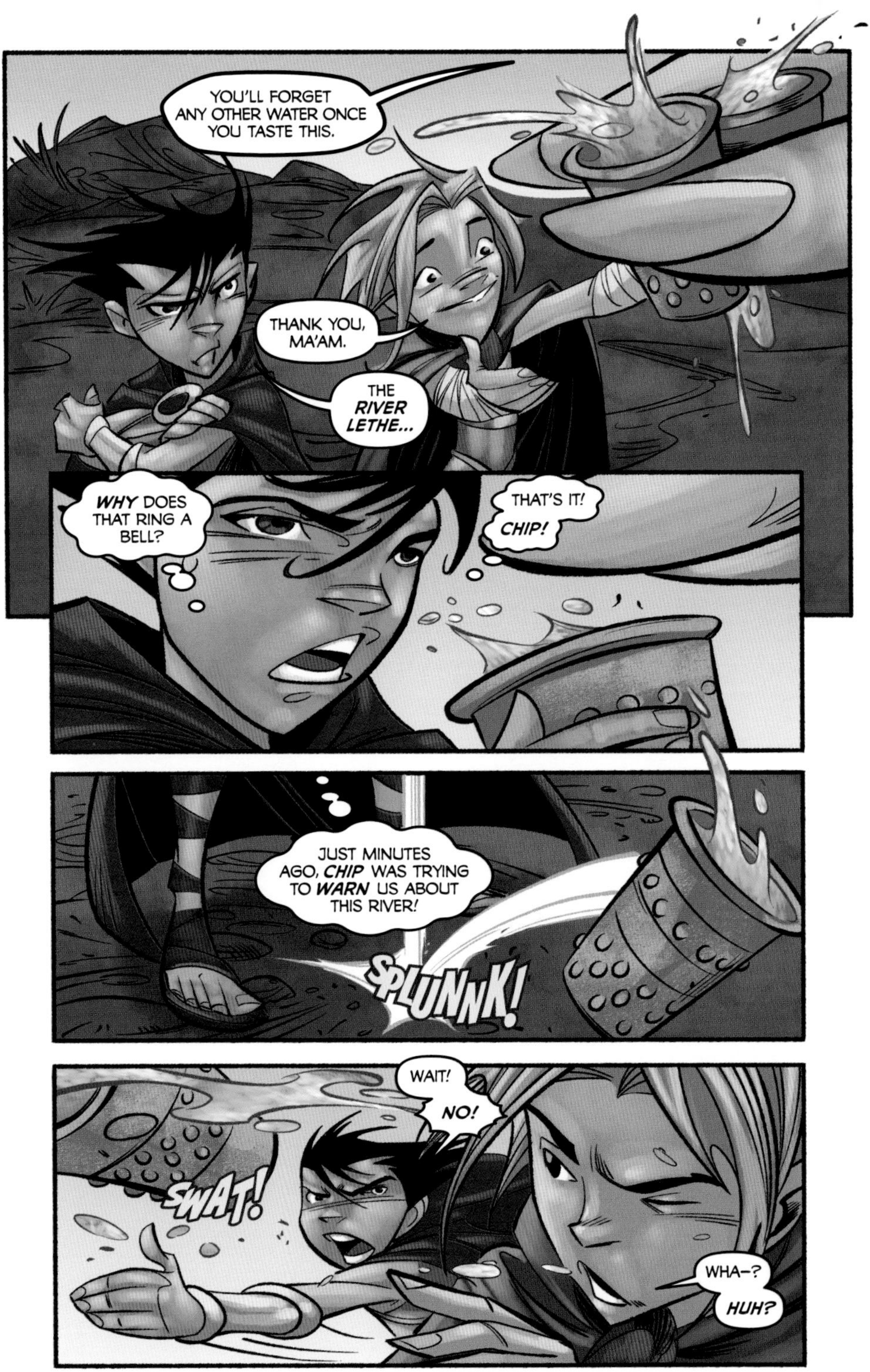
YOU'LL FORGET ANY OTHER WATER ONCE YOU TASTE THIS.
THANK YOU, MA'AM.
THE RIVER LETHE...
WHY DOES THAT RING A BELL?
THAT'S IT! CHIP!
JUST MINUTES AGO, CHIP WAS TRYING TO WARN US ABOUT THIS RIVER!
SPLUNNK!
WAIT! NO!
SWAT!
WHA-? HUH?

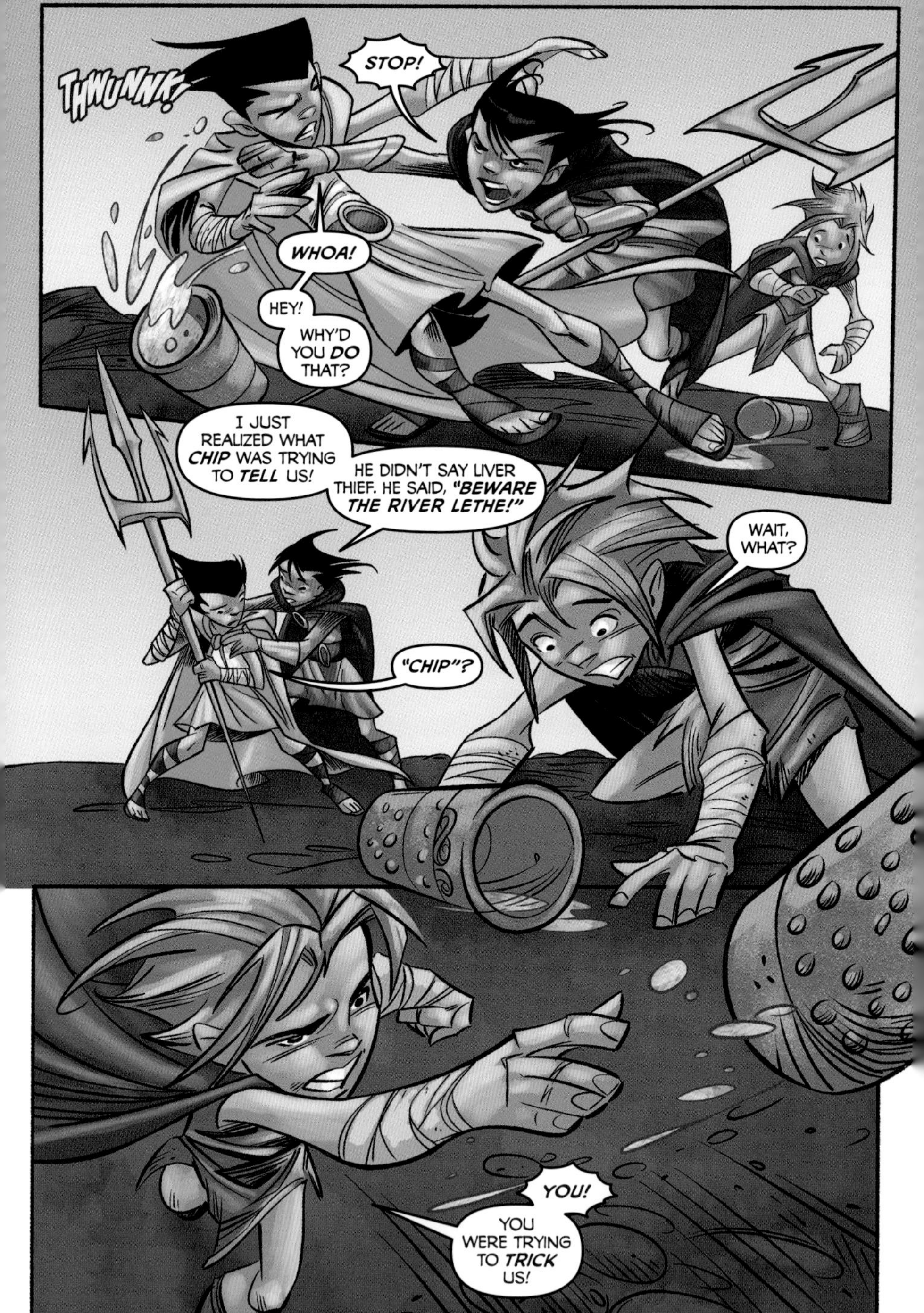
THWUNNK!
STOP!
WHOA!
HEY!
WHY'D YOU DO THAT?
I JUST REALIZED WHAT CHIP WAS TRYING TO TELL US!
HE DIDN'T SAY LIVER THIEF. HE SAID, "BEWARE THE RIVER LETHE!"
WAIT, WHAT?
"CHIP"?
YOU!
YOU WERE TRYING TO TRICK US!

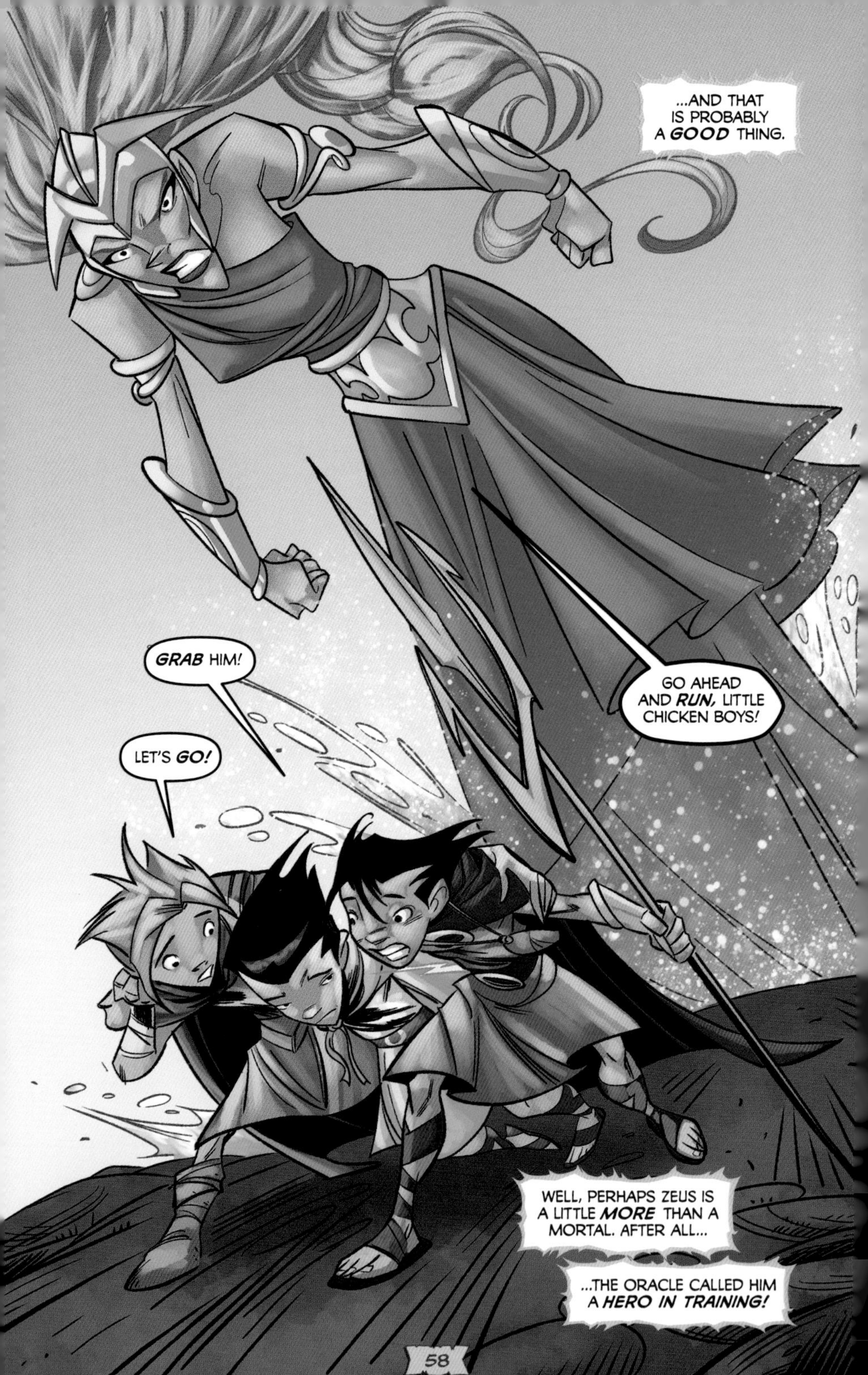
...AND THAT IS PROBABLY A GOOD THING.
GRAB HIM!
GO AHEAD AND RUN, LITTLE CHICKEN BOYS!
LET'S GO!
WELL, PERHAPS ZEUS IS A LITTLE MORE THAN A MORTAL. AFTER ALL...
...THE ORACLE CALLED HIM A HERO IN TRAINING!

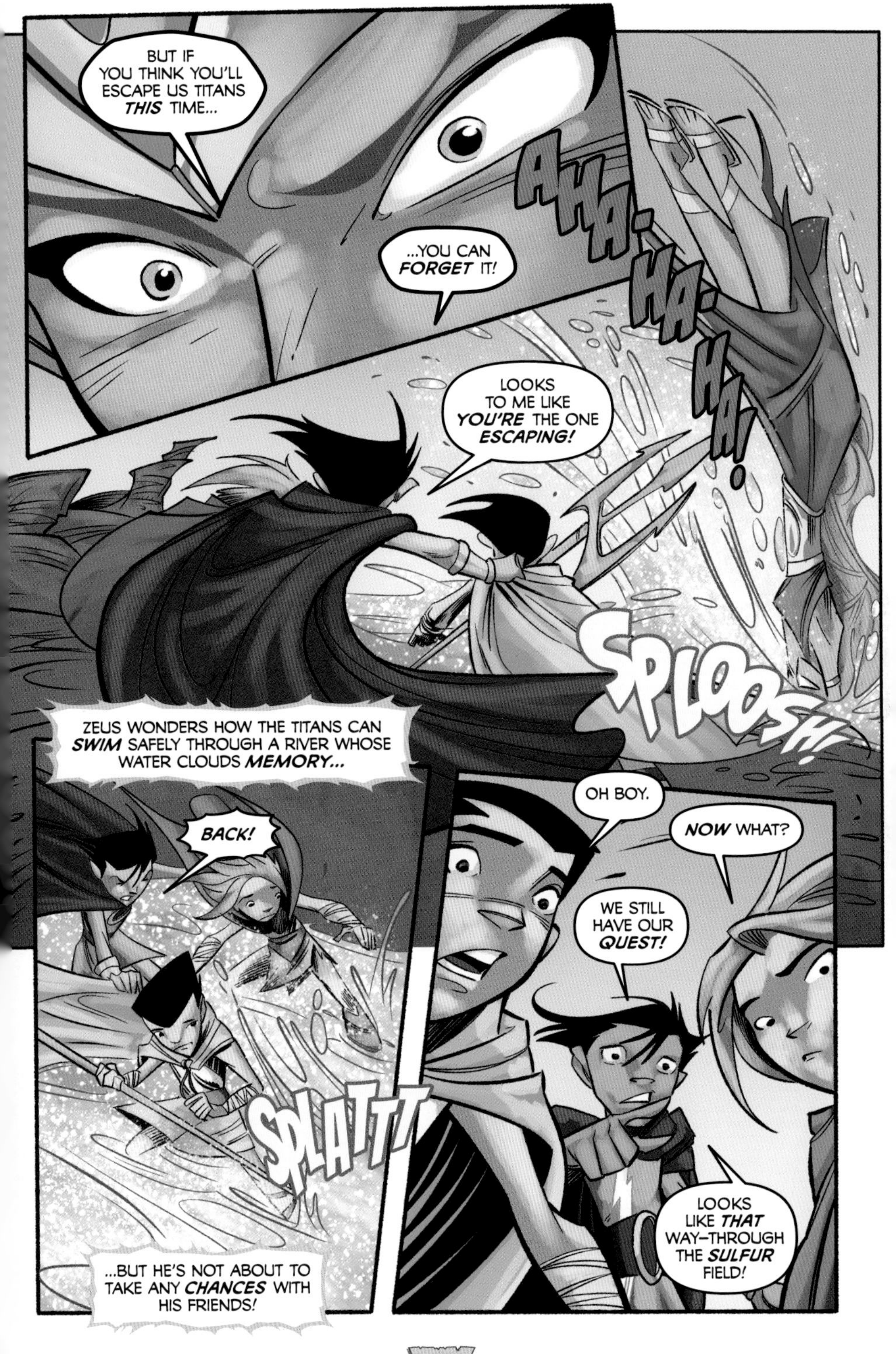
BUT IF YOU THINK YOU'LL ESCAPE US TITANS *THIS* TIME...
...YOU CAN *FORGET* IT!
AHHA-HA-HA-HA!
LOOKS TO ME LIKE *YOU'RE* THE ONE *ESCAPING!*
SPLOOSH!
ZEUS WONDERS HOW THE TITANS CAN *SWIM* SAFELY THROUGH A RIVER WHOSE WATER CLOUDS *MEMORY...*
BACK!
SPLATTT
...BUT HE'S NOT ABOUT TO TAKE ANY *CHANCES* WITH HIS FRIENDS!
OH BOY.
NOW WHAT?
WE STILL HAVE OUR *QUEST!*
LOOKS LIKE *THAT* WAY—THROUGH THE *SULFUR* FIELD!

CHAPTER FIVE:
FORGET IT

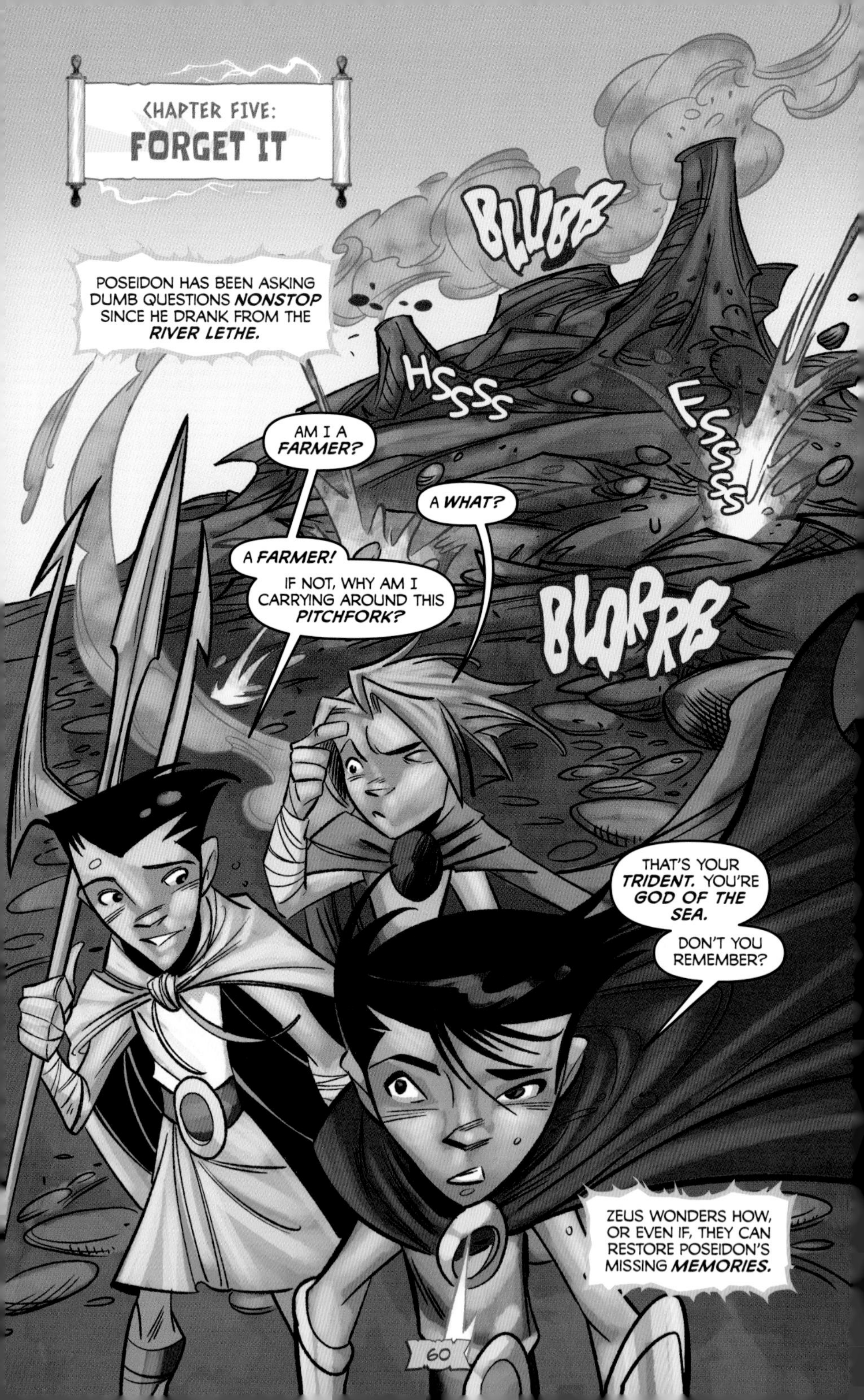
POSEIDON HAS BEEN ASKING DUMB QUESTIONS NONSTOP SINCE HE DRANK FROM THE RIVER LETHE.
BLUBB
HSSSS
ESSSSS
AM I A FARMER?
A WHAT?
A FARMER!
IF NOT, WHY AM I CARRYING AROUND THIS PITCHFORK?
BLORRB
THAT'S YOUR TRIDENT. YOU'RE GOD OF THE SEA.
DON'T YOU REMEMBER?
ZEUS WONDERS HOW, OR EVEN IF, THEY CAN RESTORE POSEIDON'S MISSING MEMORIES.

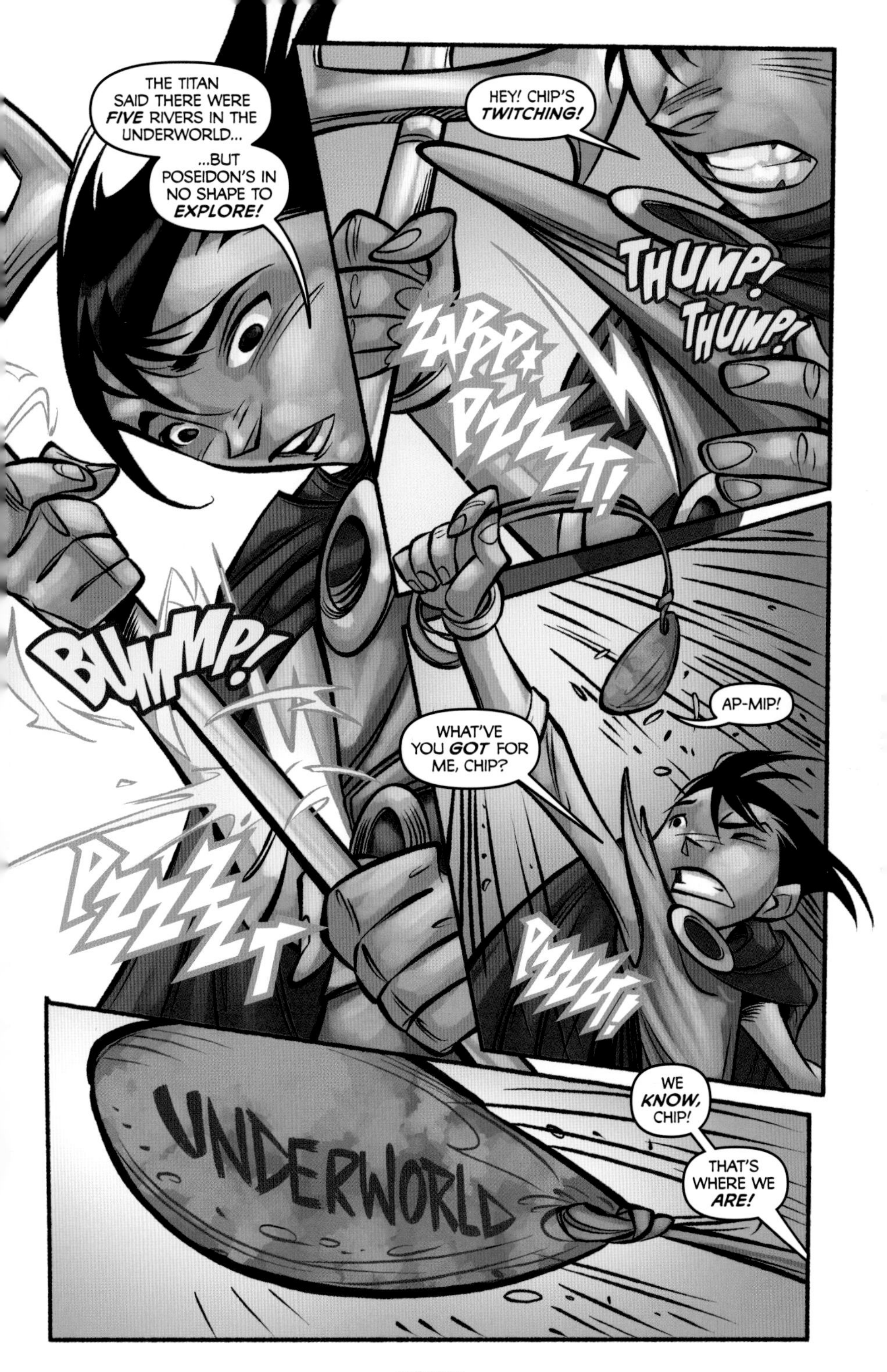
THE TITAN SAID THERE WERE *FIVE* RIVERS IN THE UNDERWORLD...
...BUT POSEIDON'S IN NO SHAPE TO *EXPLORE!*
HEY! CHIP'S *TWITCHING!*
THUMP! THUMP!
ZAPP-BZZZT!
BUMMP!
BZZZT
AP-MIP!
WHAT'VE YOU *GOT* FOR ME, CHIP?
BZZZT!
UNDERWORLD
WE *KNOW,* CHIP!
THAT'S WHERE WE *ARE!*

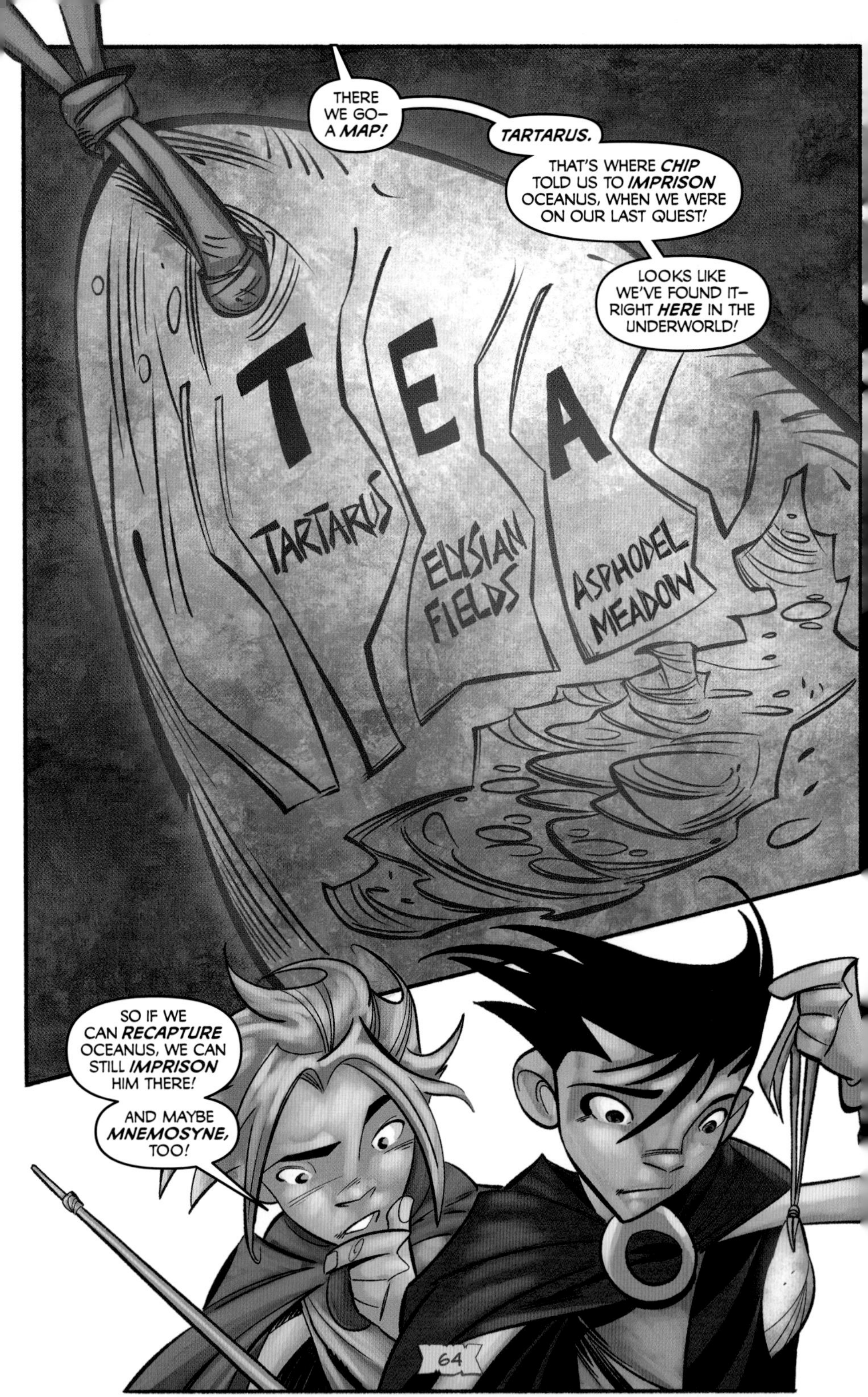
THERE WE GO– A MAP!
TARTARUS.
THAT'S WHERE CHIP TOLD US TO IMPRISON OCEANUS, WHEN WE WERE ON OUR LAST QUEST!
LOOKS LIKE WE'VE FOUND IT– RIGHT HERE IN THE UNDERWORLD!
T
E
A
TARTARUS
ELYSIAN FIELDS
ASPHODEL MEADOW
SO IF WE CAN RECAPTURE OCEANUS, WE CAN STILL IMPRISON HIM THERE!
AND MAYBE MNEMOSYNE, TOO!

MIND IF I LOOK?

GO AHEAD!

T...

E...

A...

THAT SPELLS "TEA"!

OR, IF YOU ARRANGE THE LETTERS DIFFERENTLY...

...THEY SPELL "EAT"!

LIKE THE SIGN AT THE FRONT OF THE LINES!

I'LL BET "EAT" IS ANOTHER OF MNEMOSYNE'S MNEMONICS...

...TO HELP SHADES REMEMBER THE LAYOUT FOR THE UNDERWORLD.

E FOR ELYSIAN FIELDS.

A FOR ASPHODEL MEADOW.

T FOR TARTARUS.

SO THAT'S WHY THE DOG WAS MAKING THREE LINES?

YEAH. THAT MUST BE THE THREE PLACES WHERE THE DEAD GO.

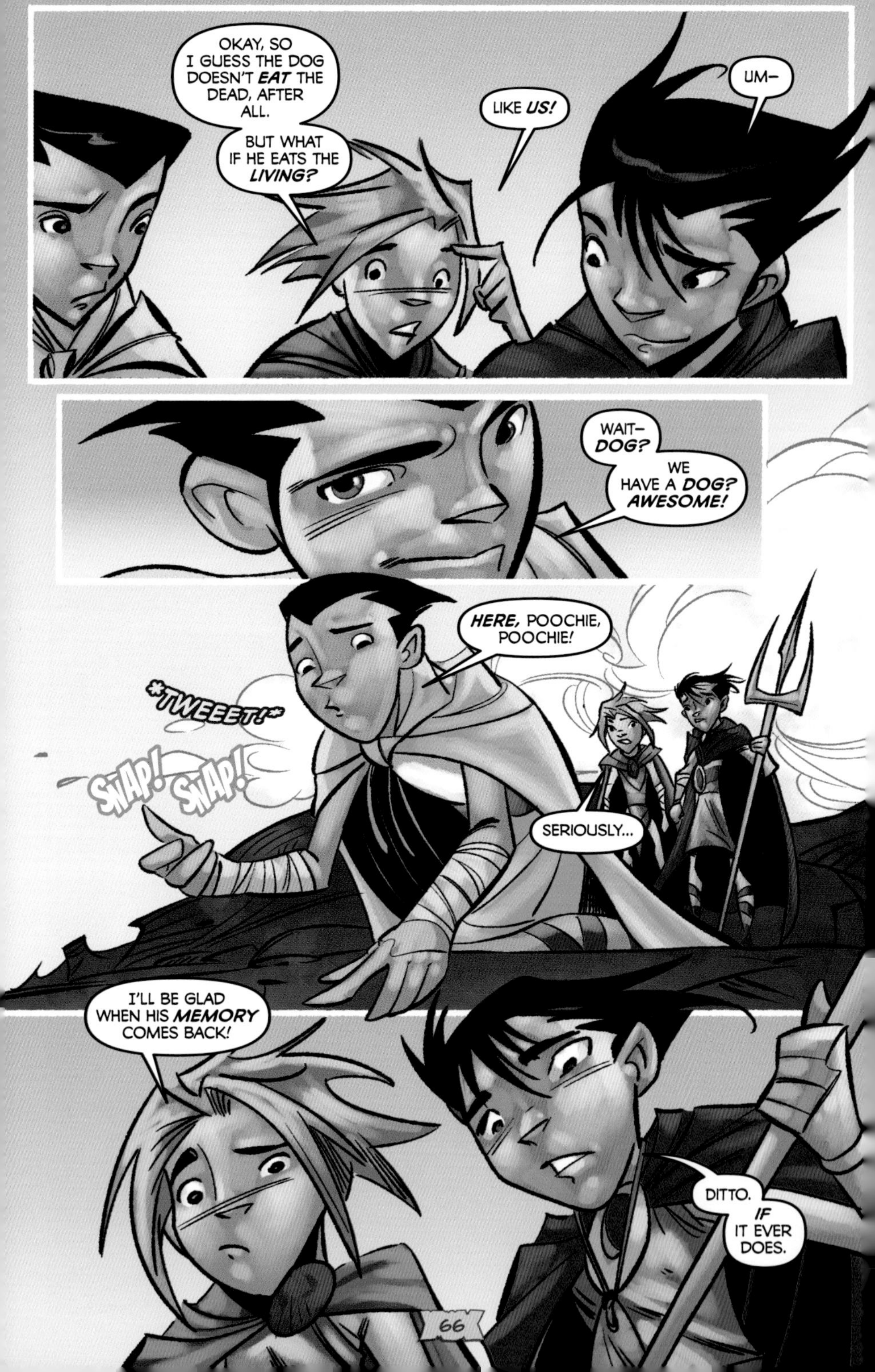
OKAY, SO I GUESS THE DOG DOESN'T *EAT* THE DEAD, AFTER ALL.
BUT WHAT IF HE EATS THE *LIVING?*
LIKE *US!*
UM—
WAIT— *DOG?*
WE HAVE A *DOG? AWESOME!*
HERE, POOCHIE, POOCHIE!
TWEEEET!
SNAP! SNAP!
SERIOUSLY...
I'LL BE GLAD WHEN HIS *MEMORY* COMES BACK!
DITTO. *IF* IT EVER DOES.

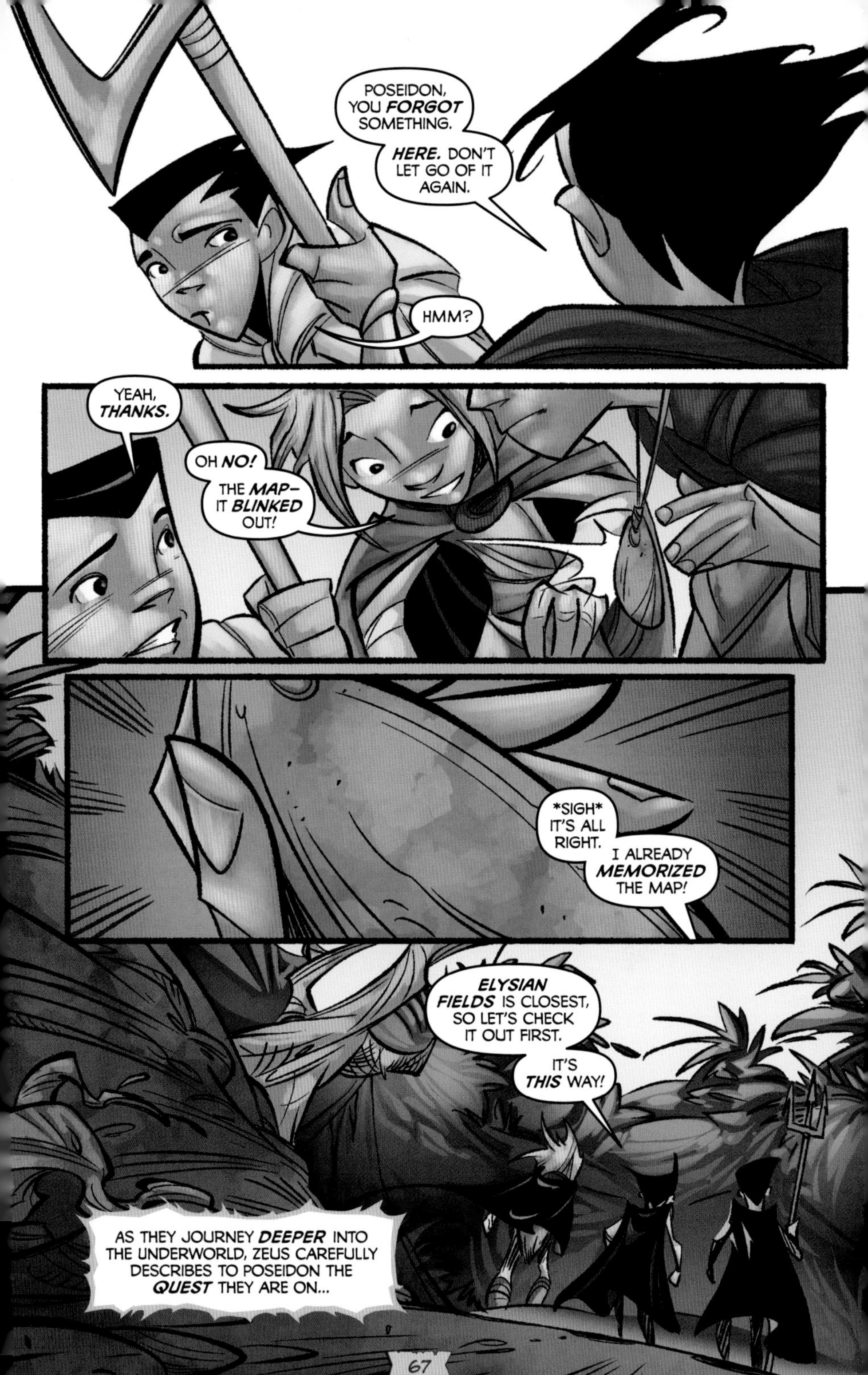
POSEIDON, YOU FORGOT SOMETHING.
HERE. DON'T LET GO OF IT AGAIN.
HMM?
YEAH, THANKS.
OH NO!
THE MAP— IT BLINKED OUT!
SIGH IT'S ALL RIGHT.
I ALREADY MEMORIZED THE MAP!
ELYSIAN FIELDS IS CLOSEST, SO LET'S CHECK IT OUT FIRST.
IT'S THIS WAY!
AS THEY JOURNEY DEEPER INTO THE UNDERWORLD, ZEUS CAREFULLY DESCRIBES TO POSEIDON THE QUEST THEY ARE ON...

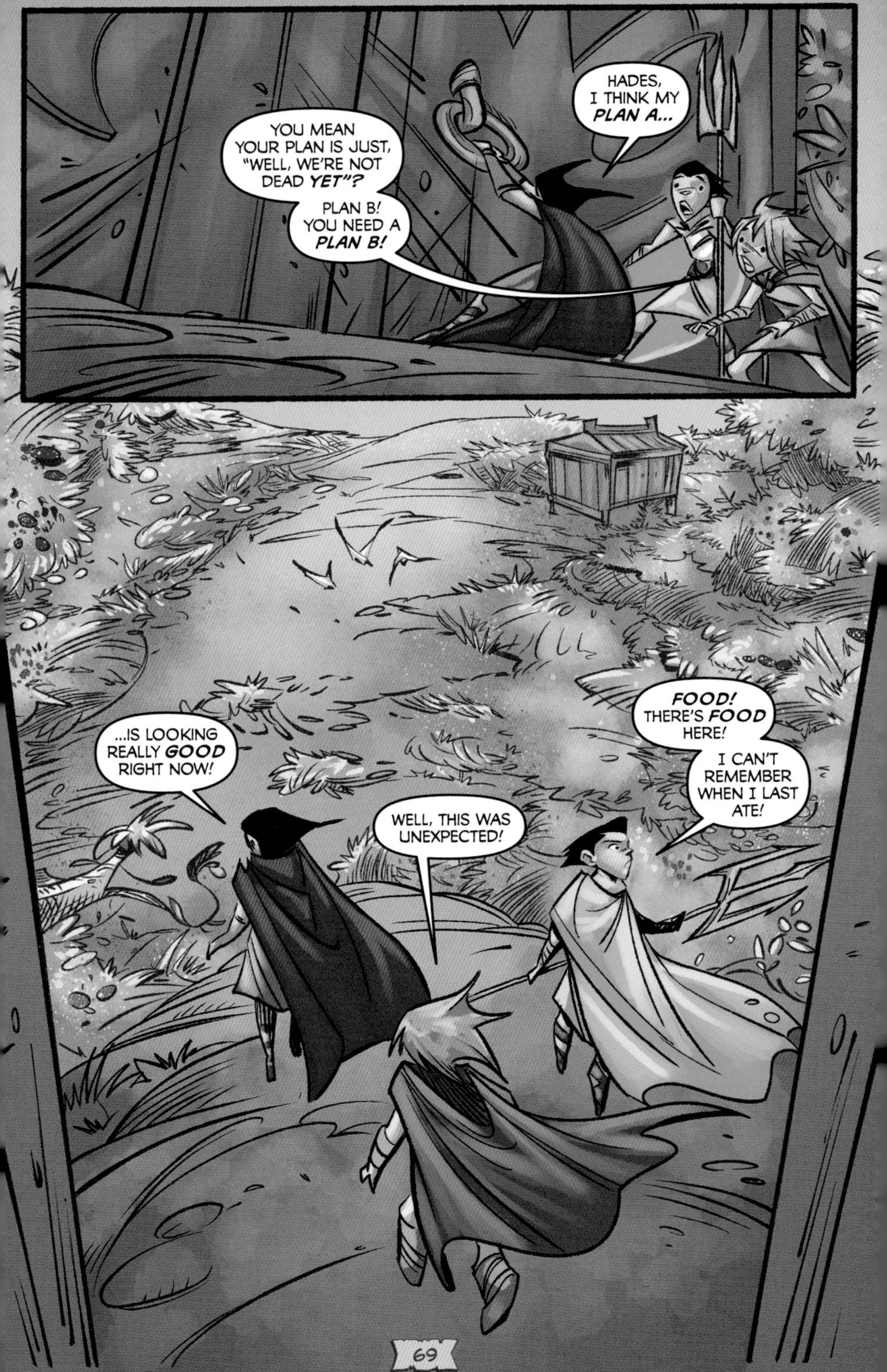
YOU MEAN YOUR PLAN IS JUST, "WELL, WE'RE NOT DEAD *YET*"?
PLAN B! YOU NEED A ***PLAN B!***
HADES, I THINK MY ***PLAN A...***
...IS LOOKING REALLY ***GOOD*** RIGHT NOW!
WELL, THIS WAS UNEXPECTED!
FOOD! THERE'S ***FOOD*** HERE!
I CAN'T REMEMBER WHEN I LAST ATE!

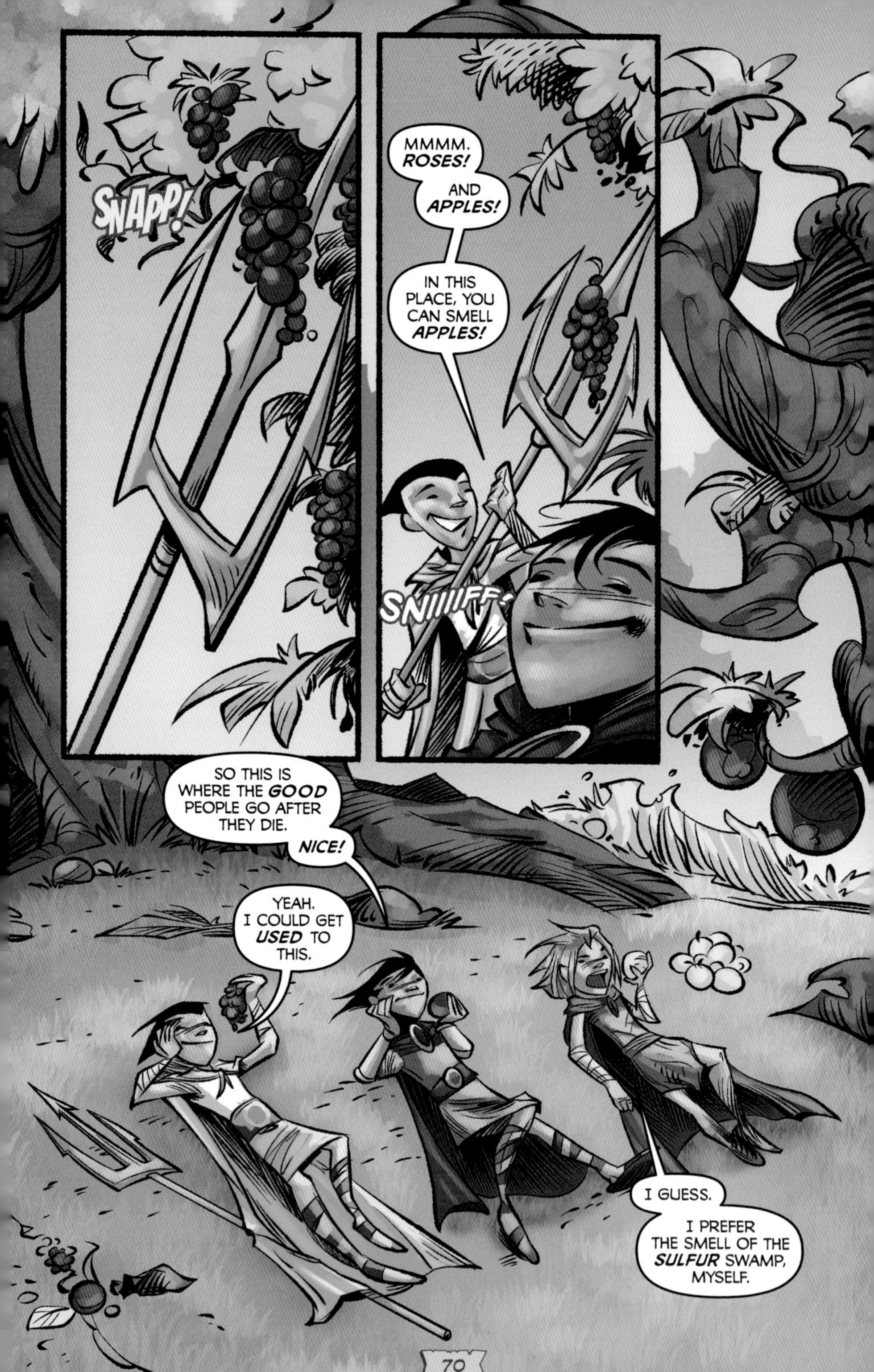
SNAPP!
MMMM. ROSES!
AND APPLES!
IN THIS PLACE, YOU CAN SMELL APPLES!
SNIIIIFF!
SO THIS IS WHERE THE GOOD PEOPLE GO AFTER THEY DIE.
NICE!
YEAH. I COULD GET USED TO THIS.
I GUESS.
I PREFER THE SMELL OF THE SULFUR SWAMP, MYSELF.

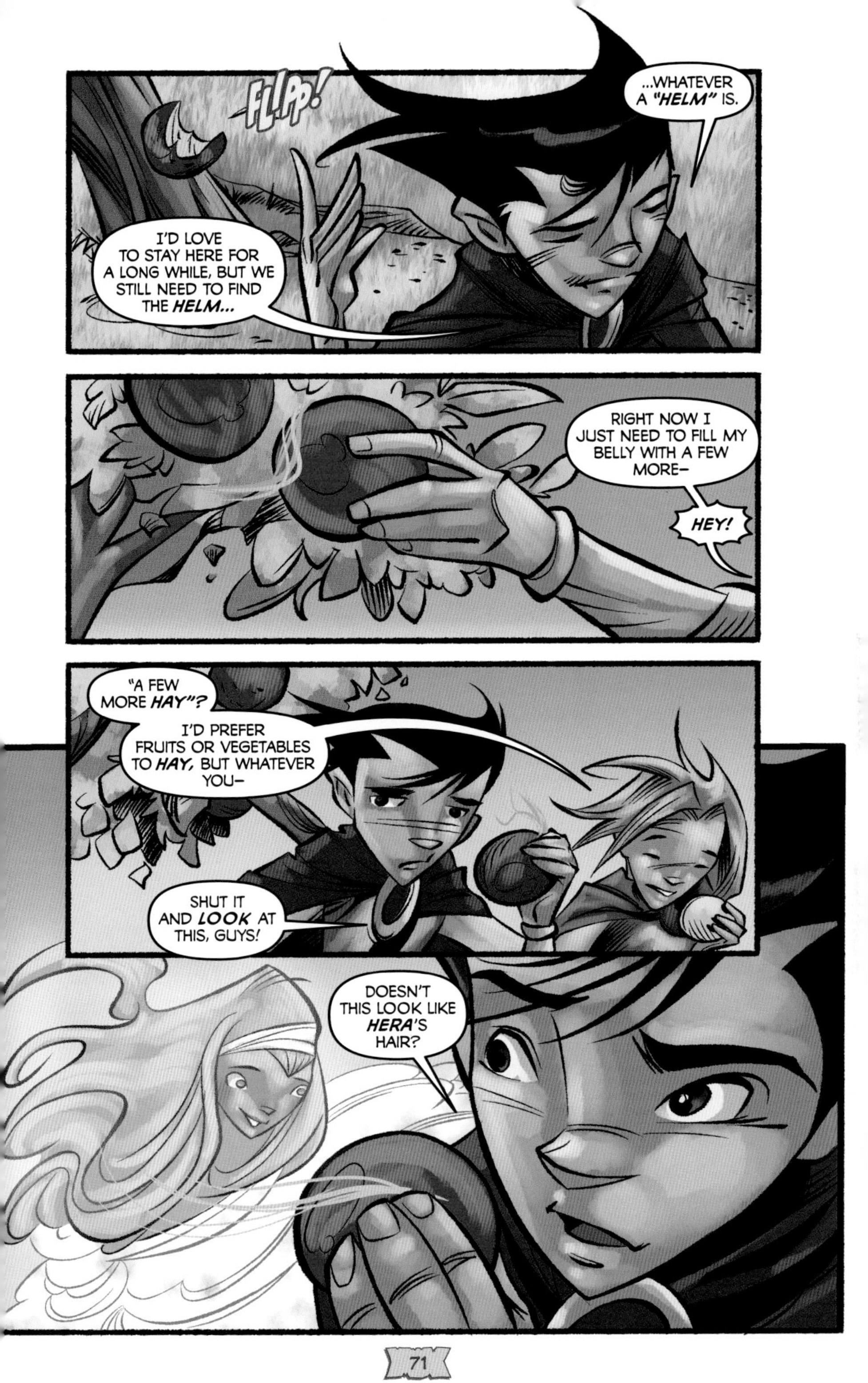
FLIPP!
...WHATEVER A "HELM" IS.
I'D LOVE TO STAY HERE FOR A LONG WHILE, BUT WE STILL NEED TO FIND THE HELM...
RIGHT NOW I JUST NEED TO FILL MY BELLY WITH A FEW MORE–
HEY!
"A FEW MORE HAY"?
I'D PREFER FRUITS OR VEGETABLES TO HAY, BUT WHATEVER YOU–
SHUT IT AND LOOK AT THIS, GUYS!
DOESN'T THIS LOOK LIKE HERA'S HAIR?

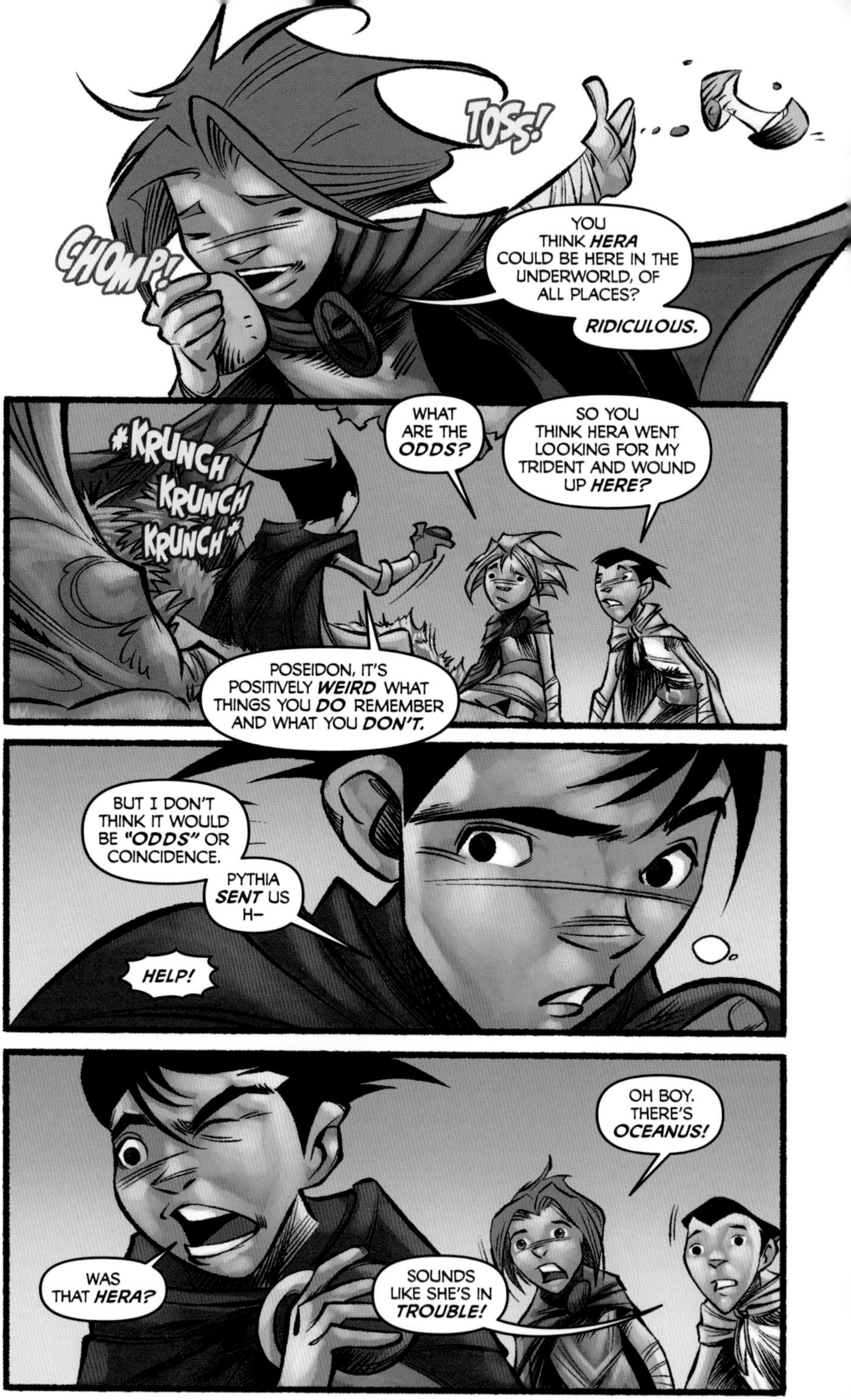
TOSS!
CHOMP!
YOU THINK *HERA* COULD BE HERE IN THE UNDERWORLD, OF ALL PLACES?
RIDICULOUS.
KRUNCH KRUNCH KRUNCH
WHAT ARE THE *ODDS?*
SO YOU THINK HERA WENT LOOKING FOR MY TRIDENT AND WOUND UP *HERE?*
POSEIDON, IT'S POSITIVELY *WEIRD* WHAT THINGS YOU *DO* REMEMBER AND WHAT YOU *DON'T.*
BUT I DON'T THINK IT WOULD BE *"ODDS"* OR COINCIDENCE.
PYTHIA *SENT* US H–
HELP!
WAS THAT *HERA?*
SOUNDS LIKE SHE'S IN *TROUBLE!*
OH BOY. THERE'S *OCEANUS!*

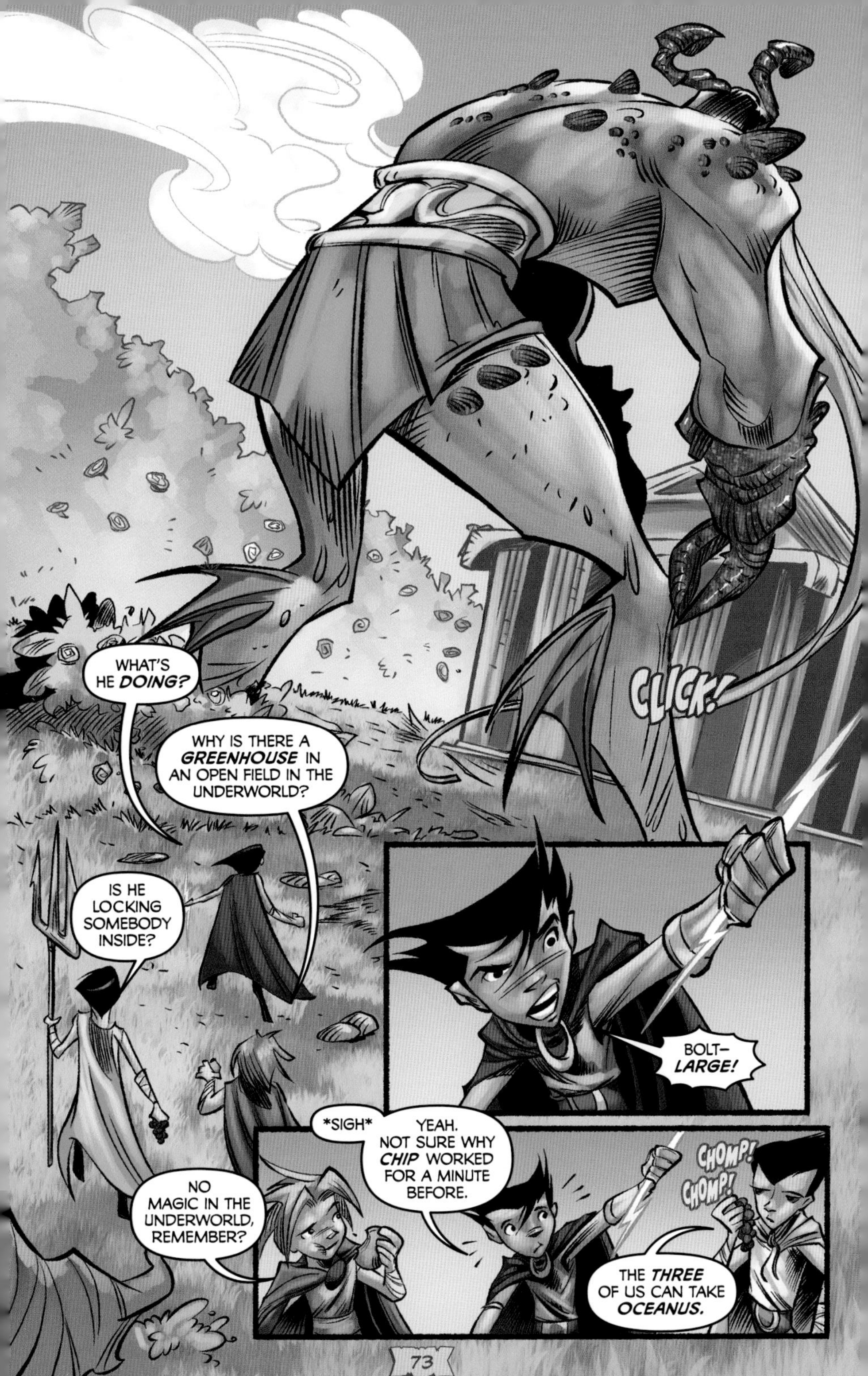
WHAT'S HE *DOING?*
CLICK!
WHY IS THERE A *GREENHOUSE* IN AN OPEN FIELD IN THE UNDERWORLD?
IS HE LOCKING SOMEBODY INSIDE?
BOLT— *LARGE!*
NO MAGIC IN THE UNDERWORLD, REMEMBER?
SIGH
YEAH. NOT SURE WHY *CHIP* WORKED FOR A MINUTE BEFORE.
CHOMP! CHOMP!
THE *THREE* OF US CAN TAKE *OCEANUS.*

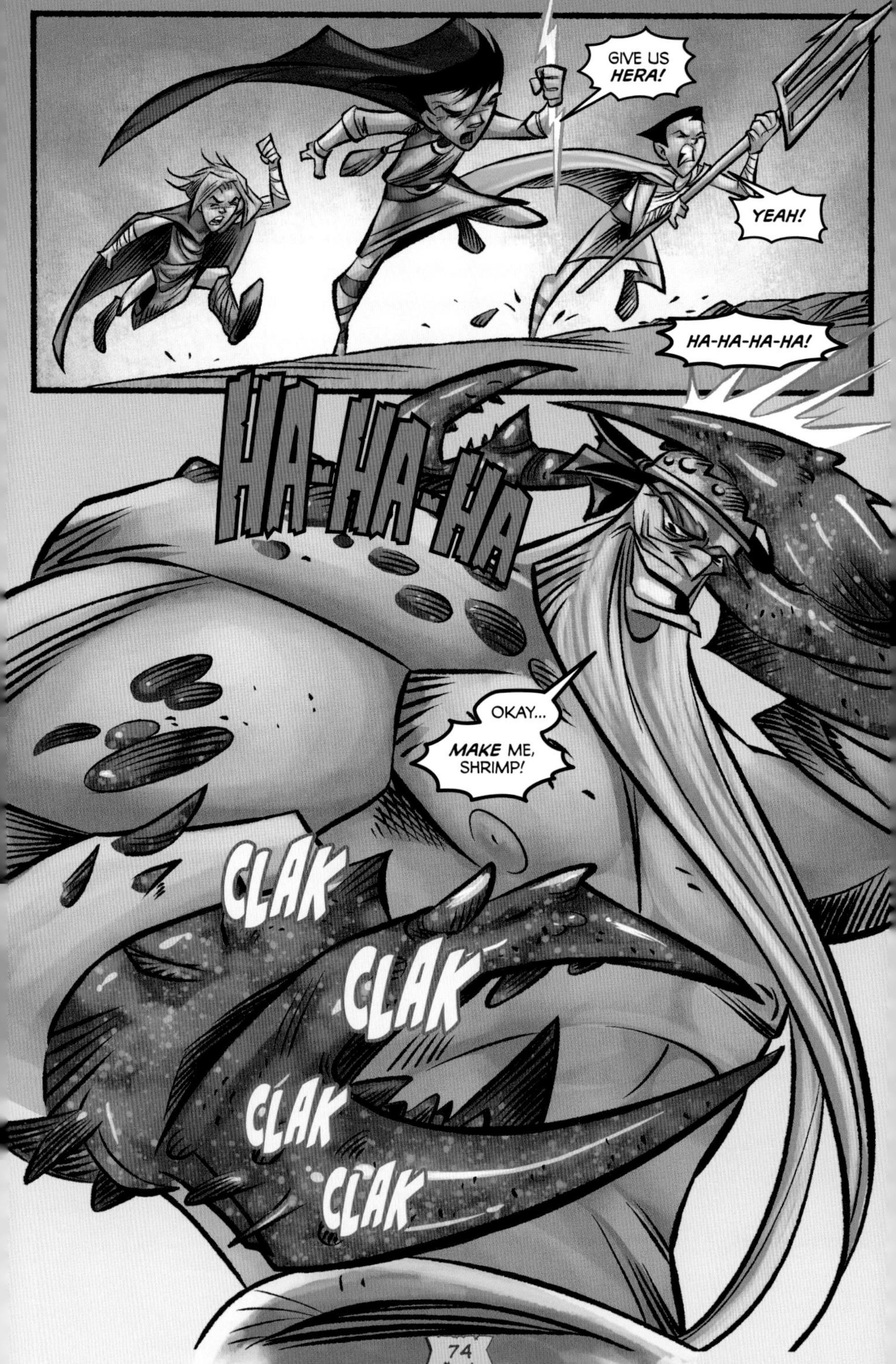
GIVE US HERA!
YEAH!
HA-HA-HA-HA!
HA-HA-HA
OKAY...
MAKE ME, SHRIMP!
CLAK
CLAK
CLAK
CLAK

CHAPTER SEVEN:
THE HELM

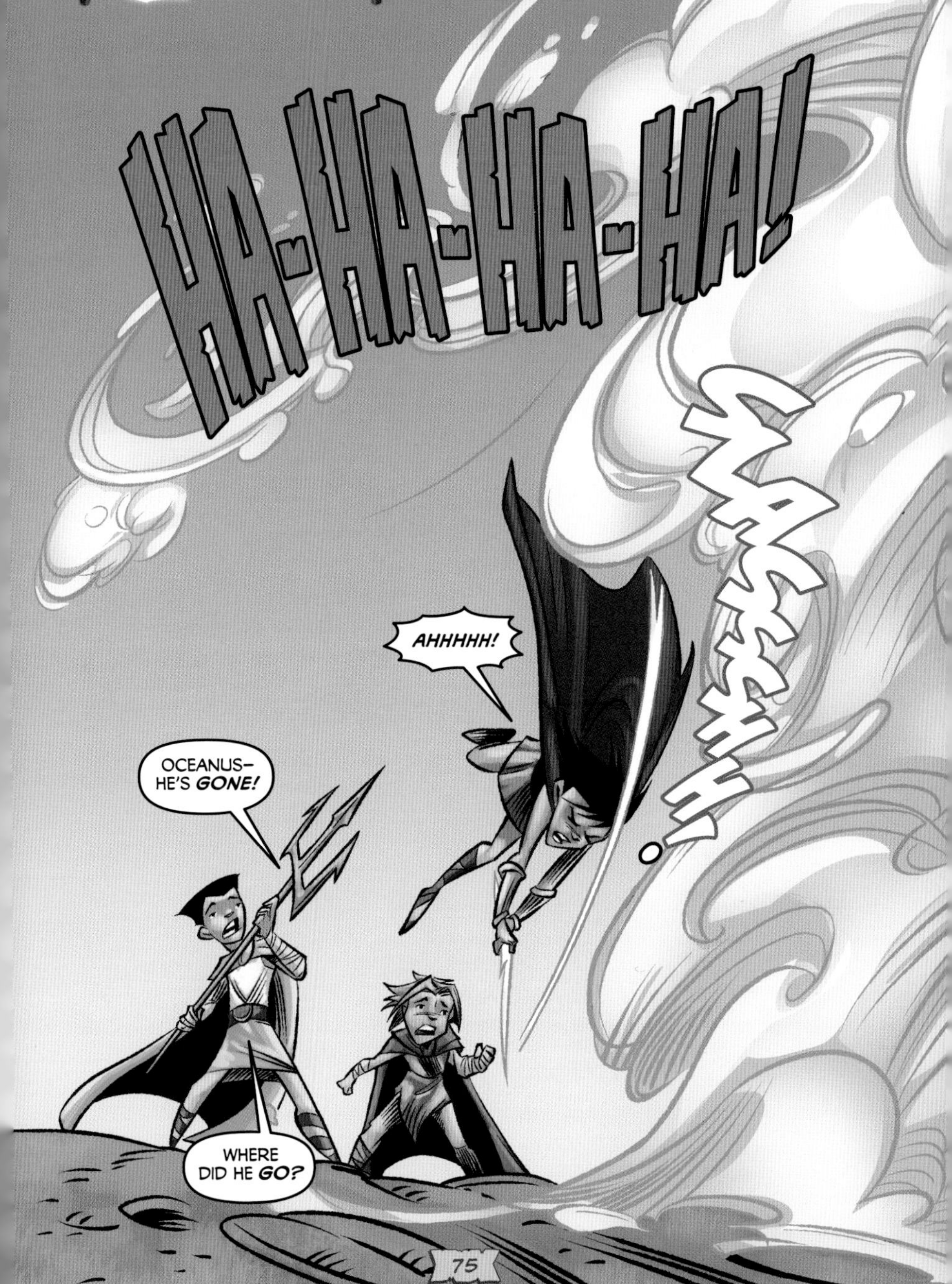
HA-HA-HA-HA-HA!
SWASSHH!
AHHHHH!
OCEANUS—HE'S GONE!
WHERE DID HE GO?

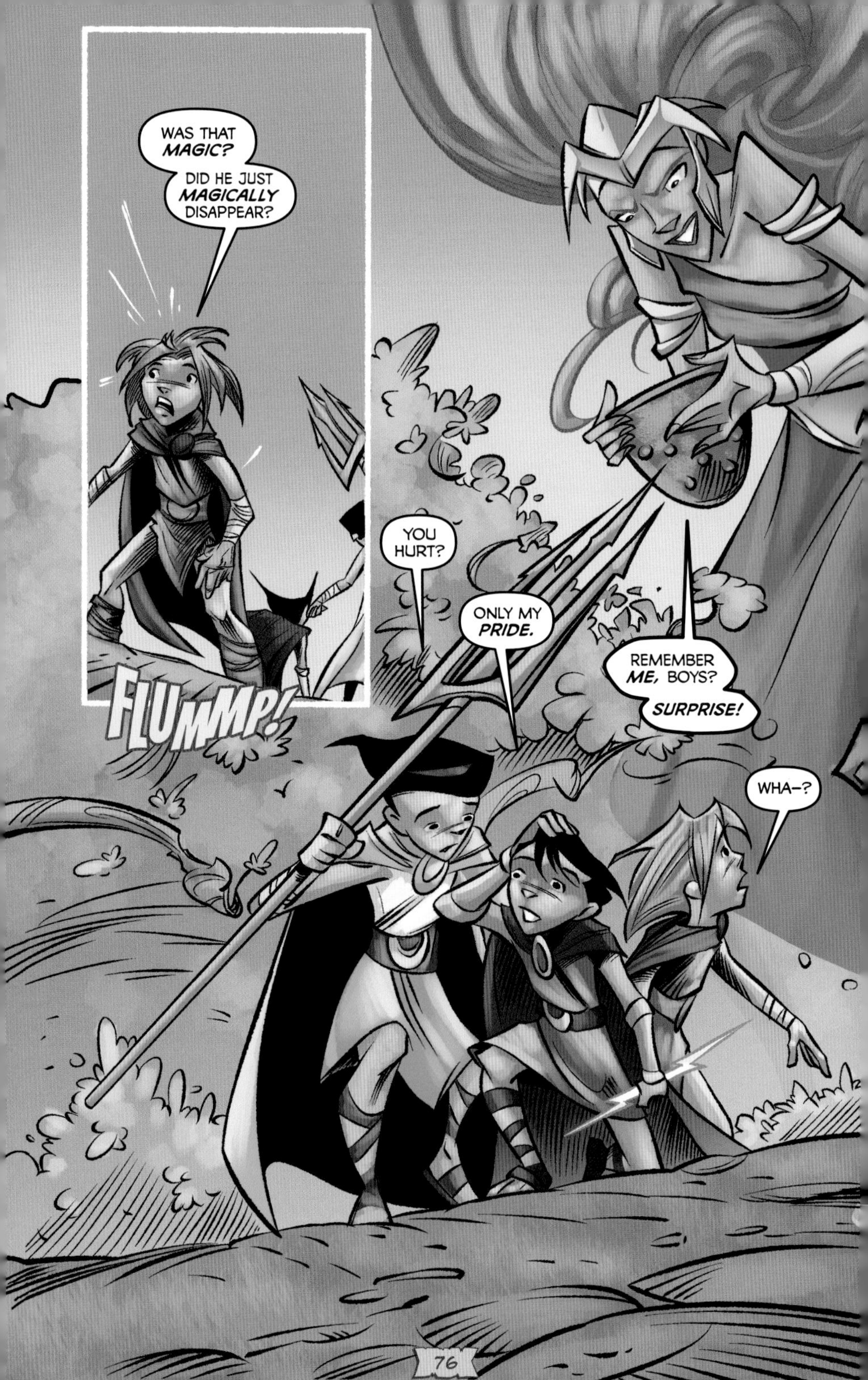
WAS THAT MAGIC?
DID HE JUST MAGICALLY DISAPPEAR?
FLUMMP!
YOU HURT?
ONLY MY PRIDE.
REMEMBER ME, BOYS?
SURPRISE!
WHA-?

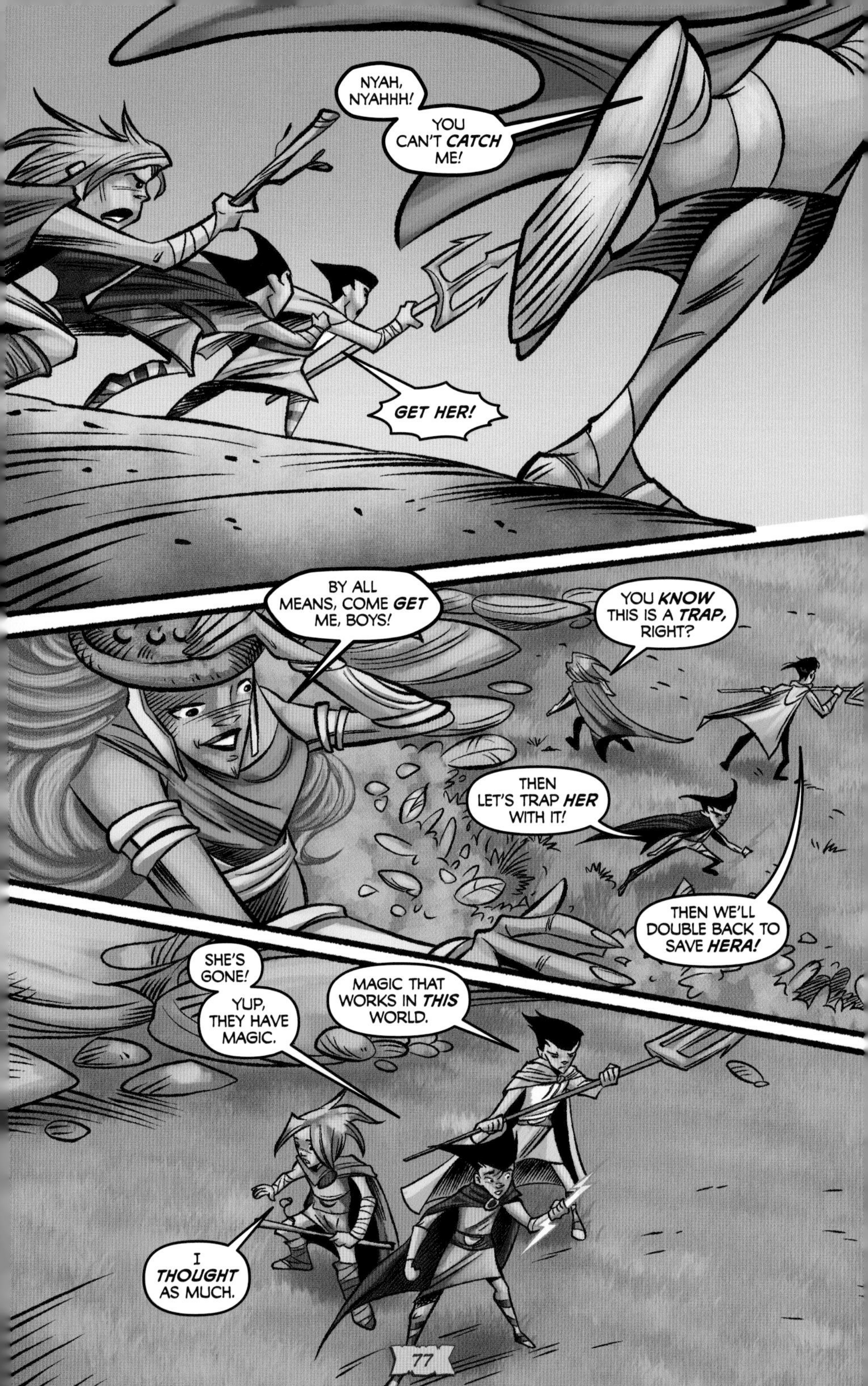
NYAH, NYAHHH!
YOU CAN'T CATCH ME!
GET HER!
BY ALL MEANS, COME GET ME, BOYS!
YOU KNOW THIS IS A TRAP, RIGHT?
THEN LET'S TRAP HER WITH IT!
THEN WE'LL DOUBLE BACK TO SAVE HERA!
SHE'S GONE!
YUP, THEY HAVE MAGIC.
MAGIC THAT WORKS IN THIS WORLD.
I THOUGHT AS MUCH.

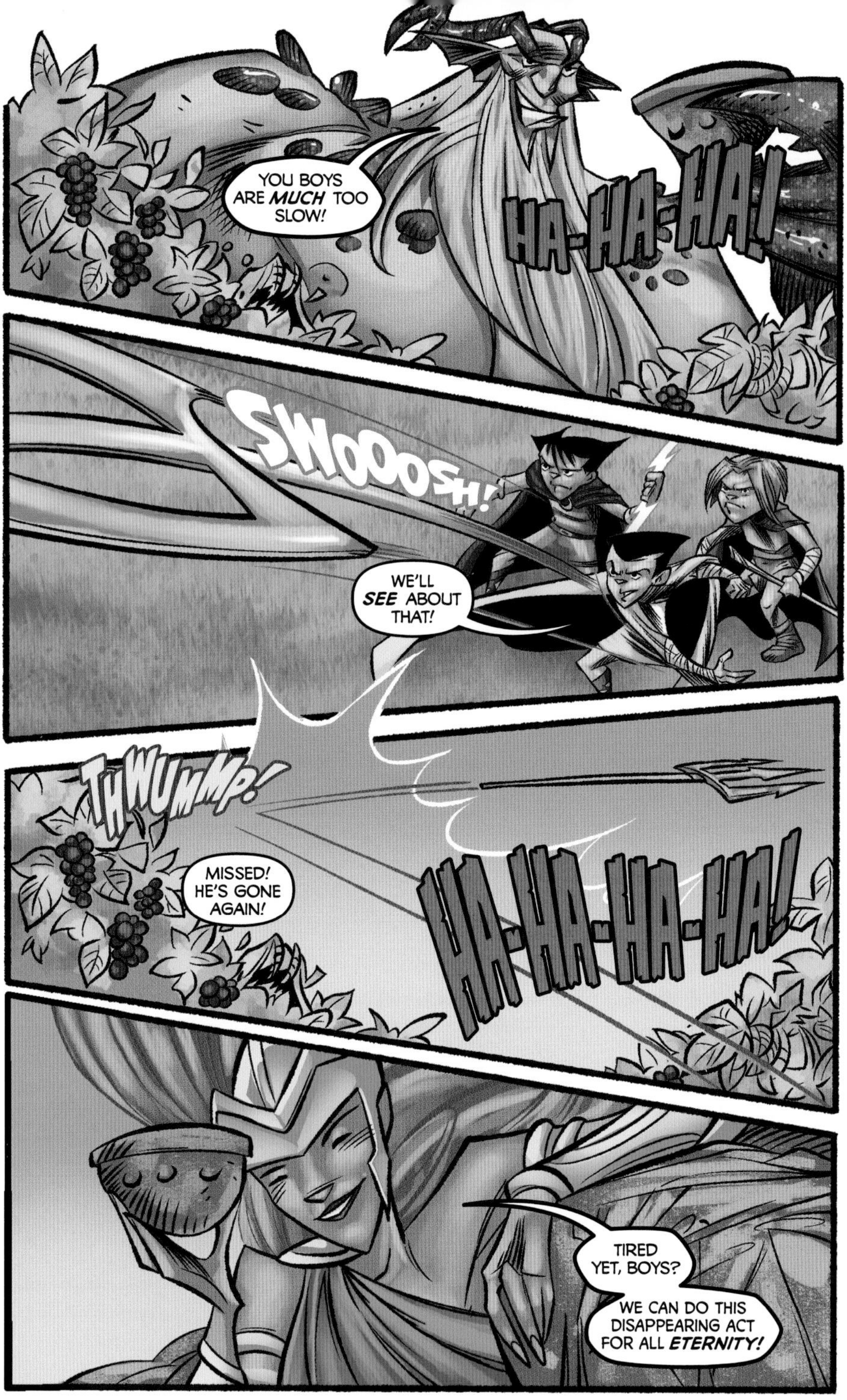
YOU BOYS ARE *MUCH* TOO SLOW!
HA-HA-HA!
SWOOOSH!
WE'LL *SEE* ABOUT THAT!
THWUMMP!
MISSED! HE'S GONE AGAIN!
HA-HA-HA-HA!
TIRED YET, BOYS?
WE CAN DO THIS DISAPPEARING ACT FOR ALL *ETERNITY!*

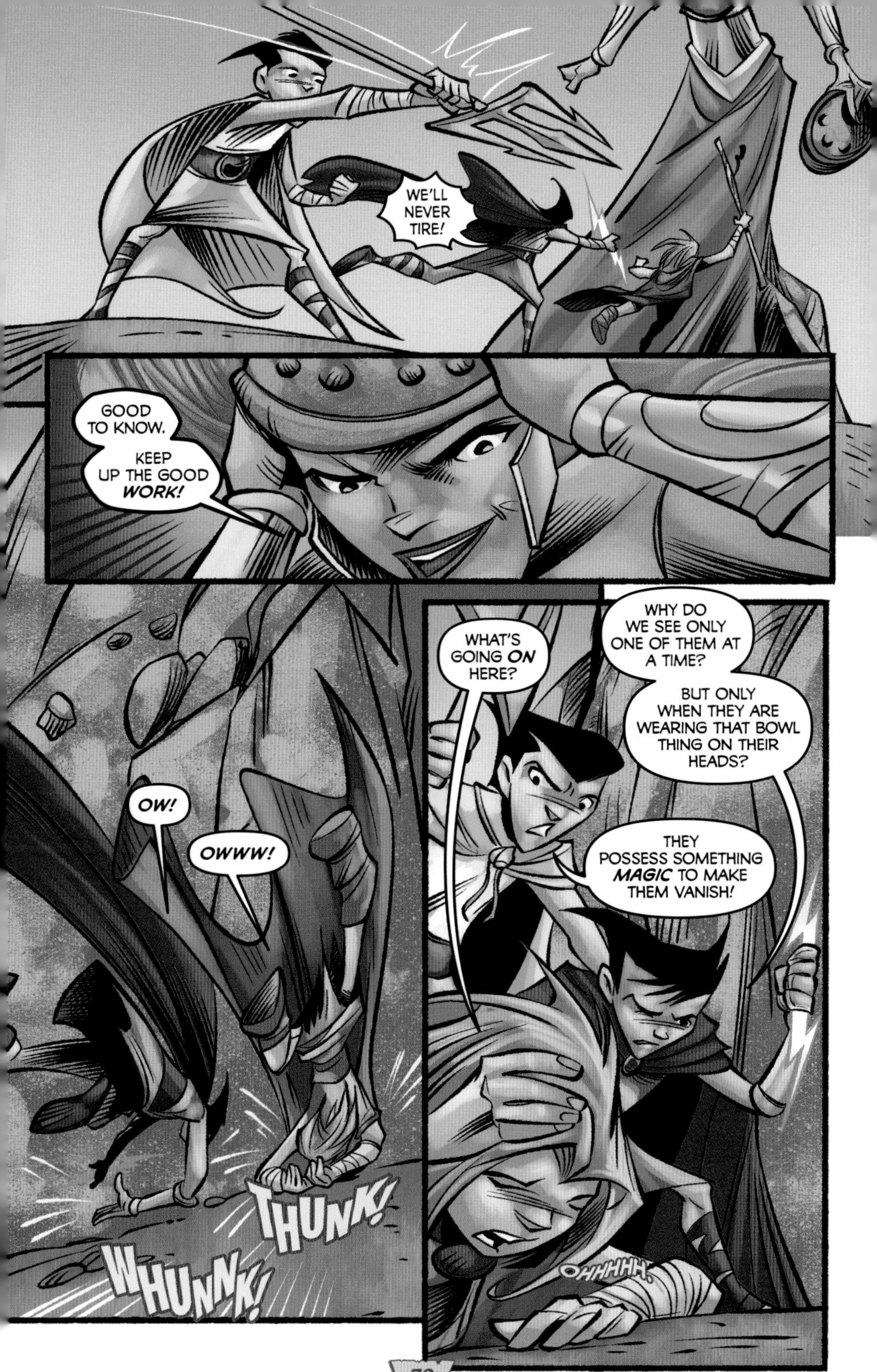
WE'LL NEVER TIRE!
GOOD TO KNOW.
KEEP UP THE GOOD WORK!
OW!
OWWW!
THUNK!
WHUNNK!
WHAT'S GOING ON HERE?
WHY DO WE SEE ONLY ONE OF THEM AT A TIME?
BUT ONLY WHEN THEY ARE WEARING THAT BOWL THING ON THEIR HEADS?
THEY POSSESS SOMETHING MAGIC TO MAKE THEM VANISH!
OHHHHH

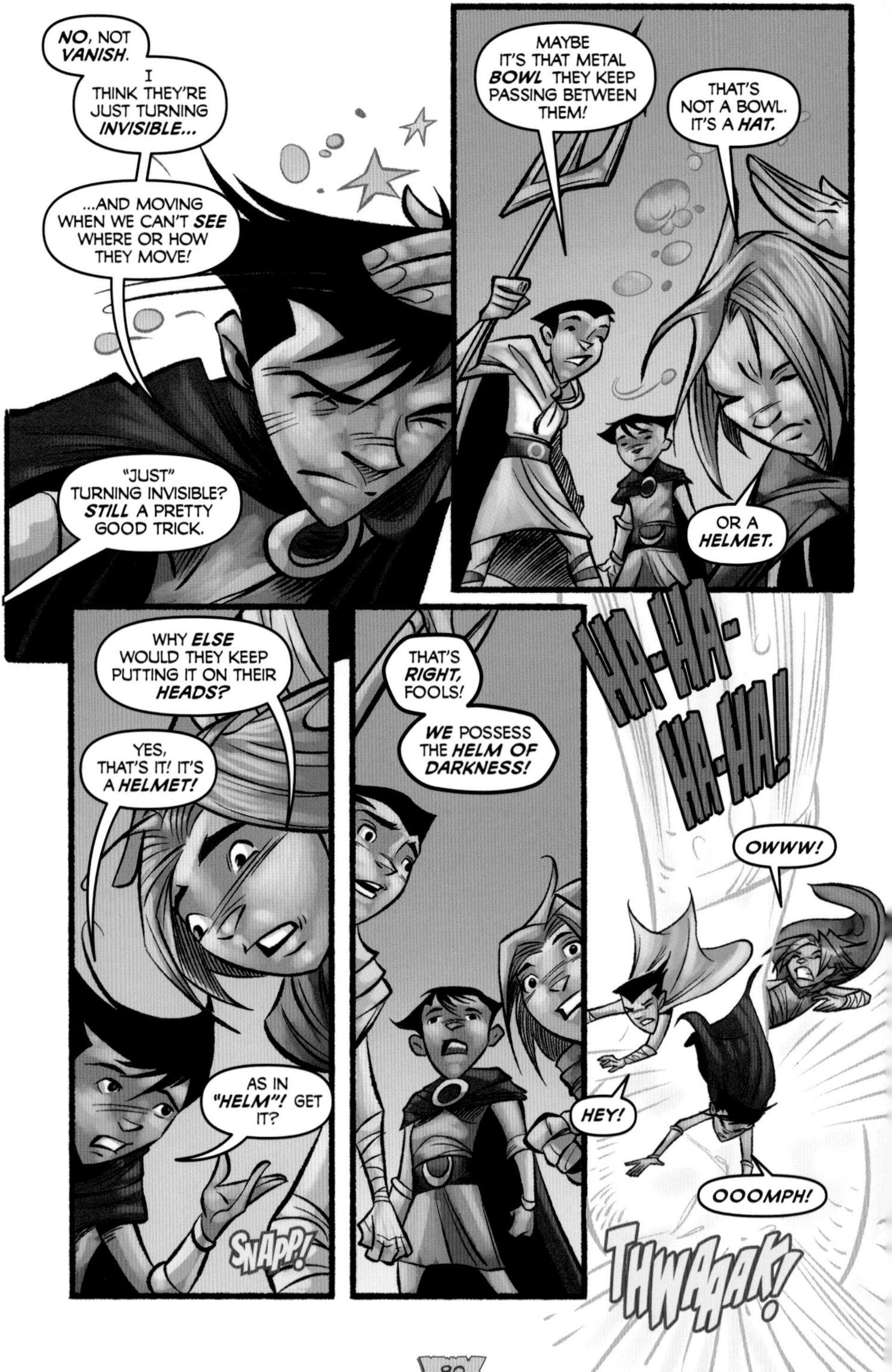
NO, NOT VANISH.
I THINK THEY'RE JUST TURNING INVISIBLE...
...AND MOVING WHEN WE CAN'T SEE WHERE OR HOW THEY MOVE!
"JUST" TURNING INVISIBLE? STILL A PRETTY GOOD TRICK.
MAYBE IT'S THAT METAL BOWL THEY KEEP PASSING BETWEEN THEM!
THAT'S NOT A BOWL. IT'S A HAT.
OR A HELMET.
WHY ELSE WOULD THEY KEEP PUTTING IT ON THEIR HEADS?
YES, THAT'S IT! IT'S A HELMET!
AS IN "HELM"! GET IT?
SNAPP!
THAT'S RIGHT, FOOLS!
WE POSSESS THE HELM OF DARKNESS!
HEY!
HA-HA-HA-HA!
OWWW!
OOOMPH!
THWAAAK!

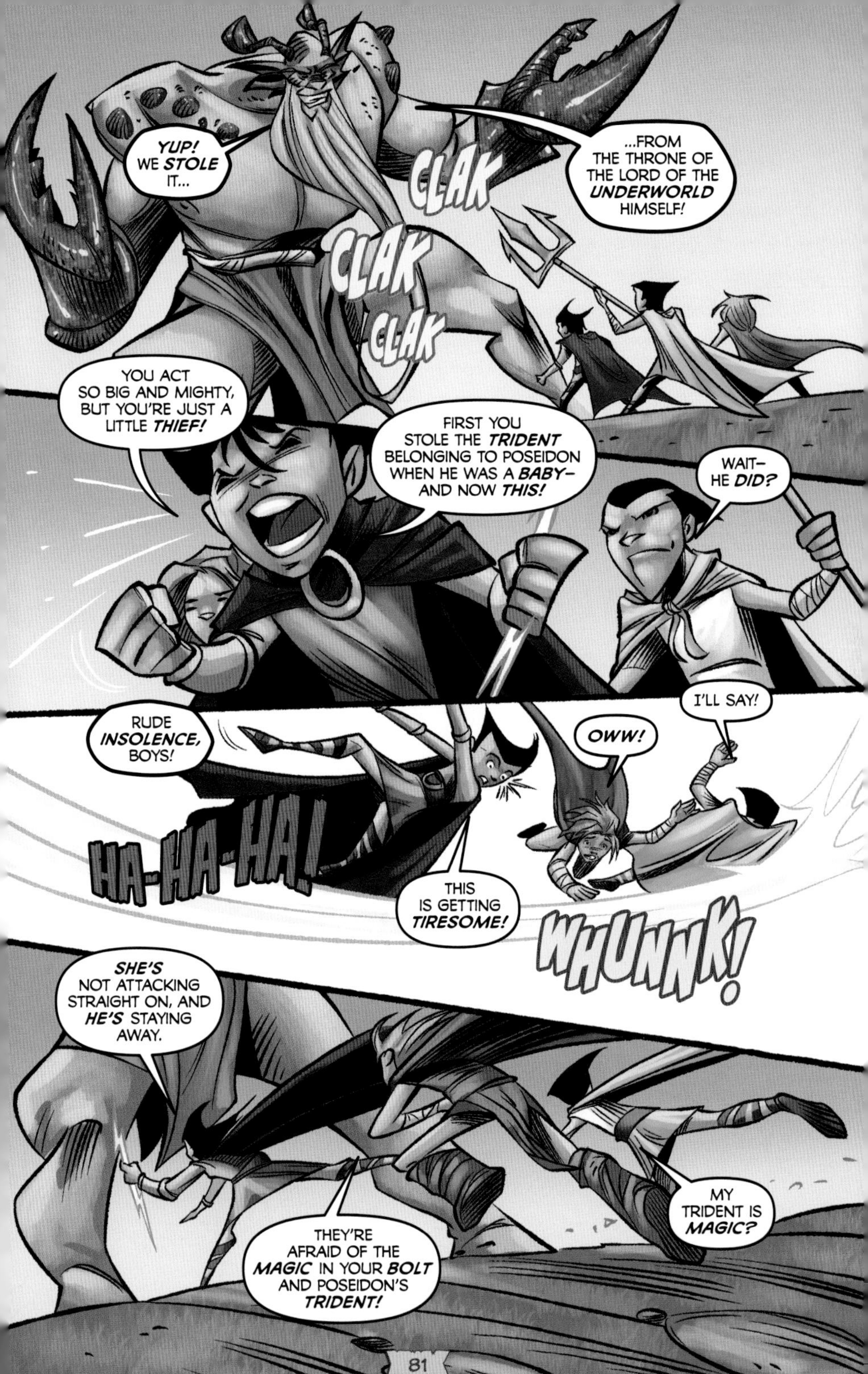
YUP! WE STOLE IT...
...FROM THE THRONE OF THE LORD OF THE UNDERWORLD HIMSELF!
CLAK
CLAK
CLAK
YOU ACT SO BIG AND MIGHTY, BUT YOU'RE JUST A LITTLE THIEF!
FIRST YOU STOLE THE TRIDENT BELONGING TO POSEIDON WHEN HE WAS A BABY— AND NOW THIS!
WAIT— HE DID?
RUDE INSOLENCE, BOYS!
OWW!
I'LL SAY!
HA-HA-HA!
THIS IS GETTING TIRESOME!
WHUNNK!
SHE'S NOT ATTACKING STRAIGHT ON, AND HE'S STAYING AWAY.
THEY'RE AFRAID OF THE MAGIC IN YOUR BOLT AND POSEIDON'S TRIDENT!
MY TRIDENT IS MAGIC?

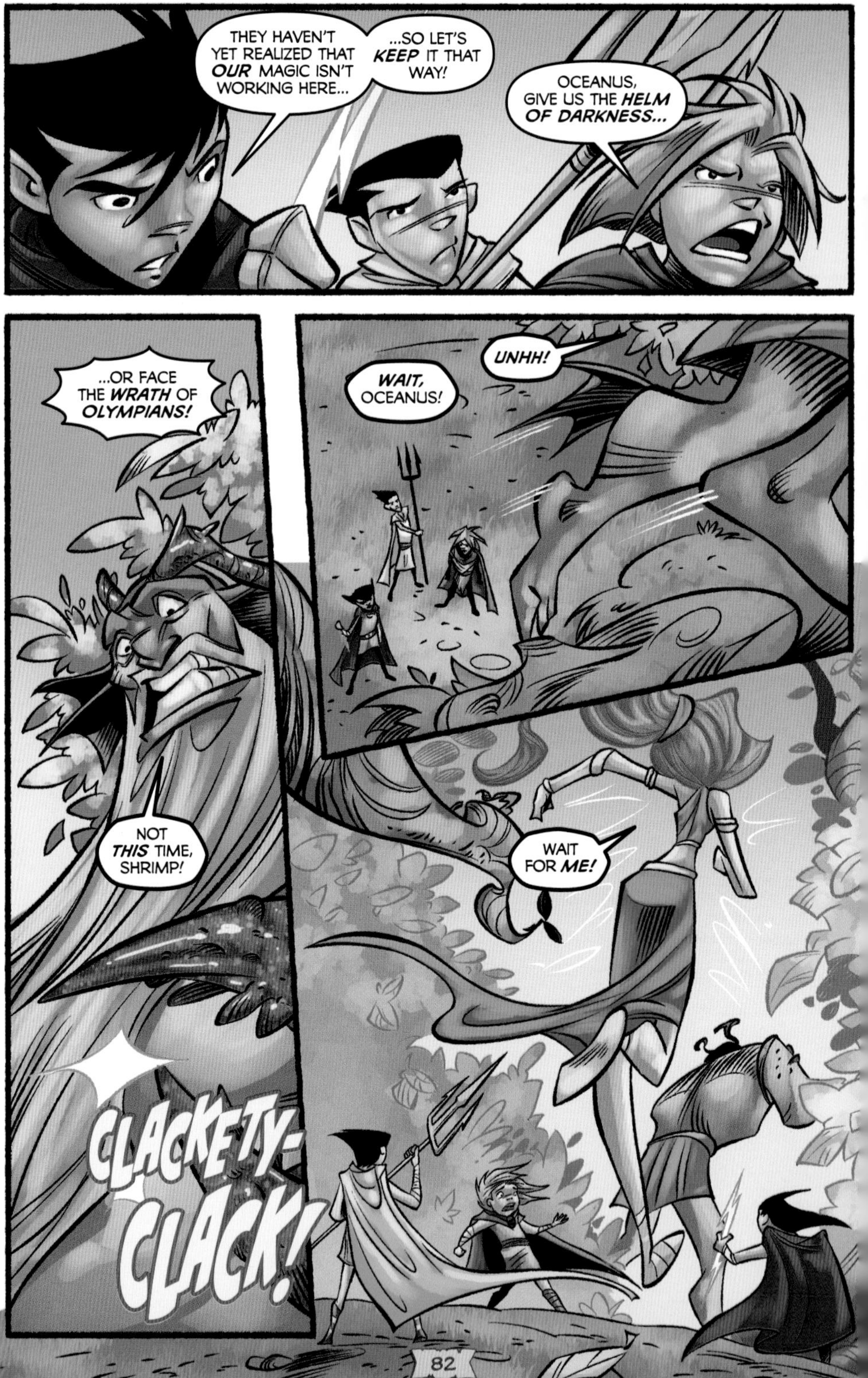
THEY HAVEN'T YET REALIZED THAT *OUR* MAGIC ISN'T WORKING HERE...
...SO LET'S *KEEP* IT THAT WAY!
OCEANUS, GIVE US THE *HELM OF DARKNESS...*
...OR FACE THE *WRATH* OF *OLYMPIANS!*
NOT *THIS* TIME, SHRIMP!
CLACKETY-CLACK!
WAIT, OCEANUS!
UNHH!
WAIT FOR *ME!*

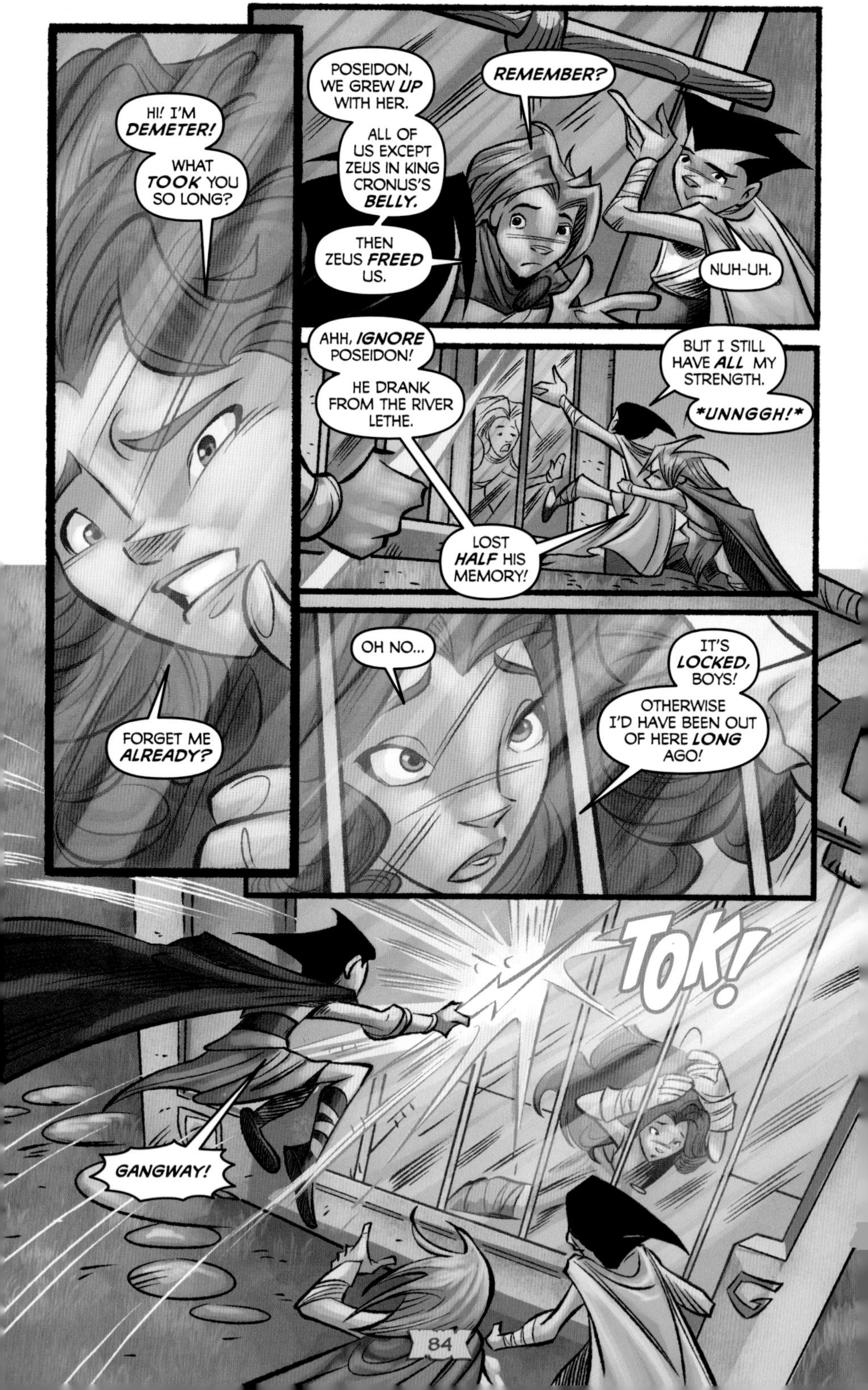
HI! I'M DEMETER!
WHAT TOOK YOU SO LONG?
FORGET ME ALREADY?
POSEIDON, WE GREW UP WITH HER.
ALL OF US EXCEPT ZEUS IN KING CRONUS'S BELLY.
THEN ZEUS FREED US.
REMEMBER?
NUH-UH.
AHH, IGNORE POSEIDON!
HE DRANK FROM THE RIVER LETHE.
LOST HALF HIS MEMORY!
BUT I STILL HAVE ALL MY STRENGTH.
UNNGGH!
OH NO...
IT'S LOCKED, BOYS!
OTHERWISE I'D HAVE BEEN OUT OF HERE LONG AGO!
TOK!
GANGWAY!

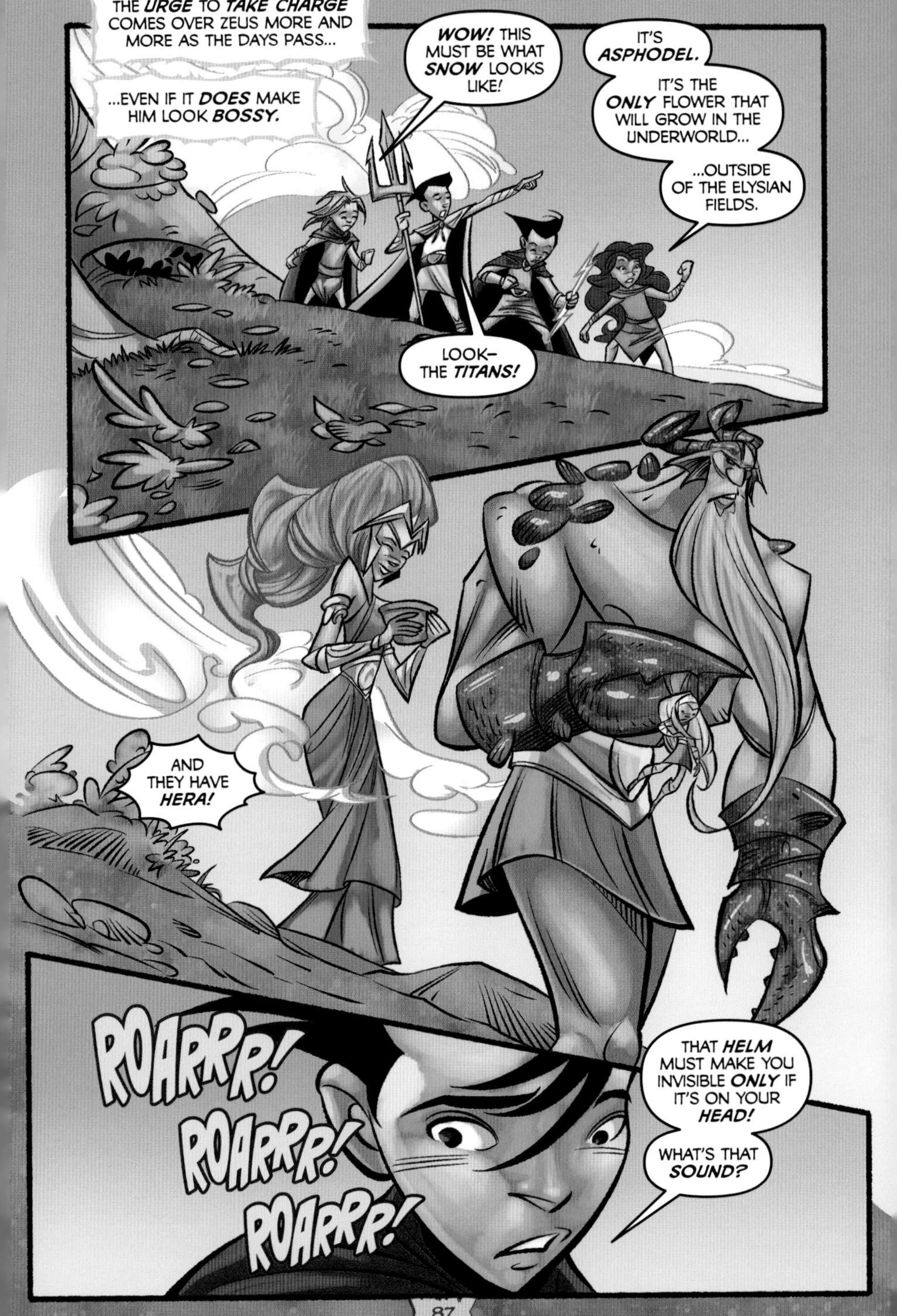
THE URGE TO TAKE CHARGE COMES OVER ZEUS MORE AND MORE AS THE DAYS PASS...
...EVEN IF IT DOES MAKE HIM LOOK BOSSY.
WOW! THIS MUST BE WHAT SNOW LOOKS LIKE!
IT'S ASPHODEL.
IT'S THE ONLY FLOWER THAT WILL GROW IN THE UNDERWORLD...
...OUTSIDE OF THE ELYSIAN FIELDS.
LOOK— THE TITANS!
AND THEY HAVE HERA!
ROARRR! ROARRR! ROARRR!
THAT HELM MUST MAKE YOU INVISIBLE ONLY IF IT'S ON YOUR HEAD!
WHAT'S THAT SOUND?

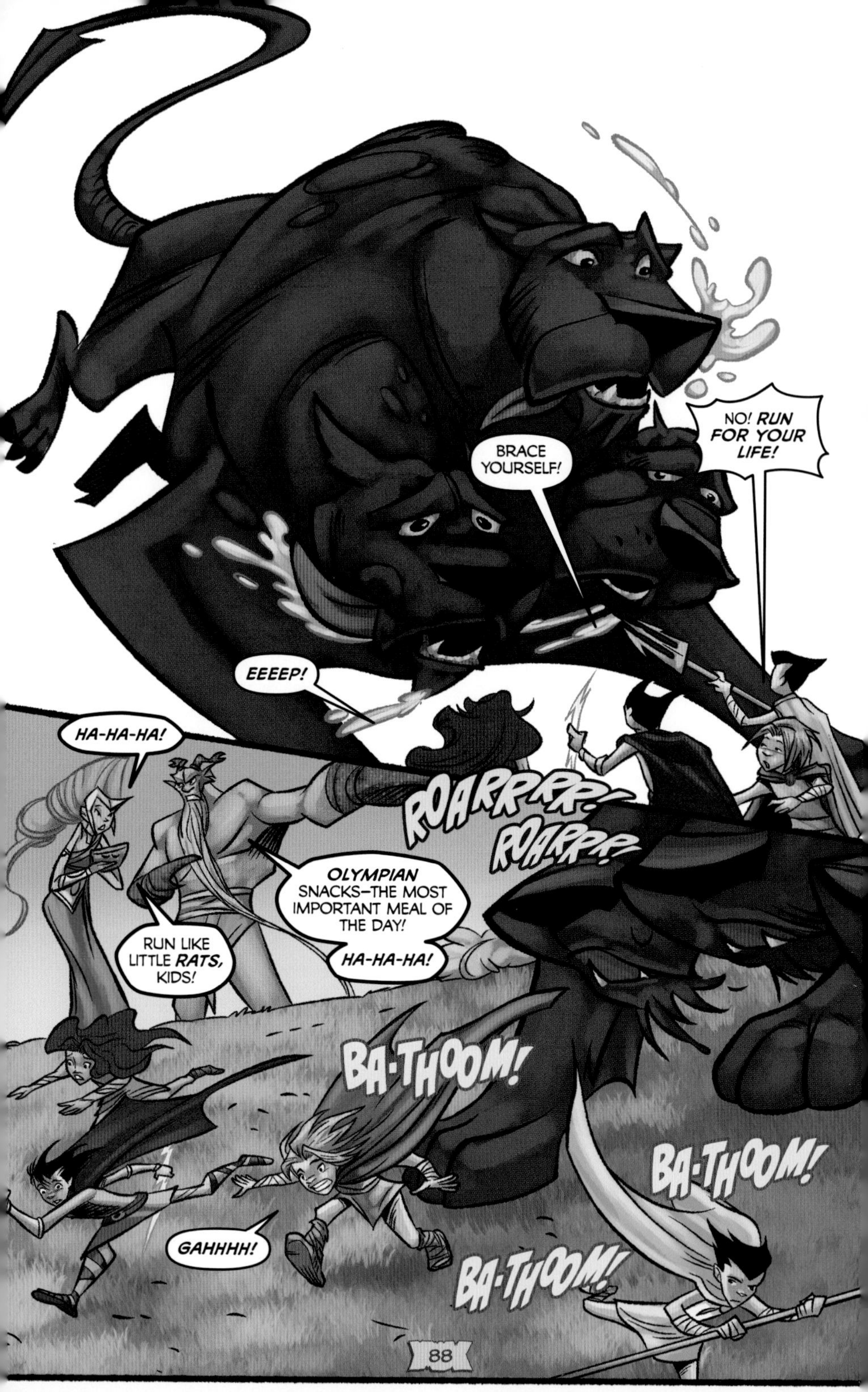
BRACE YOURSELF!
NO! RUN FOR YOUR LIFE!
EEEEP!
HA-HA-HA!
ROARRRR!
ROARRR!
OLYMPIAN SNACKS—THE MOST IMPORTANT MEAL OF THE DAY!
HA-HA-HA!
RUN LIKE LITTLE RATS, KIDS!
BA-THOOM!
BA-THOOM!
BA-THOOM!
GAHHHH!

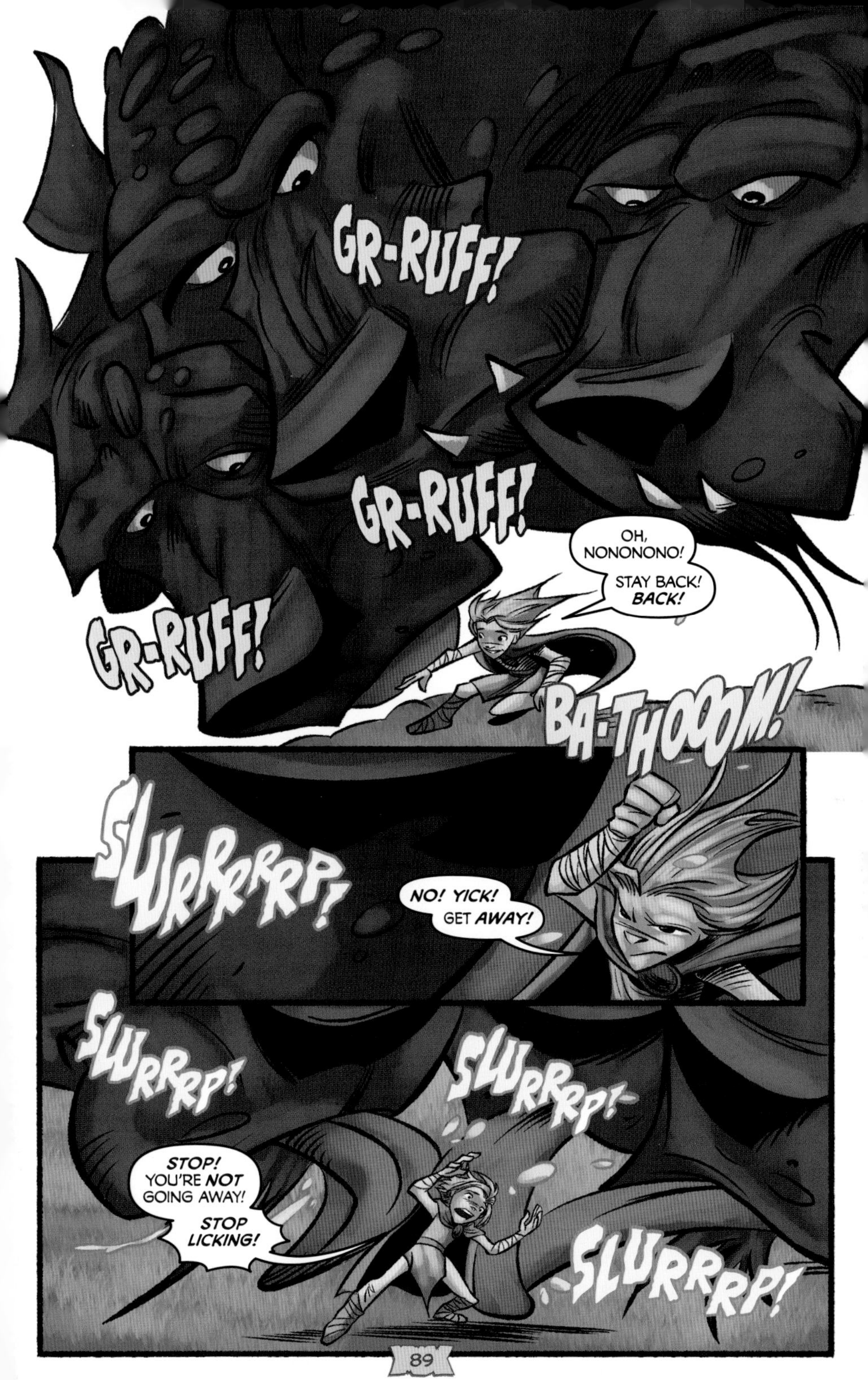
GR-RUFF!
GR-RUFF!
GR-RUFF!
OH, NONONONO!
STAY BACK! BACK!
BA-THOOOM!
SLURRRRRP!
NO! YICK! GET AWAY!
SLURRRP!
SLURRRP!
STOP! YOU'RE NOT GOING AWAY!
STOP LICKING!
SLURRRP!

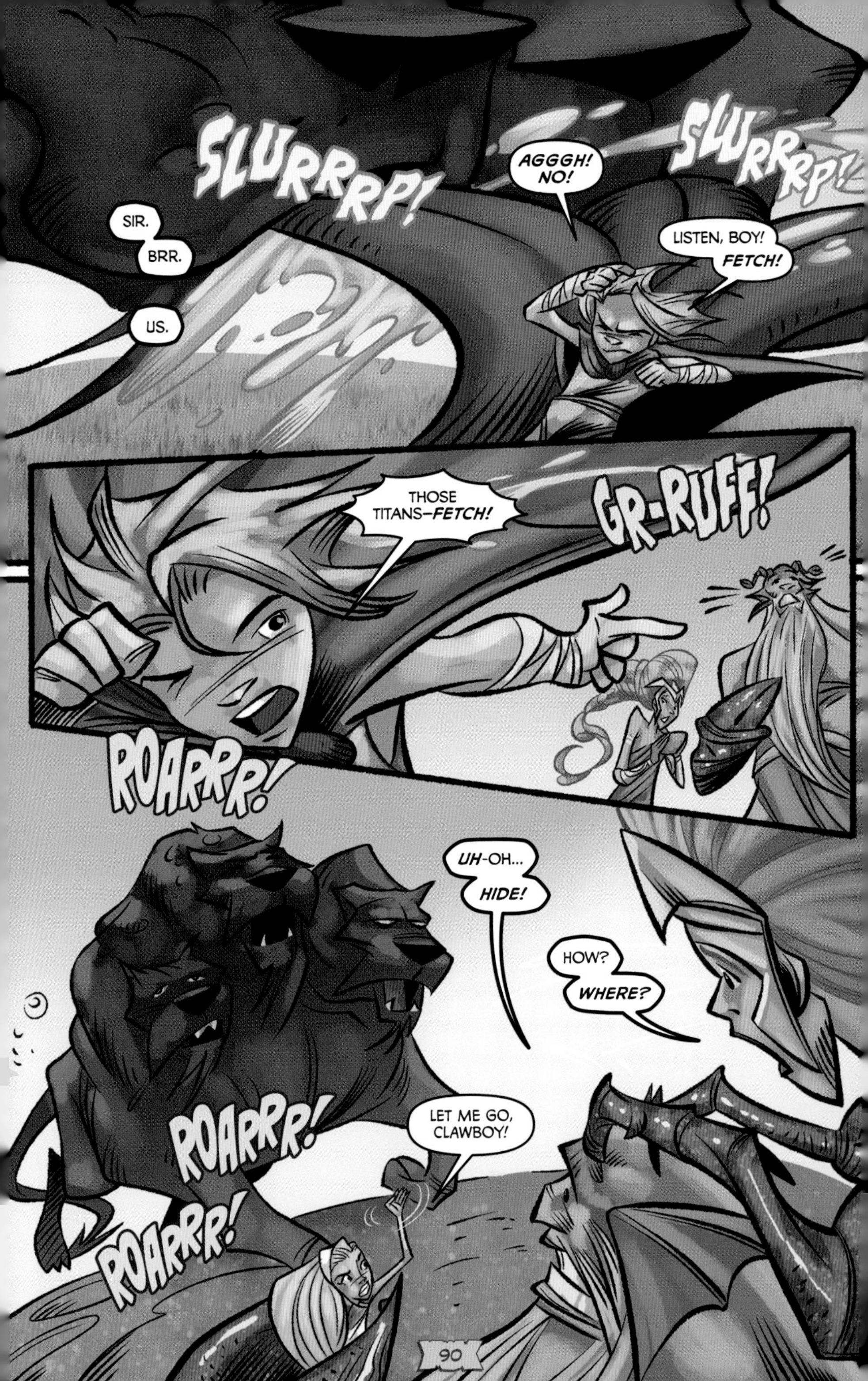
SLURRRP!
SIR.
BRR.
US.
AGGGH! NO!
SLURRRP!
LISTEN, BOY! FETCH!
THOSE TITANS—FETCH!
GR-RUFF!
ROARRR!
UH-OH... HIDE!
HOW? WHERE?
ROARRR!
ROARRR!
LET ME GO, CLAWBOY!

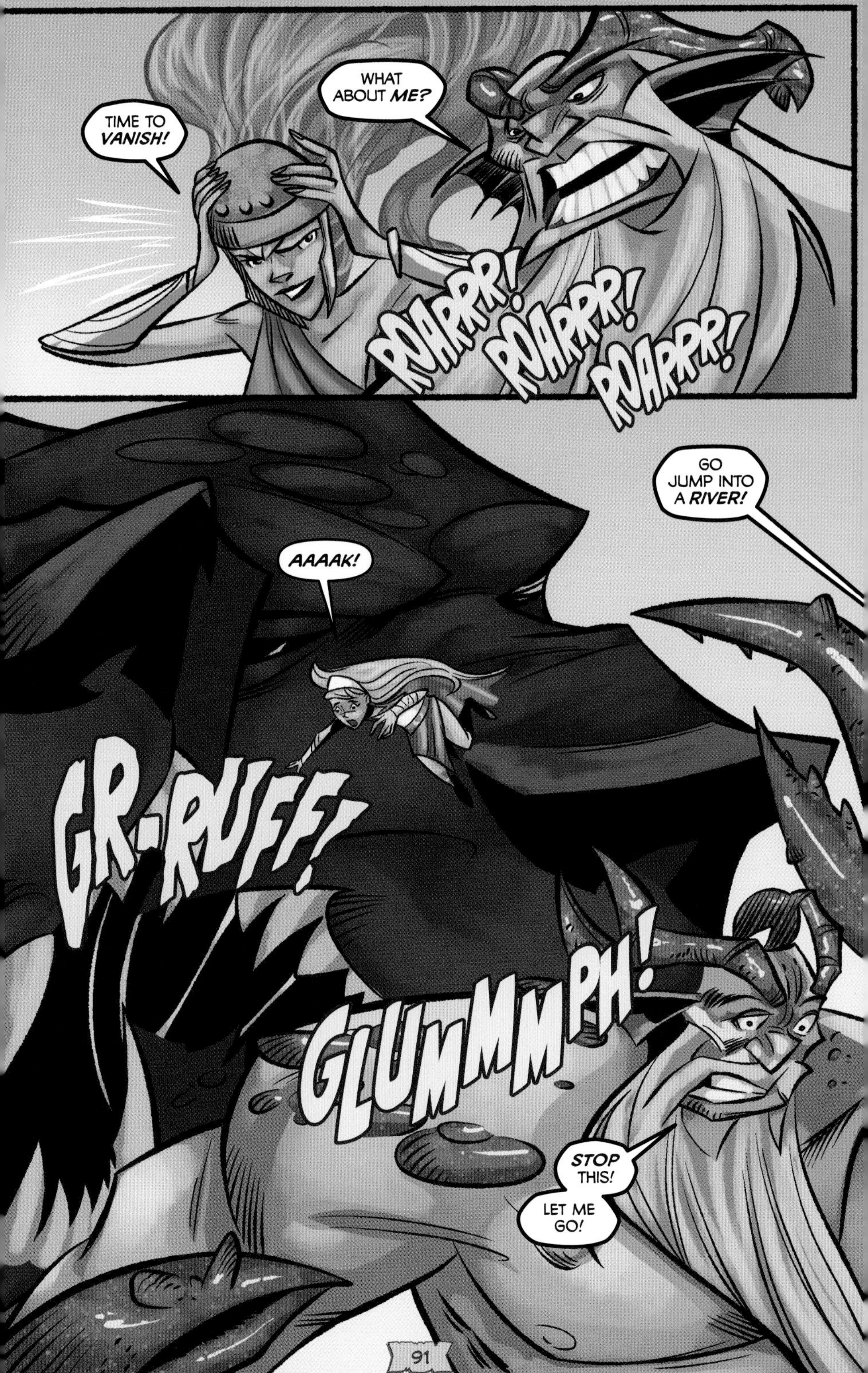
TIME TO VANISH!
WHAT ABOUT ME?
ROARRR! ROARRR! ROARRR!
GO JUMP INTO A RIVER!
AAAAK!
GR-RUFF!
GLUMMMPH!
STOP THIS!
LET ME GO!

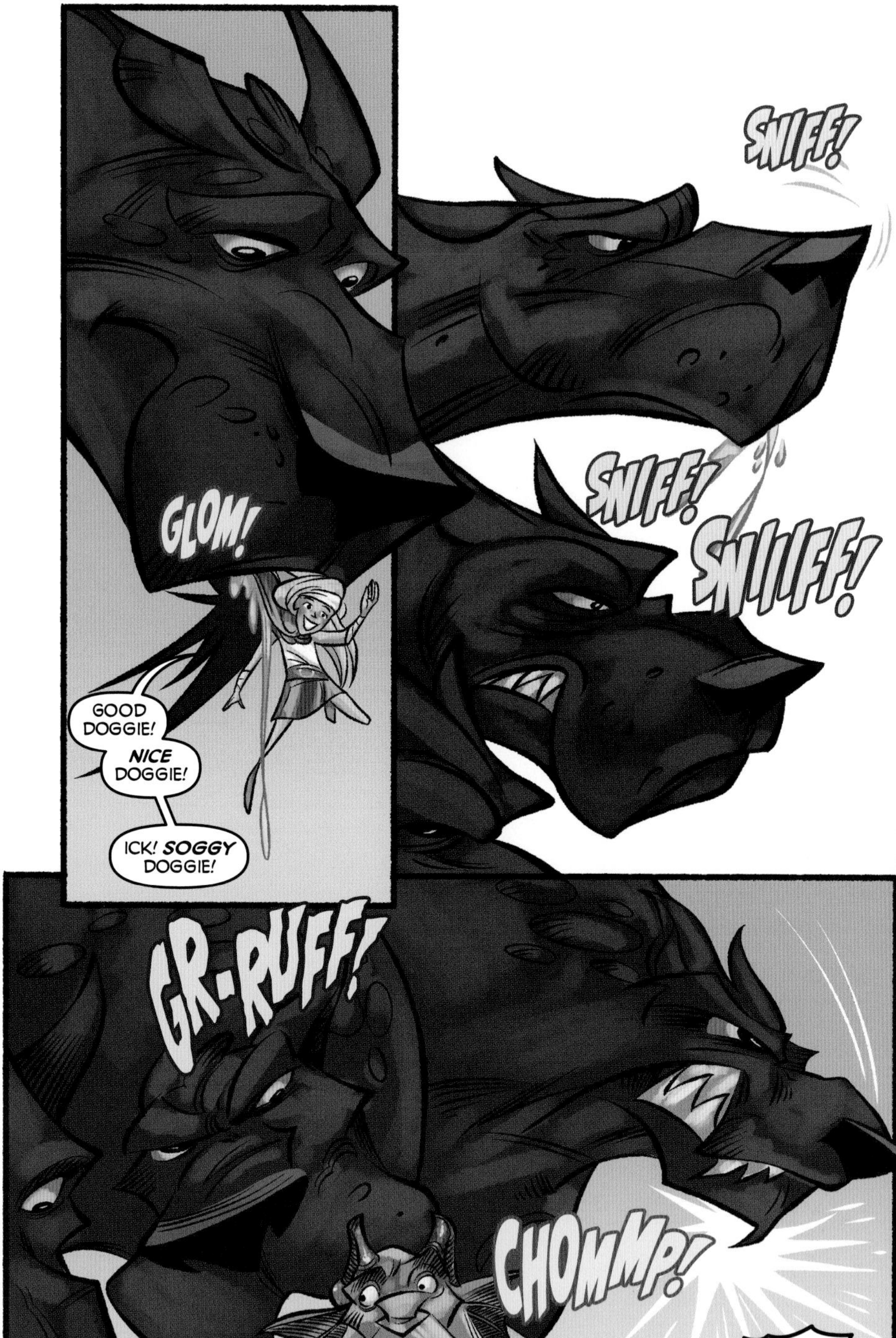
SNIFF!
GLOM!
SNIFF!
SNIIIFF!
GOOD DOGGIE!
NICE DOGGIE!
ICK! SOGGY DOGGIE!
GR-RUFF!
CHOMMP!
OUCH!

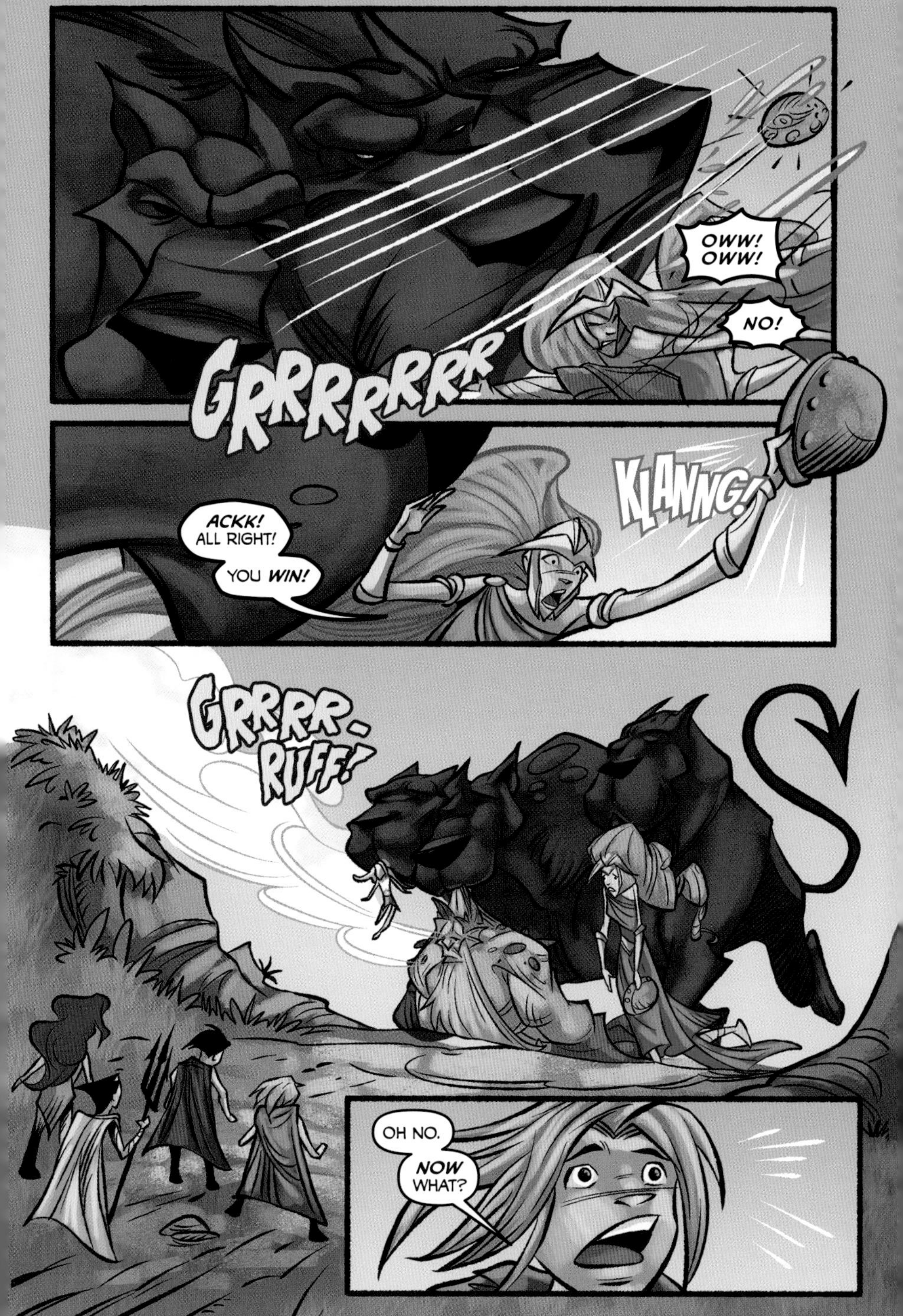
OWW! OWW!
NO!
GRRRRRRR
KLANNG!
ACKK! ALL RIGHT!
YOU WIN!
GRRRR-RUFF!
OH NO.
NOW WHAT?

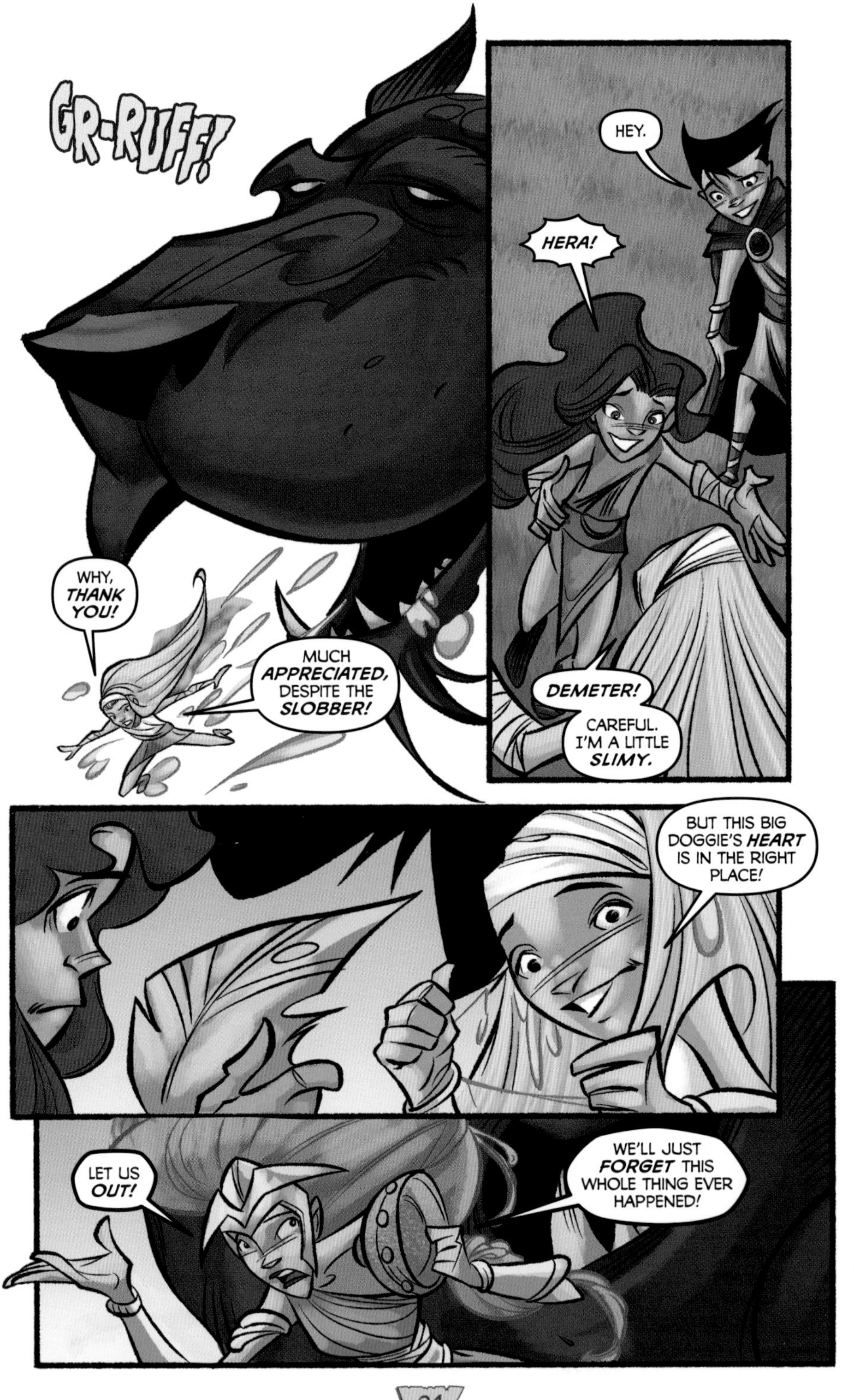
GR-RUFF!
HEY.
HERA!
WHY, THANK YOU!
MUCH APPRECIATED, DESPITE THE SLOBBER!
DEMETER!
CAREFUL. I'M A LITTLE SLIMY.
BUT THIS BIG DOGGIE'S HEART IS IN THE RIGHT PLACE!
LET US OUT!
WE'LL JUST FORGET THIS WHOLE THING EVER HAPPENED!

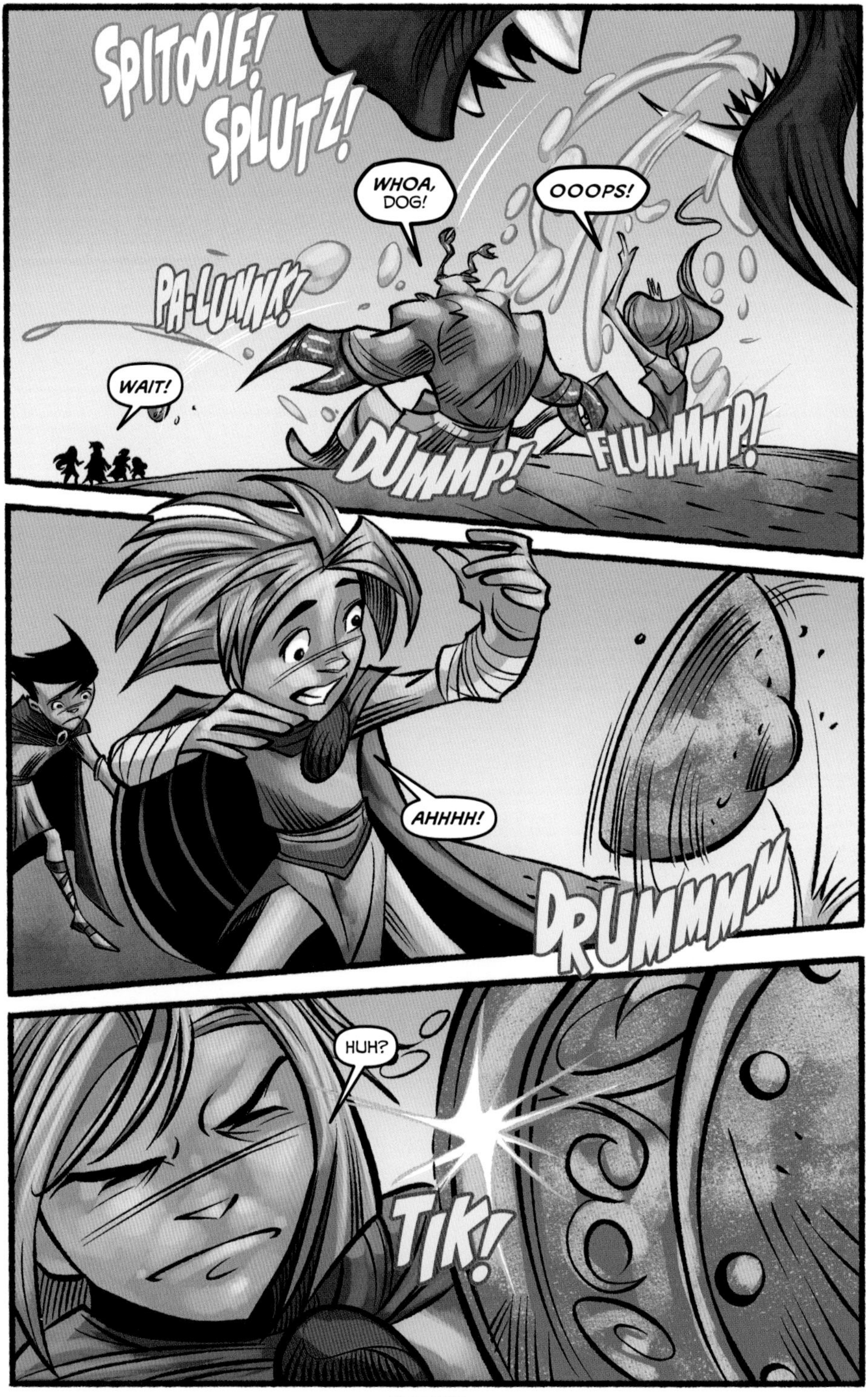
SPITOOIE!
SPLUTZ!
WHOA, DOG!
OOOPS!
PA-LUNNK!
WAIT!
DUMMMP!
FLUMMMP!
AHHHH!
DRUMMMM
HUH?
TIK!

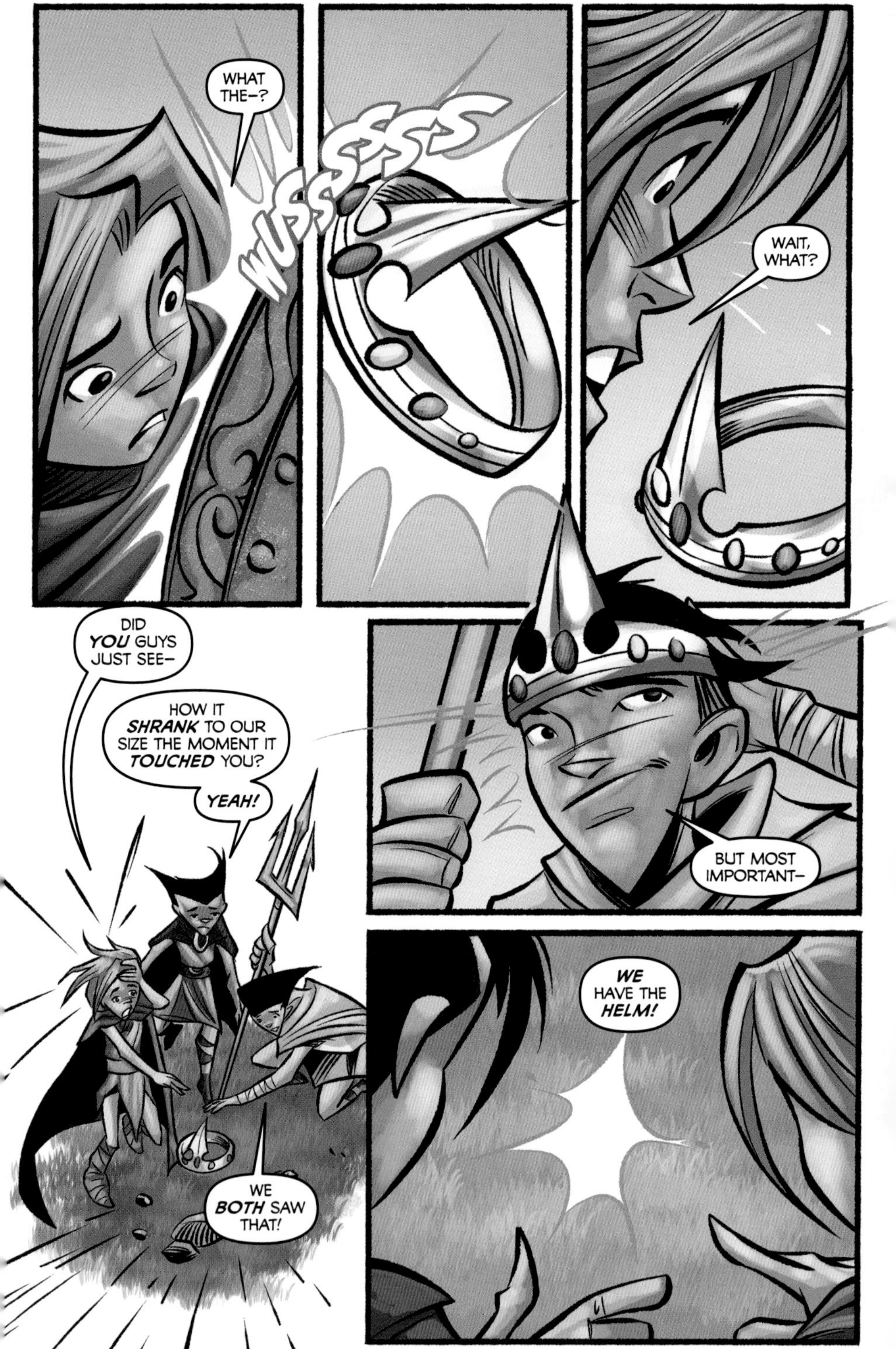
WHAT THE–?
WUSSSSSS
WAIT, WHAT?
DID *YOU* GUYS JUST SEE–
HOW IT *SHRANK* TO OUR SIZE THE MOMENT IT *TOUCHED* YOU?
YEAH!
BUT MOST IMPORTANT–
WE *BOTH* SAW THAT!
WE HAVE THE *HELM!*

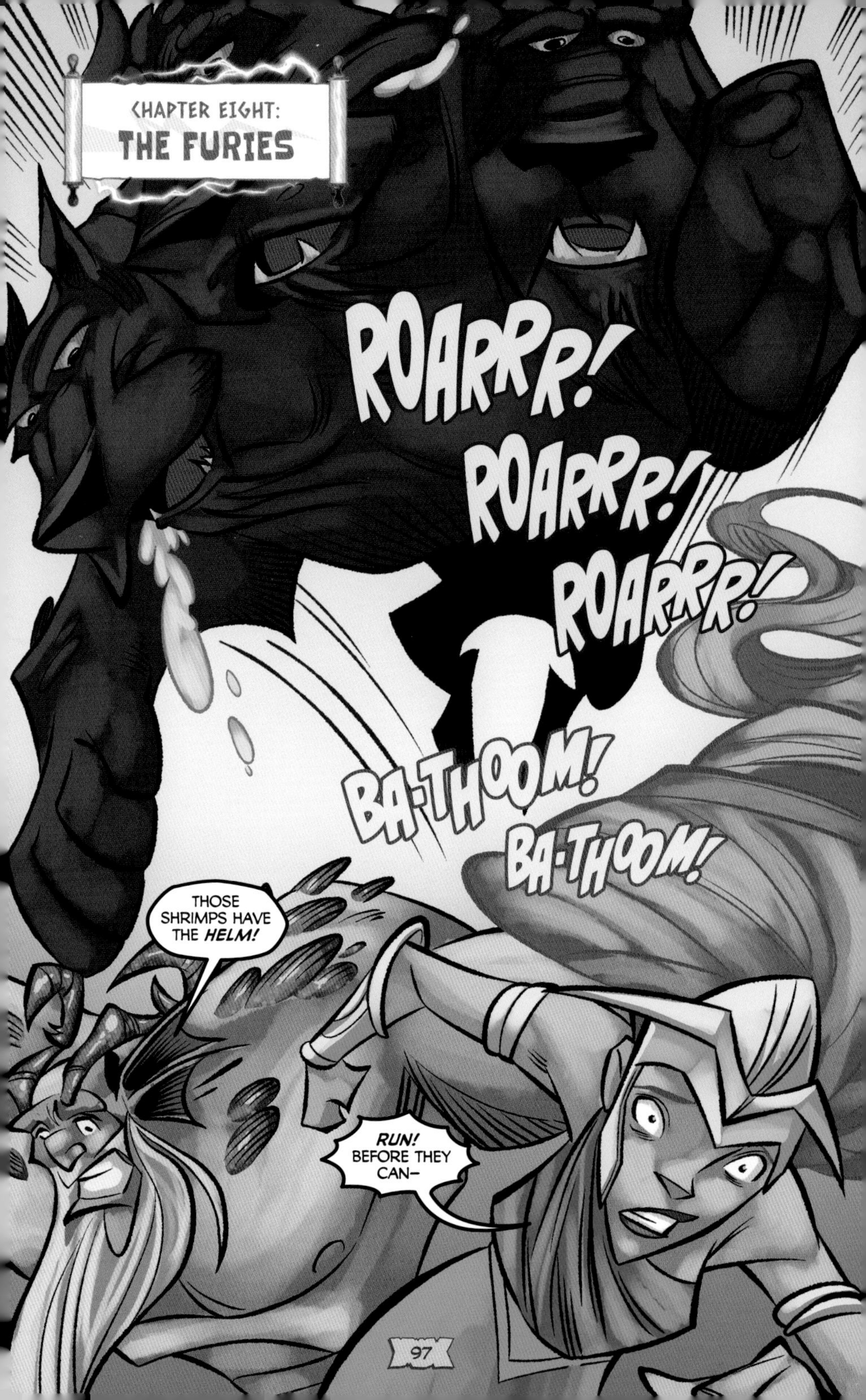
CHAPTER EIGHT:
THE FURIES
ROARRR!
ROARRR!
ROARRR!
BA-THOOM!
BA-THOOM!
THOSE SHRIMPS HAVE THE *HELM!*
RUN! BEFORE THEY CAN–

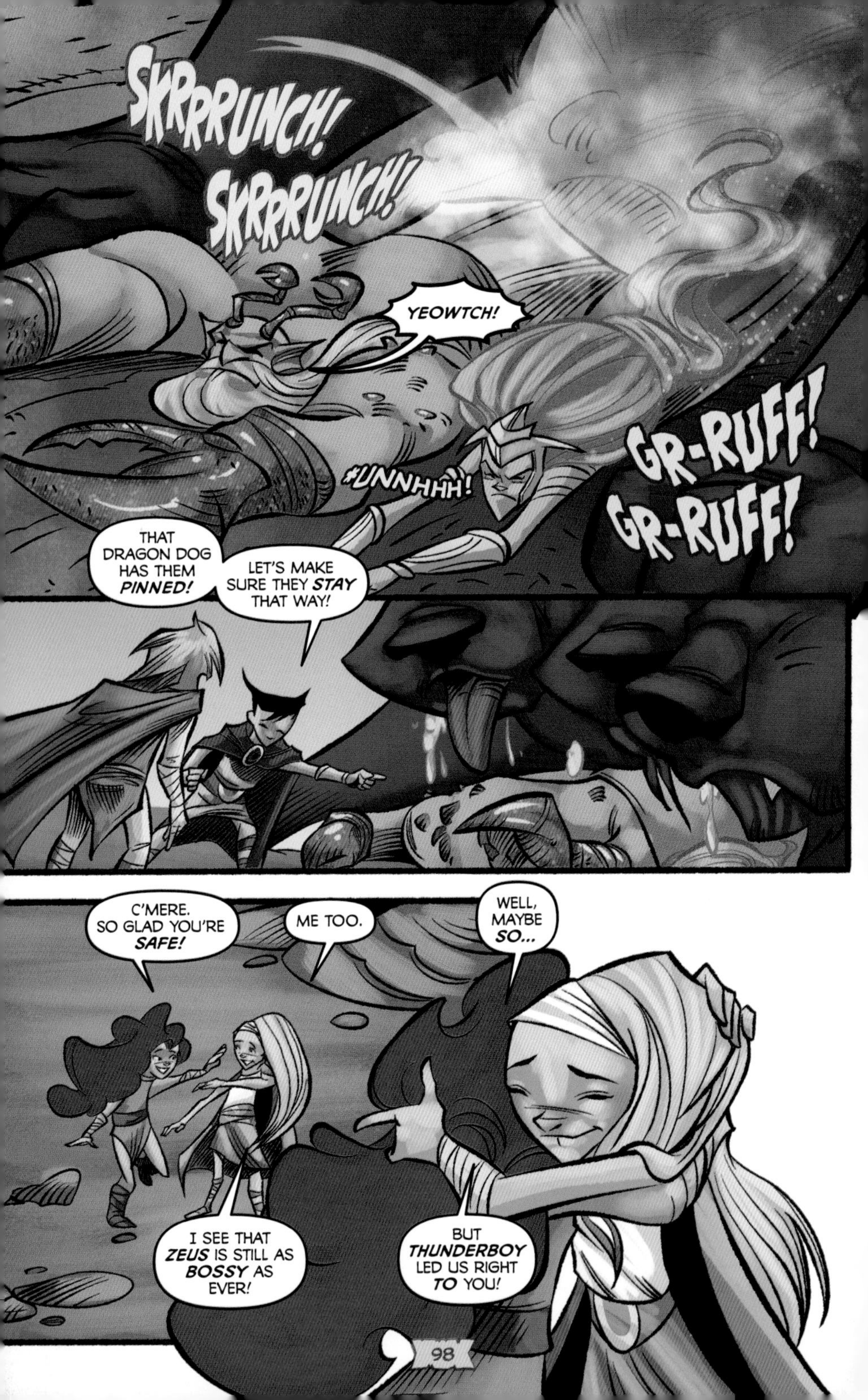
SKRRRUNCH!
SKRRRUNCH!
YEOWTCH!
*UNNHHH!
GR-RUFF!
GR-RUFF!
THAT DRAGON DOG HAS THEM PINNED!
LET'S MAKE SURE THEY STAY THAT WAY!
C'MERE. SO GLAD YOU'RE SAFE!
ME TOO.
WELL, MAYBE SO...
I SEE THAT ZEUS IS STILL AS BOSSY AS EVER!
BUT THUNDERBOY LED US RIGHT TO YOU!

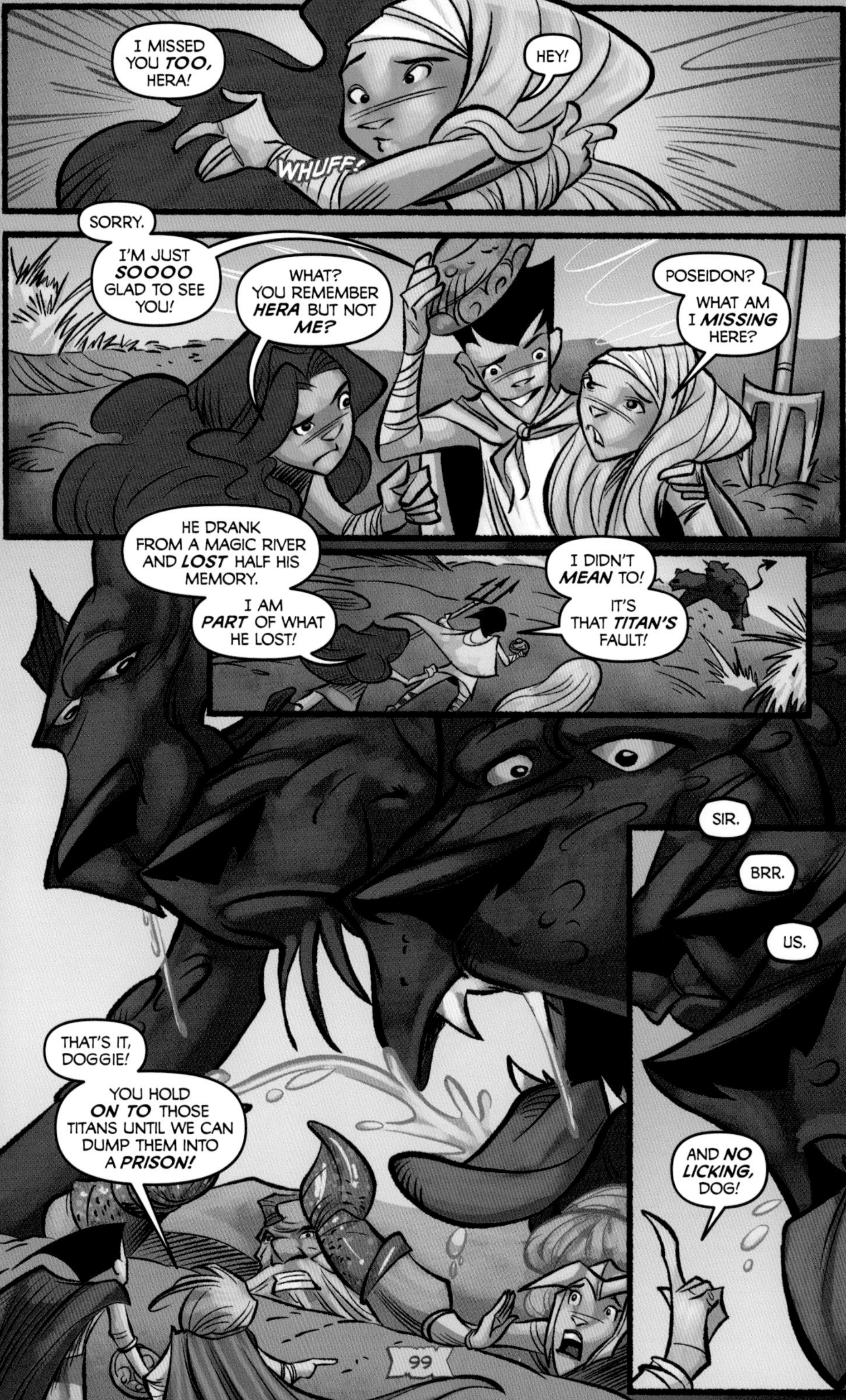

I MISSED YOU TOO, HERA!
HEY!
WHUFF!
SORRY.
I'M JUST SOOOO GLAD TO SEE YOU!
WHAT? YOU REMEMBER HERA BUT NOT ME?
POSEIDON?
WHAT AM I MISSING HERE?
HE DRANK FROM A MAGIC RIVER AND LOST HALF HIS MEMORY.
I AM PART OF WHAT HE LOST!
I DIDN'T MEAN TO!
IT'S THAT TITAN'S FAULT!
SIR.
BRR.
US.
THAT'S IT, DOGGIE!
YOU HOLD ON TO THOSE TITANS UNTIL WE CAN DUMP THEM INTO A PRISON!
AND NO LICKING, DOG!

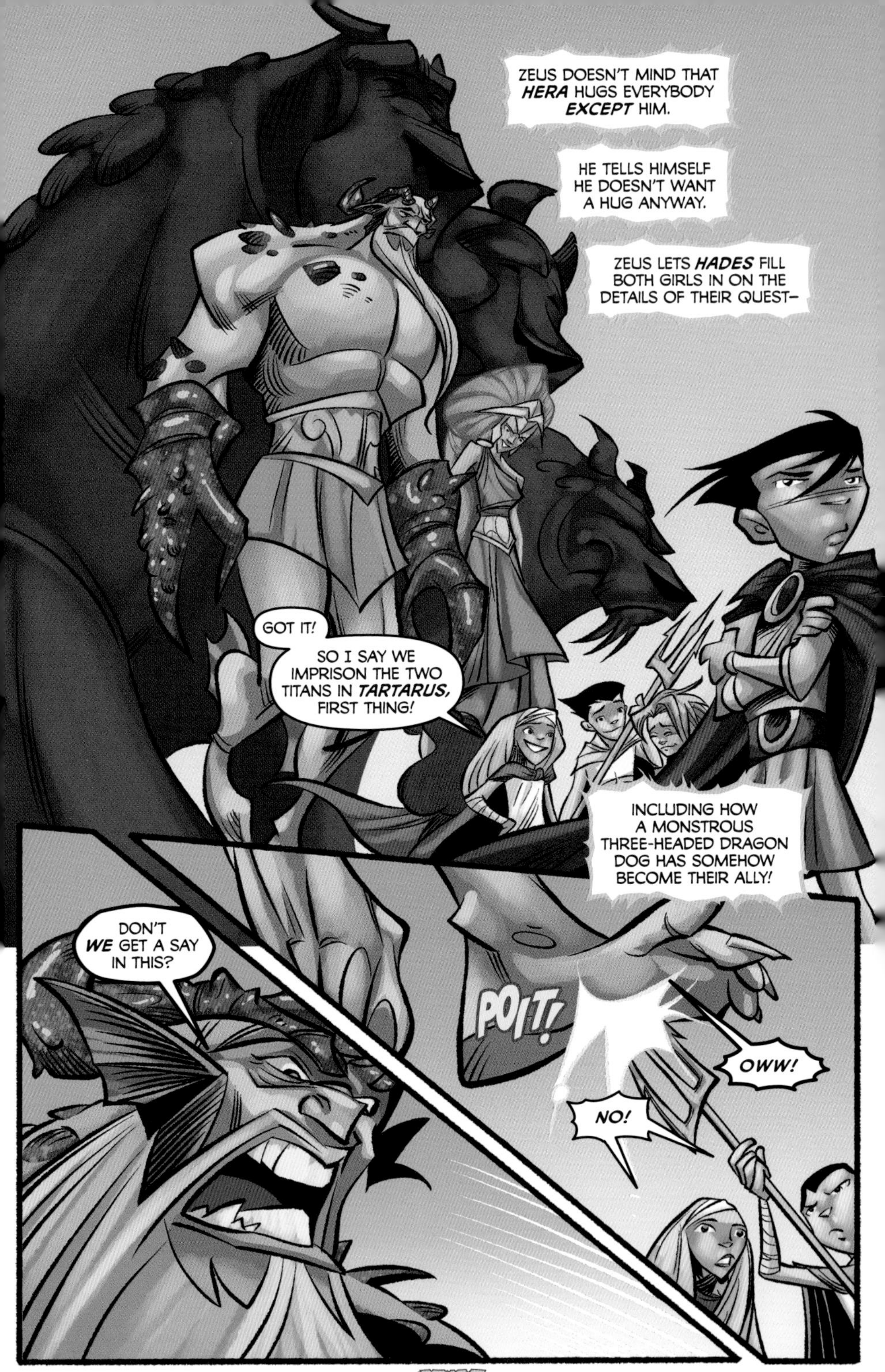
ZEUS DOESN'T MIND THAT *HERA* HUGS EVERYBODY *EXCEPT* HIM.
HE TELLS HIMSELF HE DOESN'T WANT A HUG ANYWAY.
ZEUS LETS *HADES* FILL BOTH GIRLS IN ON THE DETAILS OF THEIR QUEST–
GOT IT!
SO I SAY WE IMPRISON THE TWO TITANS IN *TARTARUS,* FIRST THING!
INCLUDING HOW A MONSTROUS THREE-HEADED DRAGON DOG HAS SOMEHOW BECOME THEIR ALLY!
DON'T *WE* GET A SAY IN THIS?
POIT!
OWW!
NO!

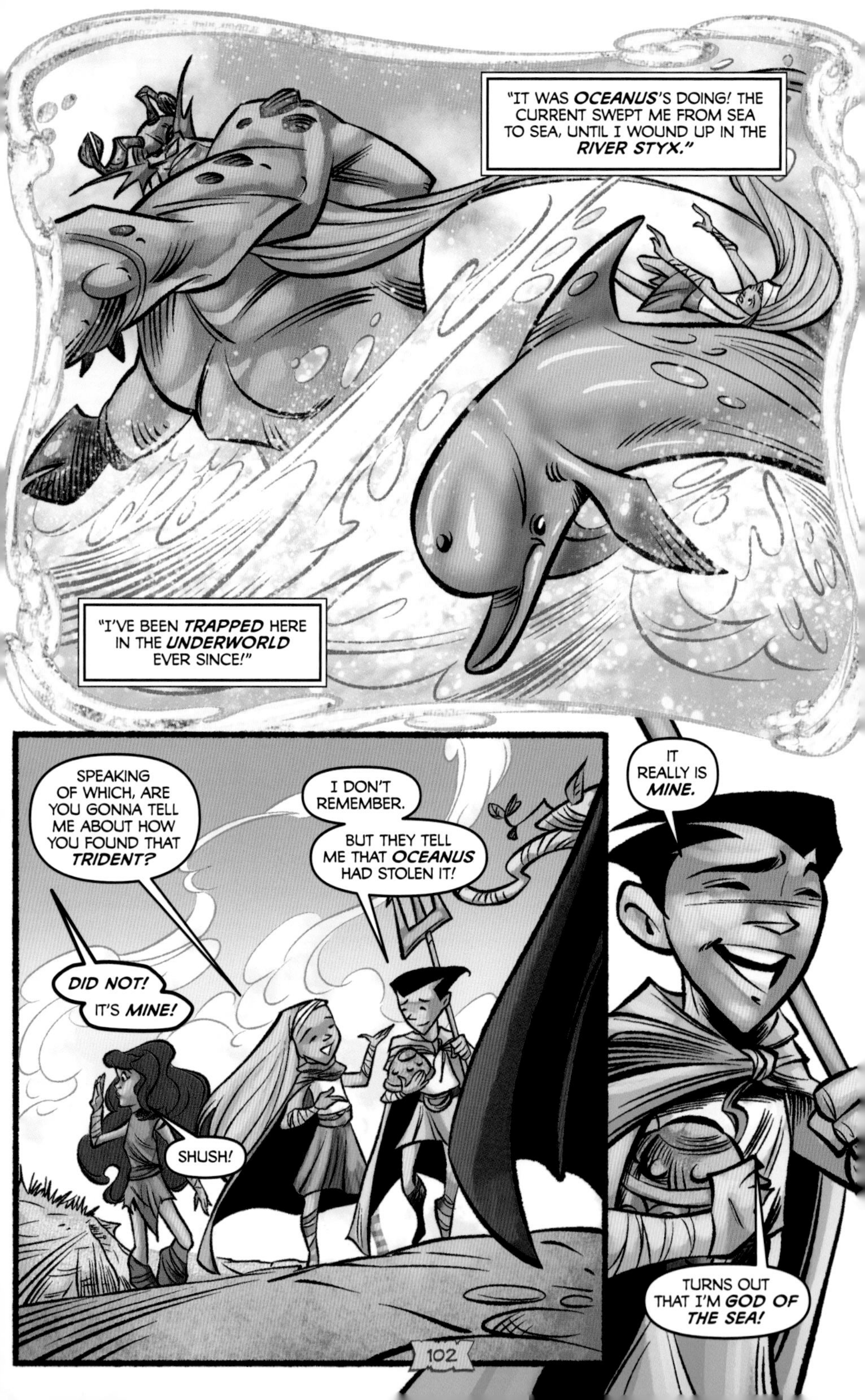
"IT WAS OCEANUS'S DOING! THE CURRENT SWEPT ME FROM SEA TO SEA, UNTIL I WOUND UP IN THE RIVER STYX."
"I'VE BEEN TRAPPED HERE IN THE UNDERWORLD EVER SINCE!"
SPEAKING OF WHICH, ARE YOU GONNA TELL ME ABOUT HOW YOU FOUND THAT TRIDENT?
I DON'T REMEMBER.
BUT THEY TELL ME THAT OCEANUS HAD STOLEN IT!
DID NOT!
IT'S MINE!
SHUSH!
IT REALLY IS MINE.
TURNS OUT THAT I'M GOD OF THE SEA!

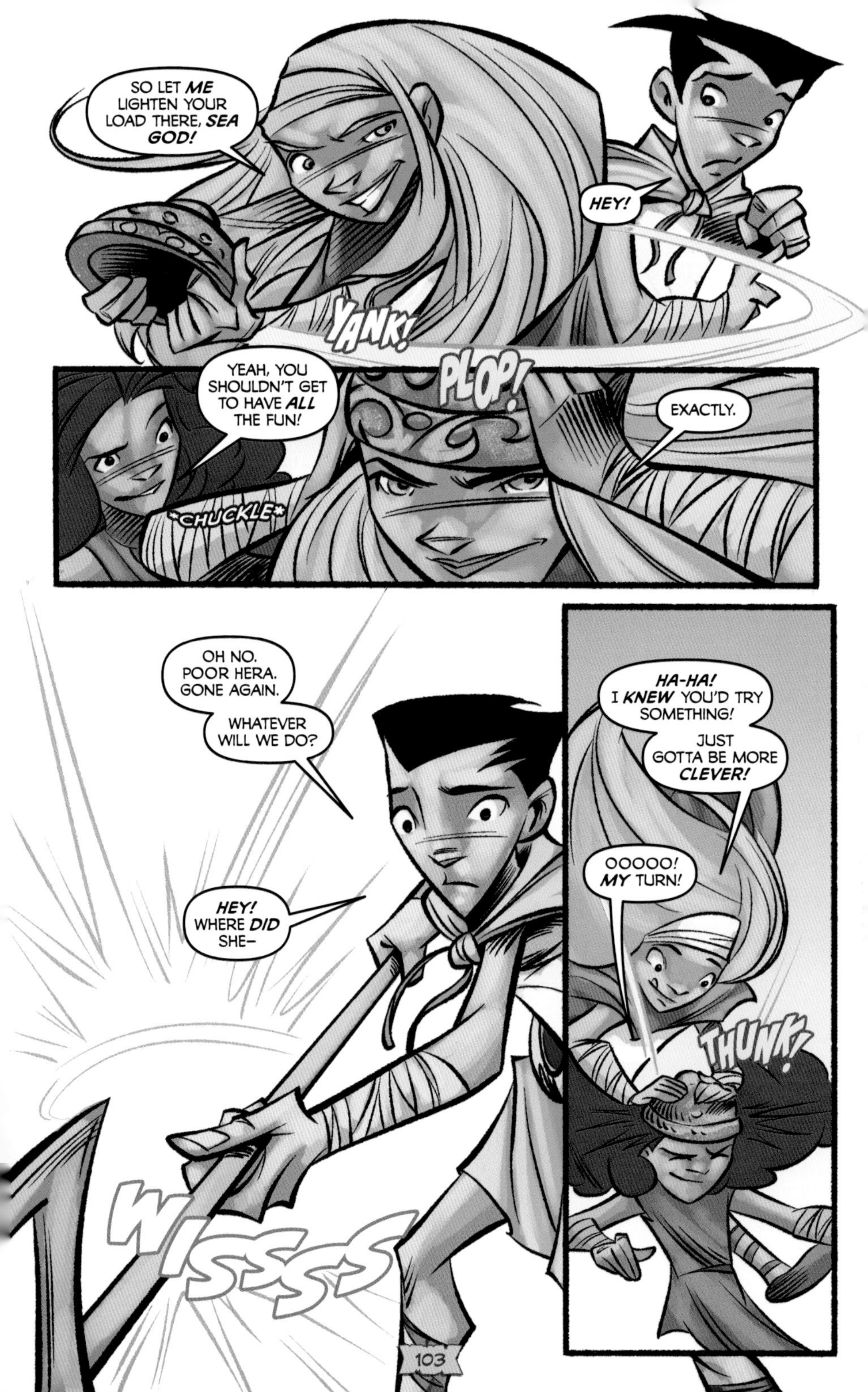
SO LET *ME* LIGHTEN YOUR LOAD THERE, *SEA GOD!*
HEY!
YANK!
PLOP!
YEAH, YOU SHOULDN'T GET TO HAVE *ALL* THE FUN!
EXACTLY.
CHUCKLE
OH NO. POOR HERA. GONE AGAIN.
WHATEVER WILL WE DO?
HEY! WHERE *DID* SHE–
WISSSS
HA-HA! I *KNEW* YOU'D TRY SOMETHING!
JUST GOTTA BE MORE *CLEVER!*
OOOOO! *MY* TURN!
THUNK!

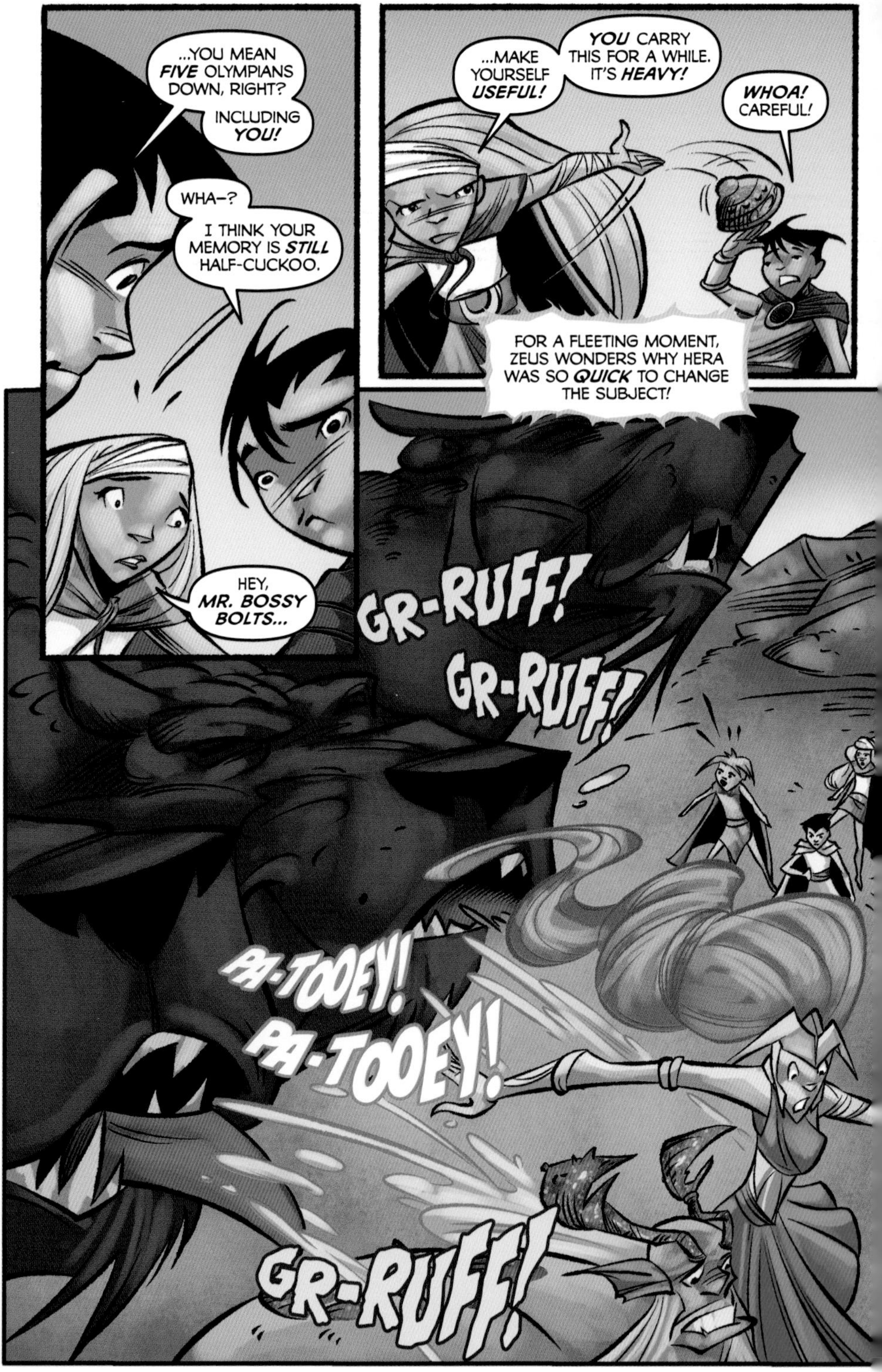

...YOU MEAN *FIVE* OLYMPIANS DOWN, RIGHT?
INCLUDING *YOU!*
WHA–?
I THINK YOUR MEMORY IS *STILL* HALF-CUCKOO.
HEY, *MR. BOSSY BOLTS...*
YOU CARRY THIS FOR A WHILE. IT'S *HEAVY!*
...MAKE YOURSELF *USEFUL!*
WHOA! CAREFUL!
FOR A FLEETING MOMENT, ZEUS WONDERS WHY HERA WAS SO *QUICK* TO CHANGE THE SUBJECT!
GR-RUFF!
GR-RUFF!
PA-TOOEY!
PA-TOOEY!
GR-RUFF!

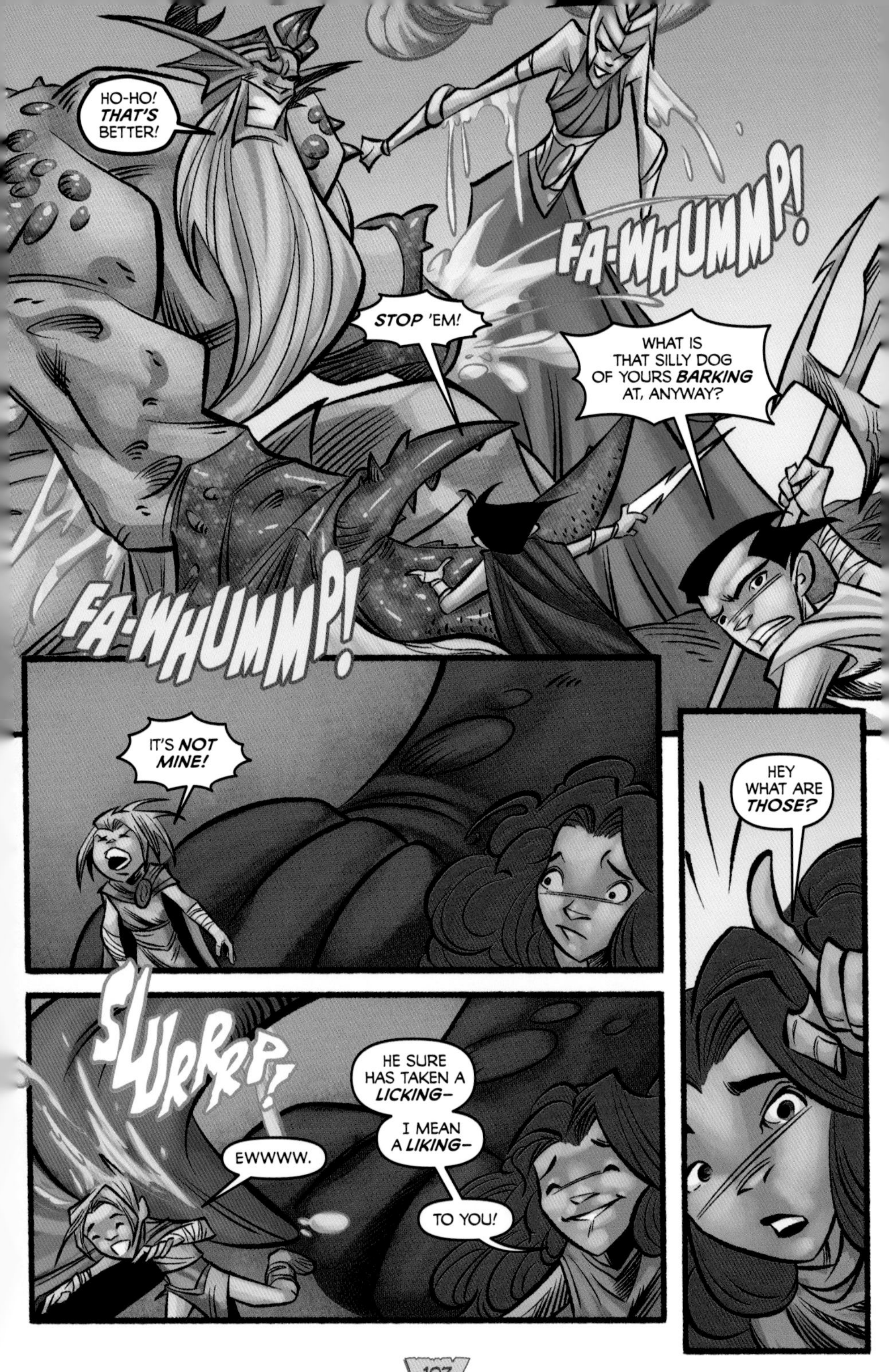
HO-HO! THAT'S BETTER!
FA-WHUMMP!
STOP 'EM!
WHAT IS THAT SILLY DOG OF YOURS BARKING AT, ANYWAY?
FA-WHUMMP!
IT'S NOT MINE!
SLURRRP!
EWWWW.
HE SURE HAS TAKEN A LICKING–
I MEAN A LIKING–
TO YOU!
HEY WHAT ARE THOSE?

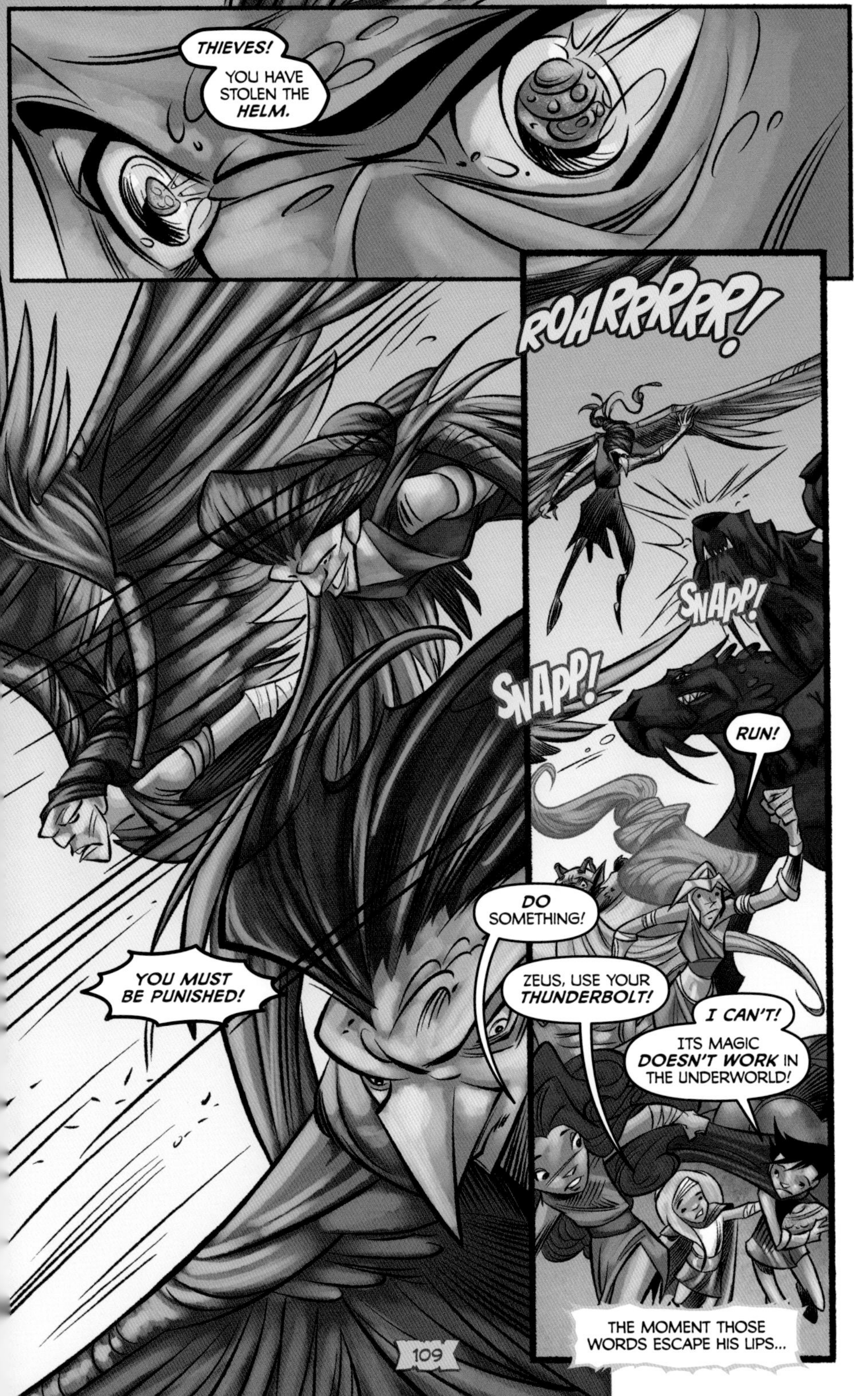
THIEVES! YOU HAVE STOLEN THE HELM.
ROARRRRRR!
SNAPP!
SNAPP!
RUN!
YOU MUST BE PUNISHED!
DO SOMETHING!
ZEUS, USE YOUR THUNDERBOLT!
I CAN'T!
ITS MAGIC DOESN'T WORK IN THE UNDERWORLD!
THE MOMENT THOSE WORDS ESCAPE HIS LIPS...

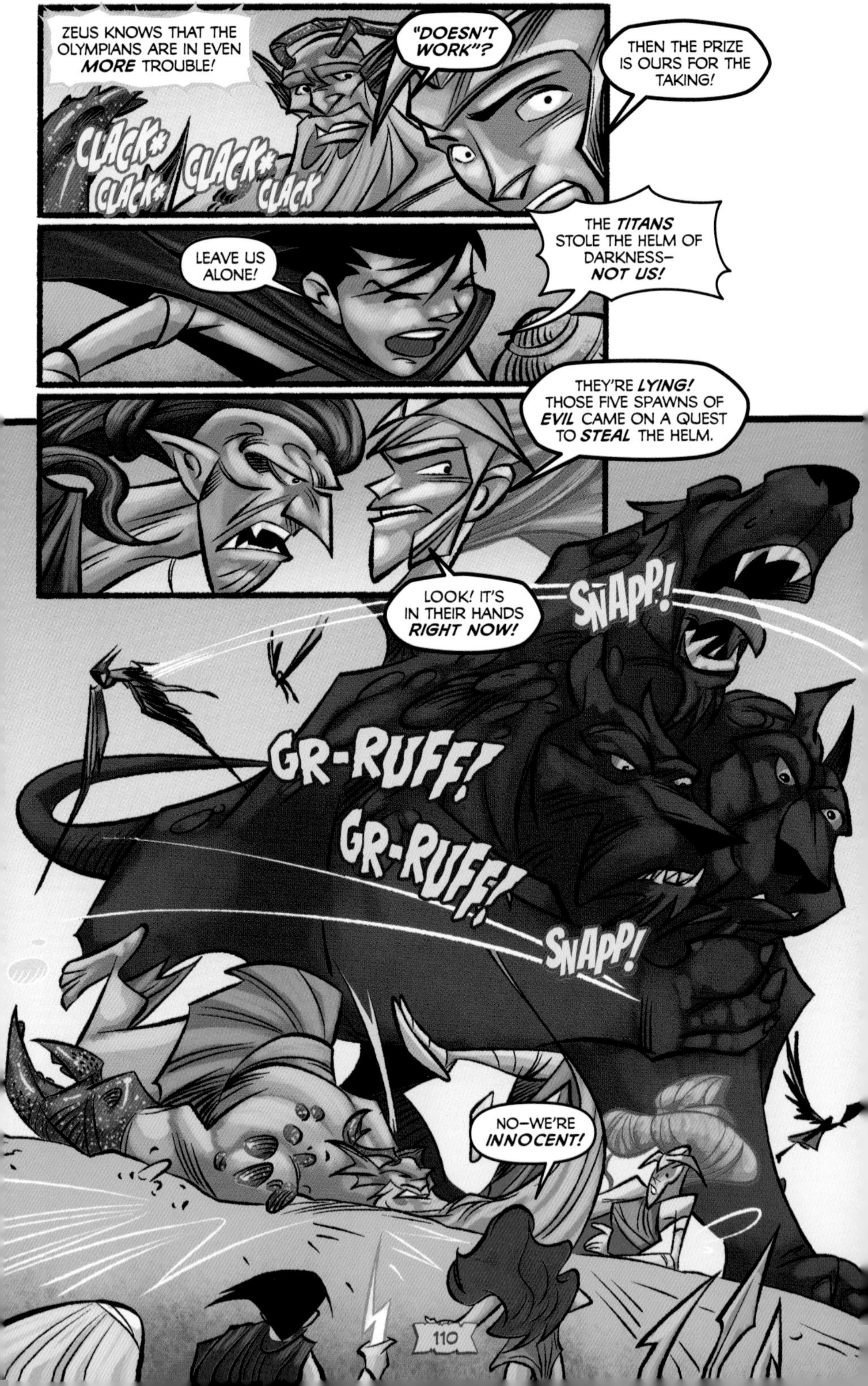
ZEUS KNOWS THAT THE OLYMPIANS ARE IN EVEN MORE TROUBLE!
"DOESN'T WORK"?
THEN THE PRIZE IS OURS FOR THE TAKING!
CLACK* CLACK* CLACK* CLACK
LEAVE US ALONE!
THE TITANS STOLE THE HELM OF DARKNESS—NOT US!
THEY'RE LYING! THOSE FIVE SPAWNS OF EVIL CAME ON A QUEST TO STEAL THE HELM.
LOOK! IT'S IN THEIR HANDS RIGHT NOW!
SNAPP!
GR-RUFF!
GR-RUFF!
SNAPP!
NO—WE'RE INNOCENT!

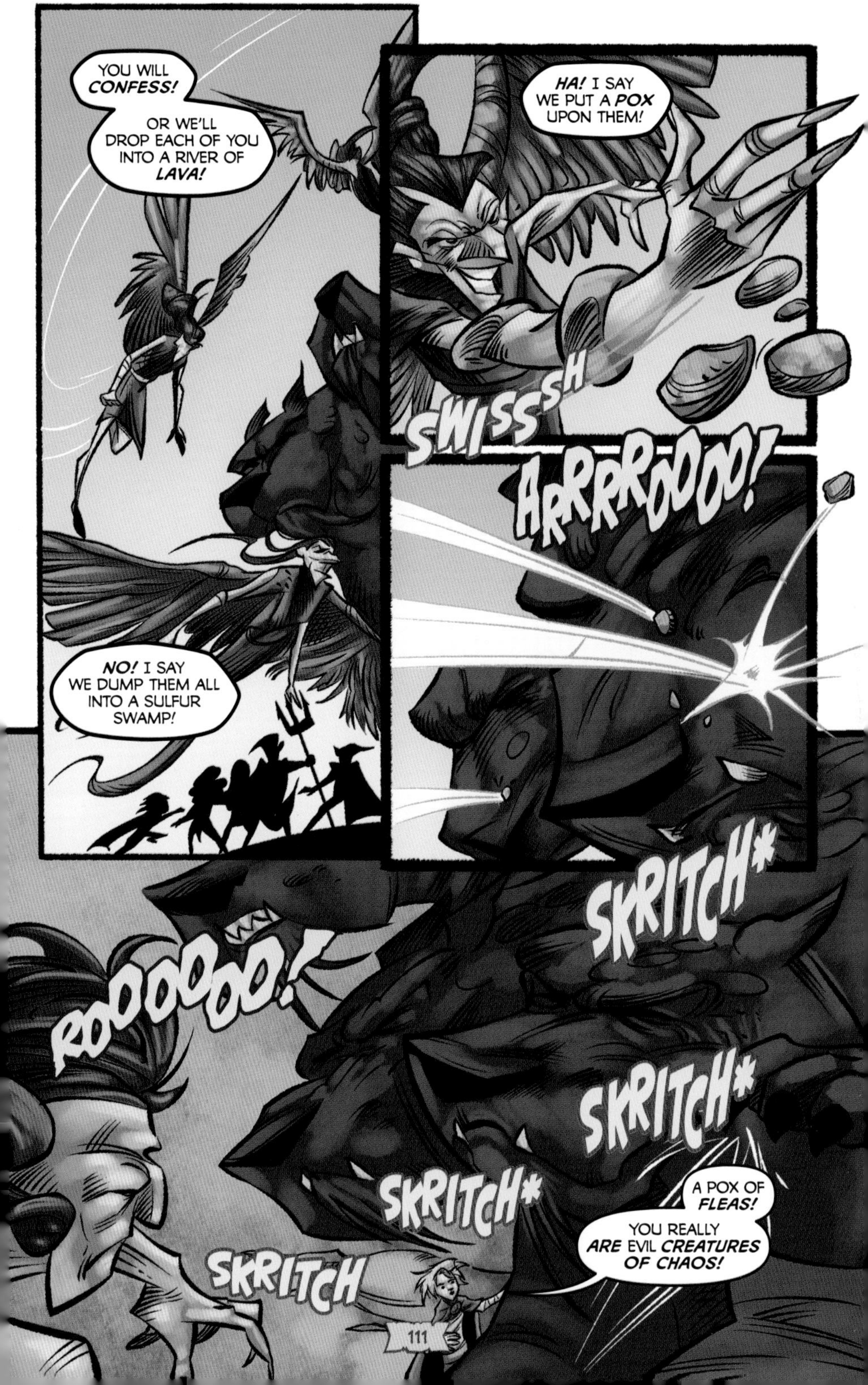
YOU WILL CONFESS!
OR WE'LL DROP EACH OF YOU INTO A RIVER OF LAVA!
NO! I SAY WE DUMP THEM ALL INTO A SULFUR SWAMP!
HA! I SAY WE PUT A POX UPON THEM!
SWISSSH
ARRRROOOO!
SKRITCH*
ROOOOOO!
SKRITCH*
SKRITCH*
SKRITCH
A POX OF FLEAS!
YOU REALLY ARE EVIL CREATURES OF CHAOS!

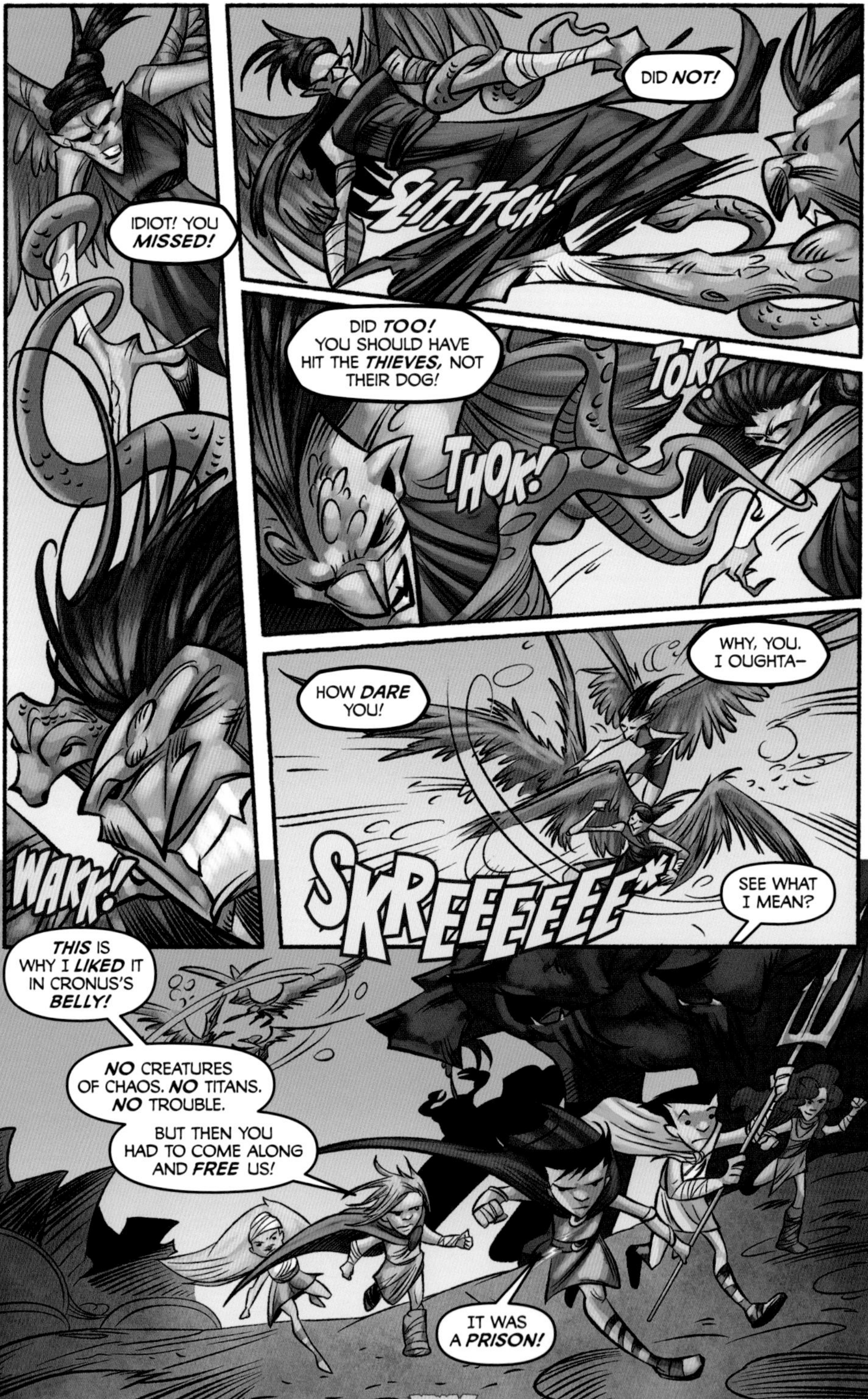
IDIOT! YOU MISSED!
DID NOT!
SLLITTCH!
DID TOO! YOU SHOULD HAVE HIT THE THIEVES, NOT THEIR DOG!
TOK!
THOK!
WAKK!
HOW DARE YOU!
WHY, YOU. I OUGHTA–
SKREEEEEEE*
SEE WHAT I MEAN?
THIS IS WHY I LIKED IT IN CRONUS'S BELLY!
NO CREATURES OF CHAOS. NO TITANS. NO TROUBLE.
BUT THEN YOU HAD TO COME ALONG AND FREE US!
IT WAS A PRISON!

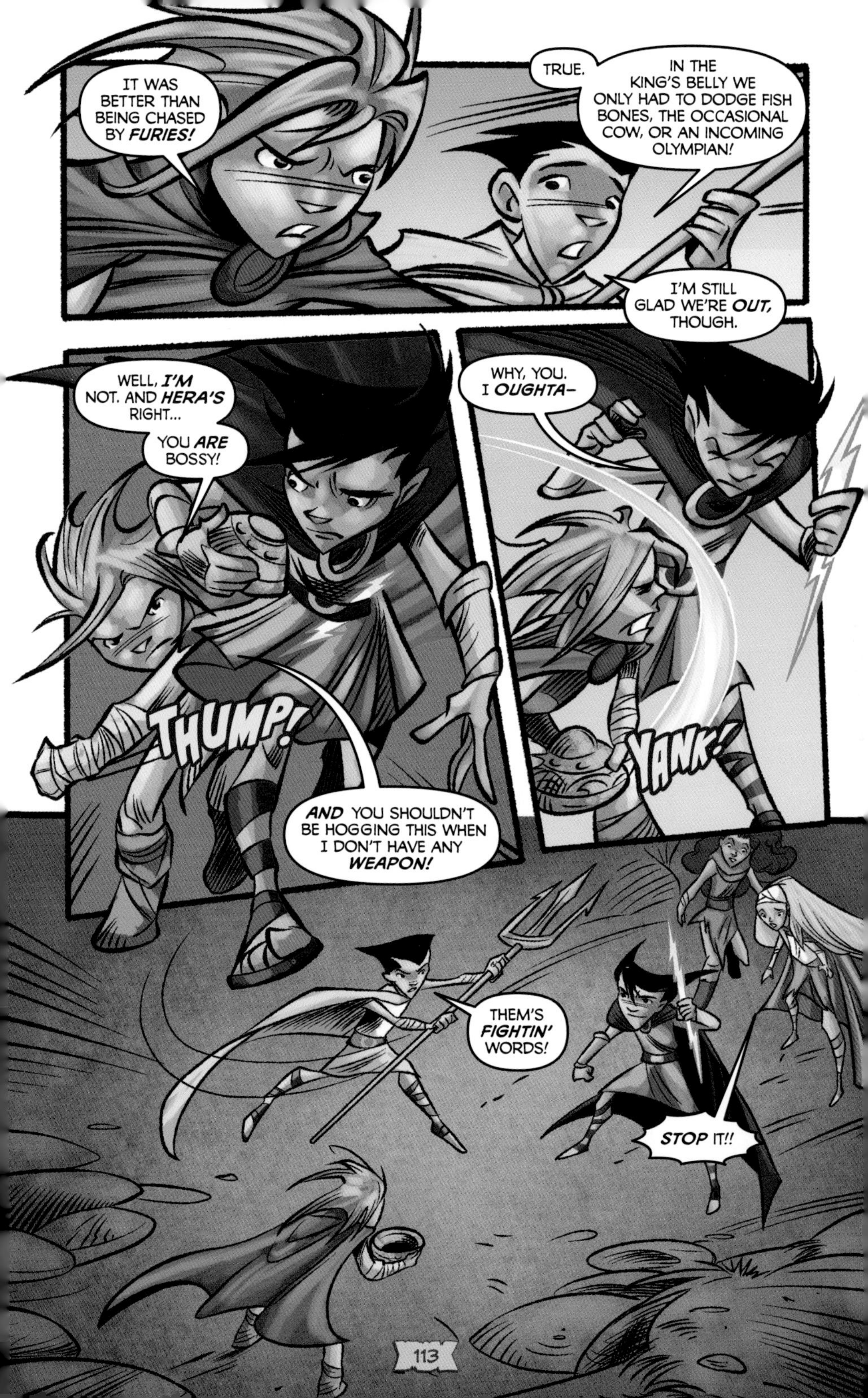
IT WAS BETTER THAN BEING CHASED BY FURIES!
TRUE.
IN THE KING'S BELLY WE ONLY HAD TO DODGE FISH BONES, THE OCCASIONAL COW, OR AN INCOMING OLYMPIAN!
I'M STILL GLAD WE'RE OUT, THOUGH.
WELL, I'M NOT. AND HERA'S RIGHT...
YOU ARE BOSSY!
THUMP!
AND YOU SHOULDN'T BE HOGGING THIS WHEN I DON'T HAVE ANY WEAPON!
WHY, YOU. I OUGHTA—
YANK!
THEM'S FIGHTIN' WORDS!
STOP IT!!

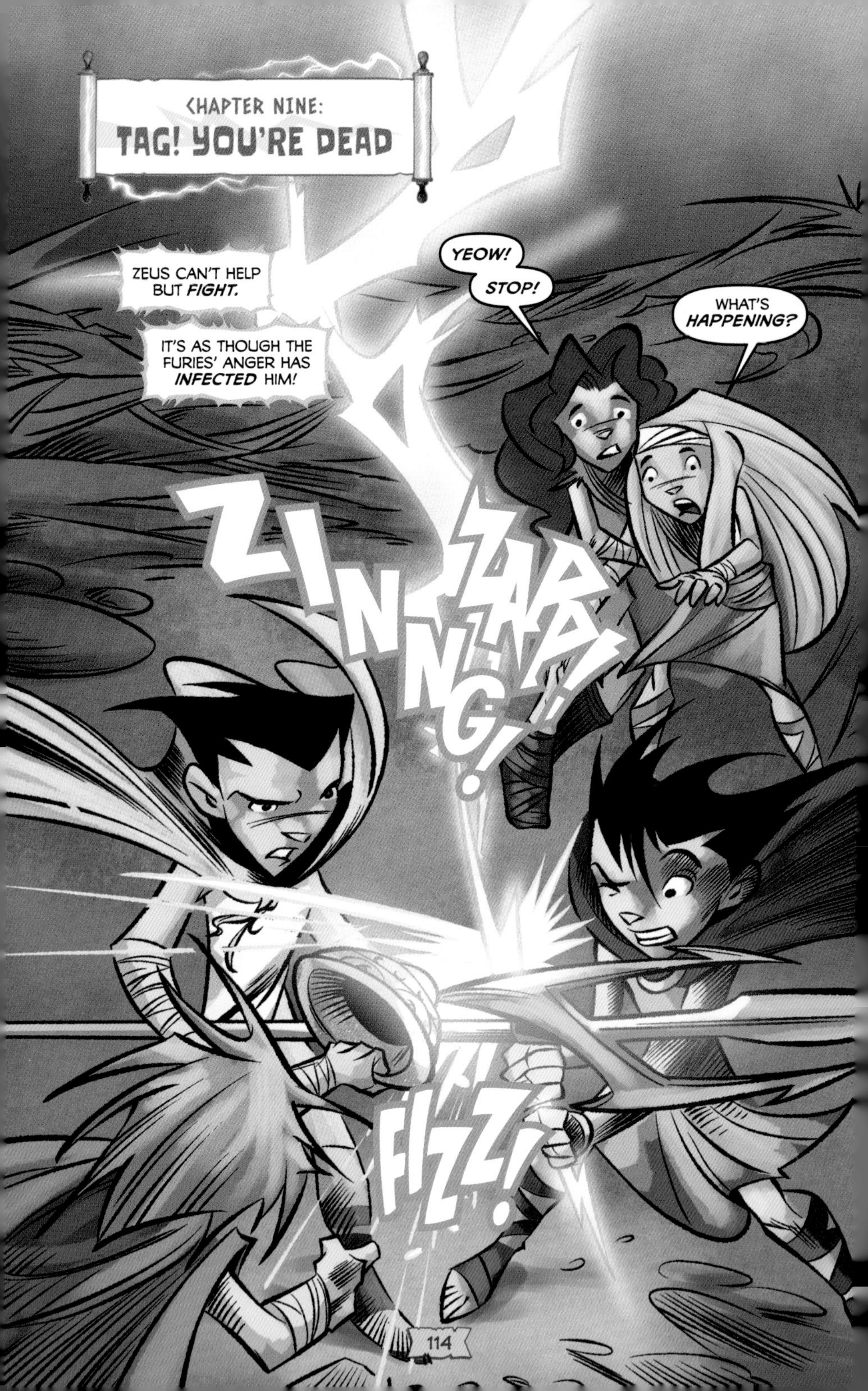
CHAPTER NINE:
TAG! YOU'RE DEAD
ZEUS CAN'T HELP BUT *FIGHT.*
IT'S AS THOUGH THE FURIES' ANGER HAS *INFECTED* HIM!
YEOW!
STOP!
WHAT'S *HAPPENING?*
ZINNNNG!
ZAP! ZAP!
FIZZ!

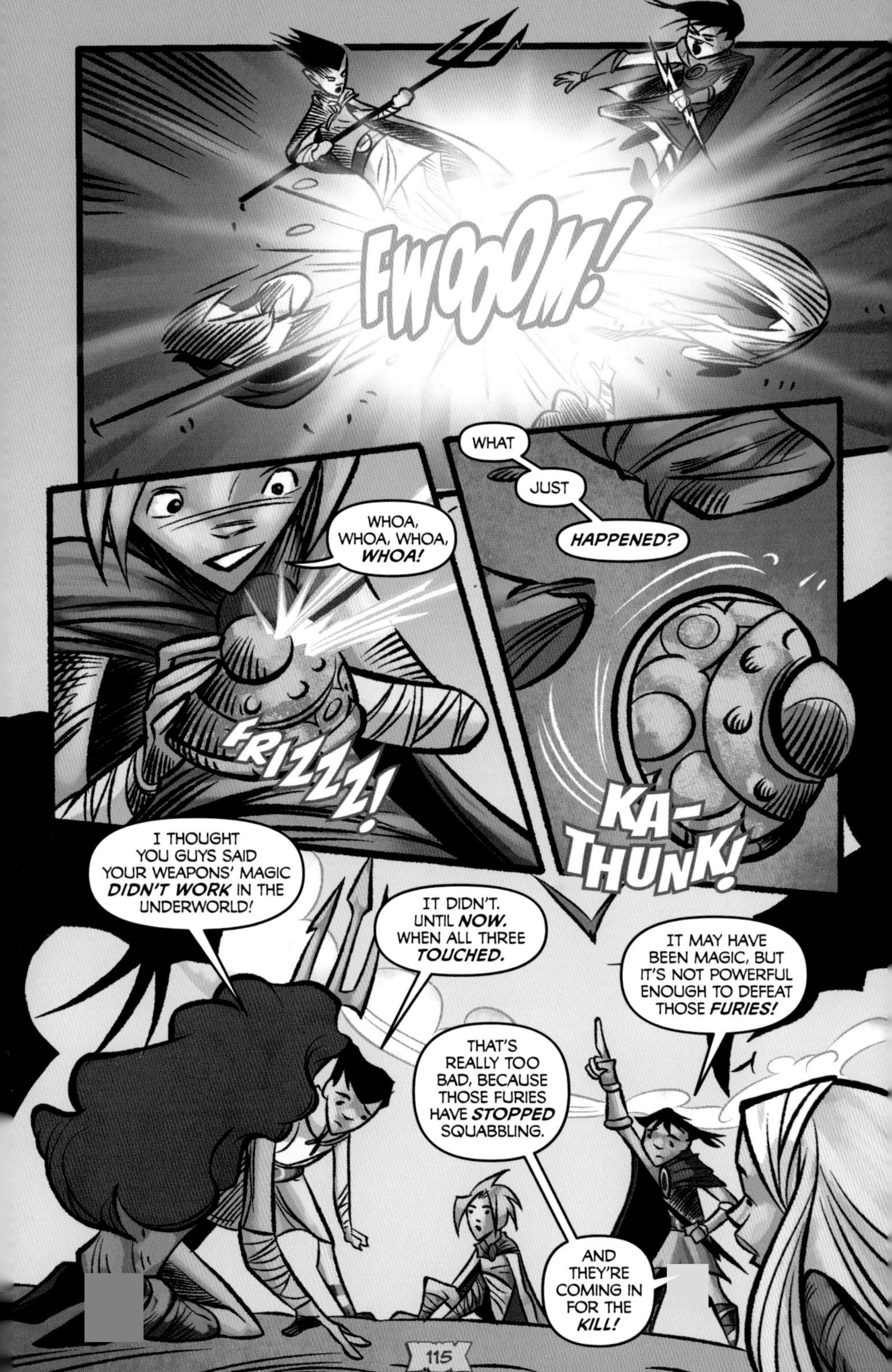
FWOOOM!
WHOA, WHOA, WHOA, *WHOA!*
FRIZZZ!
WHAT
JUST
HAPPENED?
KA-THUNK!
I THOUGHT YOU GUYS SAID YOUR WEAPONS' MAGIC *DIDN'T WORK* IN THE UNDERWORLD!
IT DIDN'T. UNTIL *NOW.* WHEN ALL THREE *TOUCHED.*
IT MAY HAVE BEEN MAGIC, BUT IT'S NOT POWERFUL ENOUGH TO DEFEAT THOSE *FURIES!*
THAT'S REALLY TOO BAD, BECAUSE THOSE FURIES HAVE *STOPPED* SQUABBLING.
AND THEY'RE COMING IN FOR THE *KILL!*

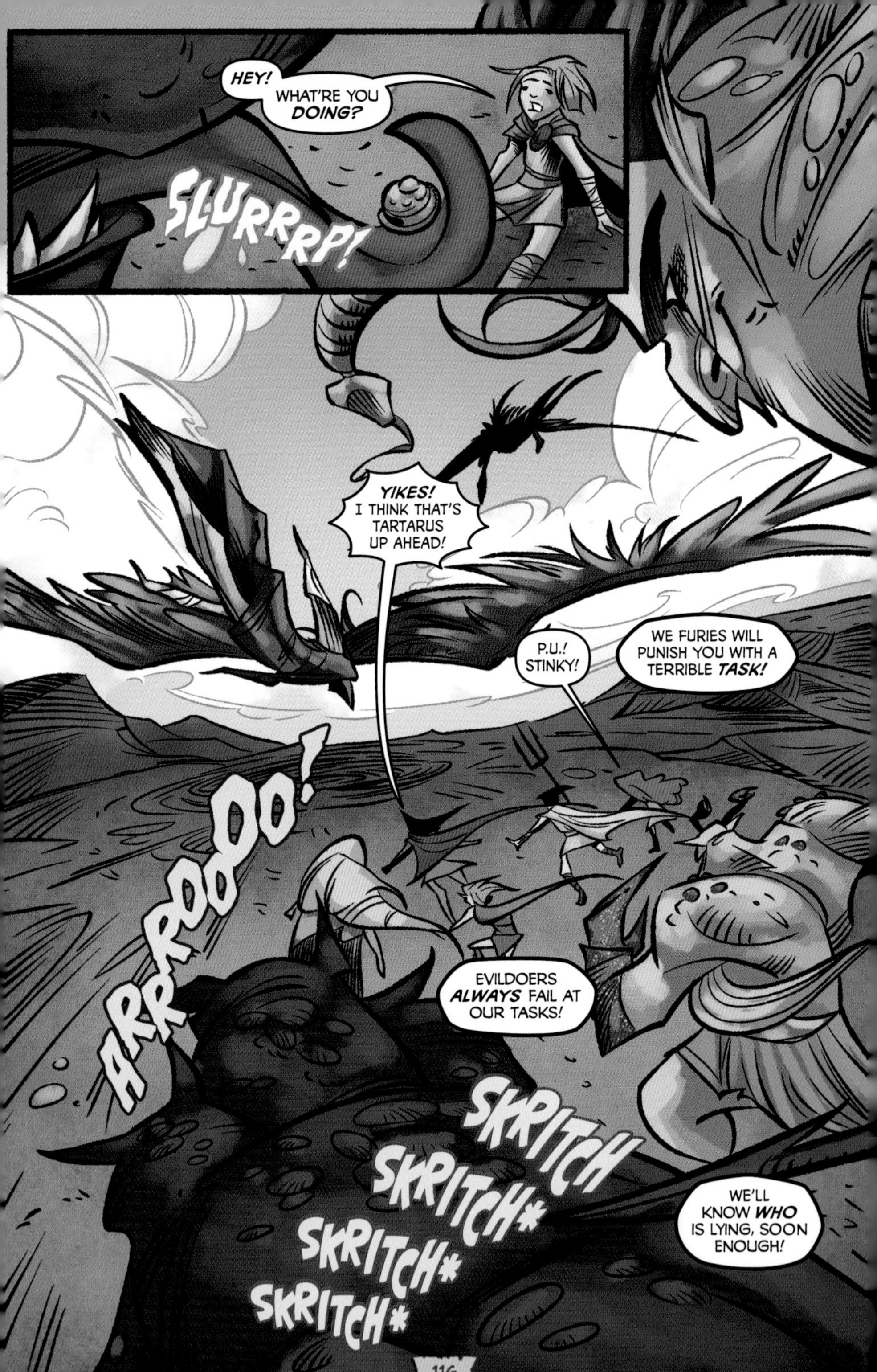
HEY!
WHAT'RE YOU DOING?
SLURRRP!
YIKES! I THINK THAT'S TARTARUS UP AHEAD!
P.U.! STINKY!
WE FURIES WILL PUNISH YOU WITH A TERRIBLE TASK!
ARROOOO!
EVILDOERS ALWAYS FAIL AT OUR TASKS!
SKRITCH SKRITCH* SKRITCH* SKRITCH*
WE'LL KNOW WHO IS LYING, SOON ENOUGH!

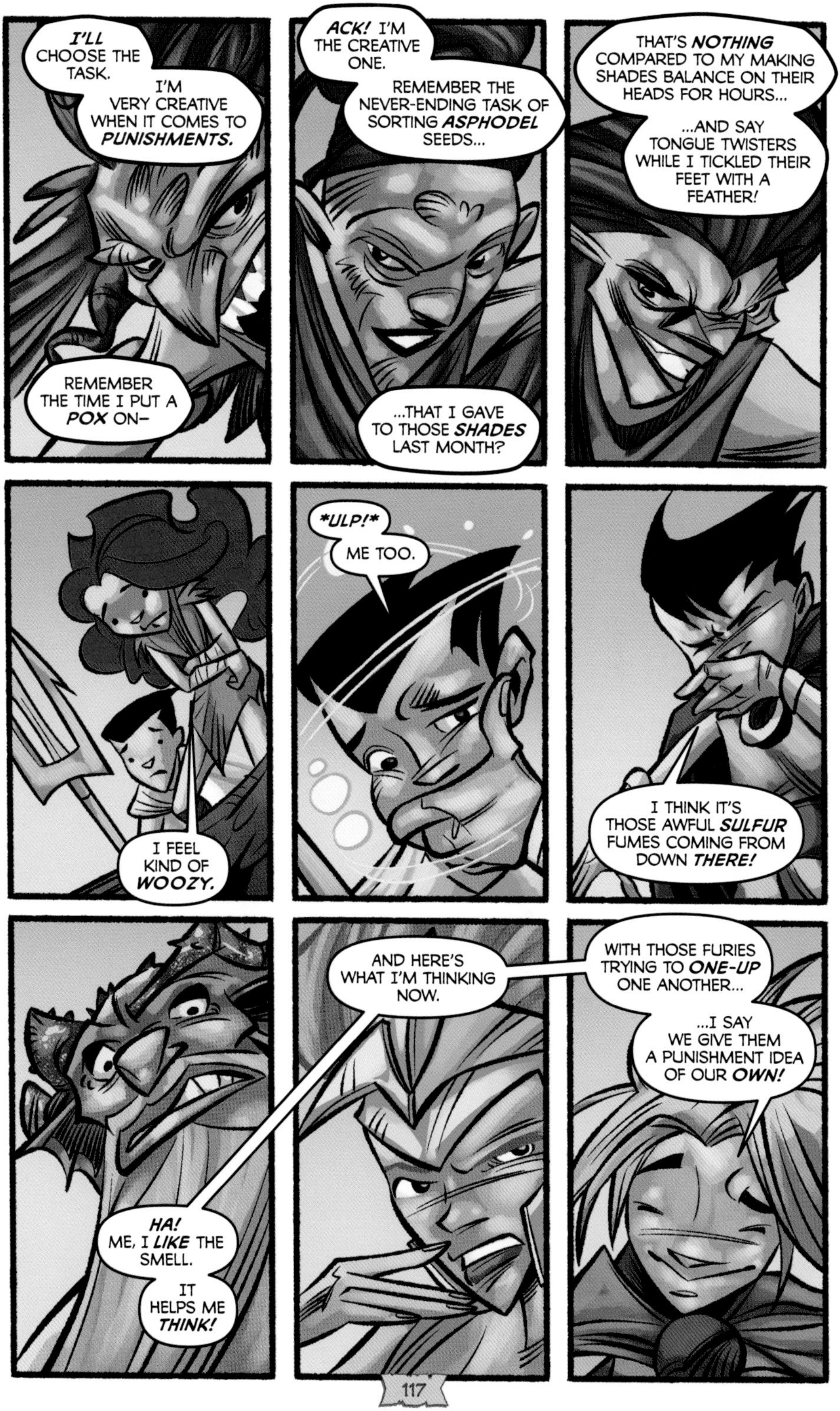
I'LL CHOOSE THE TASK.
I'M VERY CREATIVE WHEN IT COMES TO PUNISHMENTS.
REMEMBER THE TIME I PUT A POX ON–
ACK! I'M THE CREATIVE ONE.
REMEMBER THE NEVER-ENDING TASK OF SORTING ASPHODEL SEEDS...
...THAT I GAVE TO THOSE SHADES LAST MONTH?
THAT'S NOTHING COMPARED TO MY MAKING SHADES BALANCE ON THEIR HEADS FOR HOURS...
...AND SAY TONGUE TWISTERS WHILE I TICKLED THEIR FEET WITH A FEATHER!
I FEEL KIND OF WOOZY.
ULP!
ME TOO.
I THINK IT'S THOSE AWFUL SULFUR FUMES COMING FROM DOWN THERE!
HA! ME, I LIKE THE SMELL.
IT HELPS ME THINK!
AND HERE'S WHAT I'M THINKING NOW.
WITH THOSE FURIES TRYING TO ONE-UP ONE ANOTHER...
...I SAY WE GIVE THEM A PUNISHMENT IDEA OF OUR OWN!

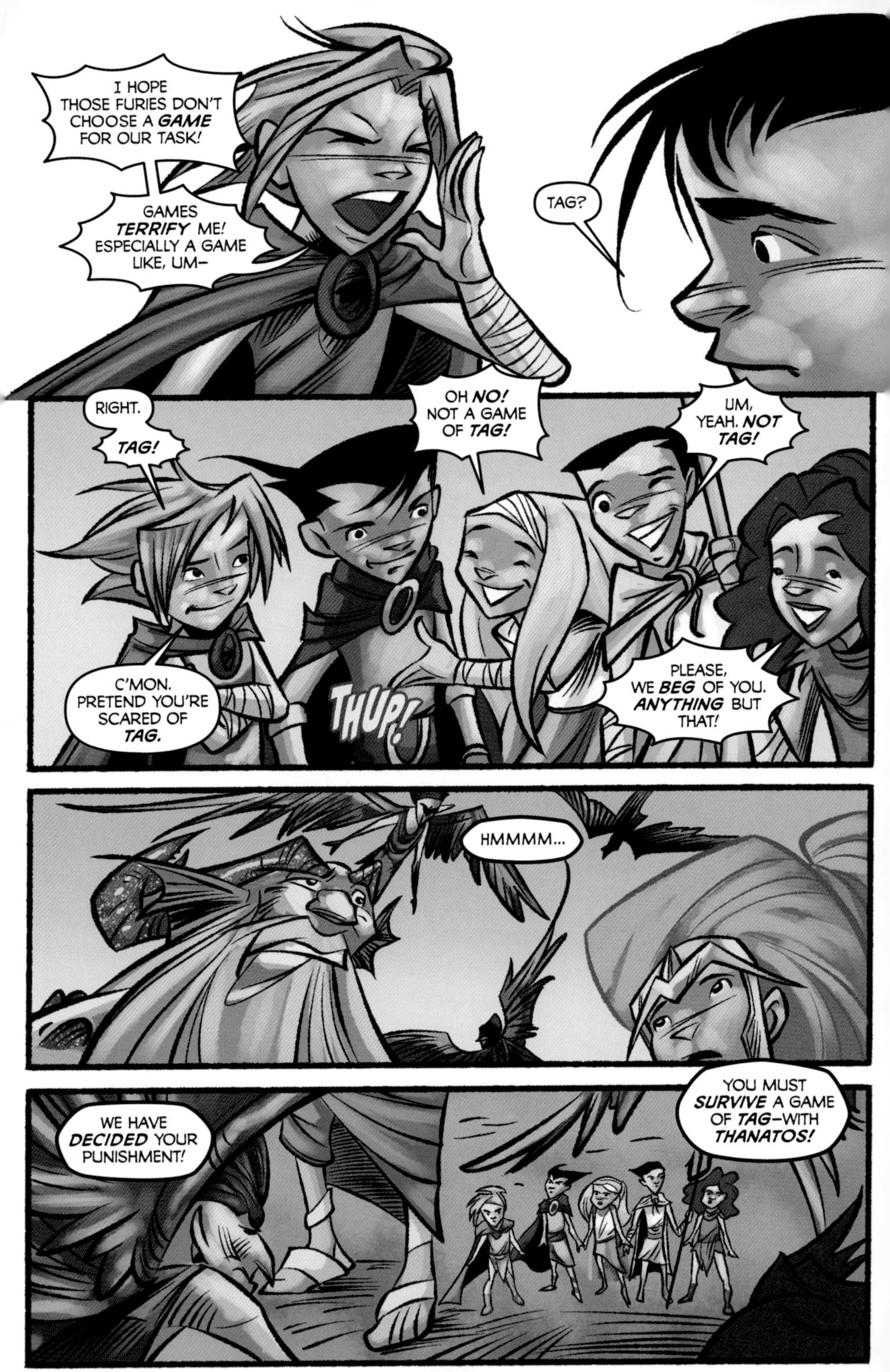
I HOPE THOSE FURIES DON'T CHOOSE A **GAME** FOR OUR TASK!
GAMES **TERRIFY** ME! ESPECIALLY A GAME LIKE, UM—
TAG?
RIGHT.
TAG!
OH **NO!** NOT A GAME OF **TAG!**
UM, YEAH. **NOT TAG!**
C'MON. PRETEND YOU'RE SCARED OF **TAG.**
THUP!
PLEASE, WE **BEG** OF YOU. **ANYTHING** BUT THAT!
HMMMM...
WE HAVE **DECIDED** YOUR PUNISHMENT!
YOU MUST **SURVIVE** A GAME OF **TAG**—WITH **THANATOS!**

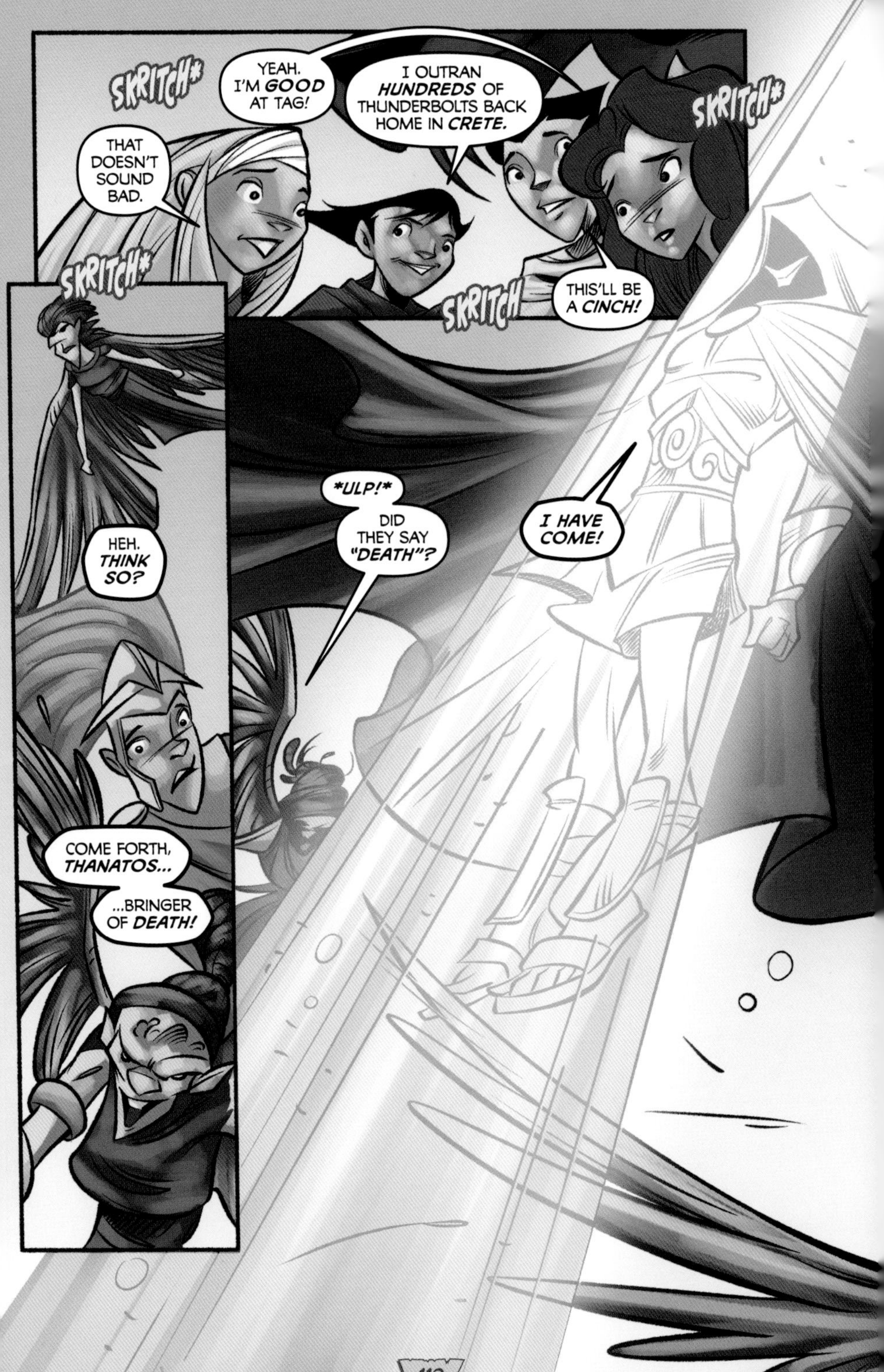
SKRITCH*
YEAH. I'M GOOD AT TAG!
I OUTRAN HUNDREDS OF THUNDERBOLTS BACK HOME IN CRETE.
SKRITCH*
THAT DOESN'T SOUND BAD.
SKRITCH*
SKRITCH
THIS'LL BE A CINCH!
HEH. THINK SO?
COME FORTH, THANATOS...
...BRINGER OF DEATH!
ULP!
DID THEY SAY "DEATH"?
I HAVE COME!

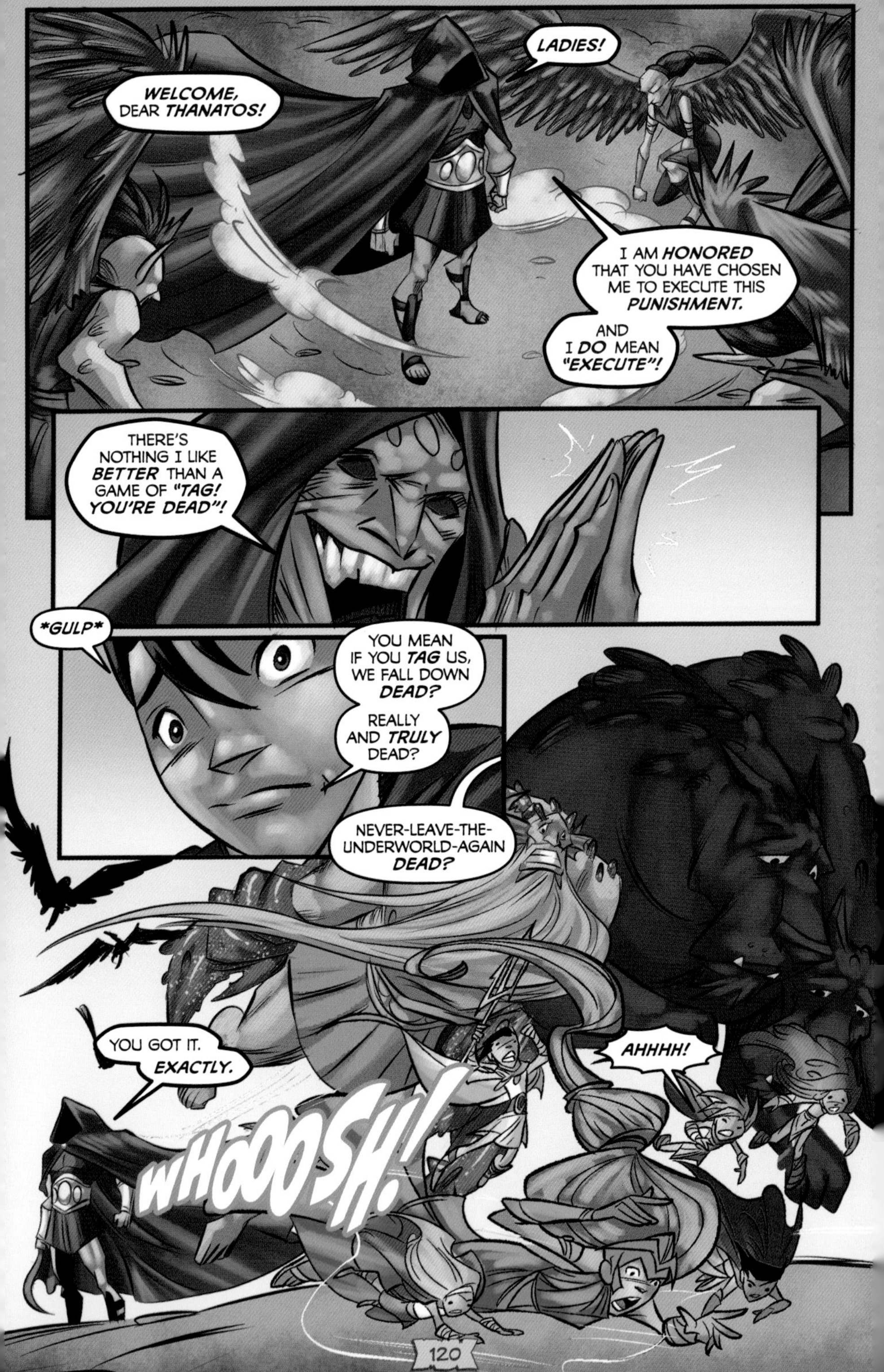

WELCOME, DEAR THANATOS!
LADIES!
I AM HONORED THAT YOU HAVE CHOSEN ME TO EXECUTE THIS PUNISHMENT.
AND I DO MEAN "EXECUTE"!
THERE'S NOTHING I LIKE BETTER THAN A GAME OF "TAG! YOU'RE DEAD"!
GULP
YOU MEAN IF YOU TAG US, WE FALL DOWN DEAD?
REALLY AND TRULY DEAD?
NEVER-LEAVE-THE-UNDERWORLD-AGAIN DEAD?
YOU GOT IT. EXACTLY.
AHHHH!
WHOOOSH!

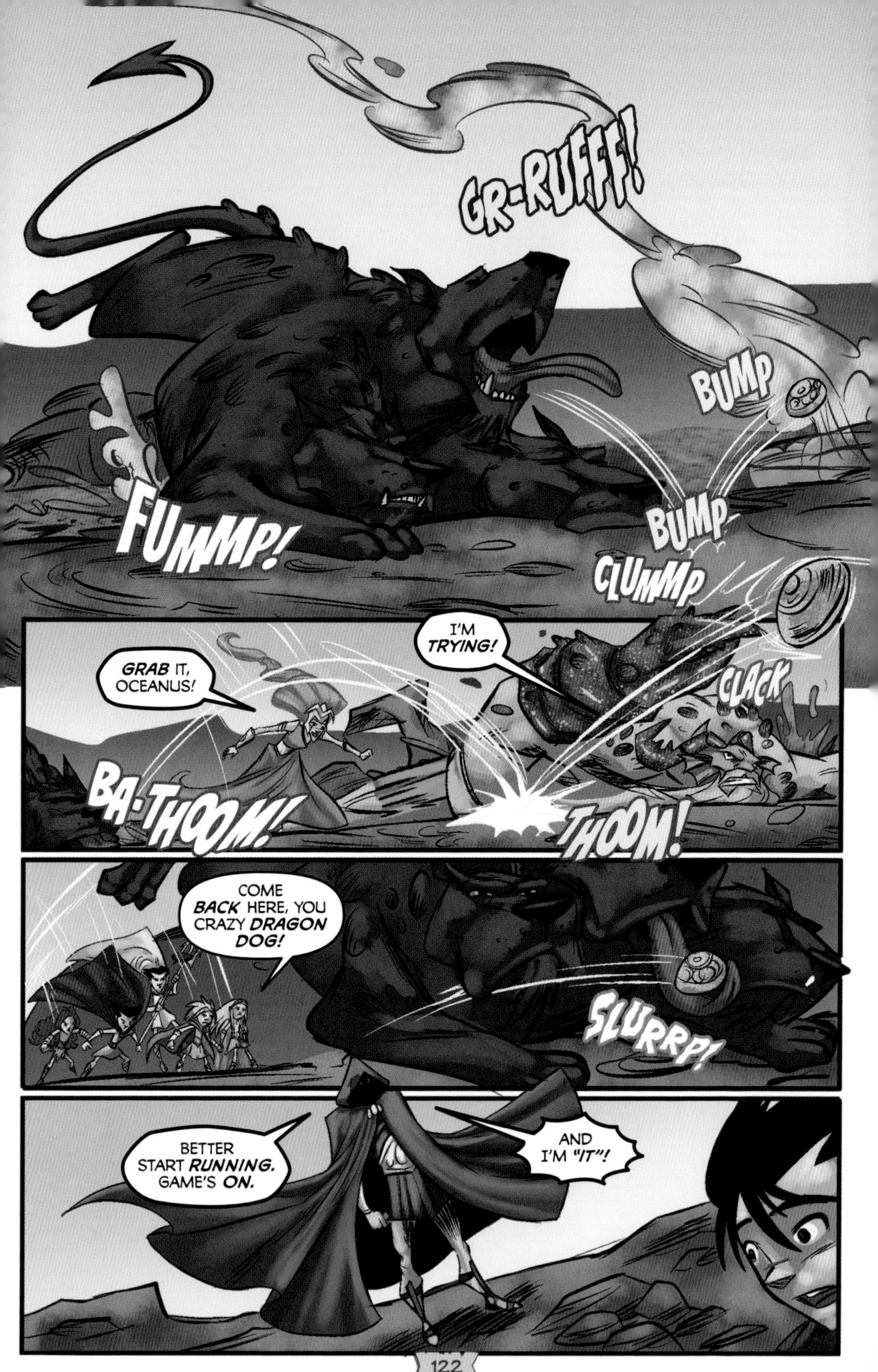
GR-RUFFF!
BUMP
FUMMP!
BUMP
CLUMMP
GRAB IT, OCEANUS!
I'M TRYING!
CLACK
BA-THOOM!
THOOM!
COME BACK HERE, YOU CRAZY DRAGON DOG!
SLURRP!
BETTER START RUNNING. GAME'S ON.
AND I'M "IT"!

WE'RE *BIG*. WE'RE BIGGER *TARGETS!*

SO TAKE *BIGGER STEPS!*

I *HOPE* THAT MEANS THANATOS CAN'T SEE THEM *EITHER!*

DEMETER AND HERA RAN SOMEWHERE ELSE. I DON'T *SEE* THEM!

KOFF KOFF

IT'S NOT A FAIR GAME, SO WE NEED NEW RULES.

THEN WE *FIGHT BACK* INSTEAD OF HIDING IN FEAR!

"SO MAYBE IF WE *COMBINE* OUR WEAPONS AGAIN, WE CAN *SPARK—*"

HERA!

RUN!

CHAPTER TEN:
LORD OF THE UNDERWORLD

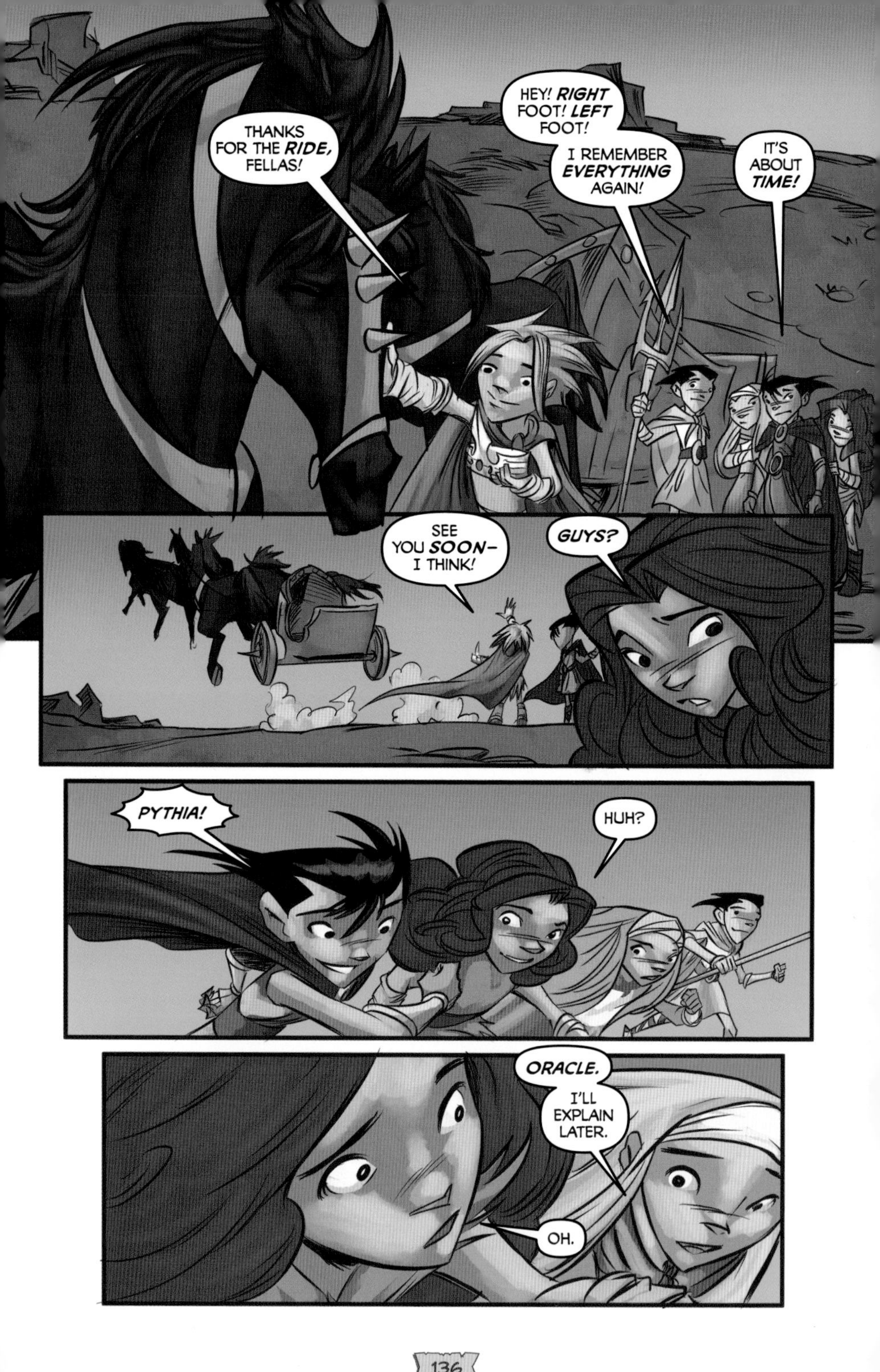
THANKS FOR THE *RIDE,* FELLAS!
HEY! *RIGHT* FOOT! *LEFT* FOOT!
I REMEMBER *EVERYTHING* AGAIN!
IT'S ABOUT *TIME!*
SEE YOU *SOON*– I THINK!
GUYS?
PYTHIA!
HUH?
ORACLE.
I'LL EXPLAIN LATER.
OH.

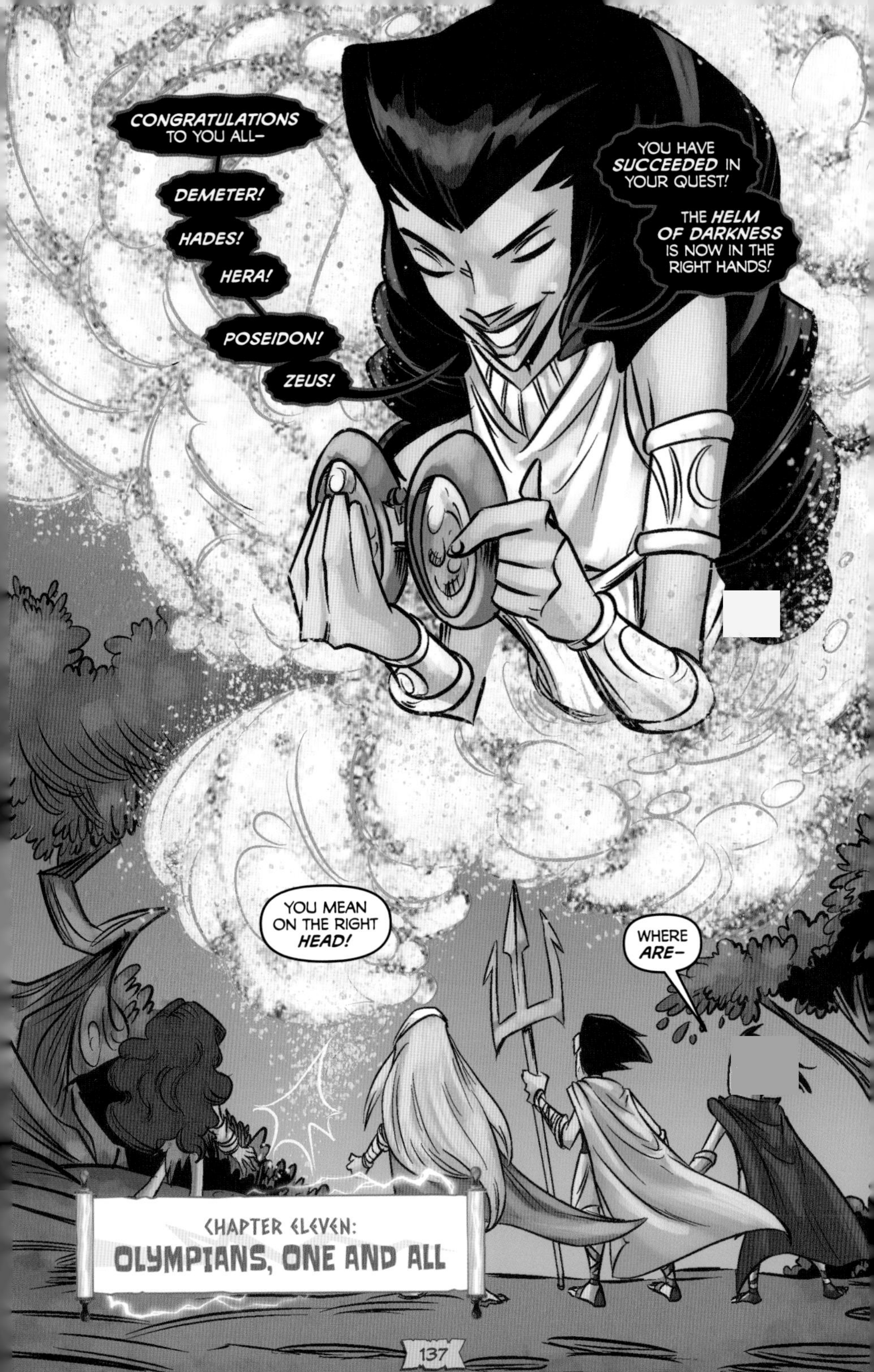

CONGRATULATIONS TO YOU ALL–
DEMETER!
HADES!
HERA!
POSEIDON!
ZEUS!
YOU HAVE SUCCEEDED IN YOUR QUEST!
THE HELM OF DARKNESS IS NOW IN THE RIGHT HANDS!
YOU MEAN ON THE RIGHT HEAD!
WHERE ARE–
CHAPTER ELEVEN:
OLYMPIANS, ONE AND ALL

I **HAIL** YOU, LORD OF THE **UNDERWORLD!**

IT IS GOOD AND **JUST** THAT YOU HAVE REGAINED YOUR RIGHTFUL **THRONE.**

THANK YOU.

AT LEAST **YOU'VE** GOT A **TRIDENT!**

WISH I HAD A THRONE.

I'VE GOT **NOTHING!**

NEITHER DOES **DEMETER.**

I GUESS IT'S OKAY.

WILL I EVER GET A MAGICAL **OBJECT** —LIKE ZEUS'S **BOLT?**

OR POSEIDON'S **TRIDENT?**

OR HADES'S **HELM?**

ZEUS FEARS THAT THE ORACLE WILL THINK THEM UNGRATEFUL FOR THE THINGS THEY **DO** HAVE...

...AND REALIZES THAT, AS A LEADER, HE NEEDS TO **SAY** THAT.

DEAR CHILD...

PYTHIA, WE'RE **GRATEFUL** TO YOU FOR OUR PRIZES AND FOR YOU GUIDING US ON OUR QUESTS.

BUT BEFORE YOU CHARGE US WITH A **NEW** ONE...

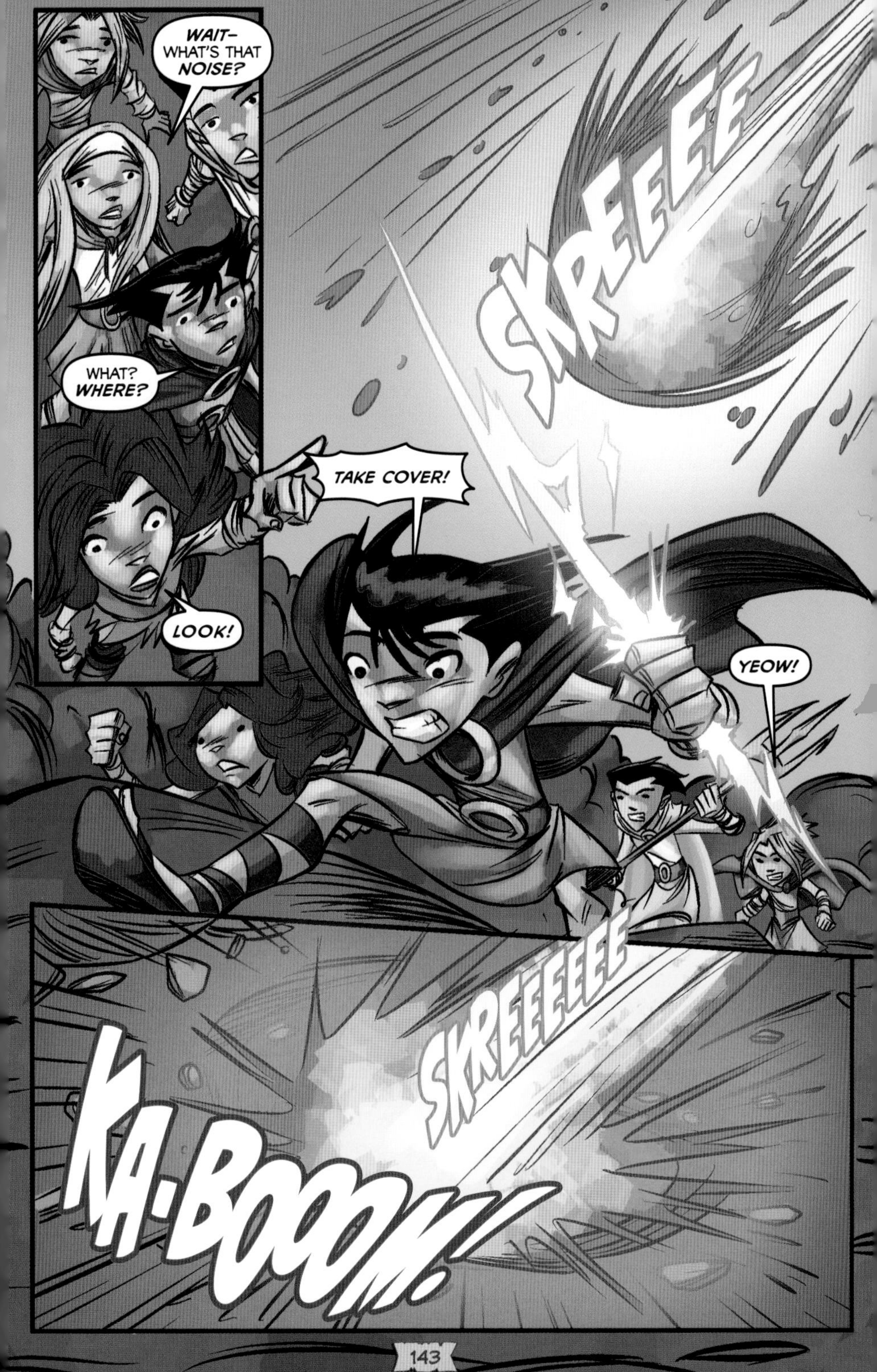
WAIT— WHAT'S THAT NOISE?
WHAT? WHERE?
LOOK!
TAKE COVER!
SKREEEEE
YEOW!
SKREEEEEE
KA-BOOOM!

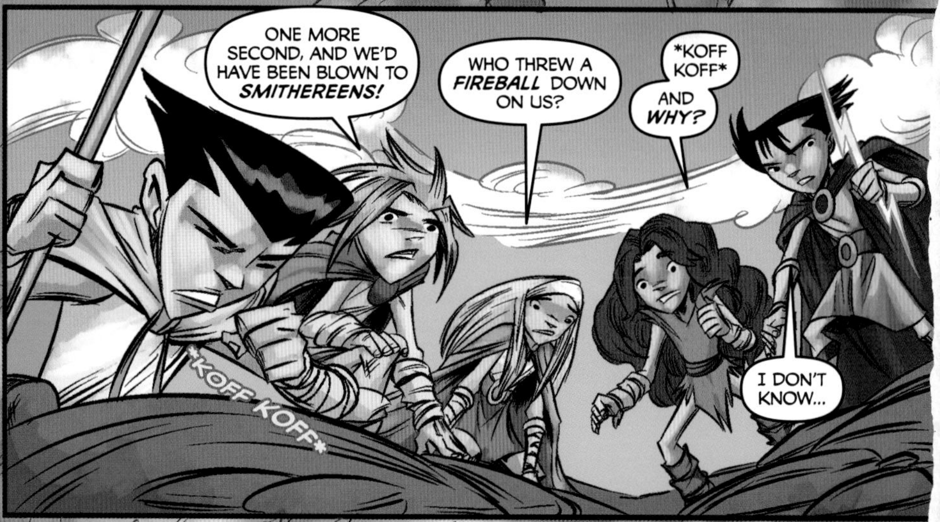
ONE MORE SECOND, AND WE'D HAVE BEEN BLOWN TO SMITHEREENS!
KOFF KOFF
WHO THREW A FIREBALL DOWN ON US?
KOFF KOFF
AND WHY?
I DON'T KNOW...

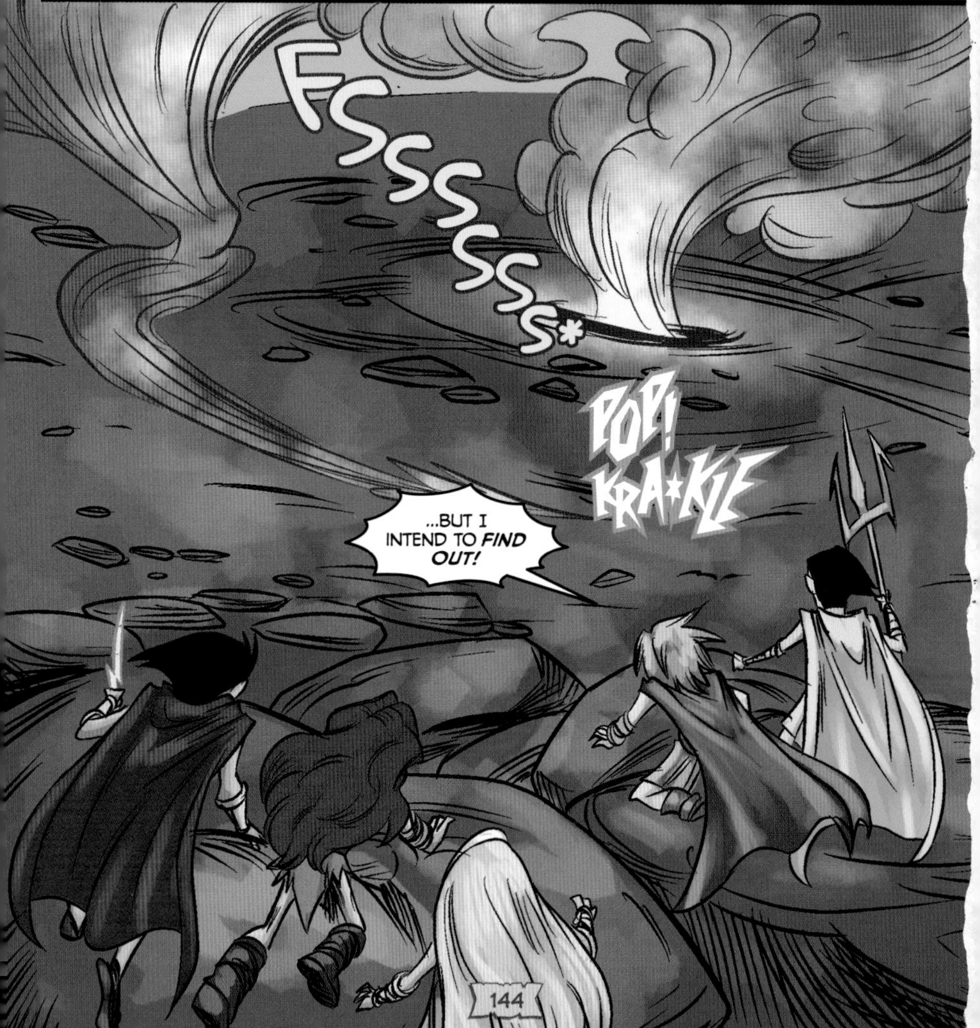
FSSSSSSSS*
POP!
KRA*KLE
...BUT I INTEND TO FIND OUT!